MARY O'SULLIVAN

POOLBEG

This novel is entirely a work of fiction. The names, characters and incidents portrayed in it are the work of the author's imagination. Any resemblance to actual persons, living or dead, events or localities is entirely coincidental.

Published 2011
by Poolbeg Press Ltd.
123 Grange Hill, Baldoyle,
Dublin 13, Ireland
Email: poolbeg@poolbeg.com

1

A catalogue record for this book is available from the British Library.

ISBN 978-1-84223-455-6

Typeset by Patricia Hope in Sabon 11/14.5

Printed by
CPI Cox & Wyman, UK

www.poolbeg.com

Note on the Author

Mary O'Sullivan lives in Carrigaline, Co Cork, with her husband Seán. Her bestselling novels *Parting Company, As Easy As That, Ebb & Flow, Inside Out* and *Under The Rainbow* are also published by Poolbeg.

You can visit Mary's website at **www.maryosullivanauthor.ie**

Acknowledgements

From author to publisher, editor, cover designer, typesetter, printer, marketing staff and retailer – the journey a book takes from initial idea to end product is helped along the way by very many people. I would like to thank the following for their support in bringing *Time and Tide* on that journey.

Firstly Paula Campbell and all the staff in Poolbeg. Thank you for the support and your faith in my work. A special word to Gaye Shortland for her editorial skills and advice.

A warm thanks to Susan and Paul Feldstein of Feldstein Literary Agency for practical advice, admirable patience and perpetual optimism.

Thanks to Karen Kinsella, Mary Lynskey and Anne Doody-Crowley who read first drafts and were so generous with their time and encouragement. Also thanks to Carmel Hemlock, Aidan Murphy, Noel Buckley and Siobhán Moloney for much-appreciated help and advice.

To my husband Seán and my family, both here and abroad, my love and thanks. To the many friends who have encouraged me, your support has meant a lot.

And to the readers who have read and continue to read my books, I am very grateful.

Dedicated to the memory of

Angela Doran

Slán go fóil

Chapter 1

It was the quiet she had longed for. Soothing. Restful. Yet not silent.

Robyn settled her bulk into the comfort of the cane chair, closed her eyes and listened. A bird was trilling. Several cheeps followed by a long note. Somewhere in the distance an answering call carried on the air. The sweetness of the communication made her think of Zach and long for him to be here with her now. She felt the baby move. Smiling, she placed her hands on her distended belly.

The conservatory where she sat faced away from the sea and south towards the fields. Acres and acres of them, gently rising to the hills. Good dairy-farming land, rare here on the west coast of Ireland, melding into sheep-rearing slopes. The perfect location for a vet to set up practice. An ideal place to rear a family. Robyn's hands moved gently over her almost full-term bump. Just over two more weeks to go until she would hold her baby in her arms. Their baby. Hers and Zach's.

She started when the doorbell rang. A glance at her watch told her it was three in the afternoon. Too early for a client in the small animal clinic. The caller could only be Tansy. Who else? The natural beauty of Felton had not been matched so far by any noticeable warmth in its citizens. Except for Tansy. Eccentric, a touch hyperactive, impractical, funny and kind.

Holding onto the arms of the chair for leverage, Robyn hauled herself up and walked to the door. The instant she opened it a pungent aroma wafted under her nose and almost made her gag. The smell was coming from whatever was hidden underneath the tea-towel-draped dish Tansy was holding in her hands.

"Here," she said, offering her dish up like a sacrificial lamb. "I've made you a casserole from my special recipe. Plenty of herbs in there for you. Borage too for hormone balance."

Robyn swallowed hard and took the casserole. "Thanks but I'm just after lunch. I'll keep it for later. Come on back to the conservatory. I'll put this in the fridge first."

Tansy shrugged and smiled. "Never mind. As my ex used to say, my cooking's an acquired taste."

Robyn opened her mouth to lie and deny, but Tansy had already gone ahead in a swirl of floating cheesecloth. The fabric was tie-dyed and splotched with random purple-pink motifs. Bias-cut and sleeveless, the dress would have been outrageous on anyone else. With Tansy's slight frame and masses of shining dark hair, it seemed just right.

"Another new design?" Robyn asked.

"Yes. One of the chain stores is showing quite an interest in my whole retro collection."

Robyn raised an eyebrow. She had thought Tansy's

new designs beautiful but not commercial. Evocative. That's what they were. All natural weave and free-flowing, like the sixties which had inspired them.

"Well done, Tansy."

"I didn't say I'd do business with them. I'd have to know where they were sourcing their materials and labour. You know how strongly I feel about that."

Robyn nodded. She did indeed know how strongly Tansy felt about almost everything. She was a campaigner for causes. Organic food, world peace, the right to live and the right to die. There was no end to Tansy's caring. Maybe not much depth either as each day seemed to bring a new passion. Robyn lowered herself carefully onto her chair again while Tansy sat on the built-in window seat.

"You're not going into labour just to avoid my casserole, are you?"

"No. Though I feel I'll never deliver the baby. I'll spend my whole life with swollen ankles and baggy maternity clothes."

"You're just missing work."

Work. The pressure. The deadlines. The bitching. Robyn closed her eyes for an instant and thought about the *Daily News* office. She had belonged there, found her niche in the cut and thrust of investigative journalism. What would she be doing now if she wasn't wedged in her chair in Felton? Following leads, editing copy, interviewing sources. Looking over her shoulder at what the other reporters were doing. Protecting her back. Avoiding Kevin Phillips. Making sure they were never alone together in the office. She opened her eyes and smiled at Tansy.

"No. I don't miss work or the city. How could I? Felton is so beautiful and peaceful. Besides, don't forget my weekly column. I haven't retired completely. I'm still enjoying writing."

"I loved your last article. You're so right about our politicians. They're not telling us the whole truth. Do you know what I think?"

"Let me guess. You think all the world's politicians are involved in a secret plot. They're planning to resettle on the Moon while leaving the rest of us here to freeze or burn up. Whichever our climate decides to do. Am I close?"

"God! I never thought of that. It makes sense. At least it would if I believed a human being had ever set foot on the moon. We haven't been there yet. I know we haven't. The 'one giant leap for mankind' was taken in a film studio."

Robyn decided to let that comment go unchallenged. Her back was aching. A dull, nagging pain. Too much sitting around.

"How would you like a walk, Tansy? Along the beach?"

Tansy stood up with a grace and litheness which made Robyn envious as she manoeuvred herself upright. With any luck it would be breezy by the sea. A cool, cleansing breeze. One that would blow away the sudden restlessness which seemed to be making her back ache and her mind wander along tracks which were best untrodden.

Even though it was over a year since she and Zach had moved into Woodruff Cottage, Robyn was still taken by surprise when she went out the front door. Today was no different. Her breath caught in her throat as she took in the scene. The Atlantic, blue-grey and restless, rolled from the outer harbour onto the shore of Felton Bay only 500 metres away from where she stood. At first glance the sea seemed to be in a playful mood, reflecting a sparkle here, a whitecap there. She held her face up to the breeze and took a deep breath. The wind lifted her blonde hair and raked it with cool fingers.

"Why didn't you build your conservatory to the front of the house? You could look at this view all day then."

Robyn pulled her cardigan more closely around her and wondered if Tansy had a point.

"It had to be south-facing to catch the sun," she explained. "Besides we're going to build a terrace out front as soon as Zach's practice is up and running. A veranda, covered in."

"I can just see you, sitting on a rocking chair, your hair in a bun, hoards of children running around – gazing out to sea and wondering what to write about next."

Unbidden, a shiver rippled through Robyn. Somewhere deep inside she felt a flash of panic. Was that it? Her future. Babies and buns. And Zach. Strong, intense, caring Zach, with his dark curly hair and clear green eyes. She turned to smile at Tansy.

"The only thing wrong with that picture is the bun. I don't think my hair suits me up. Come on. The tide will be in before we get to the beach."

Together they headed towards the strand, Robyn walking carefully down the sloping path, Tansy slowing her usual fast pace to match.

"Are you coming to the meeting tomorrow night?"

Tansy asked as they began their stroll along the water's edge.

"What meeting?"

"The one in the Community Hall of course. We don't have too many meetings here in Felton, do we? The last one was probably called during the Second World War."

"It's about the flood defences, isn't it?"

"Well, we either sit here and wait for Felton to go under or we do something to protect ourselves now."

Robyn laughed at her friend's usual overstatement, but at the same time she looked ahead to where the village of Felton squatted on a headland jutting into the sea. Boats bobbed at their moorings out from the pier while the narrow streets hugged the base of the gentle slope the locals called Lookout Hill. That's where the new Community Hall had been built. It was safe up there, if windy.

"Do you think I should ask those German people to come?" Tansy asked.

"Our very private neighbours? But you don't really know them."

"Nobody does but since they live near us I think they should come too. Our three homes are the most vulnerable."

That was true. Woodruff Cottage was one of three cottages sited close to the shoreline, originally built as summer houses for the Victorian well-to-do. Tansy occupied the house to the left of Robyn's while the Germans lived on the right-hand side.

"You're here a long time, Tansy. Do you ever remember our houses flooding? Our surveyor told us Woodruff had no damp so we assumed it has always been safe from high tides. Although the high tide this spring was uncomfortably close to our front doors."

"Don't you read your own writing at all? They've always been safe from normal high tides but we're not talking normal now, are we? Icebergs melting, sea levels rising . . ."

"Politicians going to the Moon."

"Laugh if you must but I know you're worried too. You have to be for your baby."

Robyn's hands automatically went to her stomach and cradled the child she and Zach had conceived. Unbidden, Kevin's words, spoken in anger so long ago, came back to her now: "No. No. No. You can't bring a child into this chaotic world. It's not right. Not fair." As if he, Kevin Phillips, was the arbiter of righteousness and fairness. All the old resentment against Kevin burned with a bile-like bitterness in her throat. She swallowed hard and turned her attention back to Tansy.

"Yes, of course I'll be at the meeting. Why don't we go together? And let's call to the Germans now. They should go too."

Satisfied that she had won a victory, Tansy flashed her sparkling smile as they turned and headed back along the strand.

Zach found it difficult to keep up with the little man racing ahead of him. Con Lynch was built for speed. Wiry and at least sixty-five years old, he had climbed these hills all his life and was showing no signs of slowing down. Zach glanced around him at the undulating landscape and thought that Con had no option if he wanted to make a living from all these humps and hollows.

It was very beautiful, with the high peak known as 'The 360' above them, the River Aban valley beneath and Con's farmhouse nestling cosily in the more gentle dip behind them.

"Your wife's time must be nearly here," Con called back over his shoulder.

"Two or three more weeks," Zach said, stopping and pretending to empty a pebble from his boot. He needed the breather.

"Come on, lad. Stop dragging your feet. They're just over this ridge here."

Zach's faltering breath left him altogether when they crested the hill. He took in the scene beneath him and knew instinctively that this was a sight he would always remember with dread. As if his years of study, his experience in the practice, had all been rehearsal for this very moment. The sheep were grazing in the narrow valley below. At least most of them were. Nine animals were apart, in a makeshift pen by the dried-out stream bed – some standing, some lying, all close together as if protecting each other. He was too far away to see the catarrhal noses, the sore feet, the cyanosed tongues, but he instinctively knew.

There had never been a case in Ireland. Not yet. But there was no doubt in his mind. It was here now on Con Lynch's farm.

"How many?"

"Three gone down. Six more off their feed. What do you think it is?"

"I can't say from here, Con. C'mon."

They both went downhill at a smart pace, Zach never taking his eyes off the sheep. Even before they had reached where the first ailing animal lay, he began to go over procedure for a notifiable disease in his mind. The ewe was gasping for breath, drooling, her nose runny and her face and lips swollen.

"Jesus! She's going down quick. She's worse than when I rang you and that's only an hour ago."

Zach waved his hand to silence Con as he knelt and placed his stethoscope on the animal's chest. He listened to the stertorous respiration and shook his head.

"'Tis bad?"

"Have you imported any animals within the last month, Con?"

"You know I haven't. I don't want to risk bringing any of those foreign diseases onto my farm. Anyway, the red tape involved isn't worth it. Why?"

Zach stood and looked around at the other animals Con had separated from the flock. Two were in the same condition as the one he had just examined, one was limping, while five just stood and watched with flat lifeless eyes.

"Are you sure these are all the affected animals? Could there be more?"

Con shrugged. "These are the worst. Maybe there are others breeding . . . What is it, Zach? What's wrong with them?"

Zach tried to recall every textbook and paper he had studied about this virus. A trickle of sweat ran from his hair onto his forehead. He wiped it off with the back of his arm and squinted up at the sky. It was cloudless. Azure. As it had been for the past six weeks. And that was the answer. The cause of the disease which was laying Con Lynch's sheep low. But knowing and proving were two different things. How much should he say now?

"You've a face like thunder, Zach Claymore. What's going on? What's wrong with the animals?"

"This shagging heat. That's what's going on."

"You're having me on. Next you'll be saying they should have sunscreen and . . ."

"This is serious, Con. I can't confirm until we have tests done but I'm almost certain."

Con was staring at him. Hanging on his every word. But his earlier certainty had left Zach now. Suppose his diagnosis was wrong? These symptoms could be caused by other sicknesses. But then, if he was right, the sooner procedure got underway the better. Con had given his life to the back-breaking work on his eighty acres of hill farm. This would come as a blow to him.

"I believe we're looking at BTV."

"Fuck! Bluetongue Virus! How? I haven't imported since the first outbreak in England back in 2007. It's not in Ireland. How in the hell could my sheep have it?"

"Midges. Culicoides. This heat is perfect for them. I'll have to check with the Met office but if we've had prevailing easterly winds during the past month, it's more than likely that infected midges have been blown onto your farm. They can travel huge distances in the right conditions. One bite is all it takes."

Head bowed, Con seemed to carefully examine his boots. When he looked up, he was pale, frightened-looking.

"They'll all be here now, won't they? The inspectors and officials. They'll shut me down."

"I'll have to ring in my suspicions, Con. Get priority testing. And yes, your farm will be cordoned off."

The old man nodded his head towards the animals. "Will they be culled?"

"Probably."

"The rest of the flock? What about them? They seem healthy enough."

"I can't say, Con. Bluetongue Virus is not contagious but others may have been infected by the midges. The cattle too. We have a lot of work ahead before we can make any decisions."

Con stooped down and laid his hand on the head of an ailing animal. Stockmen had no sentiment for animals, they couldn't afford it, but there was real concern for the stricken ewe in Con Lynch's touch.

"I'm sorry, Con. I'll get results as quickly as possible. I must make a few calls now and then take samples."

"Do what you must, lad."

Con turned then and strode back up the hill. Zach did what he must.

Chapter 2

Tansy's front garden was a riot of colour. Plants grew higgledy-piggledy all over the place but yet they had symmetry. Robyn and Zach's front lawn was well-tended, strewn with shrubs and flower-beds. Even Zach's purpose-built animal surgery to the back of the cottage blended in, probably because the builder had spent a long time and a lot of money sourcing old stone for cladding the exterior. In contrast, the house occupied by the German couple was dark and unwelcoming. Cypress trees, so closely planted that their lower branches intertwined, screened the house from sunlight and prying eyes.

"Remind me of the Muellers' first names," Robyn said as she and Tansy reached the gate of the third cottage.

"Horst and Ute. They arrived here about two years ago."

"They didn't plant this 'Black Forest' then. Who did?"

"The sisters. Hope and Joy Carmody. So misnamed. They were the dourest pair. I used to be terrified of them when I was small."

Robyn laughed and raised an eyebrow, trying hard to imagine Tansy ever being afraid of anything or anyone.

"It's true! I was scared. Sad though, the way they died – suffocated by carbon monoxide from their blocked chimney flue. They always pushed people away and then there was no one to help when they needed it. The inquest said they had been dead for three weeks before their bodies were discovered."

"I wouldn't like to live here, would you?" Robyn remarked as they walked underneath the shadow of the flame-shaped cypresses. "Those trees must be thirty or forty feet tall. It's creepy."

It got creepier as they approached the front door. The walls were ivy-clad, making the windows seem small and dark.

"I know he's a dot-com type – designs software or some computer stuff like that – but what about Ute? What does she do?" Robyn whispered.

"As far as I know she's a translator. Does all her work on-line too."

"They're home now," Robyn said, nodding towards the four-wheel-drive parked beside the house. "They were also here the time Zach and I called to introduce ourselves as their new neighbours. They just didn't answer the door. I might even believe that nobody lives here except that I catch glimpses of them driving past every so often."

Tansy raised her hand to the door. "Let's give them a good loud knock they can't ignore!"

The front door opened after the first rap. A tall man, brown hair thinning, blue eyes squinting through round spectacles, stood in the doorway.

"May I help?" he asked in only slightly accented English.

"We're your immediate neighbours, Mr Mueller. I'm Tansy Bingham and this is Robyn Claymore. Her husband is the new vet here in Felton."

Horst Mueller craned his head forward and stared at Robyn. Just as she was trying to decide whether he was very short-sighted or extremely rude, he smiled at her.

"I'm sorry, Mrs Claymore. We don't have any pets. I wish your husband success in his new business. Thank you for calling."

He began to close the door. Tansy put a hand on the doorknob. "No. It's not about that. We came to tell you about the meeting. We thought you and Mrs Mueller would like to come? Or maybe you know about it already? We said we'd tell you anyway."

Horst Mueller was frowning now, no trace of the smile left on his face.

Confused herself by Tansy's rambling, Robyn decided to explain to the glowering man why they were standing on his doorstep.

"There's a meeting in the Community Hall tomorrow night to discuss flood defences for the bay area. Especially the lower part of the village. And of course these three cottages are very vulnerable to high tides too."

"Do you know how many ice shelves have melted by now?" Tansy asked. "Sea levels are rising far faster than predicted and temperatures too because the exposed tundra absorbs heat and –"

"Thank you for letting us know. I'll discuss it with my wife."

Horst Mueller shut the door firmly in their faces.

"How rude!" said Tansy as she and Robyn stood staring at each other in surprise.

"I think we scared him. C'mon, this place gives me the shivers."

Even though the scent of the cypress trees was pleasant, it was a relief to leave their shade and walk again in sunlight. They stood when they reached the gate of Robyn's home.

"Would you like a coffee?"

"Thanks, Robyn, but I've work to do. And I must inspect my crop."

Robyn tried not to laugh. Tansy's crop was a row of pots in her back garden in which she had planted cotton seeds. Maybe it wasn't such a joke after all. The seeds had sprouted and were thriving. According to Tansy's climate predictions in a few short years the Irish climate would be warm and wet enough to make cotton a viable crop here. Spinning her own yarn was bound to be the next step for her. That should be fun, Robyn thought, as she watched Tansy float away in a cloud of energy, tie-dyed cheesecloth and shiny black hair.

The sun was sinking towards the horizon but the evening was still very warm. Robyn put her hand to her forehead and wondered if she was running a temperature. She immediately got annoyed with herself. Nobody had warned her that pregnancy would turn her into a hypochondriac. Every little sniffle and ache filled her with dread that the baby would be harmed by whatever ailment she imagined herself to have. An over-protective mother and the baby had not yet been born.

Needing something to occupy her mind until Zach got home, Robyn left the kitchen and wandered into the cool of the lounge. She picked up her book and began to read. The words blurred and then disappeared altogether as her eyelids closed. She jumped when her phone rang and her unread book clattered to the floor. Glancing at the screen, she saw that the caller was Zach.

"Hi. Good timing. Dinner's just ready."

"Sorry, Robyn. I'll be late. That's why I'm ringing. Are you alright?"

"Yes, I'm fine thanks. How late will you be?"

"Depends. Could be a long time. I'm at Lynches' farm. We've a serious situation here. I can't discuss it now but don't wait up for me."

"That sounds ominous."

"If I'm right, it is."

Frowning, Robyn tried to remember something about the Lynches. Sheep-farmers. Some dairy stock too but mainly sheep. Good clients since Zach had opened his practice here.

"Isn't the lambing season over? What's going on that's so serious?"

She heard Zach take a deep breath and suddenly she began to worry about him.

"Zach? Are you okay? You're telling me all the truth, aren't you? You haven't had an accident?"

"No. Nothing like that. It's just that I . . . I suspect . . . I'm as sure as I can be without test results that we have Bluetongue Virus here. We're looking at culling and exclusion zones if I'm right. It's this bloody heat."

Robyn breathed a sigh of relief. However bad BTV was for the Lynches and their sheep, at least her husband was safe. Selfish but that's the way her thinking was these days. Zoning in on her own family unit. Looking inward.

"I've had to notify the department. They're fast-tracking the tests and sending officials here."

The sound of worry in Zach's voice cut into Robyn's introspection. She began to recall details about Bluetongue Virus. She had researched it recently for her article on global warming. But she had known about it long before that. Kevin Phillips had done a series of feature articles for the *Daily News* on the largest UK outbreak some years ago when first it had spread from mainland Europe. He had told her about it. Curled up on the couch together, they had shared a bottle of wine and a discussion on BTV. He had predicted then that it was only a matter of time before Irish farms would be hit by the virus. Her relationship with Kevin had been like that. Wine and worry, love and eventually bitterness.

"Kerry will handle the clinic this evening," Zach said. "There's just one appointment anyway and that's only to remove stitches."

Robyn had forgotten about the clinic. She liked to watch clients pass the front of the house and go into the clinic, dogs on leashes, cats and birds in cages. A lot of the pet-owners were children. Zach seemed to have a way with them. Kerry, a veterinary student on work practice with Zach, was just the opposite. She could handle any animal with care and patience but children she could not tolerate.

"Have you told Kerry yet?" she asked.

"No. And I'm not going to mention BTV until we have confirmation. You mustn't either. Especially not to Tansy Bingham."

Robyn nodded her head. She didn't need to be told that. Tansy would have the news broadcast in an instant. It wasn't that she was a gossip. It was just that she had an open and generous nature which accommodated sharing admirably, discretion less so and secrecy not at all.

"Promise. Not a word," she said. "You take care. I'll leave your dinner in the fridge but make sure you don't take the casserole with the tea towel around it. That's one of Tansy's."

"God! That's all I need now. Death by Casserole. What does she put in them?"

"Everything organic. That gives her a lot of scope. Love you, Zach."

"Love you too."

Robyn was smiling as she put down the phone. Who would have thought, least of all herself, that Felton and Zach Claymore would bring her the contentment which had always eluded her in the city?

Chapter 3

Robyn had been vaguely aware of Zach, feet and hands freezing, climbing into bed beside her during the dark hours. When she next woke, sunlight was spilling through the windows and Zach was gone. Looking at her watch she saw that it was already nine o'clock. Getting out of bed these days involved an awkward combination of rolling, split timing and delicate balance. Feet finally on the floor, Robyn went to the window and looked out over the sea. It was blue but like yesterday the waves were busily pushing towards shore. The North Atlantic seemed to be in a hurry. "Another hot one," Robyn told the baby. She rifled through her wardrobe and chose a linen sleeveless top and pants. Huge top. Huge pants. In a moment of honesty, she looked in the mirror and mouthed 'Huge Robyn' at her reflection. She leaned closer to her image and examined it. Her skin had a glow. Her eyes too seemed to sparkle a deeper blue. She turned from the mirror quickly before her gaze could drop to the body which she had always so diligently kept trim and toned.

She had just stepped into the shower when the phone rang. Probably Zach to see how she was. Switching off the water, she grabbed a towel and padded to the bedroom phone as quickly as possible. Murphy's Law. It stopped ringing as she reached it. Blast! She would call him after her shower. Halfway back to the ensuite, the ringing started again. This time she caught it before it rang out. It wasn't Zach. It wasn't even someone she liked. Gemma Creedon was the office administrator in the *Daily News*. Robyn and Gemma had worked out a way to be polite to each other. They had to. But no amount of courtesy would ever disguise their mutual dislike.

"I'm sorry if I got you out of bed, Robyn. I forgot that you're living in a different time zone now."

"Good morning, Gemma. No need to apologise. I've been up for hours. And by the way, you still don't seem to understand that Felton is actually in Ireland. Hardly a different time zone."

"Still tetchy about your rural retreat! No need to be so defensive. Anyway, I've been asked to pass on a message to you. Kevin is on his way to Felton and he'd like to meet up with you."

The baby kicked and her heart thumped. Robyn, still wrapped in a damp towel, flopped onto the bed.

"Kevin coming to Felton! Why? What does he want here?"

"Stop panicking, Robyn. He's on a job. You didn't think he was going there just to see you, did you?"

The bitch was gloating. Robyn took a deep breath and tried to sound casual.

"Of course not. I'm just surprised that he's coming here. Do you know what the job is?"

"That's confidential. You should know better than to ask. How are you feeling, by the way? Not long to go now, have you?"

"I'm fine, thank you. And you? Are you still doing your language course?"

"No. I've found something a lot more interesting than Polish to study. You haven't changed your mobile number, have you?"

"No."

"Good. Kevin will ring you when he's ready. Take care, Robyn."

Gemma cut the connection. Robyn sat there in her damp towel staring at the phone. What was bringing Kevin Phillips to Felton? And why did he want to see her? As editor-in- chief of the *Daily News* he was still her boss, of course. But any discussion about her weekly column had been dealt with by email or phone over the past year. There was no reason for them to meet. No work-related reason.

The crunch of gravel on the driveway snapped her out of her shocked state. A quick shower later she arrived in the kitchen. Zach was standing at the counter, buttering some toast. He looked up and smiled as she came in.

"How's Sleepyhead?" he asked, opening his arms wide as she walked towards him.

Robyn kissed him and then snuggled into his embrace. He smelled of disinfectant and deodorant. A mixture she quite liked by now. She leaned her head on his chest and closed her eyes, enjoying the safe, warm feeling.

"Did you have an emergency call-out?" she asked.

"No. Lynches' sheep are all the emergency I can handle at the moment."

She had forgotten about Zach's problem with Bluetongue Virus. Guilty now, she looked into his face and saw worry-lines there.

"Any confirmation yet?"

"No. Not until this afternoon but the department is certain enough to quarantine the stock already. Con is very upset."

"Will he lose all his animals?"

"It depends. He'll definitely lose some but I'm hoping not all. A lot of his flock are high up on the hills. They're probably safe."

Robyn walked across to the table and sat down, a frown on her forehead. Some things were beginning to click into place now.

"Are you listening to me, Robyn? Did you hear a word I said?"

She looked up at Zach and for an instant she had a flash of déjà vu. Had she not lived this moment before? In her dreams, in her hopes for the future? She, pregnant, Zach watching over her and their unborn child. Happy, contented. No doubts. No extremes of passion. No Kevin Phillips.

"How many people know about the BTV outbreak?" she asked.

He handed her a mug of coffee and sat down opposite her with his. "You mean is it safe to tell Tansy Bingham yet?"

"No. I mean the *Daily News* rang. Kevin Phillips is on his way to Felton to cover a story. What else could it be if not the BTV?"

"He has good contacts, hasn't he? Doesn't matter anyway. The cordon is up and the police are patrolling the access roads to Lynches'. It's not a secret any more."

Robyn leaned her elbows on the table and took a deep breath.

"Kevin wants to meet up with me. I don't know what it's about."

"Don't you? Maybe he's just taking the opportunity to say hello because he's in the area."

Zach's words were clipped. His mouth, always so ready to smile, was pursed into a tight line. Robyn looked into his eyes and saw disapproval there. Even anger.

"I won't see him if you'd prefer me not to."

"Do whatever you want, Robyn. Your choice."

Her choice! When had Kevin Phillips ever given her a choice? It was always his way or not at all.

"I'm worried that he's going to axe my column. I really enjoy writing that. And the money is good too."

"That would be ridiculous. Your column sells a lot of papers. Whatever he wants, Robyn, it's not to fire you. You know that."

Zach stood up and walked to the sink. As he rinsed his mug, Robyn noted how tense his shoulders seemed. She wanted to go to him and run her hands over the knotted muscles but the spectre of Kevin Phillips lurked between them. God damn Kevin! He had no place here in Woodruff Cottage.

Zach turned to face her.

"I'll be gone for the day, Robyn. I've a few visits to make then I'm back to Lynches'. If you need me, ring."

He went then. Just like that. No hug, no kiss, leaving

her with a decision to make and a cold feeling in the pit of her stomach.

Tansy was gasping for breath. Her own fault. She had left it too late to start out on her run. The sun was already high and very hot. An idea, a fleeting thought, had woken her at six o'clock that morning and she had been working on it until after ten. Time wasted. Try as she might she could not replicate on paper the cotton jacket of her waking thoughts.

The backs of her legs ached now as she climbed the slope towards the Community Hall. This was the punishing bit of her daily circuit, the part that kept her fit. Hearing a car approach, she moved to the right-hand side of the narrow road. The engine noise got louder and then began to slow as it neared. Thinking it must be someone she knew, Tansy looked over her shoulder. She didn't recognise the red sports car.

A glance around told her she was in an isolated area. In a microsecond she imagined about ten horrific scenarios all involving her being murdered by this stranger. She began to run faster and considered scaling the ditch until she realised with a rare flash of insight that her imagination was leading her into yet another overreaction.

The car was level with her now and had slowed to her pace. The driver, elbow resting casually on the open window, leaned towards her. A blond, magnificent man. An Adonis! Tansy stubbed her toe on a stone and almost tripped.

"Are you alright?" he asked. "Sorry for disturbing your concentration."

"Yes, I'm fine, thank you," Tansy gasped, trying to maintain her momentum and ignore the pain in her stubbed toe at the same time.

"Could you tell me where Lynches' farm is, please? Con Lynch. Am I on the right road?"

"No. You've got to go back to the village and then take a right near the library."

"Damn! Does this road get any wider or do I have to reverse back down?"

A man in a hurry. The handsome features took on a more mature appearance as he frowned in annoyance. At first glance Tansy had guessed his age at about thirty-five. She could see now that he was older. He had a well-lived-in face, enhanced by laughter-lines around his blue eyes and a few furrows on his forehead too.

"You could continue on up to the Community Hall. Plenty of space there to turn."

"Thanks, but I guess I can manage."

She barely had time to notice that the arm he raised in salute was well muscled and tanned, before he took off, reversing recklessly down the hill. Show off! He would be looking over his shoulder, back towards the main road, but Tansy kept up her relentless pace anyway. Just in case he turned in her direction. She wasn't sure why she wanted to impress him except that he was the best-looking man she had seen since she had first met Ari Klum. And look how that ended, she thought as she reached the top of the hill. A peep back told her that the blond god in the red sports car was out of sight.

Hands on knees, she leaned over and took deep breaths until she could feel her burning lungs fill with air again. When she straightened up, she looked towards

Con Lynch's farm, wondering what business the red sports car and its driver could have there. Amazed, she blinked. Shaded her eyes with her hand. Blinked again. No, she wasn't imagining the cars around the entrance to Lynches' farm. A squad car, blue light revolving, was blocking the approach road and a cordon was strung across the gate. A 'scene of crime' type cordon. Jesus! A rhythmic put-putting made her look skywards where a helicopter was flying east towards Lynches'. Whatever was going on there was serious.

Confused, curious and afraid now, Tansy cut her route short and ran back down the hill. She tried to think about what she had seen – the helicopter, the squad car, the cordon. Those images faded in her mind to be replaced by one of the blond man. Her contact with him had been brief but in that short time she had sensed an extraordinary strength and energy in him. Whoever he was, this magnificent man, Tansy was determined to meet him again.

As Zach headed towards Lynches' farm he was impressed by how quickly and efficiently the area had been cordoned off. His stomach gave a nervous lurch. He was going to look a right prat if his diagnosis was wrong. A lot of manpower and money had already been expended on putting the infected animals in quarantine. He gave an involuntary groan as he saw the helicopter circle overhead. A bloody television crew!

Running over the animals' symptoms again he tried to reassure himself that he wouldn't become a national laughing stock. Had he been too hasty in assuming that Con Lynch's sheep were the first in Ireland to suffer from

Bluetongue Virus? No. It could only be BTV. Or plant poisoning, or polyarthritis, maybe pneumonia . . .

Preoccupied by his self-doubt, Zach didn't see the red sports car until it was almost too late. He stopped his dusty Land Rover just millimetres from the gleaming back fender of Kevin Phillips' Audi Cabriolet. Zach's stomach muscles knotted tighter. How that prick would love to write a caustic piece on the incompetence of the vet who had falsely cried BTV!

"*Hey!* Watch where you're bloody going!"

Kevin Phillips was striding towards his car, his face flushed with the anger which always seemed to simmer just beneath his urbane surface. Zach got out of his Land Rover and watched as the other man examined his fender minutely for any sign of damage. Kevin looked up and then walked over to Zach.

"Oh, It's you. I should have guessed. The Knight on Charging Tractor."

"I'm a vet, not a farmer. Is your memory failing?"

"Unfortunately not. I remember every detail, good and bad. So you're the vet who reported suspected BTV to the department."

With relief Zach mulled over the word 'suspected'. He could use it to make a credible case for himself, even if it turned out to be a false alarm.

"Do you know what surprises me?" Kevin asked.

Zach shook his head. Kevin Phillips had the world-weary aura of someone who couldn't be surprised by anything.

"That it's taken this long for Bluetongue to reach Ireland. Any word on the type yet?"

"There's no confirmation of the disease itself let alone

the serotype. You'll just have to have patience, Kevin. We should have word this afternoon. But you already know that, don't you? You must have some pretty high-level contacts in the department."

Kevin gave Zach one of his penetrating looks. A one-way gaze that looked right through him but did not allow him to see anything of what Kevin Phillips was thinking.

"How's Robyn?"

The question caught Zach off guard. Bluetongue he would discuss with Phillips. His private life, his and Robyn's, was off limits as far as he was concerned. Robyn would have to make her own decision on that score.

"You'll have to excuse me now. I've got work to do."

"How many animals are sick? Is it just the sheep or are cattle infected too?"

Zach shook his head as he climbed into his Land Rover. Phillips was persistent. Nothing got in the way of his story.

"You'll probably be the first to know, Kevin. And as far as Robyn's concerned, you'll find out for yourself when you meet her, won't you?"

Zach enjoyed the momentary surprise on Phillips' face. Had he thought that Robyn was going to sneak off to meet him? That their marriage was built on lies and secrets? Of course she had said she wouldn't meet up with Kevin if Zach didn't want her to. But Zach knew, they both knew, that Robyn would be there, whenever and wherever Kevin Phillips wanted her to be.

The policeman waved Zach through the cordon and into the exclusion zone. Looking in his rear-view mirror, he saw Phillips standing outside the cordon, staring after him. He shivered. He knew that Kevin always had been, and forever would be, a part of the life he was trying to build for himself, his wife and their unborn child.

Chapter 4

The black dress suited her blonde colouring but the neckline was low for daywear. While the blue top over maternity jeans emphasised the colour of her eyes, it was too casual. Not the image she wanted to convey. Robyn looked at the growing pile of clothes discarded on her bed and wondered why she was doing this. Kevin might not contact her at all. Besides, no matter what she wore she would still look like Humpty Dumpty. Her eyes fell on her peach-coloured pants and matching shirt. Popping on a white T-shirt first, she slipped into the pants and top and turned around in front of the full-length mirror. She caught her long hair and twisted it into a messy ponytail. The doorbell rang before she could decide whether she liked the look or not. Shaking her hair loose, she went downstairs to answer the door.

Tansy was shimmering on the doorstep, in a huge state of excitement even by her standards.

"Guess what!" she said.

"I've no idea," Robyn answered. "You'd better come in and tell me."

In the kitchen, Tansy threw herself onto a chair and then immediately stood up again.

"You know I said I'll never, ever again look sideways at a man?"

"In fact you've often said the world would be a better place without them."

"Well, yes. Maybe I said that but you have to understand how hurt I was after the break-up with Ari. Anyway, I've changed my mind."

"Really? Would you like a cup of coffee?"

Tansy gave a little tap of her foot which was as near as she could ever come to losing her temper.

"Don't fob me off, Robyn. I've met *the* most handsome, fabulous man I've ever laid eyes on. He's strong too. Decisive."

Robyn, tired from all her clothes-changing, sat at the table and indicated to Tansy to sit also.

"Where did you meet him and when?"

Tansy went into what seemed like a trance. She was gazing out into the garden but the smile curving her lips was obviously not for the flowers and shrubs.

"Where and when," Robyn prompted her.

"Earlier this morning while I was running on Lookout Hill. I was afraid at first, I thought he might be sinister but then I saw him. Robyn, he's just . . . just *delicious*! That's what he is."

"You seem to know him pretty well for someone you only met this morning. What's his name?"

Tansy wriggled a little on her seat and then grinned. "Okay! I admit I'm getting a bit carried away. I don't know his name or anything about him, but honest, he's fabulous, whoever he is. Even his car has class. Top of the range. And red. I love red cars. Especially sports cars."

At the mention of red sports cars Robyn felt memories surge. She remembered, how she remembered, the feel of the wind in her hair as she sat in the passenger seat of Kevin's beloved Audi Cabriolet. They had driven all over mainland Europe, the roof rolled back, sun on their faces. Happy, carefree holidays. Days enjoying the freedom of the roads, nights enjoying a passion which had touched their very souls. There had been one night in Vienna when . . .

"Oh! Robyn, I'm so sorry. Here I am being selfish again while you must be frantic with worry."

Robyn brought her attention back to Tansy who was staring at her with concern.

"Frantic with worry? Why should I be?"

"The Foot and Mouth disease of course. I heard about it. Zach must have told you that there are plans for mass slaughter of all the animals. I heard that people too will be –"

"For heaven's sake, Tansy! You've got this all wrong. It's probably Bluetongue Virus. And it's not contagious so neither other animals nor human beings can catch it from the infected animals. Besides, it's confined to Lynches' farm. So far anyway. There'll be no mass slaughter of animals in Felton. Who told you this story?"

Tansy shrugged. "Maybe I picked it up wrong. I'm glad. It would be awful if you and Zach and the baby had to leave because there were no more animals here for Zach to look after."

Robyn smiled at her friend. She meant well even though

she sometimes got her facts mixed up. She seemed quite clear though about the man in the red sports car.

"What does this man look like? The one you met this morning?"

"Blond. Blue-eyed. Vintage Robert Redford. About forty I'd say but he might be younger. He's got gorgeous arms too. Tanned, well muscled." The dreamy look left her face and her eyes widened. "My God! I just saw him sitting in his car. Suppose he's only four foot two when he stands up! It could happen, you know. He might have very short legs! That would ruin everything. He must be taller than me."

"He's six foot three," Robyn said quietly.

"What? You know him? Who is he?"

"My boss. Kevin Phillips. It must be. Red sports car, blond hair and what you so kindly call a decisive manner."

"Oh!"

"Exactly."

Tansy propped her elbows on the table and leaned towards Robyn, her dark brows drawn together. "Why don't you like him? You never said."

"I don't remember saying I didn't like him."

"You didn't have to. Your disapproving look when you say his name is enough. I had him pictured as a wizened old man with hair growing in his ears and the waistband of his trousers under his arms."

Robyn laughed and reached out her hand to her friend. No matter how confused or unhappy she felt she could always depend on Tansy to make her laugh.

"Tell you what, Tansy, I'm supposed to be meeting him today. Why don't you come along too? Wear your highest heels and see if he measures up."

"Are you sure? Won't you have business to discuss with him? Journalist talk. I wouldn't want to be in the way. Besides, I don't think he was as impressed by me earlier as I was by him. Maybe I'm better off holding on to the fantasy."

Robyn nodded her agreement. She should never have made that suggestion. Tansy was too sensitive to be exposed to Kevin Phillips' sharpness. Just as Robyn herself had been when first she had met him.

"Maybe you're right, Tansy. Anyway, I'm waiting for him to ring. He may forget or not have time. He's always in a hurry."

Right on cue, Robyn's phone rang. She stared at it as if she couldn't make up her mind whether to answer or not. Tansy gave her a dark-eyed, puzzled look and then tiptoed away. Robyn's hand shook as she picked up the phone.

"How are you, Robyn?"

She closed her eyes and allowed the richness of his deep voice to wash over her. Those were the very words he had spoken to her the first day she had met him. She had been a reporter for a provincial paper then, looking for a job on the prestigious *Daily News*. When she had gone into his office for interview, nervous and so anxious to please, he had stood, shook her hand and asked her how she was. She answered him now as she had that day.

"I'm well, thank you. And you?"

"Busy as usual. And looking forward to seeing you. If you want to, of course."

"Depends, Kevin. Business or personal?"

"Business, of course. We don't have personal any more. Remember?"

"Where will we meet? I suggest the Marine Hotel if that's okay with you."

"Perfect. I'm booked in there as it happens."

Robyn gripped the phone more tightly in her hand. Kevin Phillips was booked into the Marine? How long did he intend staying in Felton?

"Fine, Kevin. I'll see you in the Marine lobby in an hour. How's that for you?"

"See you in an hour," he said and abruptly cut the call, dismissing her as a headmaster would an errant pupil.

Sitting with the phone in her hand, Robyn's mood swung between anger and self-reproach. Kevin Phillips must be in Felton to cover the Bluetongue threat. He had no other reason to be here. So why did one part of her, that part which invaded unguarded moments, wish that he had come here just to see her?

Wearily, she got up from the table and continued getting ready for her first face-to-face meeting with Kevin Phillips in over a year.

Kevin sang as he showered off the sticky heat of driving around the environs of Lynches' farm. He usually enjoyed the sound of his deep bass, convincing himself that, under other circumstances, he could have made it as a professional singer. It was different now. His singing was an effort to drown out his noisy thoughts but the strategy wasn't working. No matter how high, low or long the notes he held, the haunting sound of Robyn's husky voice still echoed in his head and the image of her fragile blondeness was embedded in his brain. And now, very soon, he would see her, her petite frame swollen with another man's child. Zach Claymore, the curly-haired, butter-wouldn't-melt-in-his-mouth cow doctor. But Kevin knew that there was more to Zach than boyish good looks and green wellies. He had seen the flint in Zach Claymore's eyes.

Realising that his anger was spiralling, Kevin turned off the water and dried himself. When he was dressed he examined himself with satisfaction in the mirror. Not bad for a forty-year-old. Stomach flat, muscles taut, hair thick and still blond. Checking his watch he saw that it was almost time. He picked up his briefcase and the swipe card for his room, took a deep breath and went to the lobby of the Marine Hotel to meet the woman who used to be the centre of his world.

Robyn arrived early to the Marine Hotel. She had planned it that way, giving herself time to gather her troubling thoughts and steady her erratic breathing. Assuming that Kevin would be coming directly from his room to meet her, she found two armchairs at a corner coffee table in the lobby which gave her a good view of the stairs. A waiter approached as soon as she sat and took her order for a glass of sparkling water.

She settled in, her gaze wavering between the hypnotic upward motion of the gas bubbles in the water to the red-carpeted stairs which led to the guest rooms above. Her fingers fidgeted with the exquisite hand-painted scarf Tansy had given her to match her peach rig-out. Straightening out the silky folds, her fingers brushed against her stomach. Against her baby. It was a reality check. The baby needed her to be calm and relaxed. She sat back, breathed deeply and waited.

Kevin ran down the stairs, briefcase in hand. He hadn't changed. Still rushing. Still handsome. She waved as he paused at the foot of the stairs and looked around him. His face broke into the gleaming white smile she knew so well. He strode towards her and stooped to kiss her on the cheek. She inhaled the warmth and scent of him and launched into her prepared greeting before she could react.

"Welcome to Felton, Kevin. I assume you're here because of the Bluetongue Virus."

"Of course. I told you long ago it was just a matter of time before those infected midges found their way to this country, didn't I?"

"Yes, you did, but you never said they would make landfall in Felton. Careless of you."

He laughed and then called the waiter over. Robyn refused the offer of another drink so Kevin ordered coffee for himself. Turning back from the waiter he looked steadily at her. Self-conscious, she toyed with her scarf.

"Pregnancy suits you, Robyn. When is the baby due?"

"Two weeks' time. It seems forever now."

"How are you feeling?"

"A bit tired but that's to be expected. Thirty-four is probably not the ideal age to have a first baby."

"Well, you know how I feel about that. No need to go over old ground."

No, there wasn't. They had been through it for many bitter hours, months, years. Kevin Phillips had no space in his heart or mind for a baby. He obviously still believed that increasing the world's population at this time was selfish if not criminal. Staring at her half-full glass of water, Robyn watched a bubble float to the top and then burst. She lifted her eyes to the man who had brought her such happiness and misery.

"You said you had business to discuss with me, Kevin. What is it?"

"Yes, I have. It's about the last article you wrote in your opinion column."

"The climate change piece? It got a very good response. What about it?"

"I don't like the angle you took. It was biased."

Robyn was taken aback. Letters to the editor and emails had poured in after the article. The debate was ongoing. How could he not have liked it? "I don't understand," she said. "Why?"

"Because it was unbalanced and against editorial policy."

"That's not fair! You know I've never written an article without thorough research. And what do you mean by against editorial policy? *You're* the editor. Why did you let it go to print if you thought it was so bad?"

"I wasn't in the office last week. I was away. My deputy let it slip through. Besides, I didn't say it was bad – just skewed in favour of the man-has-caused-global-warming brigade."

Robyn wasn't sure how to cope with this. It was the first time in her career anyone had accused her of substandard work. Her accuracy had never before been doubted or her research called into question. She had been in touch with all the relevant experts prior to composing one word of that article. She felt a hot flush of anger and shame redden her cheeks.

"I spoke to the Met Office, the EPA, IPCC, read every

article I could lay my hands on. How could you say I wrote an unbalanced piece? I can back every prediction up with the official statistics I've been given."

"Ah! The official statistics. There you go. Where's your journalist's instinct gone? Dulled by the slow pace of Felton life and married bliss, is it?"

Both were surprised when Robyn leaned towards him with fury flashing in her eyes.

"If you have a criticism of my work, I accept that, but leave any mention of Felton or my private life out of it, please."

He gave her the look she used to think of as 'the long stare'. The one in which he read every thought in your mind and hid his own. Suddenly the white grin appeared.

"You haven't changed, Robyn. Still a calm surface and raging torrents underneath. I apologise if I insulted you."

"You insulted Felton, which I happen to like very much. But I'll accept your apology. Now tell me where, in your opinion, I went wrong and what you think I should have written about global warming."

Instead of answering, Kevin stooped down and lifted his briefcase onto the table. He snapped it open, took out a sheaf of papers and handed them to her.

"I want you to study these. Then come back to me and tell me what you think."

Flicking through the thick bundle, Robyn immediately got a sense of what all this was about.

"Yes, I've read up on some of this," she said. "So there's a debate about the cause of global warming. A few say it's part of a natural cycle but the vast majority believe our present warming is man-made. What difference does it make? Whatever the cause, the effect is indisputable."

"For God's sake, Robyn! Of course it makes a difference. All our resources are being poured into cutting carbon emissions when they're just a tiny part, if any at all, of the problem."

"In your opinion."

"In the opinion of very respected scientists who are doing independent research."

"They're researching yes. And theorising. But they have no hard evidence. No proof that solar storms or sun spots, cosmic rays or meteors are to blame for our warming planet. And the important thing is –"

"The important thing is that we should be concentrating on people, not carbon emissions. Millions, even billions, of people need to be resettled from endangered areas. Now! Food supplies will have to be secured. Our world is under threat, Robyn, and the people who call the shots are applying the wrong solutions. It will soon be too late."

Kevin's light blue eyes had deepened a shade. They were glinting with passion. Robyn had so often seen those glints as they had lain, spent and sated after making love. She blinked her eyes to rid herself of that image.

"You don't have to be an expert to see the rising seas and temperatures, changed weather patterns and melting ice caps!" she said. "Are you suggesting I should tell people to forget about energy conservation? That it doesn't matter? We're all doomed anyway?"

"You're being ridiculous now, Robyn. I never said you should scaremonger. But it's bordering on insane to tell people to cycle to work, turn heating down, plant a tree and all will be well. We can't change what's happening. We must learn to adapt. People should know the truth."

"And the truth is?"

"Whole populations are going to be wiped out. While we're patting ourselves on the back for driving electric cars and insulating our houses, people around the world are dying of thirst and hunger."

"I did mention my concerns about the vulnerability of third-world countries. I raised questions too about the scientific independence of climate reports."

"Bully for you. Now go and ask the important questions."

Robyn folded up the papers and stuffed them into her shoulder bag. Kevin had a new cause and there would be no arguing with that.

"Right. I'll read these and see what conclusions I come to. And I won't write another word about the climate. Not for the *Daily News* anyway."

"Don't go into a sulk, Robyn. You know I respect your work. It's just that you've got it wrong this time."

"Me, the world's scientists and politicians. In fact everyone except a handful of scientists and you."

He suddenly reached across the table and, grinning, caught her hand. "There was a time when you used to be afraid of me. What happened to that shy little girl?"

"She grew up," Robyn answered as her treacherous hand responded to a need no longer welcome and nestled into the warm comfort of Kevin's touch.

That was the moment when Zach, accompanied by officials from the Department of Agriculture, walked into the lobby of the Marine Hotel.

Robyn felt Zach's gaze on her before she saw him.

She snatched her hand back from Kevin but knew that it was too late. Zach had that little-boy-lost, hurt expression on his face. Shit!

She slung her bag onto her shoulder and stood.

"I'll read these and get back to you, Kevin."

He wasn't listening to her. He was leaning back in his chair, watching Zach cross the lobby towards their table.

"Any update on the rumoured BTV?" he asked as Zach reached them.

Zach ignored him and stooped to kiss Robyn on the cheek. "I hope you're not overdoing things," he said to her. "It's very warm today."

"Don't worry. I'm taking it easy," Robyn answered. "What are you doing here? Early lunch?"

"We're having a meeting but more importantly we're getting in out of the heat for a while."

"It won't be warm for much longer," said Kevin. "The weather's due to change."

Zach turned towards him and for a moment Robyn thought the two grown men might engage in a schoolboy brawl. She underestimated them both. Sarcasm was their weapon of choice. Far more mature. And more cruel.

"So you have contacts in the Met Office too," Zach said. "It wouldn't surprise me to learn you have a mole in the Kremlin."

"As a matter of fact, I watched the weather forecast on television. Why didn't you answer my question about the Bluetongue? Are you concerned that you raised a false alarm? You'll be labelled the vet who cried wolf if the tests are negative."

"I'm not in the least worried on that score. Better to be known as over-cautious rather than negligent."

"I'll go along with that. For now."

The two men stared at each other. Robyn had no doubt that Kevin would make an issue of it if Zach happened to be wrong about the BTV. A public issue with a private agenda.

"Zach! Phone. It's the lab." One of the officials was waving Zach over.

He hesitated for a moment, looking from his wife to the man who used to be her lover. He laid his arm gently on Robyn's shoulder. "Are you okay?" he said softly.

She nodded and smiled up at him, loving him for loving her.

"I've got to go now, Robyn," he said. "I'll catch up with you at home."

"I'm going to the meeting in the Community Hall tonight with Tansy. See you when I get back."

Then she stood on tiptoe and kissed him.

"Come on, Zach! They're waiting!" the phone-waver called again.

With a last look back over his shoulder at Kevin Phillips, Zach went to take the call that would either confirm or deny the Bluetongue Virus he suspected. The call that would make him the hero of the hour or an idiot whose misjudgement cost the state a lot of money. He said a quick but very fervent prayer as he took the phone. He listened intently for a few moments. Then he paled.

Chapter 5

Tansy was strolling aimlessly around her cottage. The short contact with Kevin Phillips that morning had unsettled her. He had reminded her of Ari and the bone-melting excitement of their first few years together. It had been an excitement tinged with danger. Ari Klum was a genius. A world-renowned sculptor. But he was unpredictable and at times unscrupulous. So too, she imagined, was Kevin Phillips.

Dissatisfied, uneasy, she turned to her work. The one constant on which she could rely. The jacket she had dreamt still eluded her. She squeezed her eyes shut, trying to recreate her dream. Squiggly images floated in front of her. That was it! Hieroglyphics. Ancient symbols.

In her rush to the computer she tripped over Ben, her Himalayan Persian. The cat howled in protest. Tansy scooped him up into her arms and stroked his white fur but Ben was not in a forgiving mood. He regarded her with a steady gaze from his vivid blue eyes and then leaped out of her arms, turned his back on her and strolled out of the studio. A cat treat would be needed before Ben allowed her be his friend again.

"Typical man," Tansy muttered as she booted up her computer.

Guessing that her dream of ancient symbols had some basis in reality, she checked her bookmarked pages. She bookmarked a lot of pages, always meaning to go back and re-read them but rarely getting around to doing that. There was always something newer to look up. More gripping.

As soon as the pages on Maya culture appeared, she remembered her fascination the first time she had read them. Cotton and clothes design had been as important an element of that ancient culture as it was in her life now. Fascinated, she continued reading and left Ben to his sulk.

Leaning over the rim of the rainwater barrel, Robyn debated whether she should use up what little was left for her plants. It had been six weeks since they had last seen rain. The council was rationing the supply of piped water and Zach said the stream on Lynches' farm had dried up. Water shortage was a topic which was bound to come up at the meeting tonight.

She put the lid back on the barrel again and went to check the weather forecast on the teletext. Kevin Phillips had, as usual, been right. An active weather system was moving south from Iceland and there was a possibility that it might head towards the parched island of Ireland. With any luck the plants would soon drink their fill.

Thinking of Kevin brought her attention back to the papers he had given her. She had read through some but it had been hard to concentrate. She saw Zach's worried face on every page she turned. Something was very wrong. Zach had looked shocked as he had listened to the phone call in the Marine Hotel. When last she had seen her husband, he had been hurrying out of the lobby, surrounded by officials, all looking equally stunned. Zach had mouthed to her that he would call but she had heard nothing from him since.

Robyn picked up reading where she had left off. The more she read, the more she could allow that global warming had very many causes and no simple answer. From the material in front of her, it would seem obvious that sunspot activity, first regularly recorded by Chinese astronomers in 28 BC, was an influence on Earth's climate. Closely examining an attached chart she traced the history to date of recorded warming and cooling periods which fitted snugly with increased or decreased sunspot activity.

She put down the chart. Somewhere in her own research, she had a paper proving just the opposite. If there was one thing she was sure of, it was that figures could be manipulated to prove almost any point. How was she supposed to judge? She was a journalist, not a scientist. And since the vast bulk of scientists believed that cars and planes, deforestation and coal-fired industries, were the cause of the increasingly erratic weather patterns, she would go along with their expert opinion. And yet, some of the evidence was proving to be flawed, some of the opinions biased . . .

She jumped when her phone rang. Grabbing it quickly, she was relieved to hear Zach's voice.

"How are you?" she asked. "I've been worrying about you."

"I don't have long to talk. Just wanted to make sure you were okay."

"I'm fine. What's going on, Zach? What's wrong? Do Con Lynch's sheep have Bluetongue Virus or not?"

"They do."

"That's not too bad so, is it? Cull the sick animals. Vaccinate the others. Spray the area for midges. Not a disaster."

"We can't vaccinate."

"Why? I thought that was procedure."

"This is confidential, Robyn. Not a word to –"

"I know! Not a word to Tansy Bingham."

"I was going to say to Kevin Phillips."

There was a moment's silence. Robyn's heart began to hammer. It wasn't like Zach to be melodramatic. What in the hell was going on? Was Zach jealous or was he in some kind of trouble?

"It is BTV," he said quietly. "But not a type we've seen before."

Robyn breathed a sigh of relief. She knew there had been twenty-three different serotypes of BTV identified. So what? It obviously wasn't the same variation as had appeared in the UK.

"It could be a new strain," Zach continued. "Too soon to say yet. So now you see why confidentiality is so important."

Robyn heard other voices in the background. They were calling Zach.

"I've got to go now. I may not be home tonight."

And then he was gone, leaving her with the uneasy feeling that her life was about to take a new, and as yet unknown, direction.

The sun was dipping towards the horizon as Robyn

closed her front door behind her. She looked out to sea. It was restless, at odds with the heat, tossing flecks of white foam onto the shore. The tops of the cypress trees in the Germans' house next door were waving in the stiffening breeze. Looking skyward, Robyn checked for clouds. A screech of brakes and the sound of gravel pinging against metal told her Zach's assistant had arrived.

Robyn smiled at Kerry as she hopped off her moped.

"Hi, Kerry. Here for the evening clinic?"

"Yes. Zach rang. He has to stay at Lynches' until the big noises from the Department leave. There won't be much business in the clinic tonight anyway. The whole village will be at the meeting in the Community Hall."

Robyn nodded. That was true. And anyway, despite looking no more than fourteen years old, Kerry was a very capable young woman. Robyn glanced at her watch. She had promised Tansy that she would call at half past seven and it was almost that now.

"Better run," she said and then they both laughed at the thought. "On second thoughts, I'll just walk fast."

Tansy had converted two downstairs rooms of her cottage into a light-filled design studio. As she approached, Robyn noticed that the big double patio doors of the studio were wide open. She sighed. That could only mean one thing. Tansy was working and had completely forgotten about the meeting. Now there would be at least ten minutes' delay while Tansy got herself and that big fluffy cat organised. Ben was outside the studio, sprawled on a cushion, pretending to be asleep. Robyn wasn't fooled. She had seen his whiskers twitch as she approached. She knocked on the studio door and walked in.

"Ben looks very sulky. Have you had an argument with him again?"

Tansy looked up from her computer. She seemed surprised. Then her hand went to her mouth as she remembered.

"Shit! The meeting. I forgot. I'm driving, aren't I?"

"That's the plan. Better get a move on. We need to get seats."

"Robyn, you wouldn't believe what I've been reading. It's just so fascinating. Did you ever hear of the Maya Calendar?"

"Some kind of ancient astronomical calendar, isn't it?"

"It was drawn up in ancient times, yes. Over 2000 years ago. Which is what makes it all the more amazing."

"Why don't you tell me about it in the car? We're going to be late."

"Never mind the meeting. I must tell you how clever the Maya were. They devised systems to record time from days right up to eons. The Tzolkin, which means the count of days, is supposedly based on the human gestation period of 260 days."

"They got it wrong so, didn't they? The length of pregnancy averages 280 days."

"Depends on when you count from, conception or last period and so on. Don't go all analytical on me. The calendar could also be based on the numbers thirteen and twenty which the Maya thought very significant. And right, I'll get ready now but I've loads more to tell you. Just wait 'til you hear about Ben."

Tansy dashed up the stairs, taking clips out of her hair and shaking it loose as she ran. When Robyn looked out the door she noticed that the cat had gone. She knew

Tansy would not go anywhere until she had located her cat and made sure he had his toys and his treats. They would be late for the meeting.

Felton Community Hall was only ten minutes' drive from the cottages but to Robyn it felt twice as long. Tansy talked non-stop along the way about Maya culture. By the time they pulled up in the grounds of the hall, Robyn had learned that the Maya had brewed chocolate-flavoured beer from cacoa beans, grown two types of cotton, and that the women had woven the cloth into the huipil, a loose rectangular garment with a hole cut for the head and still worn in Mexico and Guatemala.

"You can wear it loose or tuck it in. Different lengths. Plain or ornate. Embroidered, tie-dyed or sewn with pearls. It's a wonderfully versatile piece of clothing."

"So is the new Tansy Bingham range going to reflect Maya culture?"

"Maybe," Tansy answered as she steered towards a parking space which from a distance looked about half the width of her car.

Robyn closed her eyes and didn't open them until the car was safely stopped and the engine switched off. People were still pouring into the hall so at least they wouldn't be the last. It seemed that the whole population had turned up to discuss the sea-wall defences.

Robyn glanced at the hall, wondering if everyone would fit in there. It was a rectangular building, long and low, with a row of small windows so high up towards the red-tiled roof that it must have been designed by a very tall person indeed. Or else the citizens of Felton didn't want anyone peering into their hall.

"You never told me about Ben," Robyn reminded Tansy as they got out. "What did he do?"

"I can't tell you now. Not enough time. It's got to do with the Maya Long Count Calendar. C'mon quick. We must get a seat for you."

Only Tansy could relate her neurotic cat to the history of the Maya Long Count Calendar. Robyn grinned and followed along in her friend's wake.

The hall was packed to capacity. It smelled of hot bodies and occasional wafts of ozone drifting up from the harbour below. Once, a long time ago, Felton Manor had stood on this plateau overlooking the village. That had been an age when hats were doffed to the gentry and the poor emigrated or starved. Social justice had been well served by building this community-funded meeting place on the site of the old manor.

As Robyn and Tansy walked past row after row of occupied seats, it seemed that they might have to stand for the entire meeting.

A middle-aged woman Robyn knew by sight but not by name, gave the teenage boy beside her a poke in the ribs as they passed. "Get up and give the vet's wife your seat," she ordered. The boy stood reluctantly.

"I'll just go and stand at the back," Tansy said. "I'll see you later."

Robyn smiled at the boy and gratefully took his chair. He shrugged and then slouched after Tansy to the back of the hall.

"That's my son, Des," the woman said. "Awkward age."

Robyn nodded and gave an uncertain smile. How would

she and Zach cope with a teenager? She hadn't thought much about that. A baby, yes. A toddler. A young child, innocent and loving. But then her hopes and dreams had always skipped on to proud graduation days and even to grandchildren, conveniently glossing over the door-slamming, hormone-infested teenage years.

"Terrible about Lynches' farm, isn't it?" the woman said. "This bluebottle disease is a curse."

"The animal sickness is caused by midges actually, not bluebottles."

"Whatever, Lynches can't afford it. She's not strong, you know."

"Really?"

"Bad chest. Will you look at the get-up of Billy Moynihan! He must think there's votes to be got tonight."

Robyn had to shift in her seat to see around the beefy shoulders of the man sitting in front of her. She wasn't sure who the woman was talking about until she saw the table set up at the top of the hall. The members of the village council were all seated except for one man. He was fussing around, distributing sheets of paper, whispering in ears and patting shoulders. He was wearing a suit, a very bright tie and a mayoral chain. Billy Moynihan, honorary Mayor of Felton village. As Robyn watched him he went to the centre seat, tapped the microphone and then banged on the table with a gavel, his jowls shaking.

"Order! Order, please. The meeting is now open. First I'd like to convey apologies from the County Engineer. He can't be here with us tonight. Nor I'm afraid can any of our politicians."

A low booing sound echoed around the hall. Billy Moynihan raised his hand for silence.

"They've asked me to send on a report of our meeting and assured me they'll consider all our suggestions."

"Bull!" the woman beside Robyn whispered. "They've been ignoring us for years. They don't care if Felton falls into the sea."

Robyn nodded her head. The woman was probably right.

"I'm going to ask for a show of hands now," Billy said, his face taking on a sweaty sheen.

"All in favour of deferring the meeting until the officials can be here raise your hands."

Robyn looked around her and noticed only one hand go up. She glanced back over her shoulder to where Tansy was standing by the door. Tansy's hands were down. It was probable she hadn't even heard the call to vote because she was deep in conversation with Kevin Phillips. They were smiling, nodding, enjoying their chat. Robyn understood. Kevin could be the most charming of men when he wanted to be.

Billy Moynihan banged the gavel again. Robyn dragged her gaze back to the mayor.

"That's a majority for going ahead so I'll set the ball rolling. The Department for Coastal Defence has refused any further funding for Felton. In their opinion the sea wall they built five years ago is adequate to deal with any high tides that might happen in the foreseeable future."

"Rubbish! That's not what my insurance company says. That so-called wall isn't a protection!"

The angry voice came from behind Robyn. She meant

to look in that direction but instead her eyes were drawn again towards Tansy and Kevin Phillips. There was something about the way they were standing side by side, complementing each other, she so dark and slim, he blond and muscular. Kevin saw her and smiled his knowing grin. She turned back quickly, furious with herself for being caught staring.

The angry speaker from the floor was getting into his stride now.

"Five years ago we didn't have tidal surges like we had this spring. My home is on Lower Street. It was flooded out and everything destroyed. What do you want me to do? Move my home up here to the top of the hill?"

"The pier was under water. And the river topped the bridge . . ."

"My insurance premium has tripled since . . ."

The clamour of complaints mixed into one discordant sound in Robyn's head. She couldn't concentrate on what they were saying. Her mind was miles away. Years back. In a time when she had been the woman standing beside Kevin, the one he had been smiling at. And she had smiled right back at him. And loved him.

The meeting was descending into farce. Everybody seemed to have a water issue, either too much or too little of it. Tidal flooding and the threat that the local river, the Aban, could burst its banks were on the too-much side, while drought and the current water shortage were on the too little. Billy Moynihan had to do some serious gavel-banging to restore order.

"I'll take one speaker at a time, please. We'll achieve nothing with all this shouting. Raise your hand and give your name if you want to make a point. Yes, you, sir. At the back."

"Kevin Phillips, the *Daily News*."

Robyn held her breath. What was Kevin up to now? Amusing himself by getting involved in a local issue? Causing trouble because he was bored?

"Felton is a high-risk flood area," he announced. "What emergency plans do you have in place?"

Billy Moynihan instantly preened. He straightened his tie, patted his chain and threw his shoulders back, obviously wanting to impress the journalist from one of the leading national dailies.

"As Mayor, I've organised an emergency response team. We've provided a supply of sandbags for premises and homes in vulnerable areas."

"Are you confident, Mayor, that you can fight a deluge with a few sandbags?"

Robyn winced. Billy Moynihan was all bluster and bling. He had no answer to Kevin Phillips' scathing sarcasm. She felt herself stand before she had decided what she wanted to say.

"Yes. The lady in the third row," the Mayor said, relief evident in his voice. "What do you want to say?"

Robyn panicked for a moment. What did she want to say? That Kevin Phillips had no right to come here and sneer? That he had no business here at all, bringing back memories, making a nuisance of himself. She cleared her throat.

"First of all, I'd like to inform the last speaker that the village of Felton has been left almost solely to its own devices as far as flood protection is concerned. There have been official promises made but nothing done. The community is doing the best it can under the circumstances."

"That's more or less what I was pointing out," Kevin said. "The community's best doesn't seem to be good enough."

Robyn turned around to face him. He was grinning at her. She glared at him over the heads of the curious onlookers.

Billy banged his gavel so loudly that Robyn jumped.

"One speaker at a time, please. You've had your say, Mr Phillips."

Robyn bristled with resentment. This was so typical of Kevin. He could be cruel, as Billy Moynihan was learning. The Mayor was starting to look ineffectual. Bumbling. And so was she. She took a deep breath.

"The politicians are just making excuses," she said. "If we want to save Felton from rising tides, we'll have to force them to act. I propose that we bring our protest to them. If they won't come to Felton, Felton will go to them. Disturb them in their cosy little parliament!"

She got a rousing cheer and a grateful smile from Billy Moynihan.

"Go on!" the woman beside her whispered loudly to Robyn. "Give them a piece of your mind."

Robyn smiled at her and, more confident now, continued.

"We must, and we will, canvas the authorities but I think they have proved that we can't rely on them. Suppose the same situation arose here as we saw along the east coast of America a few months ago. How prepared would we be for that? Who would warn us, evacuate us? Where would we go to be safe?"

"You're scaremongering! Frightening people half to

death with speculation, that's what you're doing. Next you'll be saying we should build an ark and put two of everything in it!" The man who had spoken was standing, his face red. "You're the woman who wrote that piece in the *Daily News* about the climate, aren't you? Barely landed in Felton and you're telling us what to do. Our politicians will look after us like they've always done, long before you set foot here."

"I'm just making suggestions. Like everyone else here I'm concerned about the safety of our village."

Noise rose to an uncomfortable level as some people backed Robyn's point of view and others agreed with the angry man. Robyn sat. Her job was done. The people of Felton had taken control of the discussion – taken it back from Kevin Phillips.

"Why not make the Community Hall an emergency shelter?" Tansy suggested. "It's the highest building in Felton so unless we have a biblical flood, it's safe."

Debate went to and fro, got heated, calmed down and eventually came to a conclusion. Felton must face the threat of being overwhelmed by the tide.

Billy Moynihan, having regained his aplomb, brought the meeting to a close. The mood was positive. A new committee would be set up, including as members Tansy and the elderly GP, Dr Early. Someone would be appointed too to liaise with the Met Office on advance weather warnings.

When Robyn stood again, she felt stiff. As she turned to leave the hall, she saw that Kevin had gone. Tansy was not alone though. By her side stood the sulky displaced teenager and on her other side the German, Horst Mueller. He reminded Robyn of the cypress trees in his garden. Dark and brooding. Shadowing his surrounds. As she approached he fixed her with a stare so penetrating that she shivered. Then, like a wraith, he disappeared. The teenage boy melted away into the crowd too, probably anxious to avoid his mother.

"Very productive meeting, wasn't it?" Tansy said. "And I had a great chat with your boss. Kevin Phillips is lovely, Robyn. I can't understand why you don't like him."

Robyn shrugged. Sometimes she didn't understand either. "Forget about him. Tell me about our German neighbour. Were you talking to him?"

"Horst Mueller? No. Not a word. He just stood there and ignored me. He's very weird, isn't he? But never mind him. Wait until I tell you about Ben. You're going to be stunned."

Robyn was. A bit. It seemed that Ben was the name the Maya had given the thirteenth day of their twenty-day calendar.

"And imagine I knew nothing at all about the Maya or their calendar when I named him. Can you believe that? It's all very intriguing. Like something pre-ordained."

"How do you make that out?"

"Well, first I unknowingly give my cat a significant Mayan name. Then I dream about their signs and symbols. I look up their calendar and find out that the very last day they gave a name and date to is 21st of December 2012. I discover all this just as I attend a meeting about how crazy our weather is getting. What do you think?"

Robyn laughed. "I think you've a terrific imagination, Tansy. Did you ever consider writing science fiction?"

"Laugh if you must but you've got to admit there are

coincidences. I even share my love of cotton with the Maya. Where did that come from?"

"They can't have been that clever, Tansy. They're gone, aren't they?"

"They have descendents. But yes, their way of life and a lot of their history and culture is gone. Destroyed by war and natural disaster. And I have a feeling, a premonition, that we could end up the same."

Robyn glanced at Tansy as they headed for the car park. She looked solemn. An older Tansy without her usual child-like buzz and excitement. War and natural disaster were, after all, very grown-up topics.

In the car, Tansy put the key in the ignition and then turned to Robyn.

"Do you wonder what future generations will say about us? I mean about the people of the twenty-first century. Will they curse us for ruining the planet? Will they say we were primitive? Ignorant? Will they find bits of computers and cars and planes and put them in their museums? Reminders of a civilisation which once thrived on Earth and was then destroyed by its own success. Just like the Maya."

Robyn tried but her imagination could not focus that far ahead.

"Don't be daft, Tansy. There are challenges now. Maybe big changes. But we can cope."

"Are you sure?"

Robyn thought about that. Yes, she was sure the world would survive and prosper. She had to be sure. For her baby.

The helicopter seemed to hover for a moment, sending

eddies of wind swirling around the meadow. Then it rose and headed east into the night sky, watched by the four men on the ground.

Zach turned to the man by his side. Con Lynch had aged years in the past twenty-four hours.

"Your wife is in good hands now," Zach said, knowing his words were no consolation.

"I know that. But what if . . ."

Con didn't finish the sentence. He walked away towards the far side of the meadow, passing the red stick lights which marked the landing zone, crossing the area flattened by the helicopter which had taken his wife to hospital.

Andrew Simmons began to follow him. A Veterinary Department bureaucrat. A worried man.

"Leave him be," Zach said. "He needs time alone."

"He mustn't leave the property."

"How in the hell can he? You've the place tied up like Fort Knox."

"More like Alcatraz," Andrew said. "Did you notice how they've left all the markers they used. The red sticks and flashlights. They expect to be making more mercy flights here. I wonder which one of us will be next?"

Zach shrugged. He knew what Andrew was saying without actually uttering the words. The fear nobody dared speak. Noreen Lynch was dying. Of that there was no doubt. But from what? From a virus that rightly belonged in the animal world? The medics who attended her, swaddled from head to toe in protective clothing, must certainly have believed so. The specially adapted night-flying ambulance helicopter just confirmed the fears.

Zach watched the stooped figure of Con Lynch trudge through the field. He tried to imagine what the old man must be feeling and he tried to forget the image of Noreen Lynch, cyanosed and fighting for breath, being carried onto the rescue helicopter. He failed on both counts.

"How soon will we know?" he asked.

He was met with shrugged shoulders and worried faces. Andrew Simmons didn't know nor did Dick Maloney. There was no one else to ask. It was just the four of them imprisoned here on Lynches' farm: Andrew Simmons from the Veterinary Department, Dick Maloney from the Department of Agriculture, Zack Claymore the vet who first suspected the dreaded Bluetongue Virus, and Con Lynch, farmer and grieving husband, maybe soon to become widower of the world's first human victim of the mutated Bluetongue Virus.

Zach headed back to the farmhouse and threw himself down on the couch in the small sitting room. The place which would be his home until they knew the truth about Noreen Lynch's sickness. He feared for Con Lynch and his wife, he feared for the people of Felton. Most of all he feared for his wife and his unborn child.

Chapter 6

Zach had not been home at all last night. It appeared that, like the sheep, he was quarantined on Lynches' farm. It had been very late when he rang to tell Robyn not to expect him in Woodruff Cottage. He had seemed distracted, disinterested in her account of the meeting in the Community Hall. Robyn usually liked being alone, enjoying the time and space to wonder at life's quirky twists and turns. When she chose. Her aloneness now was not of her choosing.

She had spent the morning struggling to write an article on cloning. It was an interesting topic but not gripping enough to concentrate her thoughts. She had missed Zach's arms around her last night, missed seeing his slow smile this morning, missed the safety of his quiet strength. She thought of ringing him but knew he was probably busy.

When Zach finally rang he sounded tired. Stressed.

"I don't know when this is going to be resolved, Robyn. It might be a while yet. I could ask Kerry to move in with you until I get back. What do you think?"

"No! I don't need a baby-sitter. Not yet. Tansy is right next door and you know she's always hopping in and out. Besides, you won't be away that long, will you?"

There was silence on the line.

"Zach? What's going on? You'll be home soon, won't you?"

"I hope so. We should learn more today. I'll let you know."

"What about a change of clothes? Your shaving gear? Will I drop them up to you?"

"Stay away, Robyn! Don't come near Lynches'."

"Why? What's going on up there? Are the sheep radioactive?"

"This is serious, Robyn. It's very important that you stay away. Promise?"

Why would he not want her to call to the farm? Yes, it was quarantined but surely she could hand in clothes for her husband. Yet Zach was not given to hysterics. He must have a good reason.

"Alright, Zach. I promise."

"I'll ring later. Take care."

He had gone then, leaving her with suspicions and fears. There were things Zach either wouldn't or couldn't say. They had been apparent in his pauses and silences. So the sheep had an unusual form of Bluetongue Virus. Why all the secrecy? What was so earth-shattering about this animal virus? Costly for the Lynches, yes. A threat to local and national livestock, certainly. But it wasn't even contagious, like foot and mouth would have been. At least, the common form of the virus wasn't . . .

There was more to this. There had to be.

Restless now, Robyn gave up on her writing. She

wandered out to the front garden. It was a near perfect day. Sunshine, blue skies, white clouds and a cooling breeze. Walking over to the flower-beds, she noticed plants beginning to wilt. She squinted up at the wispy clouds and wondered if they might, at last, deliver some badly needed rain. Kevin know-all Phillips had forecast a change in the weather, hadn't he? It probably would rain soon, just to prove him right.

Glancing into Tansy's house, Robyn noticed the studio doors were open. Tansy would be absorbed in her work. Not to be disturbed. Robyn needed somebody to talk to. She needed company. She also needed a newspaper. Zach always brought the daily home from his early calls. She thought of how they shared the paper, Zach starting from the sports at the back and she from the front page. They met in the middle, she and Zach. On everything. They had forged solid middle-ground.

The baby kicked. Robyn smiled. She had company.

"We're going into the village, baby," she whispered. "No more football for a while. Okay?"

The walk into the village took Robyn along a narrow winding road. The hedges were coated with a fine film of dust. Ditches which flooded with run-off from winter rains were dried-out ruts now. Yet the air was filled with the fragrance of honeysuckle. Everywhere there were clumps of daisies and buttercups, bindweed and speedwell. A wealth of plant life surviving the drought. Along this particular stretch of road, growth seemed as vibrant as it had always been.

The road widened, turned a sharp corner and brought a different scene into view. Here the hedges were lower and Robyn had full view of the sloping fields to her right. They were charred where one week ago a raging gorse fire had burned for three days and nights. On the hillside the fire-blackened ruins of the old chapel stood stark against the blue sky. It had long since been abandoned as a place of worship. Just as well the new chapel was sitting serenely in a field five miles outside the village. The site had been donated and the Church had gladly accepted the gift. Felton was like that – puzzling until you learned the inside story.

Ahead lay the old stone bridge which spanned the River Aban as it coursed towards the sea. Robyn stood on the bridge and looked into the river beneath. Reduced to a narrow channel in the middle of the dried-up river bed, the Aban was no longer coursing. Trickling would be a more accurate description. The water was languid. Dirty. Choked with algae. A family of swans sailed single file down the central channel, the cygnets paddling furiously to keep up with their parents.

"You'll do yourself damage leaning over that far, Mrs Claymore."

Robyn looked up to see the woman from the meeting last night standing beside her. The mother of the sulky teenaged son.

"The water's very low, isn't it?" Robyn remarked, embarrassed that she didn't know the woman's name.

"Yes. Do you feel a bit silly now writing about floods and talking about sea defences when all the time a lack of water is our problem?"

"Remember last spring? Felton was under three feet of water then."

"I remember it well. I live on Lower Street with my son. The downstairs of my house was destroyed in that flood."

"I'm sorry to hear that. Anyway, what I wrote was that we would have alternating floods and droughts. I didn't think it would happen so quickly though."

"It's all our own fault, Mrs Claymore. We should have seen it coming."

Robyn thought about her research. She was less sure now than she had been that the changing climate was something mankind had caused and could control.

"I don't really believe so. Of course greenhouse gases have added to the effect but I think there's a good case for . . ."

Robyn stopped mid-sentence as the woman laughed heartily.

"I'm not talking about carbon dioxide or any of that nonsense," she said. "I mean Billy Moynihan. Why we elected him Mayor, I don't know. He couldn't organise a card game, let alone protect a village. And by the way, my name is June Varian." She stuck her hand out and gave Robyn a firm handshake. "I read your column every week. I enjoyed it until you started on all the climate doom and gloom."

"I'm afraid, June, there's no avoiding it any more. We'll just have to face up to it. And call me Robyn, please."

"I s'pose you're right. Are you going into the village, Robyn?"

They walked together over the bridge which led them onto Lower Street, Felton's main shopping area. A cobbled street, it curved gently towards the pier at one end and to access Middle Street at the other.

"Oh, look! He seems fit to burst," June said as she peered along the length of Lower Street.

Mayor Billy Moynihan was standing outside Cantillon's supermarket, his head buried in a newspaper. Even from yards away, it was obvious that he was angry. His whole body was rigid and his face was a shade of puce which clashed with his royal-blue T-shirt. As they approached he lifted his head. When he saw Robyn his temper went into overdrive.

"Did you know about this?" he demanded, waving his copy of the *Daily News* at her.

"Billy Moynihan, control that temper of yours!" said June. "You've no call to be shouting at a pregnant woman."

"I have every right if she had anything to do with this scurrilous piece. You write for this rag, don't you? Why did you let him run Felton down like that?"

It didn't take too much reasoning to figure that Kevin Phillips was the cause of Billy Moynihan's anger. Robyn took the paper and read the lead article. It was, of course about the Bluetongue Virus. It raised questions about the secrecy surrounding the outbreak and the lack of information from government sources. So far, nothing to complain about in the article. Then Kevin had decided to sharpen his pen and report on last night's meeting. Describing Felton as a 'sleepy backwater', he had written a vicious account of the meeting in the Community Hall. By the time Robyn had finished reading it, she was almost as incensed as Billy Moynihan.

"He's saying we're all ignorant morons, incapable of organising our own lives, let alone a flood defence," Billy spluttered.

This time, Robyn could not disagree with him. She understood that Kevin's main target had been the politicians who had neglected Felton, fobbed it off with promises of assistance. But in doing that he had implied, and at times stated, that the population of Felton was gullible and incapable.

"He's trying to force the politicians to take responsibility for our safety," Robyn said, wondering why she was coming to Kevin Phillips' defence.

"By pointing out that the Mayor, the first citizen of the village, is a pantomime character who wears a chain, bangs a gavel and knows nothing about government policy or climate change? That the most radical suggestion for action at our meeting came from yourself, an outsider? *I'm* not saying you're an outsider, Mrs Claymore. I'm quoting him. He's made us look like fools. Makes it seem like the world would be a better place if the sea just rolled over Felton and swept us all away."

"I live in Felton too, you know. I don't consider myself an outsider. I'm as furious as you are."

Billy Moynihan squinted his eyes and peered at Robyn. Then he nodded. He believed her.

"So what can we do about it, Mrs Claymore? Will you talk to him? Get him to write an apology?"

"The best thing we can do is prove him wrong. Get ourselves organised. Put emergency measures into place and step up our campaign to have our sea wall strengthened and our drainage system updated."

June rubbed her hands together and smiled, her eyes gleaming with the light of battle. "This calls for coffee. C'mon. We'll have a meeting and plan our revenge on that smart-ass from the city."

"My place," Billy said as he led his little army up to

Middle Street and into the backroom of his fishing-tackle shop. There was a bounce in his step again, an urgency in his plans to make the people of Felton safe from death by drowning and humiliation by criticism. And that, Robyn thought, as she trailed along in his wake, is what the astute Kevin Phillips had set out to do.

It would have been better if he had cried. Easier to understand. More comfortable for the onlookers. Anything would have been better than the paralysing grief which glazed Con Lynch's eyes and drained his face of colour. Even though he was sitting in the kitchen of his own home, he looked like a man who was completely lost.

"I don't understand," he said. "She's had chest infections before. She's never got as low as this with them."

Andrew Simmons and Dick Maloney exchanged glances – 'my department has no comment to make at this time' looks. They were hovering by the door like security guards, as if they thought Zach or Con might decide to jump up from the kitchen table and make a run for it.

Con turned towards Zach.

"What's going on, Zach? What's happening to my wife? What are they doing to her in Dublin?"

Ignoring the officials, Zach leaned towards Con and put his hand on the old man's arm.

"I'm very sorry about Noreen, Con. The truth is, we don't know what's wrong with her yet."

"It's my fault," Con said and his frame seemed to shrink under the weight of his guilt.

"Don't be daft, man. Of course it wasn't your fault. How could it be?"

"I should have insisted on calling her own doctor. Dr Early has been treating Noreen for the past thirty years. He understands her weak lungs. He would have known what to do for her."

"This is different, Con. You know it is. She needs specialist care and that's what she's getting. The very best of it."

"I shouldn't have listened to these gobshites here with their fancy suits and their technology. My wife is in a strange place on her own because of them. Noreen and me went through everything together for nearly fifty years and I'm not there now when she needs me most. I . . . I . . ."

The tears came then. Not gushing but welling up in the pain-filled eyes. Con turned his head and looked out over the fields. Following the direction of his gaze Zach saw that the old man was staring at the cleared patch in the meadow where the helicopter had landed and taken off yesterday, taking his wife to the isolation unit in a leading city hospital. Con's eyes were riveted to the spot, as if he was seeing again the rotors spinning and the craft ascending.

"I should never have allowed them to take her away. She must have been terrified."

"She's very peaceful now. She's in a deep sleep."

"How the fuck do you know?"

"I was speaking to one of the specialists working on her case."

"You're as bad as them," Con said angrily, nodding in the direction of the two officials. "Since when is my wife 'a case' as you put it? She's Noreen Lynch and don't forget that!"

"I'm sorry, Con. I didn't mean to be insensitive. But you do realise the situation is very delicate."

"You mean my Noreen could have got Bluetongue Virus from the sheep? Is that what you're all hinting at? Pussy-footing around. Thinking I wouldn't understand."

"That's a possibility we're investigating," said Andrew Simmons. "Of course we can't be sure yet."

"I want to see my wife."

More exchanging of glances and foot-shuffling from the officials.

"We'll arrange that as soon as we know it's safe," said Dick Maloney. "We have to assume the worst scenario until we're told otherwise."

Zach heard Con's sharp intake of breath.

The old man spoke quietly but with intense anger. "The worst scenario is that my wife will die without me by her side."

"I'm afraid strict isolation is necessary for now, Con," said Andrew.

Con stood then and walked out of the kitchen, brushing past the officials without even a glance in their direction. The three men listened until they heard the back door close. Con Lynch was gone to walk the hills.

"Is there any hope of a preliminary report from the labs?" asked Zach. "They must have an indication by this stage."

"Of course they must have an idea which direction things are headed by now but they have to confirm before they say anything, don't they?" said Andrew. "The hospital is working as fast as they can on virology and the vet lab on serotype. The only thing confirmed is that the sheep definitely have a virus of the Bluetongue variety. Mutated maybe to infect humans, but Bluetongue nevertheless. And as for the old woman, we just don't know, do we?"

"What we do know, without a doubt, is that we're stuck on this farm until we find out more," said Zach.

"You're not complaining about that, are you?" asked Dick "We can't risk spreading a disease which may very well be fatal. Think of your family."

Zach glared at the man and agreed with Con Lynch. Both these men were gobshites. As if Zach needed reminding of his family. Of beautiful delicate Robyn and the baby she was carrying. He would live out the rest of his days on Lynches' farm rather than put either of them at risk.

"How soon can Con get to see his wife?" he asked. "What's the situation?"

"No decisions until the results are in," Dick pronounced.

"Surely he could see her if precautions were put in place? Protective clothing or whatever."

"He may already be infected," said Andrew. "We might be too. This is a big unknown, Zach. Our priority is to limit the possibility of spread."

Zach stood and stretched his arms. He felt tired and stiff. And suddenly old. He had overseen culling, supervised the spraying of midge-breeding sites and broken the news of a wife's potentially fatal illness to a heartbroken man. All in a time-frame which seemed at once instant and endless. Numbness was setting in. He must ring Robyn. Make doubly sure that she came nowhere near Lynches' farm. But first he must sleep.

He walked into Con Lynch's sitting room and threw himself down on the couch which had become his bed. Before he closed his eyes he looked long and hard at the black-and-white portrait of Noreen and Con Lynch's wedding. She had been a very attractive girl with dark curly hair and Con had been a strapping young man. They were gazing at each other in the photo, smiling, eyes shining, the promise of happy-ever-after in their closeness. Zach remembered his own wedding day and what a beautiful bride Robyn had been. How ecstatically happy he himself had felt. Just like Con Lynch had been on the day of his marriage to Noreen.

Zach began to understand the true depth of Con Lynch's grief.

By the time Robyn left Billy Moynihan's fishing-tackle shop she and June Varian had been co-opted onto the Flood Defence Committee. Nobody would argue with the Mayor's decision. Robyn felt she could make a good contribution – she liked organising and had a bent for making lists and getting things done. The three of them, June Varian, Billy Moynihan and herself, had agreed that their fight to make Felton safe from worsening weather would have to be two-pronged. Political agitation and self-help. The need to show Kevin Phillips he had underestimated them was good motivation too.

As Robyn went to the supermarket to get her paper and some groceries, she felt more a part of Felton than she ever had before. Maybe she had mistaken the locals' natural caution for coldness.

Out on the street again, she hesitated. She could walk home by the road. The way she had come. Or else she could go down to the pier and follow the path which led to the strand. Feeling hot now, the thought of taking off her sandals and paddling in the cool sea was tempting.

She headed towards the pier and stood for a while looking along its dilapidated concrete length. The monotony of cement was broken here and there by embedded bollards used for tying up boats and by Felton's stunning Public Convenience, built towards the left-hand side of the pier, fronted by tubs of flowering primula, and most unexpectedly of all, painted a deep crimson. Robyn smiled as she squinted her eyes against the red glare and wondered just who had decided on that god-awful colour for the WC. Over to the right-hand side, the boatshed with rusted galvanised roof and weatherworn timber doors could have done with some of the same loving, if tasteless, attention. A steep slipway led from the boatshed down to the shore, its end disappearing into the shallow waters of Felton Bay. Beyond that the waters of the outer harbour were deep blue and sparkling. Robyn hated to think how deep the harbour must be. The bay the natives referred to as shallow was more than deep enough for her not very skilful swimming.

She watched now as a man and boy docked a small rowboat. The blond-haired child was a miniature of the blond-haired man. Father and son, out for a day's fishing together. She smiled at them as they proudly unloaded their catch of silver-scaled mackerel and landed it on the slipway. Gulls wheeled overhead, squawking loudly as they circled the boat. Her smile deepened as she imagined Zach and their child sharing the same camaraderie in years to come.

As she walked on, Robyn recalled Billy Moynihan saying that he was concerned about the soundness of the pier. It had not been inspected since the spring floods, despite several requests to the authorities. Another item for the list.

A flight of stone steps led from the pier to the strand. Robyn counted. Six shallow steps. Standing at the bottom she looked back at Felton village centre. It was no more than eight feet above sea level. In fact Lower Street dipped a little below that. There were no cliffs. Fields and village all sloped towards the shore. Only the sea barrier constructed five years ago protected Felton from high tides. Robyn looked at the wall of boulders packed into wire-mesh cages snaking along the foreshore and wondered how anyone could ever have thought it a proper sea defence. It was too low and too unstable. It was indeed the joke Kevin Phillips obviously thought it to be.

A short walk over rocks and pebbles brought Robyn onto the beach. Slipping off her sandals she wriggled her toes into the warm, soft sand. She wallowed in the sights, sounds and sensations. The whisper of sea, the sun on her face, the excited screech of gulls, a bracing smell of seaweed, a feeling of belonging. She felt the peace which had first attracted her and Zach to Felton. That and a vacancy for a vet.

Rolling up the legs of her pants she waded into the sea. The water was icy at first on her warm feet. Her toes curled until after a few steps she acclimatised to the coolness. Her mind wandered as waves lapped gently against her legs. She thought about the interesting detail June Varian had revealed at the impromptu meeting. Her niece was working in the Met Office. She was part of a research team monitoring climate change. June had agreed to ask her niece about setting up a weather alert for Felton. A hotline from the Met Office to give advance warning. From what little Robyn had seen of June, her niece would have no option but to cooperate.

Robyn was smiling at that thought as she rounded the curve on the shoreline which would bring her home into view. Her smile faded. Woodruff Cottage sat as serenely beautiful as ever, the German's house as darkly sombre. It was Tansy's cottage which made her stand and stare. A bright red sports car was parked in the driveway. From this distance, Robyn could see two people sitting at the garden table. One dark-haired and slight, the other blond and well-built. What in the hell was Kevin Phillips doing in Tansy Bingham's house? Robyn's first thought was flight. Escape. Go back to the village.

A frond of seaweed touched her feet and she jumped. The reaction brought her to her senses. Why should she run? This was her home. Kevin Phillips was the intruder here, amusing himself until he got the information about Bluetongue Virus he needed to sell his papers. User.

Taking a deep breath, Robyn squared her shoulders and waded purposefully towards home and Kevin Phillips.

Chapter 7

Tansy was standing by her gate as Robyn reached it.

"I wondered where you were, Robyn. I called for you. Come on in and join us. I've a visitor."

"I know. What's he doing here? What does he want?"

"Nothing. He just happened to drive by. I saw him and invited him in."

"You don't just happen to drive by our cottages. He came here for a reason."

Robyn glanced past Tansy. Kevin Phillips was sitting at the garden table, his face in the shadow of the parasol but Robyn felt his stare and imagined his ironic grin.

"Come in and have some lemonade," Tansy coaxed. "The real McCoy. Home-made."

"I'll have some water, please," Robyn said very quickly. She had drunk Tansy's lemonade once and that had been an unforgettable, and never-to-be-repeated, experience.

"Herbal tea? That would cool you down. You look flushed."

Great! She looked like a big red balloon. What a contrast to Tansy, who was lean and tanned and wearing shorts and a strappy T-shirt! Tansy caught her by the elbow and steered her in the direction of the garden table. Kevin Phillips' gaze didn't waver for a second as Robyn lowered herself onto a garden chair and dropped her shopping on the ground beside her.

"More lemonade, Kevin?"

"I will Tansy, please. It's very refreshing."

Beaming, Tansy scurried off to get the drinks. Robyn smiled. At last she knew something Kevin Phillips did not. He would spend hours in the bathroom later if Tansy's lemonade worked its evil magic on his digestive system.

"That's one of the pluses about what's happened in the past few years."

Robyn raised an eyebrow. What was he talking about? He obviously still had the annoying habit of thinking everyone else should be on his wavelength without any hints. But there had been a time when she could read his mind. Understand him.

"What do you mean, Kevin? Are we talking weather, the economy or Tansy's lemonade?"

"I'm talking self-sufficiency. The way scarcity and rising prices have forced people to do things for themselves. Like growing their own fruit and veg. And yes, making their own lemonade."

"Tansy was ahead of the posse. She never bought into the 'plastic food' as she calls it. By the way, I read your report on the Community Meeting last night. Why did you have to be so scathing? You took the easy option, didn't you? It's much simpler to criticise than be constructive."

Kevin put his elbows on the table and leaned towards

her. His eyes were narrowed now and the casual demeanour had gone.

"I wasn't taking the easy option. You know that. For God's sake, look around you! Your house is on the edge of the ocean. The village you live in is almost at sea level with little or no protection. Wake up, Robyn. Haven't you read any of the material I gave you? The Atlantic is warmer now than it's been for thousands of years. The North Pole has decreased ice cover. The Gulf Stream is under threat –"

"And you hold the people of Felton responsible for all this? I don't know what you're trying to say, Kevin. If everything is as catastrophic as you point out, then the best thing we could do is take to the hills. Abandon our homes and our village."

"Now you understand."

He sat back, sticking his thumbs into the belt of his chinos in a way she used to find so attractive. She looked out over the bluey-green sea as it rippled placidly. It seemed so docile now. Harmless.

"Proper sea defences would make a difference," she said.

"Be realistic, Robyn. You know the national resources are being used to protect centres of big population. Felton is at the bottom of a very long list."

Tansy emerged from the house carrying a tray and trailed by her fat cat.

"A Maya god, I believe," Kevin said, nodding his head at Ben.

"Did I hear 'Maya'?" Tansy asked, placing the tray on the table and sitting herself down. "I've loads more to tell you about it."

"Did you tell Kevin about the calendar? The one that ends on 21st of December 2012?"

"She did and I found it very interesting. I'm going to do a bit more research myself."

Robyn searched Kevin's face for signs of mockery. There were none. He was serious.

"You can't believe any of that, can you? Are you losing your cynical edge?"

"Put it like this, Robyn. Everything I see around me, the climate, the economy, our energy resources, our entire way of life, is under threat. What makes you think the Maya were wrong?"

"Ireland's agricultural economy is doing very nicely, supplying food to countries who can no longer grow their own."

"But we're also trying to absorb thousands of climate refugees. And, unless we come up with a viable energy source soon, what industry we have left will grind to a halt. Everything will, just like the Maya predicted."

"They didn't say the world would end on that date," Tansy pointed out. "They just said it would change beyond recognition. That's different."

"Yes, it is," Kevin agreed. "And that calendar gives us something we don't have a lot of now. Hope. A change could only be for the better."

He smiled at Tansy. They exchanged a look of understanding and something else. Friendship? Attraction? No! Not Tansy. Robyn could not allow Kevin Phillips to hurt her friend. There was no doubt in her mind that he would. The climate might be warming, the world racing towards destruction, but Kevin Phillips would never change. Robyn made up her mind.

"How is your wife, Kevin? Well, I hope."

His smile faded quickly and was replaced by an angry glare.

"You're married?" Tansy asked him, as if she had not believed Robyn. "You never said."

"You didn't ask," Kevin answered curtly. "Does one need to fill in personal details to have a conversation in Felton?"

Robyn nodded, satisfied that she had informed Tansy, annoyed Kevin and got herself onto the Flood Defence Committee. A good morning's work. All that achievement was tiring. She stooped down, got her shopping and stood.

"Excuse me. I need a rest. I'll leave you both to your fascinating discussion about the Maya."

Then, head in the air, she went home.

Sitting in her favourite cane chair in the conservatory, Robyn put her feet up on a stool. Her ankles felt swollen. Eclampsia! My God! She leaned forward and peered at her ankles and calves. They looked normal. Just to be sure, she examined her fingers and slipped her wedding ring over her finger joint. It fitted as comfortably now as it had the first day Zach had put it on her finger. "More hypochondria," she muttered, then closed her eyes and tried to sleep.

A sour taste at the back of her throat was preventing her from drifting off. It could be indigestion or it might be the bitter aftertaste of spite. She shifted in the chair to get more comfortable, but the troubling thoughts lingered. Had she mentioned Kevin's wife because she wanted to warn Tansy or because she had needed to irritate Kevin?

Spoil his plans. He definitely fancied Tansy. It was obvious by the way he looked at her and the attention he paid to her. So what? Tansy was wise enough to take care of herself, even if a little too trusting. A voice Robyn would rather have ignored whispered that she was jealous. How could she be? It was she who had ended the relationship with Kevin. If it could be called that. Liaison was probably better. A horrible three-in-a-marriage, destructive, hurtful affair. But it was over now. She loved Zach, tolerated Kevin Phillips as her boss, looked forward with all her heart to holding her baby. Robyn Claymore was, at last, happy. So why couldn't she sleep when every cell in her body was exhausted?

Restlessly, she stood up and decided to go into the garden. She told herself she needed to see some flowers, breathe fresh air. She didn't admit that she wanted to peep into next door's garden, even as she stood by the dahlias casting sidelong glances towards Tansy's garden table. She could hear them laughing, Kevin heartily and Tansy happily. They were obviously having a wonderful time. Getting to know each other. Just wait until Tansy discovered how obstinate and downright selfish Kevin Phillips could be. How very . . .

The phone rang. Robyn hurried to answer it, hoping it would be Zach. She needed to hear his voice now. It was Zach but the voice she listened to didn't sound like him at all. It seemed to belong to a much older man. A depressed man. Robyn understood why when he told her Noreen Lynch had been airlifted to hospital. He didn't say what was wrong with Noreen but, when he warned Robyn again not to come near the farm, she knew that he was trying to shield her from danger. And from the truth.

June Varian slammed the rolling pin down on the counter and walked over to where her son was bobbing his head, oblivious to everything but the music blasting through his earphones.

"The phone!" she roared. "Get it. I'm busy."

He looked at her blankly. June rubbed her floury hands on her apron and snatched the phone from the receiver.

"June Varian. Yes?"

"Aunt June, I was told you were trying to contact me. Is there something wrong?"

"Oh, Chloe! Sorry for the snappy greeting. No, there's nothing wrong, at least not with the family. Unless you count your cousin's obsession with music a problem. I do."

"How is Des?"

"He's a teenager. That should tell you everything about him. I'm looking for a favour, Chloe."

"Of course. If I can."

June could hear the steady throbbing of Des's music. It was getting on her nerves and making her worry about what it was doing to his brain. She waved him out of the kitchen before she continued with her conversation.

"I was wondering, Chloe, about the possibility of getting a weather forecast for Felton. What with you working in the Met Office I thought you could help."

There was a pause and June knew Chloe was throwing her eyes up to heaven. She wasn't the most obliging of girls. A bit like her mother.

"Why are you ringing now? Did you hear something? Who told you to contact here?"

The cheeky little bitch! June changed her mind instantly. Chloe wasn't in the least like her mother. She was just plain rude. But she could be useful. June counted silently to three before she continued.

"Nobody told me to ring. Believe it or not, I did that completely off my own bat. It's just that we are setting up our own flood-watch committee here. You know we got a real fright last spring. The tide covered Lower Street and went onto Middle and even Upper Street too. We weren't prepared. We don't want that to happen again."

"So you're on the committee, Aunt June? You'll soon have them sorted out."

"The weather forecast?"

"I'm not sure what you mean. All the information you need is broadcast every day on the radio and television. What is it exactly you want me to do?"

"I want you to tell me if there's the slightest risk that Felton might flood. A warning well in advance. I don't mind if it turns out to be a false alarm but we need to be told. Especially for the low-lying part of the village. You know what the sea wall is like. A glorified sandcastle."

"You can get the long range on radio or television too."

June was beginning to regret phoning her niece at all. Chloe had been a spoiled little child and she had obviously grown into an even more spoiled woman.

"Do you have an email address?" Chloe asked.

"I do. But don't bother yourself. I'll do as you say. Listen to the broadcasts. It was a silly idea anyway. Sorry for taking up your time."

"Are you having one of your hissy fits, Aunt June? I'm just trying to think of the most helpful way to deal with this. I have to talk to someone. I'll ring you back."

June ran back to her pastry as soon as she had put the phone down. It was a hot and sticky mess by now, breaking into clumps as she tried to roll it out. She kneaded it into a ball, rolled it in greaseproof paper and put it into the fridge.

The heat of the kitchen and the endless summer was magnified as a hot flash flooded her neck and face. She sat, suddenly feeling her energy draining away. What kind of twisted evolutionary process had decreed that some mothers suffer hot flashes, night sweats and galloping weight-gain just as their offspring enter the teen years? Menopause and adolescence under the one roof was a recipe for mayhem. Only a male power could have allowed such an aberration of nature. Cooler now, June felt guilty. Des was a good lad really. Just very sulky and very needy. And that bloody music!

The phone rang again. June picked it up, glad of the distraction from her self-pitying thoughts. It was Chloe.

"Aunt June? I've just spoken to my supervisor and got permission to pass on information to you. I've some news I think you should hear."

By the time Chloe was finished, June understood why she had at first been reluctant to talk. The news made June forget her hot flash. She now had more immediate problems to worry her.

Chapter 8

It seemed to Robyn as if Woodruff Cottage was being invaded that evening. First Tansy arrived with a secret smile and a list of questions about Kevin Phillips. Hot on her heels came June Varian and Billy Moynihan.

"I'll tell you all about Kevin later," Robyn whispered to Tansy as she ushered June and Billy into the kitchen.

Glancing at her fellow committee members, Robyn was glad to see that they were both more flushed than she. Billy Moynihan had a bigger bump too.

"Sorry for launching in on you like this," June apologised, "but something's come up."

"Something very important," said Billy, seating himself at the head of the table in his natural chairman position.

"Do you all know each other?" Robyn asked. "This is my neighbour Tansy Bingham."

"Yes, we do," Tansy answered. "For a long time. Is this private? Would you prefer I left?"

"Sit down," Billy ordered. "The more input we have, the better. Tell them, June."

"I rang my niece in the Met Office, like I said I would. She told me there's a lot of concern in the Met Office about an Atlantic depression that is deepening very rapidly. A number of factors could possibly come together to make it a big threat. The really bad news is that it might to be heading towards us."

"What does that mean? A big storm? Rain? What?" Tansy asked.

June opened her bag and put an email printout on the table. "Chloe sent this on so that we'd understand just how serious the situation could be. I'll read the important bits."

There was another pause as June poked in her bag for her glasses and put them on before finally starting to read.

"This system is quickly gathering speed and strength. Its path is unpredictable but there is a possibility that it could head towards the west coast. Since the Moon is in the full phase, tides will be higher and unfortunately the estimated storm landfall date coincides with what we call perigee. That is when the Moon is at its closest point to the Earth in its orbit and therefore has increased –"

"Cut the science stuff," Billy said impatiently. "The bottom line is we might have a combination of storm surge, spring tides and heavy rain thundering into Felton in a few days. What are we going to do about it?"

"Take to the hills," Robyn suggested, remembering Kevin's words.

"You should be the last to scoff," Billy said sharply. "The previous high water came up to the front doors of these cottages."

"No, of course I'm not 'scoffing' as you put it, but

really I'm at a loss as to what we can do in a couple of days. All the plans we discussed this morning are more long-term."

"Anyone like lemonade?" Tansy asked, ignoring looming storms and floods. "It's home-made and delicious."

"No lemonade, thanks," June said so quickly that she must have suffered a previous bout of post-Tansy's-lemonade agony. "But I'd kill for a cup of tea," she added.

Billy nodded agreement.

Robyn busied herself putting on the kettle and getting mugs, milk and sugar. Her head felt muzzy and she wondered if her blood pressure was high. Then she glanced over her shoulder and saw the little group around her kitchen table desperately trying to outwit the weather. Her husband was holed up on a farm with dead sheep and her friend seemed set to fall for Kevin Phillips just as she herself had done. And there was also the question of Noreen Lynch's emergency admission to a city hospital. No wonder her head felt muzzy.

"The priority is to make sure everyone knows about the threat," Billy announced.

"The priority surely is saving lives," Tansy said quietly.

They were all silent as they looked at Tansy and absorbed her words, each thinking of recent storms which had taken thousands of lives in Norway and Sweden and on the east coast of the United States. It felt as if the tide was already rushing around their feet. The discussion became a lot more urgent.

It was a vibrant sunset. The kitchen grew orange-tinged as the light outside faded towards dusk. The meeting was making slow progress. Planning for an unfamiliar event with unthinkable consequences, on an unknown date, was proving to be a huge challenge. Robyn had her laptop open on the table, making lists and noting suggestions which seemed to be getting ever more surreal.

"I'll have to go home soon," June announced. "God knows what my son is up to while I'm missing."

"You can't go anywhere until this is finished," Billy ordered. "Now, Robyn, water. Bottled water. Did you put that in?"

Robyn scrolled through the document on her laptop. No. They had not mentioned bottled water.

"We can't have people going to the Community Hall for safety only to have them die of thirst. Or contamination. We couldn't drink the village supply if the treatment plant was out of action. We'll have to buy in a stock of bottled water. And tinned foods. We can use the money set aside for landscaping the green."

June stared at Billy in surprise and then laughed out loud. "How long do you expect this storm to last? If in fact it happens at all. Sounds as if you're planning for forty days and forty nights."

"Whether this system hits us or not, we must plan for the worst scenario. Isn't that Rule One of emergency planning?"

"Rule One," June answered, "must be to make sure people watch the forecast and are aware of the storm threat. And then of course that they evacuate to the Community Hall from the low-lying areas if needs be."

"Pity we don't have local radio. Could you, as mayor, Billy, do anything about that?"

"We can't get a proper sea wall, let alone our own

radio station, Tansy. Anyway June is as good as any radio at broadcasting."

June glanced at Billy Moynihan, not sure if his comment was meant to be an insult. She had no more time to waste anyway. Des could have half the young girls in the village pregnant by now. He was like a young ram. His father, Des senior, had been the same at that age. It was as if he had always known he would have to pack his living into a short life-span. June said a quick prayer to her long-dead husband to look after their son and keep him out of harm's way. She stood up.

"We'll all have to do our bit to pass on the news. Should we meet again tomorrow?"

"The Community Hall. Two o'clock," Billy decided. "We'll have a good look around there and see if this idea can work at all."

"It will have to. It's the only one we've got," June said as she walked to the kitchen door.

"We should use the Bluetongue Virus," said Robyn.

They all looked at her as if she had gone mad.

"What are you talking about? Use it how?"

"For publicity, of course. For the first time ever national media attention is focused on Felton."

"You're right," Billy agreed. "And just look how they're representing us. Like that scurrilous piece on the *Daily News*. The sooner we realise the rest of the country don't give a damn about us, the better. Their only concern is that the Bluetongue would spread and affect the price of their lamb chops. We look out for ourselves from now on. Sink or swim on our own."

Standing by the kitchen door, June sighed impatiently.

"Ah! Stop with your dramatics, Billy Moynihan. C'mon. You're driving me back to village."

Billy did as he was told.

Robyn closed her laptop with a sigh of relief, then she and Tansy looked at each other and laughed.

"That was intense," Tansy said. "Is it all mad? An overreaction? Is Felton at risk at all?"

Robyn put her hands onto the lower part of her back and massaged her aching muscles. She closed her eyes, remembering the climate facts and theories she had recently read. Opening her eyes, she looked solemnly at Tansy.

"I don't know about the danger from this current weather system. And I don't know the reasons behind what is happening. But I do know, Tansy, that Felton is at high risk from rising temperatures and sea levels. If not now, in the very near future."

"Maybe the 21st of December 2012."

Robyn laughed. "Do you really think the Maya calculated their intricate Long Count Calendar just to predict the demise of Felton?"

"Why not? They were clever people. Anyway, enough of the doom and gloom. I want all the goss on Kevin Phillips."

The ache in Robyn's muscles stepped up a gear. What should she say to Tansy? How much? The realisation that she was trying to protect herself rather than Tansy was uppermost in her mind. Felton had been, up to yesterday, her Kevin-Phillips-free zone. She most certainly did not want him to have an interest which brought him here on a regular basis. Especially right next door. Nor did she want to see Tansy hurt.

"You've had a chance to talk to him, Tansy. What's your impression?"

"I think he's witty, clever and very good-looking. And married. Why didn't you tell me earlier? Before I had agreed to have dinner with him tonight."

"Dinner?" Robyn sat up straighter. This was fast work, even for Kevin. She tried to disguise her dismay. "It's very late for dinner now, isn't it?"

"He'd something he had to do. Couldn't make it earlier."

Typical Kevin, thought Robyn. Everyone had to march to his tune.

"The Marine will still be serving," Tansy said and paused, meeting Robyn's gaze. "Don't look at me like that. It's just dinner. We enjoy each other's company. There's nothing more to it."

"There's always something more with Kevin Phillips. An ulterior motive. Don't wait long enough to find that out."

"Did you?"

Robyn stood and arched her back. She walked to the patio door and looked out into the back garden. The flowers and shrubs were fading into shadow. Her gaze was drawn towards the hills where Zach was camped out in Lynches' farmhouse. He would be worrying about her and the baby, about Noreen and Con Lynch, about the whole farming community of Ireland. Zach was kind and generous and caring. The antithesis of Kevin Phillips. She turned to face her friend.

"Yes, I did, Tansy. It took me a long time to get to know the real Kevin. A big chunk of my life."

"And you still hurt."

"No! He means nothing to me now. Except of course that he's my boss."

Even to her own ears, Robyn's denial sounded too strident. Too contrived. Too false. She sat at the table again. "Just be careful, Tansy. That's all I'm saying."

Tansy reached for Robyn's hand and held it. "Of course I will and I appreciate you caring enough to warn me. But I've learned lessons from my turbulent marriage to Ari. I can fend for myself. What about Mrs Phillips? You didn't say anything about her. How long are they married?"

"He and Lisa are together a long time."

"So you and he were some time ago or else . . ."

"We had an affair. I was the other woman."

"I see."

Robyn shook her head. Tansy didn't see. How could she? Only someone who had gone through the same situation could understand the excitement, guilt, passion and frustrated hopes of such a relationship.

Tansy peered at her watch in the now-dim kitchen and jumped up.

"Lord! I'm really late! See you tomorrow."

Sitting alone in the dusk, Robyn could not prevent her thoughts going back to her first date with Kevin. He had taken her to dinner too. They had laughed and shared histories and opinions. And then they had kissed with a searing passion which had left them both breathless.

Moving more quickly than she thought she could, Robyn got up and switched on the lights. Unwanted memories burnt off in the glow. She rang Zach. Just to say goodnight. Just to hear his voice. Just to tell him that she loved him.

Zach switched off his phone and tried to sleep again. After a few minutes he admitted defeat and sat up on

Con Lynch's couch. He had heard the panic in Robyn's voice. She was eight and a half months pregnant and alone. He had promised her that he would always be there for her and now, when she needed him most, he was breaking that promise.

Her pregnancy or her aloneness was not the problem. He had asked Kerry to keep a careful check on her and he knew she was physically well. But he could not safeguard her against her own reaction to Kevin Phillips' presence in Felton. She would have to sort that out for herself. Judging by the edge of hysteria in her voice, she was not coping very well.

Zach jumped as the door to the sitting room was thrown open. The flushed face of Andrew Simmons loomed large in the dusk.

"Where's Con Lynch? Do you know?"

"Didn't he go out on his own? I assume he's somewhere on the hills. Why?"

"His wife's not responding at all to treatment. They're trying to decide now whether to fly him up to her."

Zach stood. He was pretty sure Con would have gone to the highest point on his land, to the beautiful spot known as The 360.

"I'll go get him," Zach volunteered now, glad to be leaving the confines of the house but dreading telling Con the news.

"There's a chopper on stand-by in Dublin. Myself and Dick will get the landing lights set up in case we need them. Be quick."

It was a beautiful night, the darkness lit by a full moon, the absorbed heat of the day still warming the air. Halfway to the apex of The 360, Zach had to take off the jacket he was wearing. He heard rustles as foxes and rabbits scurried and once the eerie cry of a curlew.

Con was leaning against the weather-beaten granite boulder which sat at the top of the hill. Zach stood beside him and gazed down at the sea. Moon-silvered, it rippled towards Felton, like a giant blanket underneath which creatures of the deep breathed rhythmically.

"You must come back to the house, Con. The hospital needs to talk to you."

The old man slowly turned his face towards Zach. It was full of shadows. And pain.

"I don't want to talk to them. It's too late."

"No. You must come back. They're considering taking you to Dublin. There's a helicopter on stand-by. You want to see Noreen, don't you?"

Con suddenly stood up straight and took a step towards Zach, his anger intense.

"There's no point now. Don't you see? She's dead! My Noreen has died surrounded by strangers. I'll never see her again. Why couldn't ye have left her here to die in peace?"

"No, Con. She's not dead. But she's not responding to treatment. I won't deceive you. Her condition is very critical but there's still hope."

Con kicked a stone. It skittered down the hillside and disappeared into the darkness.

"My wife is dead. I can feel it in here," he said, raising his hand to his heart.

Zach caught him by the arm. "Come on, Con. We'd better get back. Every minute counts now."

The anger seemed to leave the old man. Without further protest he began to walk downhill. When he sniffed, Zach glanced at him and saw tears, bright with moonlight, glisten on the wrinkled cheeks. He tried to think of some consoling words, something comforting to utter. He listened to the little sounds of the night and knew their whisper meant more to Con than any words he could say.

They both started when Zach's phone rang. Con continued walking as Zach stood and took the call.

"She died ten minutes ago," Andrew Simmons said. "Is he with you? We're taking him up to Dublin. The chopper's on its way. Get back to the house as quickly as possible."

Zach switched off his phone and stared into the gloom. Con was continuing his steady downhill pace, his shoulders hunched and his head bowed. Striding quickly to catch up, Zach tried to prepare what he would say. How did you tell a man his wife was dead? And that you didn't know why she had died and that maybe everyone in contact with the infected sheep would die too. What would the bad-news bearer say to Robyn? 'Very sorry, Mrs Claymore. Zach is dead. We did everything we could. Pity he'll never see his baby.' Zach shivered and walked faster.

Con heard Zach approach and stood to wait for him.

"I'm very sorry, Con. I've some bad news. I . . ."

"I know, lad. I told you. It's like this – Noreen and I were born within six months of each other, we lived in the same village, went to the same school, married when we were little more than children. Don't you think I'd be the first to know when her heart stopped beating and her soul left her body? I felt her with me on the hilltop there. She came to say goodbye to me."

Zach passed no comment. If the old man got comfort from believing he had said his goodbyes to his wife, then that could only be good.

"They'll need to do an autopsy," Con said. "I want to see her first."

Con's blunt practicality took Zach by surprise, though it should not have. It was the essence of his character. There was relief too in not having to explain the necessity for autopsy.

"The helicopter's on its way. You realise the precautions in the hospital will be strict. They're still working on finding out the cause of – of – why Noreen died."

"I knew she should have seen Dr Early. He would have known what to do. He understood her weak lungs."

Con began to walk again, proud and stiff and full of pain. Zach followed in silence, admiring the other man's dignity and feeling helpless in the presence of such profound grief.

"That was good," Kevin said, pushing his scraped-clean dessert plate away from him.

"Additives and dyes," Tansy remarked, her words as vehement as curses.

"Well, how about we have our next meal in a place of your choice? Obviously you're not too keen on the Marine Hotel. A fresh-food, organic restaurant? You find one and I'll take you there."

"Who said we'll be dining together again? You're making assumptions, Kevin."

"Oh? Are you telling me you didn't enjoy this evening?"

Tansy looked across the table at him and was struck

yet again by his blond good looks. And yes, she had enjoyed his company. He was a good conversationalist. Entertaining, lively, funny. But impersonal. Of course they had only just met. It would be silly to expect heart-to-heart revelations. Yet he was lying by omission and Tansy had had enough of that with Ari Klum.

"Tell me about your wife," she said. "Does she work at the *Daily News*?"

"No, she's not employed there. She owns it. It was her father's."

Tansy stared. Robyn had neglected to mention that vital fact.

"But she stays away from the day-to-day drudgery of it," he went on.

"I see. Do you have children?"

"What's this? Why the twenty questions, Tansy?"

"Touchy, aren't you? What's wrong with asking a married man if he has children?"

He sat back in his chair and fixed Tansy with the penetrating blue-eyed gaze she was beginning to know. It seemed to reach into the most secret depths of her mind.

"You've been talking to Robyn, haven't you?" he asked.

"We're best friends. Of course we talk to each other. About everything. Not much about you though. Why should we?"

"Maybe because Robyn and I had an affair for almost ten years."

Ten years! Tansy shifted uncomfortably on her chair. Why had Robyn not told her that? Ten years wasn't an affair. It was a full-blown relationship. Could Kevin

Phillips be the reason why Robyn sometimes seemed to ooze sadness, to be alone while surrounded by people? Why had she stayed so long as 'the other woman' as she herself had put it?

"That's your business and Robyn's," she said. "It's just that I don't like secrets. My ex-husband kept too many from me."

"You must have been very shocked when he left you for a man."

Tansy blushed. Of course Kevin would have read the press reports. Maybe he had written some of them. *'Internationally renowned sculptor leaves wife to set up home with male partner.'* It had been a joke, an amusing aside. And Tansy had been the butt of that joke. Kevin leaned forward now and reached across the table for her hands.

"I'm sorry, Tansy. I shouldn't have mentioned that. It must have been awful for you. I've long believed that some truths are best left unspoken."

She looked down at their hands, hers small, nestling underneath his strong tanned ones. She smiled at him. "The hurt is gone. Only the embarrassment remains. And yes, the truth can often be uncomfortable, but never as destructive as deceit."

"So, where does that leave us? Dinner? I promise I'll eat pulses, lentils and seeds."

Tansy excused herself and stood. She needed a visit to the Ladies' room to gather her thoughts together. Once inside the beige-tiled and mirrored room, she sat on the spindly chair beside the potted palm which was the designated rest area. She was thankfully alone.

What was she to do? Her instinct told her that Kevin

Phillips was a man she would like to get to know. The same treacherous instinct which had drawn her to Ari Klum. But then, what about Robyn? She was married to Zach. Yet there was a wistfulness about Robyn which could mean that she had unfinished business with Kevin Phillips. How would she feel about Tansy taking up where she had left off? Besides, there was Kevin's wife to consider. Although why should she consider Lisa Phillips when Kevin obviously didn't? Maybe the woman had relationships of her own. A very open, modern marriage. Convenience. Sham.

Tansy stood and examined her face in a mirror. She was no longer young. Minute lines laced their delicate threads around her eyes and on her neck. Imperceptible unless you looked closely but their embryo existence foreshadowed age. She had been smooth-skinned when she had fallen in love with Ari. Carefree and vulnerable. Each line represented a hurt. A betrayal.

Decision made, she walked back into the dining room where Kevin was waiting for her. Ignoring her chair, she stood beside him.

"I enjoyed the evening. Thank you, Kevin. I assume you'll be in Felton until the animal-virus thing is under control. I'll probably see you around."

"No coffee? No after-dinner drink?"

"Not for me, thanks. I must get home to Ben. He doesn't like being left alone for too long."

"I've never been abandoned in favour of a cat before."

Tansy looked at him as he smiled at her and wondered if she was being too hasty. Too honest. She still thought him a very handsome man. Exciting. Dangerous.

"Ben isn't just a cat, Kevin. Remember? He's a Maya god. Goodnight."

She turned then and walked away before the blue eyes, tanned skin and strongly muscled body of Kevin Phillips tempted her to stay.

Chapter 9

Robyn knew the news could only be bad when Zach rang at six thirty the next morning.

"Noreen Lynch died last night," he said without preamble, the weariness in his voice telling of a sleepless night.

"Oh, that's awful, Zach! What happened to her? How is Con?"

"He's in Dublin. At the hospital. He was flown there last night."

"Was he with her when she died?"

Zach hesitated, remembering Con saying that his wife had come to say goodbye to him on The 360. Who was he to judge whether that could have been so or not?

"Yes and no," he answered. "Con feels they were together last night on The 360 and that's comforting to him now. An autopsy is to be carried out today. We should know then why she died."

"Is the cause of death not clear?"

Zach's silence in answer to her question frightened

Robyn. The pieces of a horrific jig-saw began to slot together. Pieces she had seen in isolation but had not allowed herself to link. Dead sheep; a rare virus, maybe mutated; Lynches' farm quarantined; helicopters buzzing over Felton; Zach's repeated warnings to her to stay away from the farm; and now a dead woman. Her heart gave a sudden lurch and her hand automatically went protectively over her baby. She tried to steady her now fast breathing before she spoke.

"Are you in danger, Zach? Could you get the same sickness as Noreen Lynch?"

"Rob, I just don't know."

Robyn heard the agony in her husband's voice. He would want to protect her. That was his way of showing his love. But he would want to be honest with her too.

"Any progress on classifying the virus?" she asked.

"It's definitely Bluetongue."

"But with a twist?"

"You could say that," Zach admitted, sounding relieved that she understood the gravity of the situation. "Everyone on the farm who had contact with the infected sheep is to have a full medical today. They're flying a specialist in. We may be put on precautionary treatment."

"For what? An unidentified illness? What could they give you?"

"Maybe antibiotics, steroids. I don't know. I'll leave all that to the medical doctors. I'm too tired to think now. I just wanted to tell you about Noreen myself before you heard from someone else. Kevin Phillips is bound to pick up on it soon. In fact he probably knows already."

Of course Kevin knew. He had spies everywhere, hadn't he? People who owed him favours or those who just wanted to wallow in the light of his approval. Just as Robyn herself had done for so long. Silly, needy Robyn. But not any more.

"You take care of yourself, Zach. You should try to sleep now. You sound exhausted."

"You're right, I'm exhausted. I'll sleep for a while. Are you going out today?"

"I'm going to the Community Hall for a meeting. Didn't I tell you I'm on the Flood Defence Committee now?"

Zach laughed. It was good to hear his deep chuckle. "I knew you'd eventually start running the village. What took you so long?"

"I had to wait to be asked, didn't I?"

"Enjoy your meeting but take care. It's getting quite windy up here. I'm going to ask Kerry to organise the sandbags around the front of our house. Just in case."

"This is what the committee needs. A trial run to test our sea defences."

"Never mind the committee. Bad weather is what we all need to ensure a new batch of cursed midges don't cause more mayhem."

For an instant, Robyn wondered if it was too late for Zach. Was he already harbouring a killer virus in his bloodstream? A minute evil presence replicating itself, sucking the life from him. No! Not Zach! She banished the thought, fearing that thinking disaster would conjure it into being.

"I love you very much," she said, her voice shaking with fear. "We both do, me and the baby."

"I love you too. Go back to sleep now. I'll ring you as soon as I have news about Noreen's autopsy."

Then he was gone. Robyn got out of bed and padded into the back bedroom, from where she had a good view of Lynches' farm in the distance. She stood there, gazing at the hills and fields in the morning light, the white farmhouse nestling in a hollow, and she imagined Zach, stretched out, already asleep, his long lashes casting shadows, his curly hair enhancing his boyish looks. He would have one arm thrown behind his head. He always did when he slept. The longing to touch him, to run her fingers through his hair was so strong that Robyn reached out, her fingers hitting against the cold plate-glass of the window. She stayed like that for a long time.

Coming out of her reverie, Robyn realised she was cold. She folded her arms across her chest, noticing for the first time that dark clouds now stained the sky and the trees and shrubs bustled in a breeze. With a last glance towards Lynches' farm, she hurried back to bed and snuggled under the duvet. Cold, lonely and worried, she eventually fell into an uneasy sleep.

When Robyn woke the room was dim. Disoriented, she sat up in bed and rubbed her eyes She remembered talking to Zach earlier on. How much earlier? Glancing at her watch, she saw that it was ten o'clock. She had slept most of the morning away. Easing herself out of bed she went to the window and looked out towards the ocean. The tide was far out. Silt, sea and sky had merged into one grey vista. Just as she was about to turn away from the window she saw Tansy, wrapped in a big woolly sweater, dash from her house and head towards

Woodruff Cottage. Robyn grabbed her dressing-gown and went downstairs to let her in.

"What do you think, Rob?" Tansy asked breathlessly. "Looks like June's niece is right about a big storm on the way, doesn't it?"

"There's certainly a change. I miss the sun already."

"Don't be daft. This is fabulous. We could have rain and we need it so badly."

"Badly needed, yes. But fabulous? Don't think so. Come on in."

"But look how the plants and crops need it. And just think, the river will run again. I missed it, you know. The Aban. I love the sound it makes when it rushes under the bridge."

They went into the kitchen and together got coffee and toast ready. When they were sitting at the table, Tansy leaned forward, her dark eyes questioning.

"Well, don't you want to know how I got on with Kevin Phillips last night? Would you prefer not to mention him at all?"

About to bite into a piece of toast, Robyn stopped. She had forgotten. For once she had completely forgotten about Kevin and what he was up to. She smiled at her friend now.

"Go on, Tansy. Tell me all. I'm dying to hear."

"Not much to tell really. We got on well but I'm not seeing him again."

"Really? I thought he was the most handsome man you had ever met. An Adonis, if I remember correctly."

"He is but there's something about him that makes me uncomfortable. He's closed. Even a bit cold. How did you stay with him for ten years?"

"So he told you? What else did he say about me?"

"Nothing. And nothing about his wife either except that she owns the *Daily News*. Is that why he stays with her?"

"He should have told you she owns just half the paper. He owns the other half. If he divorces Lisa his shares revert to her. All part of the pre-nup. Her father insisted on that when he handed the business over to her and Kevin."

They were both silent then. Testing their friendship. Tansy obviously wanted to know more and Robyn equally obviously wanted to drop the subject.

"Just one more question," Tansy said. "Does he have children? He didn't really answer when I asked him."

"He's good at that, isn't he? No, he and Lisa never had children. Nor are they likely to now. Kevin thinks we're over-populated anyway and that bringing more children into the world is irresponsible."

"What a pompous ass!"

"Agreed."

"It's a nice ass, though."

"Also agreed. Now are we going to talk about something else?"

Tansy took a sip of her coffee and then smiled at Robyn.

"We could talk about the weather alert for Felton. The advance warning of floods. I've had an idea."

"I thought June Varian was looking after that."

"She is, but, don't you see, we should have a system that reaches everyone. June might not, even with the amount of time she spends talking."

"So what do you suggest?"

"That you get dressed as quickly as possible. We'll go to visit our neighbour."

"Horst Mueller? What do we want to see him for? I don't feel like having a door slammed in my face again."

Tansy stood up and began to pace the kitchen, her hands gesturing as she talked excitedly.

"We've no local radio, a newsletter that's issued only once a month and a population scattered around a wide area. It's not just the village at risk, you know, in an extreme weather event. The Aban could flood too. And maybe landslides and rock-falls from the hills. Anything could happen if the predictions for climate change are right. People must have a reliable source of information. He could set it up for us."

"Who? The grumpy German?"

"Well, he's a computer person, isn't he?"

Robyn made sense of it now. Tansy wanted Horst Mueller to set up a web page. A site dedicated to weather warnings.

"You want him to set up www.feltonweather.com. Is that it?"

"Yes! Why not?" Tansy asked, coming back to sit at the table. "It can't be that complicated and anyway he's an expert."

"Are you sure?"

"Get dressed and we'll go and find out. And hurry. His gas-guzzling off-road car is there now. We don't want to miss him."

Robyn thought she did indeed want to miss the chance of another encounter with Horst Mueller but she went to get ready anyway while Tansy used up some of her boundless energy tidying up the kitchen.

Robyn wrapped her cardigan more closely about her as

she and Tansy stood on the doorstep of the Muellers' cottage, waiting for a reply. And waiting.

"They must be home," Tansy said, looking at the massive black four-wheel-drive, a Hummer, parked close to the side of the cottage.

Robyn stepped back and glanced at the windows. The curtains were drawn back downstairs but upstairs they were closed. As she was about to return to the doorway, a movement caught her eye. Just a little twitch. The merest flutter.

"Someone is watching from upstairs," she whispered to Tansy. "I saw a curtain move. Let's get out of here. It's giving me the creeps."

"Just one more try. I'll give a long ring this time."

Tansy put her finger on the doorbell and leaned against it as if added weight would make the ring louder. It might have because the door suddenly opened and Horst Mueller stood there, looking very angry.

"You two again. What do you want?"

"We'd like to talk to you about flood defences, Mr Mueller. Presumably you're interested since you attended the meeting last night."

"I didn't think going to the meeting meant having you on my doorstep morning, noon and night. My wife's sleeping. You disturbed her with your ringing."

"We're very sorry for waking Mrs Mueller," Robyn said, catching Tansy by the arm and trying to pull her back from the glowering man. "We'll just go and leave her to rest. You know where we are if you want to discuss flood defences."

Tansy pulled her arm away impatiently from Robyn's grasp and leaned in closer to Horst.

"Could you set up a web page for us? A site where Felton people could go to see if there are any weather alerts for the area?"

"I could."

Both women looked at him in surprise. Even Tansy had expected a battle from this peculiar man. She smiled at him.

"That's great, Horst. Is it okay to call you that? A site where everyone could be kept informed would make such a difference. And we could put other local news on it too. Things like –"

"I said I *could*. I didn't say I would."

"Oh!"

"Now please go away and leave us alone. People call here by invitation only and I certainly won't be inviting either of you."

This time Tansy saw the anger in his eyes. Robyn didn't have to tug very hard to pull her away. The door slammed even before they had turned to leave.

"I'll never, ever, call here again," Tansy said as they hurried off underneath the cypresses.

"Me neither," Robyn agreed.

Having the eerie feeling of being watched, Robyn glanced back towards the Muellers' cottage. As she did her attention was caught by the curtain upstairs, still twitching. She shivered and turned quickly away.

"Have you ever seen her, Tansy? Mrs Mueller, I mean."

"Just passing in the car. Always with him."

"Me too. She seems small and brown-haired from the glimpses I got."

"I wonder where they do their shopping. Not locally anyway. I've never seen them in the village."

"Forget about them," said Robyn. "I think the website's a good idea. We'll bring it up at the meeting today."

"Look at that," Tansy said, pointing out to the sea. "The swells are big. I don't like the colour either. It's greeny-grey."

Robyn squinted her eyes, trying to see what Tansy was pointing out. It amazed her how people born near the sea seemed so in tune with the subtle signs of the ocean's changing moods. She nodded, not willing to admit that the water still looked flat and grey to her eyes.

"We'd better strengthen our flood defences pretty soon," she said.

"Oh! My crop!" Tansy wailed. "I'd better run and bring it into shelter. See you at quarter to two. Will you drive? My car's low on fuel."

Robyn waved and then smiled as she watched Tansy scurry to save her six pots of cotton plants.

Inside Woodruff Cottage again, Robyn's worries about Zach returned. The house seemed empty and cold without him. For a panicky moment she wondered if he would ever be back. She shivered and turned on the heating. At least that was one blessing from the six-week drought they'd just gone through. The solar system had stored enough energy to meet their needs for some time.

While getting her laptop and notes organised for the meeting in the Community Hall, Robyn's attention strayed back to her neighbours. There was something very intimidating about Horst Mueller. The way he stared and his anger which seemed to flare without provocation. Maybe that was why she had formed an impression from the few glimpses she had of Mrs Mueller that she was a frail woman, physically small and somehow scared-looking. Cowed. Overshadowed by towering cypress trees and her husband's rage. Just what was making Horst Mueller so defensive?

A glance at the clock told Robyn that she had better stop wondering about her odd neighbours and get a move on. She would need to make lunch before the meeting. The Felton Flood Defence Committee had a lot to discuss. It could be a long afternoon.

Chapter 10

Billy Moynihan and June Varian were already in the Community Hall by the time Robyn and Tansy arrived.

"Ye timed it well," Billy said sarcastically. "June and I have just finished stacking the chairs away after last night's meeting. Come on into the conference room." He led them across the vast expanse of oak flooring towards one of three doors at the top of the hall.

Robyn jumped when a sudden loud banging sounded behind her. She turned to see Tansy doing a very individual interpretation of River Dance, her black curls bouncing, her timber clogs beating out the rhythm of the music she was humming.

"You're daft!" June laughed as they all stood to watch.

"You're marking the bloody floor," said Billy, bringing a sudden end to the impromptu show.

June gave Billy a friendly but firm tap on the arm. "Leave her alone. We all need a bit of cheering up on this sad day." She turned towards Robyn and gave her a very penetrating look. "I suppose you know Noreen Lynch died?"

"Yes, I know about Mrs Lynch. It's terrible for her husband."

"That's awful! Poor Con!" Tansy gasped, still breathless after her dancing efforts. "If you knew about it, Robyn, why didn't you tell me?"

Robyn began to feel uncomfortable. What could she say? That Noreen Lynch might have died from a disease normally associated with sheep and cattle? That Zach too could now, at this very minute, be dying from the same disease. That the cause of the old woman's death was still being investigated and was very, very, confidential. June saved her from having to decide on an answer.

"Stop, Tansy Bingham! Don't you know it's bad luck to talk of death around a woman in Robyn's condition?"

"No. I never heard that. I think you made it up just now, June. Besides, it was you brought up the topic."

"So I did. Noreen was a good friend of mine. I'd have gone to visit her in hospital if I'd known she was there. I haven't an idea what's going on up at Lynches' farm but whatever it is seems to be kept well under wraps."

June was directing her remarks to Robyn and equally obviously implying that Robyn did know what was going on. And that surmise, thought Robyn, can only be true if Zach has told me everything about the goings-on in Lynches'.

Billy Moynihan had had enough. "If ye want to have a mothers' meeting, ye should go to the hotel. I came here to try to sort out the sea defences."

He stood in front of them, glowering and pointing to the three doors lining the top of the hall.

"Left to right: kitchen, storeroom, conference room.

If you can tear yourselves away from the gossiping, the meeting will be in the conference room."

The three women watched as he stalked towards the door on the right and flung it wide open. They smiled at each other and then followed him in. This small space, grandly named the conference room, like the rest of the hall smelled of newly cut timber and freshly applied paint.

"Magnolia, I bet," Tansy said, examining the neutral cream tones of the walls.

Billy must have chosen the paint because he gave Tansy a very disdainful glance before seating himself just inside the door at the top of the long, enormously wide table which took up most of the available space.

"You take the other end of the table, Robyn," June advised. "Give yourself a bit of wriggle-room."

It would have been more logical and a lot more comfortable for Robyn to sit where Billy had parked himself but as she squeezed her bulk between chairs and the wall, she realised that his sense of importance would never allow him cede the top chair no matter what the circumstances. Eventually she arrived at her place, put her laptop on the table and switched it on.

"Will you take minutes?" Billy asked.

Robyn nodded her agreement but Tansy immediately objected.

"I thought this was just a brainstorming session. A think tank. Why are we going all formal with minutes? That's just time-wasting."

"Time-wasting is dancing and gossiping. I now declare this meeting open," Billy said, taking a biro from his pocket and tapping the table-top. "I've prepared an agenda and it reads like this . . ."

Like a magician pulling a rabbit out of a hat, Billy swooped on his inside pocket, whipped out a sheet of paper and began to read.

"'*One: assess the suitability of the Community Hall as an emergency shelter in the event of village flooding. Two: discuss provisions and other items necessary to keep people safely here should the need arise. Three: since we share a fire service with our neighbouring village we should contact them and see if they have any better procedures in place than they had during the last flood.*' Remember, the flood waters were receding by the time the fire brigade got here."

Tansy held up her hand, like a schoolchild asking for the teacher's permission to speak. Billy didn't give her the go-ahead but she spoke up nevertheless.

"Four: set up a weather-alert web page."

"That's a great idea," June said enthusiastically. "How would we go about that? My son has taught me to go on-line and send emails but I couldn't set up a web page – could any of you?"

"What do you know about the Muellers?" Tansy asked, leaning towards June.

"That they're a very unfriendly couple. They don't mix locally at all. Do you know they go to Galway to do their shopping? I saw them there myself. I saluted them but they ignored me."

Robyn and Tansy exchanged glances. At least one of their Mueller mysteries was cleared up.

Billy was breathing heavily at the top of the table. "Ladies –"

"What's Mrs Mueller like?" Robyn asked as Billy glared.

"I'm surprised you don't know since you live beside

her. She's a mousey little thing. Afraid to look you in the eye. He's not though. He'd stare you down."

"'Twould be a brave man who'd stare you down, June," Billy remarked but the women ignored him.

"What does Horst Mueller do?" Tansy asked. "I'm not being nosey, it's just that I understand he's a computer expert. I thought, we thought, Robyn and me, that he might help set up our website."

June shook her head. "No. I don't think he is. Who told you that? I heard he used to trade in stocks and shares until the stock-market collapse. He set up some kind of on-line consultancy business then. That's how he makes his living so he must know his way around a computer alright. But that doesn't make him a computer engineer or a software designer or whatever it is these experts do."

"He's not willing to help anyway. He put the run on us, didn't he, Rob?"

Billy dropped his page on the table, pushed his chair back noisily and stood up.

"The Muellers just mind their own business," he said crossly. "It would be no harm if ye did the same and got on with our job here. Besides, the whole idea is silly. There are already more than enough on-line weather forecasts. It's getting people to look them up is the problem."

"So that's why we need feltonweather.com. They'd be more likely to go to that, wouldn't they? And we could put on announcements. Like births, marriages and deaths. Maybe a jobs page and –"

"I don't know about you lot," said Billy, "but I'm walking around the hall and making a list of what facilities we have and what we'll need to get."

Robyn sighed. She had plenty of space to push her

chair back behind her but walking the length of the table was going to be a narrow squeeze again. She just about managed it.

Like junior class on a field trip they all traipsed behind Billy back into the hall, stopping as he pointed out the door at the top right-hand side of the hall which served as an emergency exit.

"We'll have to practise our emergency drill too," he said. "If there's a fire here we don't want people getting squashed in a stampede to evacuate."

Having dropped that little bombshell, he brought them on a conducted tour of the bathroom facilities which were tucked away to the left of the entry door – two ladies' toilets, one gents' and a shower. Then back to the top of the hall where they were faced again by the three doors. The first led to the kitchen – basic but roomy with cooker, sink and microwave, two kettles, a tall fridge and an assortment of ware. The centre door opened into a store which was shelved around three walls and stocked with nails, screws, spare bulbs, fuses and coils of electric cable. They stepped inside. Cartons of every shape and size were stacked up against the back wall, so high they almost reached up to the level of the small windows. There were some free-standing shelves in the centre, piled with paint tins, many of which had dried dribbles of Magnolia hanging like stalactites over their rims.

"Just what we'd need in an emergency," Tansy said. "A bit of DIY to keep us occupied until we can go out again."

"That's not the kind of attitude . . ." Billy began but

abandoned his sentence when the front door of the hall suddenly opened.

Cold air swirled towards them. The door closed again and footsteps sounded on the timber floor of the main hall. As one, the group moved towards the door of the store-room and looked out to see who was there.

"What are you doing here?" Billy asked as Kevin Phillips strode towards them.

"Well, hello to you too, Mr Mayor. Am I interrupting something important?"

The way in which he said the words set Robyn's teeth on edge. He was laughing at them again. She glared at Tansy who shrugged and held her hands up in a helpless gesture. Robyn still glared. Who else could have told Kevin about this meeting if not Tansy? Billy walked towards the smiling, or was it sneering, journalist.

"If you don't mind, Mr Phillips, we're busy. Excuse us, please. And close the door after you on your way out."

"Not so quick, Billy. I came here to help. And to warn you."

"If we needed your help, we would have asked," Robyn said, furious that a blush was beginning to creep up along her neck. The last impression she wanted to give Kevin Phillips was that he affected her in any way. The blush increased in intensity as Kevin came to stand right in front of her, forcing her to look up at him.

"I have contacts, Robyn, as you well know. One of them happens to be in the Met Office."

"So have we."

"So you realise what's on the way then? And you know how to deal with it?"

"Depends what you're talking about. What's on the way?"

"A vicious weather system they've been keeping an eye on. No doubt now that it's headed directly for us. The Met issued a weather alert this afternoon, especially for the west coast, though this system is so intense it will affect the whole country."

Robyn turned to June Varian, an eyebrow raised in query. Flustered, June did a little jig of her own, shuffling her feet and clearing her throat.

"I – agh – I – I didn't have time to check my emails today. Maybe my niece sent something else from the Met Office. But we know what she said anyway, about the tides and the moon."

"That's right," Kevin agreed. "It seems a massive tidal surge could be on the cards. So how would Felton cope with that?"

"I'm sure you're going to tell us how we should," Robyn said. "Whether we want to listen to you or not."

"Amazing how well you think you know me, Robyn. You really don't know me at all, do you?"

As she and Kevin stood there, tension sparking between them, Robyn felt like they were reliving one of the many arguments which had spiced their relationship. Except that this time there would be no passionate making-up.

Without another word, she turned and trudged back to the conference room. The others followed on, Kevin Phillips bringing up the rear.

The power struggle between Kevin Phillips and Billy Moynihan would have been amusing to watch except that the conference room seemed too small to contain their egos. The meeting had been going around in circles for the past hour. The storm was an estimated two days away and all they had established so far was that the village would most definitely flood if the predicted five-metre sea-surge occurred. Kevin sat back in his apparently bored pose but Robyn realised he was as sharply observant as ever. He glanced around the table from one to the other of them and she felt he found them all lacking. He sat up again and leaned forward, addressing Billy directly.

"The clock is ticking and all you can say at this stage is that you don't know how many people would need to be evacuated to safety, you have no generator in this hall should electricity fail and no emergency supplies on hand if you need to provide shelter to people made temporarily homeless. Do you even know what time high tide is due in two days' time?"

"We all know what we haven't got," Robyn said. "If you really want to help like you said then give us the front page of the *Daily News* tomorrow."

"Felton's been the lead story ever since the cordon went up around Lynches' farm. What do you want? A pull-out feature on a village with a population of little more than three thousand?"

"What with emigration that's nearer 2,500 now," Billy said but Robyn didn't look in his direction, her angry gaze never leaving Kevin.

"What are you doing here if you think Felton's so insignificant and in such imminent danger? Why don't you go back to the city?"

June looked at them both and shook her head. "Tut, tut, children! Stop! We're not going to get anything organised if we're just arguing with each other."

Tansy glanced from Robyn to Kevin, a frown on her forehead, then she smiled brightly.

"I think Robyn has a good idea. The newspaper of choice in Felton is the *Daily News*. Suppose it carried an announcement tomorrow about expected bad weather. That would be our best and quickest way to make sure everyone knows what to do."

"That's only fair," Billy pointed out. "The *Daily News* has made plenty of money out of Felton. The whole country seems to be obsessed about Con Lynch's sheep."

"We're not the only press here," Kevin said defensively. "Bluetongue Virus, if that's what it is, is of national interest."

"But Felton's coastal defence is not?"

"Alright, Robyn! Alright. I'll give you a front-page space. But keep it short. Remember it's a national paper. People in Cork or Dublin won't want to read about your sea wall. They'll be worried about their own patch. This storm is going to threaten the whole country. Anyway the Felton story could be even bigger tomorrow, depending on why the farmer's wife died. You wouldn't know anything about that, would you, Robyn?"

"Noreen was her name. Noreen Lynch. And no, I don't know anything about it. As far as I'm aware nobody does yet."

Kevin glanced at his watch and then stood. "You'll have to excuse me, I've a few calls to make. A seven o'clock deadline for that piece, Robyn. Four or five hundred words, no more. I'll call to your house to edit it before submission."

Without waiting for a reply, Kevin pushed back his chair and walked out. The tension went with him. The little group breathed a collective sigh of relief and then began to work in earnest on their emergency-supply list. By the time they wound up their meeting they had cobbled together a comprehensive list of everything they might need to keep storm-refugees warm and safe until flood waters receded. Tansy volunteered to print out posters which Billy would tack up in appropriate places in the village and June would distribute door-to-door the leaflets which Tansy would also print.

"Could you make copies of this too, please?" Billy asked, handing her a plan of the hall. "If we hand them out as people come in it'll save us having to tell everyone where the emergency exit and the loo are. Copy both sides because the emergency evacuation drill is printed on the back."

"Candles," June said. "In case the electricity goes."

"We can't have naked flame in the hall, woman. Do you want us all to go up in a blaze?"

"Do you want us all in the dark?"

"What about food if the fridge isn't working? Should we get some powdered milk?"

They looked at each other then and there was bewilderment on each face. They still didn't know how bad this storm would be, or if indeed there would be any storm at all, they had no idea how many people would evacuate to safer inland areas and how many would need the shelter of the Community Hall and they had absolutely no clue where to source powdered milk.

"We don't know an iota about what we're doing, do we?" Tansy asked.

Nobody disagreed with her.

Chapter 11

Cloud cover seemed to have thickened over the afternoon. As Robyn and Tansy drove back, they had to switch on dimmed headlights to negotiate the rutted road leading to the cottages. When they got out of the car, they both automatically turned to the sea, frowning as they noted the sound of waves slapping against outlying rocks.

"It's really going to happen, Rob, isn't it?"

Robyn shrugged her shoulders helplessly. It could be that Felton would be deluged by a massive flood. Then again, maybe a wind shift, the natural anti-clockwise motion of the Northern Hemisphere, a miracle, would take all this threat away from Ireland and bury it deep in the North Atlantic. Perhaps in the Sargasso Sea, that coastless, mysterious sea of currents and seaweed.

"We can only pray that it won't and prepare as if it will," she said.

"But two days! Jesus!" Tansy stopped then and laughed. "Listen to me. Giving up before we've even started. Of course we can do it. Can't we?"

"We'll have to. Will you come in with me?" Robyn asked, aware that she sounded pathetic.

"Kevin Phillips? You don't want to be alone with him when he calls. Is that it?"

Robyn nodded.

"I must feed Ben and let him out. I'll do the templates for the posters and leaflets too. Say an hour? You can be writing your piece for tomorrow's *Daily News*."

"Thanks, Tansy. See you in an hour."

"Don't bother cooking. I've a stew ready to heat up."

Robyn opened her mouth to make an excuse but her answer was blown away on the wind. She looked helplessly at Tansy's retreating back and then turned for home.

Before doing anything else Robyn booted up her computer and logged onto the Met Office. She stared at the weather charts and satellite pictures for a long time. You didn't have to be a meteorologist to see how closely packed the isobars were on the Atlantic storm system. North-west of Ireland it was a mass of angry swirls on the screen which seemed to be developing a discernible eye. A criminal fingerprint on the ocean. She read the report on the projected storm path. If the forecast was right, the savage winds and water walls would sweep headlong into Felton. Over Felton.

She switched on the television just in time to catch the news headlines. Five more dead in Afghanistan, fifty in Iran and one hundred and twenty-six in Kazakhstan where Russia and China were locked in battle. One hundred and eighty-one young people whose families had proudly waved them off to war. Young people who had not so long ago been safely cosseted in their mother's wombs. Just like their baby now. Hers and Zach's.

She switched off the television. Grabbing her phone, she pressed a speed-dial number. Zach answered the phone on the first ring.

"Zach? I'm worried."

"What's wrong, Rob? Is it the baby?"

"The storm, the virus, you, the baby. It's everything. I miss you, Zach. I miss you so much."

"I'm so sorry, Rob. I wish I could be with you but . . ."

Robyn regretted her impulsive, self-pitying call now. Zach sounded so sad. So guilty. She tried to put a lighter tone in her voice when she spoke again.

"I'm just being silly, I know. Getting everything out of proportion. It looks like the forecasted storm is going to be big but we're making plans to evacuate to the Community Hall if necessary."

"You might be safer going to stay with your mother until it blows over. She's well inland."

Robyn had an image of being trapped in the Old Rectory with her mother, wind keening around the high chimneys and her mother constantly criticising. She shuddered.

"No, I won't do that. It's too far away from the hospital if the baby decides to make an early arrival. I'm only forty-five minutes from it here. I'll play it by ear and go to the hall if I need to. Anyway, the storm is two days away. Surely you'll be back by then?"

"I hope I will. For all our sakes. Just waiting on a call. As soon as we can confirm cause of death for Noreen, we'll know where we stand."

"No news yet so?"

"Nothing definite. It's looking good so far, from what I've been told. But they must be very sure before they issue any results."

Of course they had to be sure. The consequences of discovering a new lethal disease, a killer of animals and people alike, were huge. Perhaps a killer of husbands before they even laid eyes on their newborn children. Fear wracked Robyn so strongly that her knuckles were white as she gripped the phone and she couldn't think of one word to say to Zach.

"Has Kerry put the sandbags at the doors?" he asked.

Robyn put her fear on hold and managed to get the 'I'm coping well' tone back into her voice. "No need yet. She has them ready."

"With any luck, I'll be there to do that job myself."

"I can't wait for you to be home. I'd better get down to work now. I'm writing a front-page piece about the storm for tomorrow's *Daily News*. Seven o'clock is my deadline. Love you, Zach. Take care."

There was a second's pause, a little beat of time while Zach absorbed the information about the *Daily News*. Kevin Phillips' name had not been mentioned but it echoed down the line as loudly as if it had been shouted.

"Bye," was all Zach said before cutting off the call.

Robyn sat staring at her computer screen but not seeing anything. Would Kevin Phillips always haunt her life, make her uneasy, guilty, uncomfortable with her feelings? Sorry that she had ever met him and perhaps more sorry that she had ended their relationship. But had she? If she was really and truly finished with him, why was she still working for the *Daily News*? She had a good reputation as a journalist. She could get other work. Freelance maybe. Then she would never, ever, have to lay eyes on Kevin again. It would be just Zach and her and their baby. And Felton. No highs but no heartbreaks either. No cheating and grabbing stolen moments.

She shook her head as she wondered yet again why her affair with Kevin had gone on for so long. What had she thought? That he would leave Lisa? Abandon her to the alcoholism which had destroyed their marriage and was now destroying her? Yes, Kevin would probably have done that. It was his fifty per-cent share of *Daily News* he couldn't bear to leave behind. No Lisa, no shares. It was all in black and white and legally watertight.

Restless, Robyn got up from her desk and went upstairs. She felt cold. In need of a comfortable, cosy cardigan. She got her blue angora and cuddled into it. As she left the bedroom, she glanced at the bed and imagined Zach's curly head on the pillow. Kind Zach. Loving Zach. She blushed with shame for her thoughts of another man who was neither loving nor kind.

On the landing, Robyn stopped by the window which overlooked the Muellers' cottage next door. It was dark already, the sky smothered in cloud. Lights shone from the back upstairs rooms of the cottage and Robyn wondered if Mrs Mueller was still in bed. Maybe she was sick. Although the twitching curtain had been at the front of the house this morning. Perhaps their office was upstairs in the back. Or it could be they just liked turning on all the lights to shine into their back garden. Robyn stood on tiptoe and craned her neck, suddenly very curious about the Muellers' back garden. She had never seen into it because it was completely screened from view by the cypress trees. For one mad instant, she considered getting the stepladder and trying to peer over the trees. What had she been expecting to see there anyway? Rows of cannabis plants? Or maybe the peculiar Horst had built a nuclear shelter there. Then she smiled at the thought of being a nosy neighbour. She truly belonged in Felton now.

Just as she was starting down the stairs again, she heard a loud knock on her front door. Tansy! She hurried down and opened the door, a smile of welcome on her face. Her caller immediately dashed into the hall, the collar of his coat pulled up around his ears.

"Whew! I can't get acclimatised to this cold. I dread to think what's on the way."

"It's not seven yet," Robyn said. "What are you doing here? I haven't even started my piece for the front page."

"Thanks for the welcome, Robyn. It's nice to be wanted."

Wanting Kevin Phillips wasn't something Robyn was prepared to consider now.

"Hang your coat on the stand there," she said as she turned her back and led the way into the kitchen. She had the kettle on by the time he came in and sat himself at the table.

"Coffee?"

"Yes, please. And I have something to say to you. I know how stubborn you are so don't interrupt me until I'm finished."

Robyn put down the mugs she had in her hand and stood with her back to the counter. Kevin's windswept blond hair gave him a rakish look. Made him even more appealing.

"Have you seen the news this evening?" he asked.

"I switched it off after the headlines. Too depressing."

"You didn't see the forecast then. The Met are advising all occupants of coastal properties to prepare for possible evacuation. I want you to leave here, Robyn. Come back with me or go to your mother until this weather threat is over. You have your baby to think of too. It's not safe to stay in Felton."

The kettle boiled and clicked off. Still Robyn stared at Kevin, her anger growing every second. How dare he! How dare he show concern now when he had never cared enough. How dare he try to take responsibility for her safety and for Zach's baby. How dare he tell her what to do! He grinned at her, that cheeky white flashing smile she used to love so much.

"You're furious with me, Robyn. I can tell. But just think about it. Felton could be under water in two days' time. Or even sooner."

She took a deep breath and turned on the kettle again. She had to get her breathing back under control. She made coffee and brought it over to the table.

"My welfare and my baby's is none of your business, Kevin. Zach and I will make whatever decisions need to be made. Thank you for your concern but it's not necessary. Or appreciated."

"Oh, for heaven's sake, Robyn! Don't go all snooty on me. Of course I'm worried about your safety. You're about to give birth, a deluge is forecast and your husband is holed up in a godforsaken farm. Surely our history gives me the right to care."

Robyn laughed as she sat opposite him. Incredibly, he looked sincere and even hurt by her laughter.

"Our history, Kevin, tells us nothing except that you didn't care enough. How do you think that gives you any rights?"

He bowed his head. She had a sudden urge to touch his hair. She picked up her mug of coffee to occupy her hands – just in case. Kevin looked up slowly and for the first time she saw vulnerability in his eyes.

"I'm sorry, Robyn. Truly sorry. I should have let you go. I should never have started a relationship which had no future."

"You didn't have to let me go. I went myself. Remember?"

"Yes. Of course I remember. It was quite a row, wasn't it? Our last one."

Robyn blushed, recalling how she had picked up a vase from their suite in the Paris hotel and smashed it on the floor. She had never before or since so completely lost control of her temper. She had flounced out then, caught a plane home and begun to live a Kevin-free life. Almost.

He laughed now. "Did I ever tell you that vase cost me three hundred euro?"

"Several times. But you never did answer the question I asked you then. Why don't you want to have children? And don't trot out the same old 'I can't bring kids into a hostile world' argument."

The vulnerability vanished. It was as if a shutter had come down over his eyes. His mouth closed in a tight line. It was the same argument they'd had so often and this silence had always been his way of coping with it. Robyn wondered now, as she had countless times, if Lisa had asked him the same question. Had his wife too, longed to have his child? Had she been met with the same wall of silence when she pursued the subject?

"How's Lisa?"

Kevin relaxed a little, obviously relieved that she was moving on from the baby question.

"The same as usual. One minute in recovery, swearing she'll never drink again and the next being picked up off the street somewhere in a drunken stupor."

"Poor Lisa. She really does try to control her problem."

"She must. Her liver is calling time up. She's been warned. She's dry at the moment because she's in a clinic again. I hope to God she'll stay that way but, well, you know her history."

To Robyn's shame she knew Lisa's history intimately. She had even sat and waited in Kevin's car when he had gone to visit Lisa in hospitals and clinics. Had Lisa known that her husband's girlfriend was waiting outside? Did she drink to find comfort, oblivion? The only saving grace was that Lisa had been well on her way to alcoholism long before Robyn had slept with her husband.

It was a guilt too far for Robyn. She stood.

"I'd better write that piece. Could you give me your contact in the Met Office first? I'd like to get confirmation before I cry wolf. Or flood."

She pushed a pen and paper towards Kevin just as she heard a rap on the front door. Tansy. At last. She ushered Tansy plus stew into the kitchen.

"Ben refused to go out," she complained. "He's in a big tantrum. Blaming me for the cold."

"You spoil that cat," Kevin said. "You should show him who's boss."

"I do. I obey all his orders."

Both Tansy and Kevin laughed then. Robyn took the page with the Met Office number written on it and went to the study. She felt neither of them had noticed her leave.

The article took Robyn some time to write. She was trying to strike the right balance. Too much detail and people would not bother to read it. Too little and they wouldn't realise the urgency of the situation. Nor had Robyn truly understood until she had spoken to Kevin's contact in the Met Office. The girl sounded young. And in Robyn's momentary flash of jealousy she somehow sounded beautiful too. Why was this girl giving Kevin personalised forecasts? How well did he know her? Then the news about the approaching storm soon rid Robyn of all silly jealous thoughts.

"It's not *if* anymore but when," the girl said. "We're as certain as we can be that, barring some unforeseen event, this system will make landfall off the west coast and will sweep over the entire country."

"So you're advising mandatory evacuations of low-lying areas?"

"That's right. Dublin, Cork, Limerick and Galway all have vulnerable areas. The emergency services are meeting tonight to co-ordinate efforts. We'll be issuing hourly bulletins all day tomorrow. Shipping and flights will be curtailed or stopped completely. This could be the biggest we've ever seen. The worst on record. It could be even more devastating than the famous storm of 1839 or Hurricane Charley in 1986."

Robyn thought of the emergency services in Felton and she shuddered. The local GP, Dr Early, two policemen – one of whom was just a raw recruit, a fire brigade in the next town, and of course the coastguard. There was a lifeboat, whatever use that would be in a flooded village. And flooded it would certainly be if the projected high tides, heavy rains and storm-force winds all combined as predicted.

"What about coastal areas with smaller centres of population? For instance Felton. What are the emergency plans for those areas?"

The girl laughed as if the question Robyn had asked was stupid.

"I don't know. I'm in the Met Office, remember. We just deal with the weather. Maybe you should ring your local police."

Robyn thanked her and put the phone down. The thing which worried her most was the unpredictability of the storm. It might hit the coast in two days' time, or it could come crashing in tomorrow. There was still a chance it would veer away and miss Ireland altogether but that possibility was looking less likely by the hour. Since the jet stream of westerly winds, which would normally have an influence, was sitting stubbornly south of Ireland out of range of the oncoming storm, there didn't seem to be anything to slow its progress or divert it away.

Glancing up on the wall, Robyn read the number of the police station from the Felton calendar and dialled. The phone rang out. Bloody great! A monster storm churning up the North Atlantic, emergency services in all the city centres preparing evacuation procedures and Felton police station was closed for the night. Nothing for it now but to take the responsibility on her own shoulders.

Bending over the laptop, Robyn's fingers flew over the keyboard. She wrote about the threatened storm, about its predicted fury and damage capability, about the planned evacuations in major centres of population and the total lack of any plans for Felton.

'*We must protect ourselves,*' she wrote. '*We will have to prepare for the worst. You must listen to the weather alerts and be ready to evacuate. Go inland. Beg, steal or borrow safe accommodation until this storm is over. If you cannot do that then go up to the Community Hall. Bring provisions with you to last at least two days. Contact Mayor Billy Moynihan for more instructions on what to bring and when to evacuate.*'

She printed out the piece and read the hard copy. It was alarmist, yes, but that's how she meant it to be. As she walked back out to the kitchen, she remembered the nursing home. A beautiful old house at the far end of the village. It had landscaped gardens and a sea view. A comfortable retirement home one hundred metres from the sea. A death trap in a sea surge.

When she opened the kitchen door the air was thick with the aroma of heating stew. Tansy and Kevin were deep in conversation. Their elbows on the table, they were leaning towards each other. Robyn heard the word "Maya" and wondered again how Kevin, always so cynical, was finding Tansy's latest fad so riveting. Tansy was waffling on about astronomy while he listened attentively.

"This alignment of the centre of the Milky Way and the winter solstice sun that's due to occur on December 21st 2012 – it's a one in 25,800-year event and yet the Maya predicted it with almost pinpoint accuracy."

"What I find fascinating too is the fact that they seem

to have known about the existence of black holes. Portals into space."

"Now do you believe me?" Tansy said. "It's taken centuries of study and billions in research to prove what the Maya knew."

"I give in, Tansy," he said. "You've convinced me. Armageddon just before Christmas 2012."

Robyn walked to the table and put her report in front of Kevin.

"We won't have to wait that long for catastrophe. It's heading right towards us at this minute. I've been talking to your friend in the Met Office."

Kevin picked up the page, glanced at it and then back at her. "What did I tell you? You should leave Felton until this storm blows over. You too, Tansy."

Tansy stood suddenly and dashed towards the oven. "Oops! Almost forgot our dinner. Would you get plates and cutlery, Rob, and we'll serve up?"

Robyn glanced at Kevin. He seemed unperturbed by the fact that they would have to eat the concoction which was filling the kitchen with a sharp smell. She shrugged and got the ware. They were silent as the three of them ate. To her surprise, Robyn found the tangy flavour tasty.

"This is good! I know there's chicken. What else? What are the seeds?"

"That's not chicken. It's rabbit. The other ingredients are secret."

Robyn had just put a forkful in her mouth. She almost gagged, imagining grey fur clinging to the cubes of meat. With great effort she swallowed and pushed her plate away from her.

"Delicious, Tansy," Kevin added. "Very creative."

Tansy and Kevin smiled at each other and Robyn was revisited by the notion they had forgotten she was in the room. Not wanting to analyse her feeling of disappointment, she immediately changed the topic.

"How many people are in the retirement home, Tansy? Do you know?"

"Usually only about twelve. I know it looks big but it's not really. Oh, lord, we didn't think of them, did we?"

"We didn't and now I'm thinking disaster. Those old people will have to be evacuated. They're too near the sea. Who's in charge there?"

Kevin put his knife and fork together on his empty plate and sat back.

"Isn't that just the problem? Who's in charge? The Mayor? I don't think so. The police, all two of them? The Village Council? Here, read this." He pushed Robyn's report towards Tansy.

Tansy scanned the page and then stared, white-faced, at both of them.

"It's not just a storm, Rob, is it? The Atlantic is going to roll in on top of us."

"That seems to be a possibility."

"What are we going to do? We can't just sit here and wait for the village to go under."

"Exactly what I said," Kevin agreed, staring at Robyn. "Get out while you can."

Tansy sat up straight and glared at him. "You go. This is not your place. I was born here. I'm not going to abandon Felton now."

"Me neither," Robyn added.

Kevin, for once, seemed to be struck dumb. Tansy stood and began to clear away the plates.

"We'll make coffee, Robyn, and put our heads together. Make a list of all the people we need to contact. Do you think we should call Billy Moynihan and June Varian over? And ask June to check with her niece in the Met Office. Just to be doubly sure."

"I'll do that. I think we should contact Dr Early too, don't you? He attends the retirement home. And he knows how many sick and vulnerable would need priority evacuation. He can give us facts and figures."

Somewhere in between coffee-making and drawing up plans, Kevin Phillips left Woodruff Cottage. He too had some calls to make.

Chapter 12

June Varian was frowning as she put down the phone after talking to her niece. The sense of excitement she had felt about organising shelter from the coming storm had suddenly become fear. She rang Billy Moynihan but got no answer. She walked upstairs and hammered on the door of her son's room. Eventually he heard her through the din of his music and opened the door a slit.

"I'm going out for a little while," she said. "Don't dream of putting a foot outside the door. I won't be long."

He nodded and quickly closed the door again.

June threw on her coat and ran up to Middle Street where Billy Moynihan lived in the flat over his shop. He had obviously been snoozing in front of the telly because his hair was tousled and his eyes sleepy. June went in the door without being invited.

"Get yourself together, Billy Moynihan. Tansy Bingham has been trying to ring you and so have I. We're calling a meeting. This storm is worse than the forecasters thought it would be. It's a monster and it's heading in our direction. We're going to the vet's house so make yourself decent."

"Why are we going there? Can't you ask them to come over to us?"

"Just like you to drag a pregnant woman out at night! You're a very selfish man. You should be ashamed of yourself."

Quickly and without any further objections, Billy got ready and they drove to Woodruff Cottage.

Tansy opened the door for them and led them into the kitchen.

"My niece said –"

"We know, June," Tansy interrupted. "We just have to assume the worst now and prepare for it."

"Jesus! Why?" Billy asked crossly. "Just because June's niece said so? What does she know about Felton?"

"My niece is in the Met Office, for heaven's sake, Billy. What more do you need to convince you? The sea sloshing around your shop?"

Billy glowered at June, then dropped his gaze. Like a chastised child he hung his head and muttered, "All we have is the Community Hall. No sea wall to talk of. No government help, no –"

"Complaining won't get us anywhere," Robyn said. "Nor can we depend on outside help at this stage. We must work out how to help ourselves. We can do it."

"Can we? Do you think?"

"We have to. We don't have a choice."

A knock sounded on the front door. "I'll get it," Tansy offered. She went out and returned with the elderly Felton GP.

"It's not your time, is it?" June asked, ignoring Billy Moynihan's panicked stare in Robyn's direction.

Robyn smiled at them both. "No. Don't worry. I asked Dr Early to sit in on our meeting. We'll need medical supplies and help with evacuating the retirement home."

"I'll be glad to do whatever I can to help," the old man said, "but I understand you're talking about this storm hitting the day after tomorrow. I'm not sure exactly what we can do in that short length of time."

"Neither are we," said June and on that negative note the meeting started.

"This will finish them off," Dick Maloney said as he pulled on a woolly sweater and rubbed his cold hands together to heat them up. "The little feckers can't survive once the temperature drops."

"I assume you mean the midges," Zach remarked.

The other man just glared at him. They were enclosed in a kind of hell in Con Lynch's kitchen. Neither man liked the other but they were forced to spend hour after mind-bending hour in each other's company. The Veterinary Department official, Andrew Simmons, had the tremendous advantage of being able to sleep through most of the tedium.

"There's worse forecast," Dick continued. "The best thing that could have happened to finish off the Bluetongue threat. It's gone. Over. They'll have to let us out of this fucking jail soon."

Zach sighed. They must have had this same conversation about a thousand times.

"You know we're here until they confirm cause of

death for Noreen Lynch. You hardly want to be responsible for spreading a new virus, do you?"

"Jesus! How long does it take? Surely be to Christ they have some idea by now? They said her heart was weak, didn't they? And her lungs. She was a sick old woman for God's sake! These guys are just trying to justify their existence. Coming here in their spacesuits, taking blood samples from us like we were an alien species."

Without opening his eyes, Andrew stirred on the couch.

"Shut the fuck up, Maloney. We'll know soon enough. They're just waiting on one result. We'll have that tomorrow. Then we're either under death sentence or we're free."

Zach shivered. That was a stark choice. He was beginning to imagine pains, aches and fevers.

"I feel fine. Not a thing wrong with me," he announced to reassure himself. "Except for a sore arm from all the blood tests."

"I wonder will Con Lynch be allowed bring his wife's body back here for burial?" said Dick.

Andrew, eyes still closed, muttered, "They may insist on cremation in Dublin if she died from mutated Blue-tongue."

Zach stared at the man sprawled comfortably on Con Lynch's couch and wondered how he could be so sanguine. If Noreen had died from this virus, then they three most likely would too. And Con Lynch. They had all been in close contact with the diseased animals. The fingers of his right hand automatically went to the wedding band, still new and shiny, on his left ring-finger.

He turned it round and round, remembering that day, thinking of Robyn and the baby he might never see.

Gemma Creedon was the most efficient administrator the *Daily News* had ever employed. She was also a pain in the butt, Kevin thought as he listened on the phone to her clipped voice run through lists of to-dos.

"When are you due back from Felton?" she asked. "I've had to reschedule several of your appointments already."

"Can't say. There's more to come on the Bluetongue story. I must be here when the results of the local woman's autopsy are released. Anything else I need to know about?"

"Nothing work-related but we did have tickets for the theatre last night. You obviously forgot."

Shit! Yes, he had forgotten. In fact, this whole developing relationship with Gemma Creedon was something he would rather forget altogether. It wasn't working. Not for him. It had been a mistake. Desperation.

"I'm sorry, Gemma. I hope you used the tickets, brought a friend along."

"I wouldn't do that, Kevin. I understand you have to stick with the Bluetongue story. Although I wonder why you don't send one of our reporters down there. You can't enjoy being in that backwater."

"I'm quite liking Felton, actually. It's a nice village. That reminds me, make sure we have plenty of cover on the evacuation plans for the cities. Bring in some freelancers if you need to. I've already spoken to the front desk about it but keep on eye on it for me."

"The storm isn't due until the day after tomorrow.

Surely you'll be back. You're not thinking of staying on the coast, are you?"

Kevin couldn't reply to that question because he didn't know the answer. He should have left Felton yesterday. Gone back to Dublin, the office, Gemma Creedon, his alcoholic wife in the clinic overseas and his busy life. Gemma was right. A junior reporter could cover this story on the ground. The real drama was in Dublin now, in the hospital where Con Lynch's wife had died and in the labs where the cause of her death was being investigated. Yet Felton, with its beautiful scenery and slower pace, was hard to leave.

"It's Robyn Claymore, isn't it? That's why you're staying there."

Gemma's sharp tone cut right through Kevin's hazy thoughts. With a start he wondered if she was right. Had he come to Felton because Robyn was here and was that the reason he was reluctant to leave? Robyn, very pregnant, was more beautiful than he had ever seen her. And there was Tansy too. Scatty, eccentric Tansy. She was making him laugh like he hadn't done for a very long time. Possibly never.

"Don't be ridiculous, Gemma. You know I go where the story is. For now, and until the Bluetongue Virus is officially declared under control, the story is in Felton. Besides, I don't need to explain myself to you. Let me know if there are any problems. I'll be in contact."

Even as he cut off the call, he knew he had been unfair to Gemma. It wasn't her fault that he felt restless and dissatisfied. That he still missed Robyn.

He dialled another number. The receptionist knew his voice instantly.

"Good evening, Mr Phillips. I'm afraid your wife is sleeping at the moment. Did you want to talk to her?"

No. Kevin didn't want to talk to Lisa. Not to go through the same stilted routine over and over, listening to the sound of depression and despair in her voice, hearing her need for alcohol echo in every silence.

"Just tell her I rang, please. I'll call again tomorrow or the day after."

He switched off his phone and looked around him. This room was a clone of all the other hotel rooms he had occupied. Impersonal. Just a rest-stop in his transient lifestyle from one newsworthy crisis to the next. He glanced at his reflection in the mirror and quickly looked away. He could see it in his eyes, the loneliness, and he did not want to confront it. God damn Robyn Claymore and her horse-doctor husband! Kevin squeezed his eyes shut as a horrible thought taunted him. Suppose, just suppose, that the farmer's wife had died from some hitherto unknown form of Bluetongue Virus. The one they were whispering about behind closed doors. Suppose that Zach Claymore had the same disease. Suppose he too died . . .

Kevin opened his eyes suddenly, disgusted with this train of thought. Just to prove to himself that he was not an altogether evil person, he said a short but fervent prayer for Zach Claymore's health. Then, because he could not help himself, he headed back to Woodruff Cottage.

The meeting in Robyn's kitchen had been making slow progress before Kevin Phillips arrived back. He tried to speed things up while Billy Moynihan sank into a resentful silence.

"I can't understand why you don't have the police

here," Kevin pointed out. "They'll have to organise the evacuation, put up road blocks, ensure premises have been vacated. Why can't you go knock them up if you have to? Don't you know where they live?"

"Of course we do. They're local men," Billy said sulkily.

"Then get them here for heaven's sake! Tell them there's been a murder if that's what it takes."

"There might be yet," Billy said so earnestly that they all laughed.

Dr Early volunteered to ring the sergeant.

"What about Fr Ryan?" June said. "Shouldn't we let him know?"

"Don't be daft, woman. He's in hospital, isn't he? We don't want to be worrying him with parish business while he's so sick. We'll have to talk to The Man Above ourselves."

Robyn glanced at her watch. It was nine thirty.

"I suggest we call an end to the meeting for tonight," she said. "We've arrangements in place now to bring the residents of the retirement home to Galway by ambulance tomorrow, thanks to your intervention, Dr Early. Tansy has posters and flyers ready for distribution, the front page of the *Daily News* will tell people to leave here pronto –"

"We've organised a first-aid kit and emergency medical supplies for the hall, we've shopping lists compiled and cash on hand to buy," June added.

"Exactly," Robyn agreed. "A good night's work. Wouldn't we be better off getting some sleep now and starting early in the morning?"

"Agreed, " June said, already standing up and putting on her coat. "I must get back home and see what my hero of a son has got up to. C'mon, Billy."

"Nine o'clock tomorrow morning in the Community Hall?" said Tansy.

Everyone nodded agreement.

Robyn walked to the door with them as they left. Billy, still sulky or maybe just tired, trailed after June and Dr Early.

"You make sure he puts exactly what you wrote on the front page tomorrow," Billy warned Robyn, nodding his head in the direction of the kitchen where Kevin Phillips was still sitting at the table, his long legs stretched out.

"I will. He really wants to help us, you know. It's just that he's not good at sharing. He always wants things his own way."

Robyn stood and watched as the two cars drove away. It was cold and seemed to be getting breezy but yet she stood there, the sound of the tide in her ears and the words she had just spoken to Billy Moynihan in her head. Kevin Phillips always wanted things his own way. Wasn't that the kernel of the man? His way or not at all.

"Come in, Rob. You'll get your death of cold."

Robyn closed the door and turned to smile at Tansy.

"I'm tired. I think I'll go to bed. Will you and Kevin lock up for me when you're going?"

"Are you alright? I'll stay tonight if you want."

Robyn shook her head. She knew Tansy had other things to do. Other company to keep.

"I'm fine, Tansy, thanks. I'll see you in the morning."

She climbed wearily up the stairs and didn't look back. She didn't have to. She knew Kevin had come to stand beside Tansy, that his arm was around her shoulder and that they would spend the night together.

Chapter 13

The stillness woke Robyn. No birdsong. No breeze. Light seeped in through the curtains. Not the warm, yellow glow of sunshine but not the gloom of dark cloud either. She squinted at her bedside alarm. Seven o'clock. Easing herself carefully from the bed she padded barefoot to the window and lifted a corner of the curtain but it wasn't the glassy sea or the silver-grey sky which caught her attention. It was the red sports car parked in Tansy's driveway. She had known, hadn't she? She had seen the way Tansy and Kevin had been looking at each other, the way they touched and smiled. So why the shock, the burning twist of jealousy?

Quickly, Robyn dropped the curtain and went into the shower. She sang while she showered, talked to the baby and counted backwards from one hundred. Anything to rid her mind of the image of Kevin holding Tansy in his arms. Dressed, she drew the curtains and stood for a moment facing towards the sea, trying to absorb perspective from the timelessness of the perpetual tidal flow. Still restless, she turned her back on the sea and went downstairs.

Zach rang just as she finished her muesli.

"Any news from the lab?" she asked, wishing him to say the words she needed to hear.

"Not yet. I don't know what the hold-up is. Either Noreen Lynch died from Bluetongue Virus or she didn't. They must know by . . ."

His sentence trailed off, unfinished. Robyn could imagine him being furious with himself for worrying her more.

"I'm sorry," he muttered.

"They have to be very sure, Zach."

"I know, I know. That's what I keep telling myself and the morons I'm stuck here with. But I'm going stir-crazy. I think I might strangle one of my fellow inmates shortly."

Robyn laughed at the idea of Zach harbouring any murderous thoughts. Not Zach. "It must be awful for you. Why don't you go out and have a walk around the farm? Get some fresh air."

"I might do that. Although it's sad to see the empty stalls and sheds."

"Are all the animals gone?"

"Every last one of them. It was the only way."

She heard the devastation in his voice. The cull must have hit him hard. His whole life was about saving animals, not destroying them in one fell swoop. She tried to distract him by changing the topic.

"We had a meeting here last night about storm preparations. Although looking out the window this morning all the talk of weather chaos seems way off the mark."

"Don't be fooled, Rob. The storm threat is real."

She frowned as she heard the note of worry in his voice. "No need to fret. Our new Flood Defence Committee is getting into gear now. Dr Early came to our meeting last night. We decided to prepare for the worst."

"If the forecast is half-right, we could be in for a lashing. Is there any possibility you'd see sense and go to your mother for a while?"

Robyn decided to ignore that. She had already told him she wasn't budging from Felton.

"We've another meeting this morning. In the Community Hall."

"He's still around, isn't he?"

The question caught her by surprise. She didn't have to ask who he meant. But she did have to answer.

"Yes. Kevin Phillips is still in Felton. I wonder if he knows about Noreen Lynch's autopsy? Is that what he's waiting for?"

"Bull! That will be decided in Dublin. He'll have another reason for being here."

She had an image of Zach, tired and frustrated, trapped on Lynches' farm and imagining things happening outside. Things over which he had no control. Dishonest things. Hateful things. She rushed to reassure him.

"Kevin's around alright. His car is outside Tansy's house. I'd say it's safe to assume he spent the night there, wouldn't you?"

"Did you warn her? Does she know he's married?"

"I told her, yes."

"So she knows about you and him?"

"There's no me and Kevin Phillips. Just you and me and our baby."

An awkward second passed before Zach spoke again. "You're doing too much. You should be resting. And not here. You really should go home to your mother, Rob. At least until this storm threat blows over. You shouldn't be in Felton at all."

Robyn glanced through the patio doors at the motionless shrubs and remembered the mirror-smooth sea this morning.

"The doom and gloom forecast seems ridiculous now. But I promise I'll go to the hall if there's the slightest risk."

"Just take care. I'll ring as soon as I have any news. Or better yet I'll race home to tell you."

"Can't wait. I love you, Zach."

"Love you too."

Robyn held the silent phone in her hand for a long time after he had cut off the call.

Robyn had just finished clearing up after breakfast when Tansy arrived in. She seemed to have a particular glow about her, enhanced by the white hand-knit sweater she was wearing.

"You look very chirpy this morning, Tansy. Would that have anything to do with the fact that there's a red sports car parked outside your house?"

Tansy glanced first at Robyn and then over to her own driveway. "Oh! You mean Kevin's car. It broke down last night. I think it's gears or something. I had to drive him to the hotel."

Robyn turned away and made a fuss of getting a coat to wear in case it rained. She didn't want Tansy to see any trace of the inexplicable relief she felt. Why should she care where Kevin bloody Phillips slept last night? It was nothing to her. Not really.

"I can't remember what we decided last night," Tansy said. "Who's supposed to contact the Gardaí this morning?"

"Billy. He knows the sergeant well. They played football together at some stage."

"Billy Moynihan played football? He told you that? He was the gofer for the Felton rugby team. Fetching and carrying on the sidelines."

"That figures. He'll ring the sergeant anyway, even if he never scored a try."

As they walked out the front Robyn noticed that the pet-clinic door was open.

"I'd better have a word with Kerry," she said. "Won't be a sec."

The clinic smelled like Zach. Disinfectant and deodorant. Kerry was busy sterilising instruments.

"Morning, Kerry. Have you heard from Zach today?"

The girl lifted her head from her work and smiled.

"Hi, Mrs Claymore. Yes, I did. He's hoping to be back soon. Weird, isn't it, the way the animals are culled but the humans on the farm are still quarantined."

"Just bureaucracy. You know what these department officials are like."

"I will do soon enough. Did Zach tell you I'll be leaving today?"

Robyn was surprised. As far as she knew, Kerry should have been with the clinic for another six months. Funny that Zach hadn't mentioned anything.

"I'm sorry to hear that, Kerry. Where are you going?"

"Oh, no! I'm not *leaving*-leaving. I'm just going home to Roscommon until this storm is over. My parents insisted. Isn't that what you advised people to do in your article in the *Daily News* today?"

Robyn grinned at her. Yes, that's what she had advised in the strongest possible terms. "I didn't expect such an immediate response."

"I'll put the sandbags at the front doors before I go. Just use the back door coming and going to the house. What about you, Mrs Claymore? Where are you going to sit out the storm? Shouldn't you be near a hospital in case you go into . . ." Kerry blushed and stuttered. "I-I'm sorry. None of my business."

Robyn smiled. "I'll be staying in the Community Hall if needs be. It's all a wait-and-see game now, isn't it? Both on the storm and the baby front. I'll see you when you come back, Kerry. And thanks for organising the sandbags."

There was no sign of Tansy at the front of the house when Robyn got back there. A quick look in the direction of her cottage explained all. The bonnet of Kevin Phillips' car was up and a mechanic was leaning over the engine, closely watched by Tansy and Kevin. Robyn strolled towards her own front gate and looked out to sea. She tried to see the swells Tansy identified with ease but the water still seemed smooth to her. Barely a ripple as it ebbed its way back from the earlier full tide, leaving ever-widening expanses of wet sand in its wake. It would seem that this placid body of water had never done anything more forceful than gently lap onto the waiting sands.

Robyn jumped as Tansy spoke from right beside her.

"Look at all those gorgeous shells! I wish I had time to collect some now."

"Could the Met have got it wrong, do you think?" Robyn asked. "It wouldn't be the first time, would it?

Look at the sea, the sky. There's not a trace of a breeze let alone a major storm."

"In which case we'll look right plonks, won't we? Holed up in the Community Hall with Billy Moynihan, tins of beans and sleeping bags!"

Kevin approached, rubbing his hands with a tissue. He had obviously been poking at the greasy engine, typically not trusting the mechanic enough. "Better get a move on," he said. "Anyone want a lift?"

"So your car is fixed," Robyn said. "Where are you offering the lift to?"

"The meeting, of course. Where else?"

"Dublin, maybe."

"You wish."

Tansy stood between the two of them and caught their hands. "Stop bickering, you two. Now come on, we'll be late."

Robyn and Kevin glared at each other before turning and walking to their respective cars. Tansy shrugged. Storm first and then she would try to figure out what was going on between these two stubborn people.

The patrol car was outside the hall. So was Billy Moynihan's car and Dr Early's. Tansy put her head in her hands in a very dramatic way.

"Shit! They've started the meeting already. Billy Moynihan will be sulking all day now."

"We're only a few minutes late. Dance for him again, Tansy. That should cheer him up."

Laughing as they approached the hall door, Robyn hadn't noticed Kevin approach from behind her until he caught her arm. "I know about the conference-call today, Robyn. I hope it goes well. For everyone's sake but especially for you and Zach."

Robyn stood still and looked up into Kevin's eyes. "What in the hell are you talking about?"

"The conference. Surely you know about it? I have a contact in the hospital. Well, actually, I have contacts everywhere, as you well know."

"What conference?"

Kevin frowned as he examined her face. "You really don't know, do you? The State vet lab and the hospital virology lab are meeting today. Comparing notes. They'll be linking up with some international experts too and World Health Organisation. Then we should know if the Bluetongue mutated or not. I thought Zach would have told you."

"He did," Robyn said stoutly. It was partly true. Zach had said he would know today, hadn't he? But he had not mentioned anything about international conferences and the World Health Organisation. It seemed too surreal that midges in Felton had sparked an international crisis. That Zach was at the heart of the crisis. Robyn took a deep breath to still her panicky thoughts.

"He didn't say what time the meeting was. Do you know?" she asked.

"It will start at eleven this morning. God knows when or how it will end."

"Is there anything at all you don't stick your nose into? Who told you about Noreen Lynch?"

"Helicopters, mercy airlifts, secrecy. It was easy to put two and two together. Why do you think I stayed around here?"

Without answering, Robyn turned to follow Tansy

into the hall. A shiver ran down her spine. No wonder Zach had downplayed the whole thing. It was typical of him to want to protect her.

"Glad ye could make it," Billy greeted them sarcastically from his seat at the head of the table in the conference room.

Flanked by the Garda Sergeant and the young Garda recruit on one side, June Varian and Dr Early on the other, Billy seemed to have found a new confidence overnight.

"Sit down and let's get started. We've no time to waste. For those who don't know, this is Garda Sergeant Tim Halligan and his second-in-command Garda Seán Harte. Tim will tell ye his plans as soon as ye stop scraping chairs and shuffling around."

Despite again having to squeeze her bulk between chairs and wall and her worry of only a minute ago, Robyn felt like giggling. Maybe it was being treated like a schoolgirl that made her want to behave like one. It would be interesting to see how the newly assertive Billy Moynihan would cope with Kevin Phillips. Satisfied that everyone was now ready, Billy nodded at the sergeant to go ahead.

"We plan on closing off Lower and Middle Streets this evening. Maybe Upper Street too, depending on how the forecast is looking. Headquarters are in contact with the Met Office and my latest advice is that the storm is continuing to gather speed and strength and maintaining its course in our direction."

"We'll definitely be hit so, will we?" Tansy asked.

"That's what they say. There's a huge Atlantic swell, at least five metres. Possibly as high as ten. The wind is pushing it all towards our coast. Particularly up here in the north-west."

They were all quiet as the reality of a wall of water heading in their direction hit home.

"But it's such a mild day," June muttered, shaking her head.

"Calm before the storm," Billy announced and then repeated it for effect. "Calm before the storm."

"What about evacuations, Sergeant Halligan?" Kevin asked. "Will they be mandatory?"

The sergeant looked at Kevin as if trying to figure out who he was. Then he nodded. "You're from the *Daily News*. I heard about you. Call me Tim. Felton sea wall is a joke. The storm swell will certainly overtop it. We've no option but to get people out of the village which is why we have no time to waste now." He turned to Tansy. "I was told you have some leaflets prepared advising people to leave their homes."

Tansy reached into her bag and took out a bundle of papers. "Here they are. I advised going inland but if that's not feasible getting to the Community Hall is the next best option. I included the list of emergency supplies to bring along. The one we agreed on last night."

"Did you ask them to bring their own toilet rolls?" Billy asked.

Robyn felt like giggling again even though it was a very practical suggestion. She glanced at Tansy and saw that she too was trying to suppress a titter.

"Um, yes," said Tansy.

Tim Halligan took the pages from Tansy and glanced at them. "Thanks. I'll photocopy more in the station.

Seán and I should have them delivered to each house by noon. I'll take those posters you have there too. Stick them up in the shops."

He stood up and pushed his chair back.

"Keep in touch and check the forecast regularly. The experts tell us this storm is not behaving normally. It may veer away from us but for now we have to assume it could hit us harder and sooner than we expect. Our priority is to save lives. Every minute is vital. Get organised as quickly as possible. And, Dr Early, could I have a list from you of the patients you are evacuating to the hospitals? Just drop it by the station when you have them all packed off."

The old doctor nodded. "I'll be on my way too. The fleet of ambulances should be at the retirement home by now. I have other patients I'm concerned about. I don't think they would be strong enough to survive wet and cold. I'm trying to source suitable accommodation for them also. I'll let you know, Tim."

With a wave of his hand, the sergeant walked quickly away, shadowed as usual by the fresh-faced recruit.

They left a stunned audience behind them. June Varian let out a long sigh. "Holy shit! This is even more serious than we thought, isn't it?"

"You could say that," Dr Early agreed and then he too stood. "Come out to the car with me, Billy. I'll give you a first-aid kit and emergency medicines for the hall. Make sure they're locked away securely."

Even Kevin seemed subdued as the remaining few sat at the table.

"We don't really know what's going to happen, do we?" June asked quietly. "Chloe said – how did she put it? – that they've never seen a system 'deepen so quickly or behave so erratically'."

Kevin raised an eyebrow. "Chloe?"

"My niece in the Met Office. You're not the only one with contacts."

"We're wasting time," Kevin said sourly. "Let's get down to work."

Just as they began to go through the provisions list, Dr Early came back in the door and called to Robyn. "A word, please, before I go."

Robyn shuffled her way out of her seat and walked across to him. He led her outside the door and into the hall.

"I don't think you should stay, Robyn. You're one of the people I would strongly advise to leave Felton today, while you still can."

She shook her head, annoyed now that everyone was telling her leave. "I'm not going while Zach is still here. Anyway I'll be safe in the hall. We all will."

The doctor looked closely at her, his expression stern. "You must think of your baby. Suppose it decides to arrive early? You need to be near a hospital, Robyn."

"I need to be near my husband. Besides, first babies have a habit of being late, don't they? How long do you expect this storm to last? A month?"

"The effects of the storm may last a lot longer than a month. We don't know, do we? I want you to think about it."

He turned and walked across the hall, leaving Robyn wondering if he thought her selfish. Careless. A bad mother. Then she lifted her head. She loved the life inside her with all her heart and soul. She would never do anything to endanger her baby. She went back to the conference room more determined than ever to make the Community Hall the safest storm refuge in Ireland.

The sky seemed to be falling. As if he could touch the grey cloud blanket by reaching up his hand. Zach smiled at his silly notion, wondering if his enforced stay on the farm was affecting his sanity. It was airless and very warm on top of The 360, the place where he had last stood with Con Lynch the night Noreen had died. He sat on a rock and looked down at Felton. The town centre, as the locals so grandly called their three narrow streets, clinging to the edge of the sea. He shivered, remembering the latest weather forecast he had seen. If this storm stayed on track, it was possible Felton would be engulfed. Smothered in a wave of brine.

Zach turned his gaze towards the Community Hall on Lookout Hill. From here he could see only the back of the building in the distance. Robyn would be in there now, Tansy by her side and maybe, just maybe, Kevin Phillips on her other side. Stirring up old memories. Rekindling passions which should never have been.

Angry, Zach picked up a stone and hurled it downhill. It bounced off rocks and finally disappeared into a tuft of heather. The hillside looked bare without sheep. Like a Christmas tree without baubles. Like life without Robyn. It seemed that fate was conspiring to separate them, by one means or another. It could be that the mutated Bluetongue Virus was already coursing through his veins, burrowing into his cells, duplicating at lightning speed. Preparing to choke him as it had done Noreen Lynch. It was a possibility. The longer he waited for the phone call from

Dublin the more a death sentence by Bluetongue seemed likely.

He thought of the life he and Robyn had carved out for themselves in Felton. Just one short year. A year of warmth and sharing. Tears welled in his eyes now as he thought of the baby he might never see. Would it be a boy or a girl? They had decided not to find out from the scans. It didn't matter. They would love and welcome their baby. Just as Robyn would have loved Kevin Phillips' baby too if he had agreed to have one with her. This was the truth Zach admitted but rarely confronted. He had been Robyn's second choice. He knew that. The knowing hurt.

He stood up and turned his back on Felton. Walking downhill again, he noticed the thin trickle of water in the valley riverbed. It was as dusty and dry as the first day he had seen the sick sheep there. That seemed like a lifetime ago. The Bluetongue Virus had poisoned everything. It had taken Noreen Lynch, Con Lynch's livelihood, and brought the outside world in to poke and prod and file news reports on the place they liked to call 'a sleepy backwater'. It had brought Kevin Phillips back into Robyn's life. Perhaps he had never left.

Nearing Lynches' farmhouse now, Zach felt despair at the thought of going in there again to spend more restless hours in the company of the two men inside. He stood for a moment and then continued towards the house. The company of those two prats was preferable to the deep despair of his own thoughts.

The Felton supermarket was in chaos. The owner, Noel Cantillon, and two of his assistants ran back and forth filling trolleys while the hastily cobbled together Flood Defence Committee issued orders from a long list.

"Water. Bottled water is the most essential thing," June said. "Give us what you have." Noel let out an impatient sigh, lifted his cap briefly and scratched his head. Noel's hair, always under a navy peaked cap, was part of Felton legend. Abundant was one way of describing the bushy mane which crowned the otherwise very neat man. A hangover, Tansy confided, from his short stint as a member of a ballad group in his youth.

This shopping bonanza was obviously putting him under huge pressure.

"I can't clear out the store for you. My customers will want to buy their own supplies too. I can't let them down. The two convenience shops have already run out. Some bloody list or other instructed them all to buy bottled water in case the mains supply would be effected by the storm."

"You can't leave people stuck in the Community Hall without clean water," said June.

"Batteries. Don't forget them," Tansy added. "We'll need them for torches and the radio June volunteered to bring along."

This request seemed to be the end point for the store-owner. He did a little foot-tap, his face red. "What kind of storm are ye expecting? Armageddon? Look, I appreciate the business but I can't help feeling this is all a bit over the top. What if the storm never happens or misses us entirely? Am I guaranteed payment?"

"I gave you my word," Billy said angrily. "If you want I'll get the money out of the Community Hall account now."

Looking a bit sheepish, Noel Cantillon smiled at Billy. "No need for that. C'mon. Let's get going again. Delivering this lot up to Lookout Hill will take me a couple of trips. Tinned foods next because . . ."

He stopped talking when Robyn tapped him on the arm. "Look," she said quietly, pointing to the television screen which flickered in the corner of the storeroom.

Suddenly there was silence as all eyes were drawn towards the images on the screen. Lines of traffic snaked over bridges and motorways as people in low-lying city areas abandoned their homes and businesses. Dublin, Cork, Limerick, Galway. Captions flashed underneath the different scenes but each one told the same story. People were fleeing endangered areas.

"Turn up the sound, Noel," June ordered.

The voice-over was telling of the latest warnings from the Met Office. The biggest storm ever to hit Ireland was on course to make landfall within the next twelve hours or less, bringing with it a huge tide and winds which by now were officially hurricane force. Currently Category One with winds in excess of 120 kilometres per hour. All the indications were alarming. The system was drawing energy from the seas which had been warmed to 27 degrees surface temperature during the six-week warm spell. Pressure, too, in the eye of the storm was dropping quickly.

"See now!" Billy said. "The only way you'll save any stock from your shop is to bring it up to the hall. We're doing you a favour, Noel."

They watched in silence again, mesmerised by the continuous flow of slow-moving traffic. Train stations and bus depots were thronged with people who seemed to be carrying their homes on their backs. The queues were orderly, well controlled by a big police presence but the whole scene had an underlying tone of suppressed panic. It would take only one frayed temper to cause chaos.

"Such stupid overreaction!" Noel said crossly. "Why are people leaving Dublin and Cork? They should be safe. Isn't it the west coast that's at risk?"

Billy hissed at him to stay quiet as they listened to the sombre voice of the presenter.

"It is expected that the storm will lose some energy when it makes landfall but the meteorologists are warning of the possibility of structural damage inland. It is anticipated that some rivers may burst their banks with the heavy rains expected."

June blessed herself with the sign of the cross rapidly. "Jesus! We brought all this on ourselves with loose morals and interfering with nature. The Man Above is very angry with us."

Billy glared at her. "Agh, stop with your nonsense, June! We've too much work to do and not much time. We must get on with this order and then help the Gardaí. There's no question now but that the town will have to be evacuated. You'll have to board up here, Noel."

"I'm not going anywhere. I'll move what I can upstairs and stay there with my family."

"It's a hurricane, Noel!" Robyn pointed out. "You're on the edge of the sea here. You can't be serious about staying. What are you afraid of? Looting? In Felton?"

"I was born in this building. I've lived here through many a storm. I'm not going to be panicked into running away."

Robyn felt a shiver run along her spine as she listened

to Noel. His bravado would be echoed over and over throughout the country. For the first time she realised that there would probably be a significant death toll from this storm. Or hurricane as it had now officially become.

Suddenly Tansy squealed in that childish way she had. "My God! I don't believe this! Did you hear what he said? This hurricane is named Kimi. I don't believe it! I must tell Kevin. Where is he?"

"He said he had some business to do," June answered. "He'll be back soon. What's so amazing about the hurricane being called Kimi?"

"Kimi is the sixth day on the Maya twenty-day calendar."

The group looked at Tansy as if she had gone mad. Except Robyn, who felt annoyed, not puzzled.

"For heaven's sake, Tansy. Don't even mention that Long Count Calendar. Not now. Give this Maya thing a rest. At least until we're organised." Then she felt guilty when she saw the hurt expression on her friend's face. "I'm sorry. I shouldn't have snapped like that."

Tansy looked closely at Robyn. "You're pale. I'm taking you home to have a rest. Anyway I must change. My sweater is too heavy in this heat. Does anyone else feel warm?"

"Running off now, are ye, with so much to be done?"

Tansy caught Robyn by the elbow and smiled sweetly at Billy. "You don't want the two of us to pass out, do you? We'll be back in the hall around two. Noel should have everything delivered by then."

"But what about the cooker?" he spluttered. "You're the one who insisted we should have a gas cooker up there in case we're stuck without electricity!"

In two strides June was standing in front of him, her hands on her hips. "Billy Moynihan! Get a hold of yourself! There's one shop in Felton selling cookers. They have one model of gas cooker in stock. Now do you think you and I can manage to buy the cooker on our own or should we call the National Reserve?"

Beaten, Billy bowed his head.

"Off you go," June said. "Robyn, you put your feet up for a while."

Outside the door, Tansy took a deep breath and looked up at the sky.

"No wonder I feel warm. The sky is nearly down on top of us. I wish you'd go home to your mum, Rob. You don't look well."

"I'm not sick. Just worried. It's Zach. He's . . ."

Before she could finish the sentence, the patrol car screeched to a halt in front of the supermarket. The sergeant jumped out.

"Headquarters have just been on to me with an updated warning. The pressure inside this hurricane is dropping like a stone. As low as 938 hectopascal."

"What does that mean? Is it bad?"

The sergeant looked crossly at Tansy, as if her question was a challenge to his authority.

"If the Met thinks it's bad, then it is. As far as I know, the lower the pressure over the water, the easier it is for the sea to swell up. I hope ye're finished buying provisions because I'm going to close down all the businesses soon."

He dashed off into the supermarket, leaving Tansy and Robyn looking at each other and then at the silver-grey sky and the sea. The tide, far out in the bay, was on the turn, at the placid phase between high and low. Soon it would begin to curl towards the shore, filling the shallow inner bay before resting, turning and flowing back towards the horizon again in its perpetual twelve-hour twenty-five-minute cycle of ebb and flow. They had been at the forefront in warning about the weather and yet they could not marry the threat of imminent disaster with the calmness around them.

Tansy shrugged. "Worst scenario we'll all be holed up in the hall and Noel Cantillon will make a fortune."

They laughed then as they headed towards the car. All along the street, sandbags were being put in place, windows boarded up and cars were being packed with essentials for a trip to stay with relatives or friends inland. Everyone seemed to have an earpiece in, listening for weather updates. Faces were grim, movements hurried.

The women's laughter became a lot more nervous. It echoed with fear.

Chapter 14

Kevin glanced around his hotel room. A last-minute check to make sure he had not left anything behind. He could hear sounds from the corridor outside. The swish of luggage being pulled along and the footfalls of staff as they rushed about making sure everyone was preparing to leave. The sergeant had said he would be back by early afternoon and would expect the Marine Hotel to be empty of staff and guests alike by then.

He left the room reluctantly and went to reception to settle his bill.

"I suppose you'll head back for Dublin now, Mr Phillips?" the girl asked.

"I suppose so."

She noted his hesitancy and took it for a rebuke. She didn't ask any more questions. He walked out to the front of the hotel where his car was parked and put his luggage into the boot. He stood then, staring at the sea, trying to make up his mind. He probably should go back to Dublin. To the office, Gemma Creedon, his weekly visits to Lisa in the clinic. To the busy emptiness of it all. A flock of gulls wheeled overhead, screeching, as if they were telling him go home. He took out his phone and keyed in a number.

"Gemma? Just letting you know I'll be staying in Felton for another while. Don't expect me back today."

He listened then as Gemma unleashed a tirade. If he had any doubt before now about the wisdom of his relationship with her, that doubt was dispelled as she listed all the reasons why he should come back to Dublin. At once. He listened patiently until she got onto the topic of Robyn Claymore. That was when Kevin called a halt.

"Enough, Gemma! My friendship with Robyn is none of your business. As far as I'm aware, I pay you to run the office and that's all I need from you now. Make sure my instructions for protecting the ground floor are followed. Have everything you can removed to the first floor until the danger of flooding is past."

He frowned as he listened to Gemma again, his rising colour testament to the fact that his patience was running out.

"I know how far our offices are from the river, Gemma, but the drains may overspill so do as I ask, please. I'll cover the report from Felton. Have the other reporters left yet for their destinations? Yes? Good. That means we'll have comprehensive coverage of storm damage. If it happens. Keep in touch."

He switched off his phone and sat into his now smoothly running car. He put it in gear, drove out through the front gates of the Marine Hotel, turned left for the coast road to follow it along as far as the three cottages. Just as he had known he would.

It was peaceful and very warm in Tansy's studio. Robyn sat back into the comfortable tub chair and stretched her legs out in front of her.

"What was it you were saying about Zach before we were interrupted by the sergeant?" Tansy asked.

Robyn looked at her and wondered if she should say anything. There was a possibility Kevin had already told her. It was still supposed to be a big secret, wasn't it? Dead animals, a dead woman, blood tests and conference calls. Classified. Too big a secret for Tansy to have kept to herself. She obviously did not know.

Ben daintily licked his food from the hand-painted bowl Tansy had made especially for him. Robyn watched and thought the cat cared about nothing but his own comfort. A bit like Kevin Phillips. She took a deep breath.

"Zach may be sick. He could be. I don't know yet. He's had blood tests done. We'll get the results today."

Tansy raced across her studio and threw her arms around Robyn.

"Oh, I'm so sorry! No wonder you look pale. Has it got something to do with the sheep virus?"

Robyn nodded, impressed by Tansy's shrewdness.

"So that's why he's still on the farm, is it? He's quarantined. And Noreen Lynch. Did she – was it the same?"

"We'll know that today too. It may all be a false alarm. But they have to take precautions. The animals were infected with a mutated form of the virus. That's the problem really and why they have to be so cautious.

Nobody knows anything about the new form of Bluetongue. So please, Tansy, not a word to anyone unless we have to. There's enough panic around with this storm."

"As if I would. I know when to keep my mouth shut."

"I'm sorry, Tansy. I didn't mean it like that. Let me cook lunch for you to make up."

Before Tansy could answer they were both startled by a red sports car driving past and then swinging into Robyn's drive, barely missing the pillar at the front gate. Even Ben stopped eating.

Leaning over the sandbags Kerry had put there, Kevin knocked loudly on the front door of Woodruff Cottage. Tansy went to the studio door and called out.

"We're here, Kevin! We'll be over as soon as Ben has finished his lunch."

Kevin grinned and waved back. Tansy turned to Robyn.

"Now you'll have to make lunch for three. Do you want me to do it for you?"

Robyn hauled herself out of the chair. "No. I'm better off keeping busy. Anyway you said you want to change into something cooler, didn't you? I'll go and start lunch."

As Robyn walked towards her own cottage, Kevin stood with his back to the front door and watched her approach. The nearer Robyn got the more intense his gaze became. Eventually she was standing in front of him and they looked at each other. She saw regret and deep sadness in his eyes. He saw what could have been.

Wordlessly, Robyn indicated to him to follow her around to the back door. They went into the kitchen together and, still silent, they washed and chopped salad, sliced bread, made coffee. Side by side they worked, doing normal mundane husband and wife things. As connected to each other's thoughts as they had always been.

"I've moved on, Kevin," she said as she got out the ware. "You should too."

"I've tried. God, how I've tried!"

"Try harder."

She looked towards the back door then, praying for Tansy to bounce in, throwing some of her scatty ideas into this cauldron of intense emotion.

"I was wrong," he said. "I should have . . ."

Kevin stopped talking as Robyn put her head to one side, listening intently. She dashed past him, moving at amazing speed for a woman so pregnant. He began to follow her as she ran to the front of the cottage. Then Kevin stood back out of sight and watched as Robyn threw herself into her husband's arms.

Robyn clung onto Zach, breathing in the scent of him, holding him so tight that she could feel his heart beat.

"Zach, thank God, thank God," she murmured over and over, only now admitting the true extent of the fears she had felt for his life.

Standing on tiptoe she closed her eyes and kissed him, lost in the touch of the lips she had believed she might never kiss again. It took a few seconds for her to realise that Zach was not responding. His lips were on hers, his arms around her, but there was no joy in his touch, no answering passion. She opened her eyes. Zach was staring over her head at the red sports car parked carelessly in their driveway.

"What's he doing here? Has he moved in? What's been going on, Robyn?"

"He's just here for lunch. And Tansy too. Surely you don't think . . . ? You couldn't believe . . . ?"

Suddenly Tansy appeared around the side of the house, a huge welcoming smile on her face and Kevin Phillips by her side. They were arm in arm. A very striking couple.

"Zach! So good to have you back. Now we might see a smile on Robyn's face again."

Zach looked in surprise from Tansy to Kevin then back to Robyn. But his surprise was not near as much as Robyn's. How had Tansy managed to pull off this trick of bi-location? She must have seen Zach arrive, sneaked over the back fence and collected Kevin on her way to show him off like a trophy. Robyn threw her a grateful smile.

"Good to be back, Tansy," Zach said.

He nodded to Kevin and then stooped down to whisper in Robyn's ear. "I'm sorry, Rob. I should have known. Am I forgiven?"

"Only if you give me that kiss you were denying me."

Zach lowered his head to hers and neither were aware that Tansy and Kevin had gone back to the kitchen, that thick clouds were beginning to blacken the grey of the sky, that a breeze was stirring in the airlessness of Felton. It was just Zach and Robyn, the baby and the love which bound their little family together.

Tansy had the extra place set for lunch when Robyn and Zach got back to the kitchen. They sat around the table, the four of them: Robyn, her best friend, her husband and her ex-lover. She smiled at the oddness of it all and she smiled because she could not suppress her happiness.

"So, Zach, what happened to Noreen Lynch?" said Kevin. "Have they told you yet?"

Zach narrowed his eyes and peered at him. "I thought you had contacts. Don't you know?"

Kevin held up his phone. "Switched off. Will I have to turn it back on or will you tell me?"

"I expect you to treat this information with respect."

"I'm not going to put any private medical information on the front page of the *Daily News* if that's what you're implying. If the woman's death was related to Bluetongue Virus, then that's a different matter. I must report it."

Zack peered for a little longer before replying. "Noreen died from natural causes. Complications of emphysema. She'd been suffering from it for a long time. Her illness and death had nothing to do with the Bluetongue. Although the virus is still a major problem as far as the animals are concerned. At least until a vaccine is developed for this new strain. Noreen could have, maybe should have, been allowed to die at home as Con wanted. I don't think he'll ever get over all this."

"That's so sad," said Tansy. "So will she be coming home now for burial?"

"They're on their way. Officialdom owed it to Con to fly him and his wife's body back to Felton. It had to be done immediately they got the go-ahead. All small aircraft will be grounded soon because of the storm."

"It's officially a hurricane now, Zach."

"So I believe." He turned to Robyn. "I promised Con I'll be there to meet him when he comes home with Noreen. There are arrangements to be made. Funeral arrangements. He'll need someone with him and he doesn't have anyone else. Will you be alright, Robyn?"

"Yes, I'm fine. More than fine now that I know you're safe."

"I'll look after her," Tansy offered, as if Robyn was six years old. "We've loads of work to do yet to get the hall ready as a refuge but I'll make sure she doesn't do too much."

"So will I," Kevin added.

They all looked at Kevin, each surprised by the fact that he seemed to intend staying in Felton.

"I thought you'd be on your way to Dublin by now," Robyn said. "Don't you realise you may be stuck here for a few days at least if roads are flooded or bridges damaged? What about the *Daily News*? Aren't you going to look after your staff and your premises?"

"And your wife," Zach added.

"I pay staff to look after my business and my wife isn't even in this country at the moment. Now, any more intrusive questions? What is it about Felton that makes it so difficult to be accepted here?"

Tansy reached across the table and put her hand on his arm. "We're not like that at all, Kevin. Could it be that you ruffled a few feathers by calling us provincial and a bit behind the times?"

Kevin decided not to answer that question. Instead he just bowed his head in a humble way at odds with his normal assertiveness.

Zach stood. "I'll just grab a quick shower and change of clothes and then I'll be off back to Lynches' farm. I think I'll call to the undertaker on the way. It would be easier if he came up with me to attend to – to Mrs Lynch."

He had got just as far as the kitchen door when his phone rang. He listened as someone spoke and then agreed to leave immediately. He walked back and sat beside Robyn.

"That was Oliver Ganley at the stud farm. Someone must have put out the word that I was back in circulation again. One of his horses has gone lame. I'll have to call there before I go to Con. I'll try to get back to you as soon as I can."

Robyn lifted her hand and touched Zach's face. Such a kind man. Putting everyone else's needs before his own. Her fingers touched his hair, trailed along his cheeks, brushed his lips. She looked into his green eyes with the long curling lashes and felt a wave of love so strong that she almost gasped.

"You take care, Zach."

He stood then and dropped a kiss on the top of her head.

"Promise me you won't do any lifting or hauling. Leave that to the others."

"I promise," Robyn agreed.

She watched as he strode out through the back door, tall, lean yet somehow vulnerable. For a second she panicked. She needed him to come back to her for one more hug, one more kiss. One more chance to tell him she loved him. She heard the Land Rover start up. Leaving the kitchen, she hurried to the front of the house. She was too late. By the time she stepped outside he had already rounded the corner on the coast road.

Robyn looked up at the darkening sky and out at the now restless ocean, amazed at how quickly it had shed the placid calm of the morning. She shivered as an inexplicable feeling of loneliness brought a lump to her throat. Tears in her eyes, she stood gazing at the ocean, reluctant to turn back to the cottage and the preparations for the storm heading full tilt towards Felton.

Chapter 15

Billy Moynihan was furious. Sweat dribbled down his forehead as he rushed around the Community Hall, directing Noel into the kitchen with groceries and overseeing the delivery of the gas cooker and cylinders of gas.

"Where in the hell are the other crowd?" he shouted to June. "They said they'd be back ages ago. We're flat out here and they're off wining and dining. It's your fault. You told them take a break. And don't give me that excuse about Robyn Claymore being pregnant. She could be putting some of the groceries in cupboards."

June ignored him and continued ticking items off the list in her hand. They would have plenty of time for organising things in their proper place later. Too much time. She should tell him the latest news but one glance at his purple face told her he might get a heart attack. Or explode.

"Just going to the Ladies'. Won't be a minute," she told Noel who was busily counting tins of salmon in case he and his precious supermarket would be done out of a cent.

In the bathroom, June took out her phone and dialled Woodruff Cottage.

Tansy answered. "Robyn just popped out for a minute, June. I'll get her for you if you like."

"No. You'll do. I wanted to let you know, in case you don't have a radio or TV on, that the hurricane is now Category Two. My niece said latest monitoring puts wind-speed at 164 kilometres per hour and increasing. It's heading right towards us much faster than expected. Every report is worse than the last. It's approaching three on some hurricane scale or other. Simpson or something like that."

"Saffir-Simpson."

"Yes. That's it. I'm beginning to get really worried, Tansy. The Gardaí are evacuating the village but we still don't how many people will take refuge here. Billy is like a headless chicken. Will you be back soon?"

"We're just about to batten down the hatches here, June. Sorry we're so late but Zach arrived home from Con Lynch's and that delayed us a bit."

"Does that mean Con Lynch's sheep virus is under control?"

"Bluetongue Virus is the least of our problems now. We'll be with you soon and we can put our heads together. We have time, haven't we?"

"To be honest I think the Met doesn't know what this system is going to do or when. Chloe was talking about the historically low pressure and warm sea temperatures. I'm afraid. I just pray that the forecast is wrong or else the Community Hall is high enough."

"Of course it is! Tell you what, June, you need a break and I know you need to see to your own house and your son. We'll be up to the hall in about three-quarters of an hour. Why don't you hop home then?"

"Thanks, Tansy. Yes, I need to see Des, that little scallywag. I'll bring him back with me. A bit of hard work will do him good. Anyway, I'd be afraid to let him out of my sight until this – this hurricane, blows over. I'd go now except that Billy Moynihan would probably have a tantrum. See you soon."

It was obvious that June was much happier by the time she put down the phone. Tansy was not. Despite her cheerful tone with June, despite her hope that the hurricane might yet be driven out to sea, despite her innate belief that everything would turn out right in the end, Tansy felt cheerless, hopeless and pessimistic.

She turned back to Kevin who, unusually subdued, was still sitting quietly at the kitchen table. She tried to put a smile on her face as she sat down beside him.

Robyn just then returned, teary-eyed, to join them.

"We'd better get a move on," Tansy said. "I think Felton's in big trouble."

"What do you mean?" Kevin asked. "Has the supermarket run out of Lottery tickets?"

Tansy glanced at him, at the smile on his face not touching his eyes. She understood what he was trying to do. Lighten the mood. Laugh in the face of danger. But he was not succeeding in being funny. Just brash.

"We've got to get ourselves organised quickly and go back to the hall. That was June on the phone and she sounds very stressed. The hurricane has been upgraded again. While we're sitting here it's gathering force and energy and heading towards us. We must move. Quickly."

"From what I've seen of that woman, she lives in a state of constant stress and panic."

Both Robyn and Tansy rounded on Kevin.

"You don't know her at all," they chorused, then Tansy added. "She's worried about her son and her house. It's not fair to her. We'd better let her get home."

Kevin put up his hands in surrender. "Where's your TV, Robyn? Do you mind if I turn it on?"

"Checking the facts? Trying to prove June wrong, are you? Come on, smart guy. We'll all check."

A minute later Kevin's brashness was gone. The Taoiseach was on the national channel, his face sombre, his message even more so. Ireland was in the path of Hurricane Kimi and there would be high winds, heavy rains, possible floods and probable structural damage. The Taoiseach was reeling off lists of emergency services and the preparations they were making. "The Government's priority now is to protect life," he said. "If you're on the coast, particularly the west coast, go to high ground or move inland. If you live in a river flood basin, do what you can to protect your property but leave at the first sign of danger. Contact neighbours, especially the elderly or those living alone. The brave men and women of the emergency services will do what they can to help but each individual must take responsibility for their own safety. *Beannacht Dé orainn go léir*."

Robyn pressed the remote. The screen darkened but still the three of them sat, each trying to understand the enormity of what they had just heard.

"That makes it real, doesn't it?" Tansy said at last. "I wonder if they've known for some time and just didn't want to cause panic?"

"I'm wondering just what they do know." Kevin said. "The Taoiseach seemed very definite about the devastation. Could it be worse than what we've imagined?"

"Worse than what?" Robyn asked. "Florida, Texas, Portugal, the Netherlands three months ago? Worse than the thousands of storm deaths and billions of euros' damage? Ireland has escaped for a long time. Our warm seas were bound to cause something like this sooner or later. And the jet stream staying south has changed the balance. It's all about change, isn't it? Climate change. If only –"

A loud banging noise coming from outside the cottage startled them. Tansy jumped up from her seat.

"Jesus! What was that? Don't tell me it's started already?"

The banging got louder as the three of them went outside. A small pick-up truck was parked on the roadway and a man in overalls was hammering a lath near a window frame of the cottage while beside him lay a pile of plywood sheets.

"What are you up to, Don?" Tansy asked.

"Boarding up the windows like the vet asked me to do," the man replied gruffly. "He told me to do your cottage too."

"Don Cronin," Tansy explained. "Carpenter. And obviously now employed by Zach."

Robyn smiled. Typical of Zach to think ahead like this. She nodded at the man. "Thanks, Don."

"Are you going to secure the cottage next door too. The Germans'?"

The man looked at Tansy as if she had been stupid to ask that question. "I only do what I'm asked and what I'm paid for. I never spoke to those people in my life."

Robyn looked at the barrier of cypress trees cutting off all view of the Muellers' cottage next door and remembered the light from their house last evening.

"I wonder if Mrs Mueller is sick?"

Tansy shrugged. "Don't have an idea. Why?"

"I was just wondering."

"Ah! The return of the investigative journalist at last," Kevin laughed. "Are you stalking your neighbours?"

Robyn was about to defend herself but a sudden cold breeze blew her hair back from her face. She turned to look out to sea. The water which had so recently been placid and grey was dark and swirling.

"A rip tide," Don Cronin said without pausing in his work. "Not good."

"A rip tide?"

"Means there's big waves on the way. Those currents would pull you under. You couldn't fight them. Might as well give up. Just drown. Not a bad way to go so long as you don't fight it."

"We'd better get a move on," Robyn said, not wanting to hear any more of Don Cronin's scaremongering. "June and Billy must be having hissy fits by now. Or else they've killed each other."

"No!" Tansy objected. "They really like each other. He needs to be bossed and she needs someone to boss around. They're the perfect match."

Kevin caught each of them by the arm and steered them in the direction of the house. "I don't want to upset your cosy chat but don't you both think you should be packing what you need to bring with you to the hall? We mightn't have time later and it could be our home for the next few days."

Both women stood still and stared at him, struck forcibly by two thoughts. One that the hurricane now seemed to be a reality and two that whatever happened over the next hours and days, they would be sharing it with Kevin Phillips.

Even though the animal's death was quick and painless, Zach was saddened. The horse had been a magnificent animal. A roan mare, powerful and intelligent. And now dead. He shook his head as he drove away from Ganley's stud farm. There had been too much death in the past days. Con Lynch's livestock and now the horse. And worst of all Noreen Lynch, that quiet little lady, the centre of Con's life. That thought reminded him of Robyn. He punched the quick-dial number on his hands-free phone.

"Rob? I forgot to tell you I asked a man from the village, Don Cronin, to board up our windows."

"I know. He's already working on them. He said he'll do Tansy's cottage too. Thanks, Zach. I'm just packing a few things now to bring to the hall. In case . . . in case we have to leave Woodruff in a hurry."

"I meant to remind you of pet food. If people take shelter in the hall, some are bound to have pets with them. Any dog food or cat food on the provisions list?"

No. They had not thought of either pets or pet food. Robyn felt a twinge of panic. What else had they forgotten? Vital things. Life-saving things.

"Don't worry about it," Zach said. "I've plenty animal feed in the Clinic. I'll collect it later and bring it up to the Community Hall. I'm almost at Lynches' farm now. Keep in touch, Rob."

For the second time that day, Zach was gone before Robyn could tell him how much she loved him.

Upstairs in Woodruff Cottage, Robyn put a weekend case on the bed and began to throw some essential items into it. Things she might forget if she had to leave here in a hurry. Her book, phone charger, *Crossword Magazine*, pen, iPod, woolly socks and two warm sweaters. It would probably be cold up on Lookout Hill. Then she sat on the bed and stared at her case in confusion. How do you pack for an event like this? Just what should you bring to an emergency shelter? The wedding photo from the top of the dressing table? Certificates, insurance policies? Passports for ID.

Why would they need ID? She shivered, wondering what had inspired that thought. It must have been from listening to Don Cronin and his talk of drowning. She stood up, blinking to rid herself of the image of the Community Hall under tons of water. This cottage submerged. Every item she and Zach had so painstakingly and lovingly chosen for their home, smashed, swept away. Noel Cantillon in the supermarket said he was going to haul his precious stock to the first floor of his house. She would do the same. She and Zach, when he came home. The computers, the television, filing cabinet, their documents – all would have to be brought upstairs for dry, safe keeping. Just in case.

Going to the wardrobe she took out the bag she had pre-packed for her trip to the maternity hospital. She opened it and laid her hand on the softness of the baby clothes. Lemon and white. Fluffy. Warm.

For the first time she began to doubt her decision to

stay in Felton. Her fingers smoothed the tiny garments as she mulled over her options. She still had time to make the journey from here to Sligo. The roads would be busy but she would get there. She could drive up the tree-lined avenue of her childhood home, climb the three wide steps to the front door of the Rectory, lift the brass lion's-head knocker and rap it loudly enough for her mother to hear. She would stand and wait for Ellen to open the door and then she would stoop and kiss the cold and perfectly smooth cheek her mother would offer. Few words would be spoken. Robyn and Ellen never had much to say to each other. But the baby would be safe in the darkness and solemnity of the Old Rectory. Far from raging tides and swollen rivers. And Zach? Would he be there too, standing on the doorstep of the Old Rectory, an unwelcome and uninvited guest, just as Robyn herself would be. Disturbing Ellen's self-centred and regimented lifestyle.

A door downstairs opened and closed. Tansy had arrived back from her house where she too had been packing. Robyn heard voices as Tansy joined Kevin in the kitchen. A door opened and closed again and then footsteps came to the bottom of the stairs.

"Rob! C'mon!" Tansy called. "Kevin has just left for the Community Hall. We'd better follow on quickly to referee between himself and Billy Moynihan. I'll drive. I promised Zach I'd look after you."

Robyn closed the zip on her baby-bag and placed it on the bed beside the weekend case. She quickly threw in two sweaters for Zach in case she forgot them later and then walked to the landing.

"Be with you now, Tansy. Just ready."

In the bathroom, she brushed her hair and put on some lipstick and a spray of perfume. She was pale, worried-looking. She felt the baby kick and a slow smile eased away her worry-lines. The future was here, in her belly and in Felton. With Zach. Feeling stronger, more secure, she made her way downstairs.

June left the hall before Tansy and Robyn arrived. Her need to look after her son outweighed her sense of obligation to the community. She stood in the middle of her kitchen now and cursed. It was a new and very liberating experience for her. Her teeth cut into her bottom lip as she articulated the 'f' word, all her frustration and worry adding energy to the sound.

"I'll kill him," she said out loud. "I'll kill the little f-fucker when I catch him."

She picked up her son's cell phone off the table again as if he would somehow materialise from the slim piece of technology. She frowned as she held it. It was never out of Des's hand. He was always either getting or sending texts. Where in the hell could he have gone without it? He even brought it into class against the rules. That was his problem now. No school. The summer break seemed to be going on and on. A bit of homework and study would straighten him out.

She flipped open the phone, unlocked the keypad and then dropped it back on the table as if it was hot. It felt wrong prying into his private possessions. He was, after all, fourteen years old. But where was he and why didn't he have his phone with him? Grabbing the phone again, June went into the contact list and scrolled through it. Just to get an idea as to where he might be. Who he could be with. A list of names rolled past, most of whom she did not know. Friends from his school obviously. Des, like other second-level students in Felton had to travel to the nearest town for secondary education. A decent sea wall wasn't the only lack in Felton. There was no secondary school either.

Her finger hovered over the Messages icon. But only for a second. With another muttered curse, she opened his text messages. As she read the last text Des had received her hand reached behind her to pull out a chair. She needed to sit. The idiot! She glanced at the Sender name. Audrey. Audrey Quill. The little trollop. Leading him on. She read again, more slowly this time.

My folks busy packing 2 leave. Fancy a trip round the harbour? Meet me in the boatshed. Audrey XXX

A hurricane ready to roll in and Des decides to go for a pleasure trip around the bay! June snapped the phone shut, put it in her pocket and pranced out the front door, forgetting to close it behind her. All along the length of Lower Street people were boarding up windows, lashing down roofs and placing sandbags at doors. Cars were being loaded with clothes and things in boxes. The street was being evacuated and already had an abandoned feel to it. A few short, quick strides brought her to the terraced house next door to hers. The front door was open and the car parked right opposite it was laden down.

Just as June raised a hand to rap on the open door, Siobhán Quill came through the hall, a bundle of towels and blankets in her arms.

"Oh, June! Isn't this awful? They say now that even inland will be lashed. I 'spose we –"

"Where's Audrey?"

A look of surprise came over Siobhán's face, as if she only now realised that she had a daughter named Audrey. She looked back into the house and then shrugged her shoulders.

"I-I'm not sure. I sent her to the shop ages ago. To get sweets and drinks for the journey. We're going to Tipperary to my sister. Here, hold these," she said, thrusting the bundle of towels and blankets into June's arms. "I'll see if she's in her room. That's where she spends most of her life."

June heard doors upstairs opening and closing and then Siobhán call her daughter's name. There was no answer.

George Quill backed into the hall from the living room, hauling one side of a couch. His son staggered out after him barely holding onto the weight on his end. George nodded to June, his face red and his neck veins bulging.

"Do you know where Audrey is?" she asked.

"Why do you want her?" he asked.

"I need to speak to her."

"So do I," he said, then he shook his head and began to mutter about Audrey always disappearing when there was any work to be done. He began to huff and puff as they tried to manoeuvre the couch into the narrow hall and angle it towards the stairs.

"Trying to get as much as we can up to the first floor," he gasped. "We'll surely get flood water in downstairs. What about you?"

"I don't give a fiddler's about the furniture. I'm looking for my son. Have you seen him today?"

Siobhán appeared at the top of the stairs and her eyes widened. "You're not bringing that up here, George!

The place is overloaded as it is. Anyway we'll have to go. The roads will be busy."

June was getting so angry at this family of furniture-removers that she had to take a deep breath before she spoke.

"Where is Audrey? Have you seen Des? I think they're together."

Siobhán smiled and nodded her head. "I thought so. I had the feeling there was some hanky-panky going on between that pair. They're not here anyway."

"Does Audrey have her phone with her?"

The confused look was back on Siobhán's face again. She shrugged her shoulders. June dropped the bundle of towels, turned her back and stepped out onto the street before she completely lost her temper. Taking Des's phone out of her pocket she went through the numbers until she found Audrey. She pressed Call. That really annoying baby-chuckle ring tone sounded from inside the house. A cold sweat broke out on her back. Audrey too had left her phone behind. What were she and Des up to that they didn't want to be contacted? As soon as the question formed in her mind, June knew the obvious answer. The pair of children who thought they were adults needed some privacy and no interference from parents. She ran back into the Quills' house again.

"Look at her messages," she ordered Siobhán, who was standing at the head of the stairs, Audrey's phone in her hand and a look of bewilderment on her face.

"I wouldn't do that! I couldn't! They're entitled to privacy, you know. They're almost adults."

"Would adults go out joyriding on the sea with a hurricane forecast?"

"Don't be ridiculous. You don't really think –"

"Read her texts for heaven's sake! Or throw the phone down to me. I'll do it."

George, wedged halfway up the stairs between the couch and the wall, ducked his head as Audrey's phone sailed past. June's fingers shook as she caught the slim, pink phone. She went to Messages, then Inbox and opened the most recent text. The words danced before her eyes. She blinked and read again.

My old lady gone to de hall. C U in boatshed in 5. Des XXX

A check told her this text had been sent over two hours ago – during the time she had been arsing around Noel Cantillon's shop, counting tins and bottles and Audrey's mother had been folding sheets and towels.

"Do you still have that punt you call a rowing-boat?" she shouted up to George.

His face got redder. "It *is* a rowing boat! Why do you want to know?"

"My son and your daughter are out in it and there's a hurricane on the way. While you're saving your sofa they could be drowning. Have you any control over that girl at all? I warned Des to stay away from her!"

"How dare you! My daughter is –"

"Oh, shut up! We're wasting time arguing. Get down to the boatshed. I'm going to see if there's any sign of them on the strand."

June began to run along Lower Street. A few people stared in surprise, one asked if she was alright, but she kept running, head down, lungs bursting, muscles aching. When she reached the access road which led to the pier, she stopped, lifted her head and looked out to sea. The inner bay was rippling with white-capped waves. Beyond, the outer harbour was grey-black and heaving with eddying currents. She stood and stared, her lungs burning, her heart cold with fear. Images of Des flashed before her. Random memories from baby to toddler to teen. The flaming red hair he had inherited from his father, his first steps, the Mother's Day card he had made for her when he was only five years old. The tantrums and sulks and the light fuzz which had lately begun to shadow his no longer childish cheeks.

A flash of colour caught her attention. Someone wearing yellow oilskins was running along the pier towards a knot of people gathered there. The lifeboat crew! She looked past the pier and out to where the lifeboat was moored in deeper water. A rubber dinghy was pulled up alongside and some people were scrambling aboard. The dinghy revved up again the instant the last man had left it and, churning up spray, headed back towards the pier to collect the rest of the crew.

June knew then. Just as sure as she had somehow known that last morning when Des Senior had walked out the door to work, his lunchbox under his arm, that he would never be back again. A wailing sound filled her head and she recognised it as the sound of her own unbearable grief. She sank to her knees and keened as the bereaved have done since time immemorial.

Chapter 16

Tansy was quiet as they counted and stacked provisions in the Community Hall.

"You're not going to eat any of this, Tansy," Kevin remarked, looking at their store of tinned food. "Are you going to bring some of your own supplies with you?"

When he got no answer he went to stand in front of her. She was staring into the distance. Robyn frowned. "What is it, Tansy? What's wrong?"

Tansy started, suddenly realising that she was the centre of attention. She shrugged and smiled at Robyn. "I'm superstitious. Right?"

"You are."

"And sometimes I overreact."

"That too."

"It's just that I didn't do any packing when I went back to my cottage today. I changed Ben's litter tray and then I logged onto the computer."

"Definitely a huge overreaction," Kevin said sarcastically.

Robyn frowned at him. Tansy was worried about something so this was no time for his insensitivity.

"Go on, Tansy. What happened then? Something upset you."

Tansy nodded, opened her mouth to speak and then just as quickly shut it again. That was Kevin's fault. Robyn was furious with him.

"Carry on, Tansy. Just ignore Kevin. He might go away."

Tansy looked at Robyn in surprise. "It's not him. I don't care what he thinks. I'm not sure I should tell you, though. It's silly really but I felt creepy when I saw it."

"Tansy!"

"Okay! Okay. You know this hurricane is named Kimi and that Kimi is a Maya god."

"Right."

"He's the God of Death."

Kevin threw back his head and laughed. Robyn elbowed past him and put her arms around Tansy.

"Don't be such a goose, Tansy. This really is taking superstition too far. I know a hurricane, especially one as vicious as this one promises to be, will probably cost lives but not because it's called Kimi."

"I realise that but the coincidences are really spooking me."

"You mean your cat is another Maya god and you dreamt about the hieroglyphics?" Kevin asked.

Tansy moved away from Robyn's embrace and looked steadily at him. "Are you going to start laughing at me again?"

"No, I'm not. I apologise. Look, we're all a bit afraid. We've never been hit by a weather system like this before. Not in living memory anyway. It's only natural to be scared."

"Don't patronise me. Just because I think there's more to life than making money doesn't mean I'm stupid. Besides, I thought you were fascinated by the Maya too. Were you only pretending?"

Robyn was interested in his answer but, before he could say a word, Billy Moynihan came bustling into the kitchen.

"There's trouble in the harbour. The lifeboat's gone out. I must get down there. Ye carry on here."

Billy turned and ran, moving his bulky frame surprisingly fast. Kevin ran after him. There was drama in Felton and Kevin Phillips must always be at the centre of the action. Robyn and Tansy looked at each other and then without saying a word they too followed. Outside they saw that Billy's van had already reached the bottom of the hill, closely followed by Kevin's distinctive red Audi Cabriolet. Before getting into Tansy's car, Robyn glanced down towards the sea and shivered. The lifeboat was moored out in the harbour, white-capped waves slapping against the keel.

"I wonder if a fishing trawler's in trouble?" Tansy asked.

Tansy took off in pursuit of Billy Moynihan and Kevin, jarring gears but arriving at the pier miraculously safe and sound. They parked beside a car piled high with boxes and clothes. The doors were open as if the occupants had abandoned it in a hurry.

"That's the Quills' car," Tansy said.

Robyn raised an eyebrow in inquiry.

"June's next-door neighbours. George Quill is not part of the volunteer lifeboat crew. I wonder what he's doing here."

"June's there too," Robyn said as they approached the group of people standing at the pier head. She could see that June's head was bowed and her shoulders slumped.

Tansy suddenly stood still, a look of shock on her face.

"My God! Oh no! I hope I'm wrong. It couldn't be."

"What are you talking about?"

"The young Quill girl and June's son are an item. I'm not sure if their parents know but the pair of them have been smooching all this summer. June's here and so are the Quills. You don't think it could be Des and Audrey in trouble, do you?"

"Why would they need rescuing from the sea? They hardly went swimming today."

Tansy nodded her head in the direction of the boatshed. The doors were open.

"The Quills have a rowboat. George is always out fishing, especially when the mackerel are in."

As they approached the group a scuffle broke out. A portly dark-haired man was being held by Billy Moynihan and Kevin Phillips. He was trying to break free of their hold as the dinghy took off from the pier and headed towards the lifeboat. Although it was only afternoon, the light was beginning to fade and it was not easy to see the lifeboat clearly.

"She's my daughter!" he was shouting. "Let me go. I must try to find her."

"You'd only be in the way, George," Billy said. "Let the lifeboat crew do their work."

George Quill's body suddenly sagged. A small brown-haired woman, tears running down her face, went to him and put her arms around him.

"Siobhán Quill," Tansy whispered. "I'm right, Robyn. It must be Audrey and Des. Poor June!" She tapped the shoulder of one of the onlookers. "What's going on?"

"Young Varian and Audrey Quill took the rowboat out. They were spotted in difficulty over near the Bull Rock."

"But that's miles out. What were they doing there?"

"Strong ebb tide earlier. They must have been dragged out."

Tansy turned to Robyn, tears in her dark eyes. "They must find Des. June will never cope with this."

"Let's see if there's anything we can do for her."

"What can we do except be here?"

That was true. Robyn looked at June standing right at the edge of the pier, her eyes focused on the lifeboat, and she felt helpless. She longed to go to her, put an arm around her and tell her not to worry. That the lifeboat would rescue her son. The centre of her life. Her reason for living.

As she and Tansy pushed through the crowd towards June, a sudden squall blew in from the sea. It lifted their hair and raised goose pimples on their skin. Sheet lightning flashed, illuminating the sky, the sea, the lifeboat which was just casting off. Robyn noticed several people blessing themselves with the sign of the cross.

"Kimi," Tansy muttered.

Robyn was about to snap at her when a clap of thunder rocked Felton. The ground seemed to shake. "Right overhead," someone remarked. Robyn snuggled into her coat, regretting that she had chosen to bring such a light one. They had almost reached June when the first rain fell. It started slowly, a few lazy drops splattering onto the startled group. Hands were outstretched to feel the wetness of the rain they had not seen for over six weeks.

Upturned faces savoured the cool touch of the moisture some had believed would never fall again. "Thank God," one of the group said fervently, probably a farmer whose crops were parched in his fields.

Another flash of lightning rent the sky, fork this time, dancing through dark cloud and swishing its angry tail towards the sea-going lifeboat. Thunder followed instantly. It was so loud that Tansy held her hands over her ears and Robyn cradled her stomach in an instinctive action to protect the baby's delicate hearing from the crashing boom which reverberated through Felton. While the ground beneath their feet was still shaking the sky above opened sluice gates and lashed them with torrents of steel-grey rain. It fell in vertical bars, imprisoning the little group on the pier. The sea surface immediately in front of them was dimpled by the pile-driving rain rods. The rest of the ocean – Felton Bay, the lifeboat, the horizon – was gone from view, hidden behind the deluge of rain and the sudden dimming of light. June dropped to her knees and uttered a hair-raising keening sound. It blended into the powerful hiss of falling rain and carried on the strengthening breeze.

The rain began to fall at an angle now, blown right into their faces by the wind. Billy Moynihan reached down to June and, with an unexpected tenderness, gently raised her to her feet.

"There's a floatation device on the boat," he said. "It won't sink, even if it capsizes. They'll be fine, June. They have life jackets."

At the mention of life-jackets, Siobhán Quill began to sob so loudly that she could be heard over a peal of thunder. Billy spun around to stare at her and her husband.

"They have life-jackets, don't they, George? You said the jackets were gone from the boatshed."

Siobhán howled louder as George Quill dropped his head. "The jackets are old," he muttered. "I meant to change them. Just didn't get round to it."

"Have they crotch straps?" Billy asked.

George shook his head and Billy cursed.

"Is this bad news?" Robyn whispered into Tansy's ear.

"Yes. Crotch straps ensure the jacket doesn't come off in the water. If the jackets are old and cracked anyway, they wouldn't be much use."

"Oh, shit! Please God they won't need them."

Tansy didn't answer. Instead they both looked out into the early dusk and then went to stand by June's side. Neither spoke to her. She would not have heard them anyway. Her face had the pallor of death, her eyes were huge and glazed with shock. Surrounded by people, June was alone with her heartbreak.

"No point in staying here in this rain," Billy said. "We should go to the hotel to wait. Get in out of this rain."

"Don't know if we can," Kevin said. "They were locking up when I was leaving. Police orders."

Sidelong looks were cast in his direction, some pitying, some angry. What gave him the right to be here and to be telling them what they could and couldn't do? Felton looked after its own and no matter what the police said if June Varian needed to be in the hotel now, it would be opened for her. That's what Kevin Phillips and his likes would never understand.

Billy nodded to Robyn and Tansy who each took one

of June's arms and led her, unresisting, away from the pier.

"Do what you want," George Quill said. "We're waiting here for our daughter. I'm not budging until they bring her back."

A light sparked in June's eyes. A flash of anger. She stood in front of the Quills.

"Audrey will be back. Have no doubt of that. Her type always survives."

The shutter fell over her eyes again and her head bowed. Nobody spoke. Nobody tried to reassure June that her son too would return, as moody, loud and full of life as ever. They heard the defeat in her voice, felt her grief and held their counsel. Quietly, gently, Robyn and Tansy led her to the hotel to await the news from the lifeboat crew.

Chapter 17

Don Cronin was soaked to the skin by the time he sat into the cab of his pick-up truck. He cursed under his breath. This threatened hurricane had been a bonanza for him. He had made more money in the past day and a half, boarding up windows and securing properties, than he had made for the previous six months. He stared at the rain coursing down along his windscreen and knew that he was out of time now. The storm was knocking on Felton's door. The first flash of lightning had come while he was finishing work on the vet's cottage. It had lit up the lifeboat in the bay as the crew boarded. Don had shaken his head, remembering the rip tide. When a blast of thunder vibrated the ground under his feet he had known that Felton was in for a lashing worse than it had ever experienced before.

The rain had begun just as he was about to start on Tansy Bingham's windows. Big drops fell on the parched earth, wafting the warm scent of baked-in summer around him. He had stood for a moment, sniffing the invigorating scent and in that moment the skies had opened and spilled its six-week store of rain. Head down he had run towards his pick-up.

Poking in the glove box he pulled out a sheet of paper and glanced through the list of names. Besides Tansy Bingham's cottage he had six more households to call on yet. Seven more jobs to be done. A sudden squall off the sea rocked the pick-up. The rain battered on the cab roof, making it hard to think. He turned the key and switched on the windscreen wipers at full speed. They swished over and back but were ineffective against the torrent of rain which had been falling in vertical rods but was now slanted by the strengthening breeze. He rolled down the driver's window a crack and peered out. Visibility was limited to a few metres. He knew the sea was to his right because he could smell it on the breeze and taste its salt on his lips but he could not see it. Rain and wind both rushed in through the open window.

He closed the window quickly and looked at his list again. It was too dark now anyway to work. Sighing, he folded it and then pushed it back into the glove box. He must get home. Evie would be afraid. There was no point telling his wife that they were safe on their elevated site overlooking the village. She had been following forecasts fanatically and nagging him to board up their own house before he did anyone else's. This storm seemed to be undoing all the progress she had made over the past year. She was turning back into the jittery, nervous woman she had been before Dr Early had put her on those little blue pills. And maybe she was right. What was the point in him protecting everyone else's property and leaving his own vulnerable? And while their site was safely above the sea, the house was also very exposed to wind.

The dampness was beginning to seep through to his bones. He searched around for a sweater or jacket, cursing when he realised they were on the flatbed of the pick-up. They would be drenched by now. The quicker he got home and had a hot shower the better.

He put the pick-up in gear and pressed the accelerator. A whirring sound cut through the staccato drumming of rain on the roof. He pressed again, carefully balancing clutch and accelerator pressure. The vehicle shivered and groaned and dug in. Fuck! He should have realised. This road in front of the cottages was just a dirt track. Dust mixed with torrential rain had turned it into a mud rink in minutes.

He thumped the steering wheel in temper then took a deep breath. No point in going off in a tantrum. There were sheets of plywood in the back. All he had to do was place them so that the spinning back wheels could find traction. The instant he opened the driver's door, lightning flashed, immediately followed by thunder which ripped through the atmosphere, so loud and powerful that it seemed to bear down with a crushing weight. Don lowered his head and ran towards the back of the pick-up, dragging two sheets of plywood off the stack. The body of the truck was mud-splattered and the wheels were dug into two deep potholes. As he bent over to place a sheet of plywood strategically near each rear wheel, his phone fell out of his trouser pocket and landed with a splash in a muddy puddle. He grabbed it, rubbed it against the fabric of his shirt and shoved it into his pocket, satisfied that it had not been in the water long enough to do any damage. Plywood sheets in place, he dashed back to his cab.

Rain coursed down his face, his neck and into his

eyes. He shook himself off like a dog, spraying droplets around the cab. Searching the glove box he found a packet of tissues. They dissolved into a mushy mess when he tried to dry off his face and hands with them. He threw them on the floor and put the engine in gear again. The truck shook as the wheels dug deeper. He was stuck.

Don had not believed it possible but the rain began to fall with even more force. For some reason he thought of little birds huddling in their nests. This rain was vigorous enough to injure or even kill them. Delicate little birds reminded him of Evie. She must be terrified by now. He reached into his pocket and took out his phone. The screen was blank and there was condensation trapped inside the monitor. He pressed the On button with increasing frustration. Nothing happened. His phone was dead. Just like when he had let it fall down the toilet. He'd had to replace it that time and it looked as if he would have to do the same again.

Frustration began to turn to anxiety as Don realised he could not contact Evie nor could he ring anyone for help with freeing his truck. He had been considering asking Jeff Wilcox to bring his tractor over to haul the pick-up out. The din of rain on the cab roof was so loud now that Don found it difficult to concentrate. He could walk to the Wilcox farm but that was over a mile away. The truck rocked again as another wall of wind pushed against it. It had a keening sound this time. A brave man, a logical man, Don Cronin felt an unexpected shiver of superstitious dread as the wind howled and rain hammered. One thing he could not do was sit out the storm in his truck on the edge of the ocean. The tide would soon turn its mighty force towards the shore. He knew neither he nor his truck would survive that onslaught.

He jumped out of the cab and looked around him. He could see the vet's cottage, windows all neatly boarded up. Tansy Bingham's cottage was in view too although it was harder to make out the detail in the gloom. He turned away, knowing there was nobody home in either place. He faced towards the sea, eyes squinted, as if he could find an answer to his problem there. The foreshore was clear, seaweed glistening, sand dark-gold, but the sea was camouflaged by rain and cloud, subsumed into the blanket of grey. He knew it was gathering itself out in the harbour, swelling towards high tide.

He looked at his pick-up and cursed again when he saw the puddles and muck on the track. His attention was caught by a creaking sound. Head tilted, he traced the sound to the Germans' house. The cypress trees were groaning under the weight of the deluge. A faint light from the house shone through the trees. They must be home. Relieved, he began to walk towards Muellers' cottage. He had never spoken to them before but he was sure under the circumstances they would let him use their phone. He could contact Evie and then ring Jeff Wilcox to bring his tractor down.

Feeling more confident now that he had a plan, Don braced himself for a short but wet and windy walk to the Muellers' house.

Zach stood at the kitchen window in Con Lynch's house and stared at the rain as it pelted onto the concrete yard. Already rivulets were beginning to form in cracks and dips. The rain-barrel had overflowed in the first ten minutes of the cloudburst and was now forming a steady stream which ran underneath the hearse. Lightning flashed again and Zach smiled. It was not a smile of amusement, more an acknowledgement that he knew this surreal scene could not possibly be and that he would soon wake up. Thunder rattled the window frames of the old house. Zach felt it vibrate through his body and admitted to himself that this was indeed all real – the corpse of Noreen Lynch, still in the body bag provided by the hospital, reposing on the couch in the lounge, the coffin and hearse in the yard, Gareth Dempsey, the soft-spoken undertaker, discreetly trying to advise Con against waking his wife in the farmhouse.

"I know you'd like to give Noreen a good send-off, Con," he said. "But with this bad weather you won't get many people coming up the hills to pay their respects. Noreen would be better off in the Funeral Home where people could easily come to see her."

"Gawp at her more like. She would hate that. She wanted to be laid out here at home, in her own bed. She has the – the things she wants to wear ready."

"She can wear them in the Funeral Home too. Look, the decision is yours, Con, and I'll assist you in any way I can. But remember you'll have to cater for mourners here too. When were you planning on having the wake?"

"I wasn't planning on having it at all, you gobshite!" Con answered angrily.

Gareth Dempsey just bowed his head and stayed silent. He was used to the sharpness of the grief-stricken.

A rush of wind down the chimney brought Zach's attention back into the kitchen. He walked across to the table and sat down beside Con.

"He has a point, Con. This storm is only starting now and God knows how long it will last. From what I saw on my way here most people have boarded up their houses and left the village. The rest of the villagers will be taking shelter in the Community Hall. I don't think anyone could battle their way up here for a wake. Not until the storm is over anyway."

"What are you telling me to do, lad? Let Frankenstein there put Noreen in a fridge? Like a side of beef waiting to be butchered!"

Zach made eye contact with Gareth. The solemn undertaker nodded. Zach smiled at Con.

"I wouldn't put it like that, but yes. I think the best course of action is to let Gareth take Noreen to the Funeral Home now. He can keep her safe there until you decide exactly where and when you want to hold the wake."

Con's chair scraped on the tiled floor as he pushed it back roughly. He began to pace the kitchen, muttering to himself, his anger at his wife's death apparent in every step. He stopped in front of Zach.

"I know you think I'm being unreasonable, lad, but I let my wife down when I allowed them take her away to Dublin. I don't want to let her down again."

Zach reached out and laid his hand on the old man's arm. They were both discomfited and yet comforted by the contact.

"I understand, Con. It's just this bloody weather. We could organise everything, ham sandwiches and whiskey, whatever, if it wasn't for the storm. No one, not even the Met Office, seems to know how soon or how hard it will hit us. The shops in the village are already closed and will stay shut until the storm has blown over."

"Ironic, isn't it?" Con asked.

"How do you mean?"

"The weather killed Noreen because the heat brought the midges here and now the weather is preventing her having a dignified burial because there's a bloody storm."

Zach nodded. There was no point in arguing with Con in his present frame of mind even though the midges had nothing at all to do with her passing. A violent gust of wind whined down the chimney and Con flopped onto a chair as if it had blown him over. He looked steadily at Gareth Dempsey's professionally mournful face.

"Is Father Ryan still in hospital?"

"He is, Con. But don't worry about the funeral service. The curate from the next town is covering until Father Ryan is well again."

Con nodded then suddenly rose and came to stand in front of Gareth. "Give me a few minutes alone with Noreen before you go."

"Of course."

"Treat her with care and respect."

"You have my word on that."

"My wife was a lady."

"She certainly was."

Con walked towards the sitting room, closing the door after him. The kitchen lit up with another flash of lightning. Gareth crossed himself. Before he had finished the ritual, thunder roared overhead. It rumbled around the hilltops and echoed down the valley.

"I never heard it so close before," he said.

"It's only starting," Zach told him. "Hurricane force winds and sea surge have yet to hit us." He leaned close to the solemn-faced man in the black suit and pristine white shirt and spoke softly to him. "I have a delicate question to ask, Gareth. Your – your – storage facility. It's not in your funeral parlour in the village, is it?"

"No. The funeral parlour is just window dressing. I share a refrigerated unit with my brother in the next town. He's in the funeral business too. I'll bring Mrs Lynch there. Keep her safe from floods if that's what you're worrying about. I've already boarded up in the village. It flooded last spring, you know."

"I know. That's why I asked. What about the refrigerated unit? There could be power cuts if the storm hits as hard as expected."

"No problem. My brother has back-up generators."

They were silent then as pelting rain beat out a hectic rhythm on the slate roof and the wind keened in tune with Con Lynch's grieving for his beloved wife.

Don Cronin was smiling as he approached the door to the Muellers' cottage. He had barely entered their property before he had spotted the big four-wheel-drive parked at the side of the house. An answer to his prayers and as good as any tractor in this emergency. The man Horst was, according to local gossip, brusque and unfriendly but that didn't worry Don when he rang the doorbell. He watched the cypress trees sway as he waited for an answer. And waited. The rain was falling so strongly that it was beginning to hurt his skin so he stepped into the shallow recess of the front porch for shelter. Presuming the wind was drowning the tinkly sound of the doorbell, he knocked loudly. He must have been right because the door opened almost immediately.

"What do you want?"

So the gossip was true. The man holding the door open a crack was frowning, his face pinched by bad humour.

"I'm sorry to disturb you. My name is Don Cronin. My pick-up truck has got stuck on the road outside the Claymores' cottage."

"What do you expect me to do about it? Lift it out for you?"

"I was hoping you would tow it with your four-wheel-drive. It would only take a few minutes."

Horst leaned forward and peered into Don's face as if he had difficulty seeing even though he was wearing glasses. "Why don't you go to them for help?" he asked, nodding his head in the direction of Robyn and Zach's cottage.

"Because they're not there. If towing is too much trouble for you maybe I could use your phone to ring for help. I need to contact . . ."

Don stopped talking as the face of a woman suddenly appeared in the crack of the barely open door. She was very pale, her eyes dark and darting about as if she was trying to see everything at once.

"Go inside, Ute," Horst said. "I'll get rid of this nuisance."

That was when Don decided the gossip was wrong. Horst Mueller wasn't rude. He was obnoxious. Walking to the Wilcox farm, even in the downpour, was a preferable option to having anything further to do with the ignorant German.

"Sorry to have bothered you. If you ever need a carpenter don't call me."

Don turned on his heel and took a few steps away. The sound of a scuffle made him glance over his shoulder towards the door. Mrs Mueller, if that's who the pale woman was, her foot placed firmly in the doorway, was struggling with Horst who was trying to force the door shut.

"Ute! Stop at once! Have you completely lost your mind?"

Horst's hand grasped Ute's shoulder and hauled her back inside. The door banged shut. Don stood for a moment, confused by what he had just seen. He listened intently, trying to catch any sound from inside the house but all he could hear was the incessant drum of rain and the creak of the trees as they bent into the freshening wind. He shivered, remembering the story of the previous inhabitants of this cottage, their bodies lying here for three weeks, unloved and unmissed. There had been fear on Mrs Mueller's pale face. The same haunted expression he had sometimes seen on Evie's face before she had begun to take her pills.

Fork lightning rent the sky and Don ducked his head, certain that it was aimed in his direction. And yet he hesitated. Horst Mueller seemed capable of violence. Was his wife in danger? Maybe he should go back. Knock on the door again. Make some excuse, perhaps offer to board up their windows. A strong gust lashed the trees and dumped a torrent of cold water onto his head. That was sign enough for Don. He would do what all good Felton inhabitants did. He would mind his own business. For now that business entailed walking to the Wilcox farm, phoning Evie and rescuing his truck before the sea decided to claim it for its own.

Chapter 18

There was an open fireplace in the lobby of the Marine Hotel. Cavernous, with a mahogany over-mantel, it was a feature of the reception area. A focal point. People huddled around it now, steam rising from their wet clothes. The cheery brightness of the fire was doing nothing to dispel the gloom of the hotel which was devoid of guests and darkened by shuttered windows.

June Varian had a seat directly in front of the blazing fire. She was isolated in her grief, alone even though Tansy and Robyn sat to one side of her while Kevin Phillips and Billy Moynihan flanked her other side. A snifter of brandy sat untouched on the table beside her. Tansy picked up the glass and pressed it into June's hand.

"Take a sip of this, why don't you? It will do you good."

June blinked and turned to face Tansy. "Will it bring Des back?"

"You don't know that he's gone. The lifeboat could

be hauling him out of the rowboat now. Or maybe he and Audrey are sheltering somewhere."

June stared until Tansy looked away. Everybody else did too. Nobody could meet the hopelessness reflected in June's dark eyes, the pallor of death on her face. Billy Moynihan, who up until now had been constantly uttering comforting words, bowed his head and carefully examined the toes of his shoes.

An hour ago, when the lifeboat had cast off, there had been optimism. The pair of silly kids were probably paddling furiously, wet, exhausted, but still safe in their little rowboat. The lifeboat crew would locate them, rescue them and give them a good telling-off. As the wind strengthened, rain lashed, lightning flashed, and time crept slowly on, that scenario became increasingly more fantasy than realistic hope.

"They could have pulled into Robbers' Cove," suggested Noel Cantillon, who had just recently arrived at the hotel, having at last abandoned his stock-take in the Community Hall.

June kept staring into the fire while Robyn explained that a rowboat had been spotted out near Bull Rock.

"Bull Rock! But how . . .?" Noel stopped talking then as he began to understand the reason behind the tangible despair in the room. As if to confirm their worst fears the solid building shook when yet another peal of thunder crashed down on Felton. He remembered the rain while he was driving from the hall. He had never seen anything like it before. Already road-side channels were overflowing and the Aban was rushing down from the hills, swollen and muddied. He had not seen the sea. It was screened behind sheets of rain but he could imagine how it too was angry and flaunting its power. The Quills' little rowboat would be swatted like a fly. Squashed. Mashed against the sharp edges of Bull Rock, sucked into the currents there, which were lethal even in calm weather.

"Are you really sure about this?" Kevin asked Billy. "Who alerted the coastguard?"

"Henry Kingston. He lives on the coast. A cottage right on the tip of the peninsula."

"Henry spends his days sitting in his front window, scanning the sea with binoculars," Tansy explained to Kevin. "He was in the Merchant Navy all his life and he can't seem to leave the sea, even though he's well into his eighties now."

"Could he be wrong? At that age his sight can't be up to scratch."

The dark stares and silence told Kevin he had committed another breach of Felton etiquette. It was obvious this retired sailor was held in high esteem and that casting any doubt on his powers of observation was unacceptable. He sighed. The harder he was trying with these people, the more mistakes he was making. And yet in one short year, Robyn seemed to have found her place here. Not quite a Felton native but not an outsider either. She smiled at him now.

"Henry's sharp wits and eyesight have saved many lives. If he says a small rowboat is in trouble off Bull Rock, then it is. We'll just have to wait and see if it's the Quills' boat."

Waiting to see was the last thing Kevin felt like doing now. The lobby was oppressive. Dreary. The only movement in the room came from the dancing flames as they licked up the chimney. He stood up and took his still-sodden coat off the hallstand.

"I'm going down to the pier. I'll ring back if there are any updates."

"Sit down!" Billy said sharply. "What help do you think you'll be there? You'd only be in the way."

"Jesus, man! Do you know what it's like out?" Noel Cantillon spluttered. "You'd be drowned the second you put a foot outside the door."

The word 'drowned' echoed around the lobby and then hung in the air. June's head bowed even lower. Noel grimaced, angry at himself for his thoughtless remark. He shuffled his feet a bit and then announced he'd better get down to his shop and check that the staff had secured it properly. As an afterthought, he added that he'd better check on his wife and family too.

But Noel did not leave. Nor did anyone else. They huddled around June, as if their proximity would protect her. The little group fell silent. When Billy Moynihan's phone rang, they were all dragged back suddenly from their own thoughts.

"I see. Thanks for letting me know. We'll be there in a few minutes."

Billy switched off his phone and put his arm around June's shoulder.

"The lifeboat is on the way back, June. They'll be in shortly."

"And?"

"They didn't say. All I know is that they have requested an ambulance."

Tansy and Robyn exchanged glances. That sounded hopeful. Why would they need an ambulance if not to whisk the survivors off to hospital? Or the survivor. Or the bodies for autopsy.

"Do you want to stay here, June?" Billy asked. "I'll let you know if you're . . . if you're needed at the pier."

June stood and in robot-like fashion headed for the huge front door. Cold and rain swept into the lobby as she opened it up. Everyone else grabbed their coats and jackets and rushed to her side. Like a funeral cortege, they travelled the short distance from the Marine Hotel to the pier, pelted by rain, deafened by thunder, illuminated by lightning, buoyed by hope and bent by dread.

Zach tried his best to maintain some dignity as he and Gareth Dempsey pulled and pushed the coffin containing Noreen Lynch's body through the narrow door of the sitting-room, out into the kitchen, through the back door and into the yard. Rain tapped on the varnished lid, some of it splashing into droplets, some lodging in glistening little pools. Gareth, still managing to appear unruffled and mournful, manoeuvred the trolley so that it lined up with the back of the open hearse. Con watched from the doorway as his wife's coffin slid onto the hearse. Gareth slammed the door shut and walked back over to Con.

"I'd better be off now. If this rain keeps up the roads will soon be flooded. Just let me know as soon as you have your mind made up about the when and where of the burial. I'll look after all the details for you. You have my number, haven't you?"

Con didn't answer. He was staring wordlessly at the hearse, as if he needed to memorise every detail of Noreen's last journey from the farm.

"I have your number, Gareth," Zach said. "I'll let you know what he decides."

With a solemn wave which could pass for a blessing, Gareth got into his hearse. It rolled smoothly out of the yard and began the downward journey towards the village.

Zach caught Con by the arm, led him into the kitchen and sat him at the table. The room was cold. Going to the range, Zach noticed that the fire was almost out. Noreen would hate that. She had always kept the range well stoked, even in summer. Because of his enforced stay here, he knew exactly where to find everything, including turf and blocks. Ten minutes later the fire was red and the turf basket full. He went to the sideboard and took out a bottle of whiskey. There wasn't much left in the bottle. Andrew Simmons had discovered it early on during the quarantine and had felt entitled to it. Zach filled a glass and put it on the table in front of Con.

"Drink that. It will heat you up."

Con pushed the glass away from him and looked up at Zach.

"What are you doing here? You see the weather. You should be at home with your wife. Especially in her condition."

"I'm going now. But I don't want to leave you here on your own. Why don't you come with me?"

"What for? All I have left of my life is here. When I look around and see all Noreen's things, the ware, her plants, books . . ."

Con stopped talking then, put his arms on the table and dropped his head onto them. His shoulders shook as he wept for his wife. Zach stood awkwardly beside him, not sure whether to try to comfort the old man or just let him grieve in privacy. He cleared his throat.

"The weather forecast is very bad, Con. I know your

house is in a hollow here but it's still very high up. You'd be safer coming with me to the Community Hall until it blows over."

Con lifted his head and Zach was reminded of the raw pain he sometimes saw in animals' eyes when they were suffering. That instinctive knowing.

"You go, lad. Look after your wife and the baby she is carrying. Blessings on you for all the help you've given me but there's nothing you can do for me now. I need to be on my own and you need to be taking care of your family."

Zach nodded. The old man was right. He needed to be with Robyn now, making sure that she and the baby were safe. He had to collect animal feed for the hall too and try to shift some of the more irreplaceable items in the cottage up to the second floor. Just in case the sea decided to roll in as far as Woodruff Cottage. He put a hand on Con's shoulder.

"I wish you'd come with me but, if you're sure, I'll leave you in peace."

"I have all I want here. And don't worry. I'll lash down whatever needs securing. The work will keep me occupied. Off with you now."

Con stood and walked to the door with Zach. It was almost dark now. When Zach switched on the Land Rover's lights he sat for a moment, hypnotised by the teeming rain lashing against the windscreen and glistening in the twin beams. When he glanced back to the door, it was closed. Con had shut himself and his heartbreak off from the rest of the world. He drove carefully, wary of aquaplaning on the water-slick road. At the bottom of the hill, he indicated left to head for home.

That's when he saw the blue flashing light swirling through the darkness and rain. The squad car. It turned right and headed towards the pier. Zach followed, wondering why he was doing so, yet knowing that curiosity, fear and a primitive urge to witness disaster would not allow him do otherwise.

The three of them, Audrey's parents and her younger brother, were huddled together as they waited at the pier's edge. Siobhán saw June approach and immediately walked over to her.

"They found the boat. Off the Bull Rock, just like Henry Kingston said."

"And the children?"

Siobhán Quill began to cry, her words swallowed up by noisy sobs. Billy left the group and walked over to a man wearing a yellow oilskin jacket. A member of the coastguard. Heads close together, they exchanged a few words before Billy came back to June and, holding her by the arm, drew her away from Siobhán.

"The rowboat was capsized when the crew reached it. One of the kids was clinging to the upturned boat and was rescued."

"Audrey Quill?"

Billy nodded. He held tightly to June's arm as if he expected her to run away from the pier, the lifeboat, the awful truth. Instead she stood still, resignation in her eyes.

"They're bringing Audrey in now and going straight back out again to look for your lad. A rescue helicopter is being considered but the weather has to be taken into account."

To Billy's puzzlement June smiled at him. "I knew it. So typical of Des. He wouldn't stay there clinging onto the boat. He'd have to be the hero."

"We're not sure yet what happened. Maybe he tried to swim for the rock or he might have, he could have . . ."

"Drowned?"

"We don't know, June. It's too soon to say. We can pray."

"You can. I'm done with praying."

She left him then and returned to keep vigil with the Quills. Tansy, Robyn, Kevin, Billy and Noel Cantillon followed, huddling around the families of the two missing teenagers as if their physical closeness would lend protection.

An ambulance approached the pier just as the coastguard launched the dinghy. The outboard motor roared into life and the dinghy skimmed over the shallow waters of the inner bay and disappeared into the darkness.

The eyes of everyone on the pier strained to follow the progress of the dinghy as it sped towards the lifeboat. Everyone except Robyn. She was watching Tansy and Kevin as they stood close together. Tansy whispered something to him and he smiled at her. It was a warm smile. Too warm, too happy for rain-lashed Felton pier. Too intimate, too disrespectful to the Quills and June Varian as they waited to hear if their children had survived or not. Too inappropriate. Robyn suddenly realised she had been staring at Kevin and Tansy. She turned her head but not quickly enough. Kevin came to her side, put an arm around her and drew her close to him. She felt the heat from his body and instinctively leaned into the familiar shape of him. She was instantly warmer. Safer.

"Are you alright, Robyn? You look frozen with the cold. Why don't you go back home for a while? I'll drive you, if you like."

"No need, thank you," a voice from behind them said. "I'll look after my wife myself."

Kevin's arm instantly dropped from Robyn. She twirled around to face Zach. He looked drawn, somehow older than when she had last seen him, even though that had been only a few hours ago. She threw herself into his arms and snuggled as close as she could get with an eight-month baby-bump between them.

"I'm so glad to see you, Zach," she muttered against the stiffness of his waxed jacket. "Have you heard what happened here?"

Zach nodded. He had been talking to one of the coastguards. "It's terrible. We can only hope. Whatever happens, Rob, you shouldn't be here. You'll get pneumonia. Look at you! You're drenched. That coat wouldn't keep out a light shower let alone this. Come home with me now."

"Just what I was telling her," Kevin said.

Zach tightened his hold on Robyn. She had her back to Kevin but she knew the two men were glaring at each other, offering a challenge.

"My wife's welfare is none of your business, Kevin."

Robyn looked up into Zach's face and barely recognised the angry man she saw. For heaven's sake! What was wrong with this pair of juveniles? Couldn't they forget their pride for one minute and see that only the two missing kids mattered now? And June. Poor June. Besides, if Zach only took the trouble to look, he would see that Tansy was the new passion in Kevin Phillips' life. Maybe Kevin didn't know it himself yet but Robyn knew. She remembered all the signs and signals, all the glances and warm smiles.

"We'll go home as soon as the dinghy returns," she said to Zach. "It'll be back from the lifeboat very soon. I'm waiting in case there's anything I can do to help."

Zach silently nodded agreement and Kevin too appeared to opt for silence and a renewed interest in looking out to sea. The thunder and lightning had passed over by now but, instead of easing, the rainfall was more intense. It was being whipped by a stiffening wind and intermittent violent gusts.

Dr Early, just arrived on the pier, came to join the group around June and the Quills. He shook his head, dislodging a stream of water from the brim of the trilby he was wearing.

"In all my time here, I've never seen anything like this rain. If it doesn't let up soon we won't be able to tell land from sea."

"There won't be any land if the forecast is right," Billy said.

Nobody commented. There didn't seem to be anything to add. They all stood, staring out to sea, listening intently to catch the sound of the returning dinghy. It was difficult to discern any noise except hammering rain and keening wind.

A few minutes later Siobhán Quill suddenly cocked her head to one side. "They're here!" she cried, running right to the edge of the pier, George after her.

The sound of the dinghy motor was louder now, spray splashing as it sped towards the jetty. In unison, the rest of the group moved forward, followed by the ambulance crew. Robyn moved closer to June and reached out her hand. June's cold, shaking hand clung onto hers as together they watched the dinghy dock and a thrown rope being secured to a bollard. A foil-wrapped body was then carefully lifted up and placed on a waiting stretcher. George and Siobhán Quill immediately leaned over the stretcher and hugged their daughter until Dr Early gently but firmly pushed them aside.

"We must get her into the ambulance. I'll give her a quick check and then let the paramedics look after her. She needs to be in hospital now."

As the stretcher was wheeled past, Robyn glimpsed Audrey's face, waxen except for her blue lips. Her shock had barely registered before a flash sparked highlights on the tinfoil wrapping Audrey's body.

"What the fuck do you think you're doing?" Billy Moynihan shouted, lunging towards Kevin.

"My job," Kevin answered, deftly side-stepping Billy and holding the camera up above his reach.

Robyn looked straight at Tansy, willing her to look back, wanting her to understand the kind of man Kevin Phillips was. The type who would always put the *Daily News* and a story before anyone or anything else. Even decency. Tansy, talking to Noel Cantillon, hadn't seemed to notice what had happened. Or perhaps she just hadn't wanted to see. A tug on her hand brought Robyn's attention back to June.

"I need to talk to Audrey."

"I'm not sure that you can, June. Is she even conscious?"

"She is. I saw her eyelids flicker. I must ask. I must know."

Robyn understood. Audrey was the last person to see

Des. Of course June needed to ask if he had tried to swim for the rock or if he had been unable to cling onto the upturned boat as Audrey had done.

"We'll ask Dr Early. See if he says it's alright to have a quick word with her."

Zach, who had been listening to the conversation, nodded to Robyn to go ahead. As she and June approached the ambulance, Siobhán Quill walked forward and threw her arms around June.

"I'm so sorry, June. I'm really, really sorry."

June pushed the sobbing woman away from her. "What happened? What did Audrey say?"

"That Des said he would go to get help. The last she saw of him was when he slid off the boat and began to swim away."

"Was he wearing his life jacket? The old one with no crotch strap?"

Siobhán lowered her eyes and nodded.

"Did Audrey see him go . . . go under?"

"No. She doesn't know what happened but she said the swell is very big out along. Is he a strong swimmer, June?"

June laughed. A hysterical, horrible sound. "You stupid woman! He's fourteen years old. How could he be stronger than a hurricane?"

"But you never know. There's still hope. And they're going out looking for him again now."

"They're searching for a body. You know it and I know it. By the way, how is Audrey?"

"She's suffering from hypothermia but she'll be fine. We'll pray that Des will be too."

June opened her mouth as if to say something and

then, without warning, she sighed, swayed and fell to the ground. Robyn called as loudly as she could for Dr Early. He was there in seconds but June had already come round, bleary-eyed as she glanced at the people surrounding her. Colour flooded back into her face as she was helped to her feet. She looked from the ambulance to the crowd on the pier, then turned and looked out to sea. Her face crumpled as she remembered why they were all gathered here. All except Des. Her son. Her life. June screamed her anguish into rain and wind.

Chapter 19

Billy Moynihan took charge on the pier in a way which surprised everyone. After a quick consultation with Dr Early, he thrust June, now trance-like, in Tansy and Robyn's direction. "Take her away out of this rain. Get her dry and try to make her rest and have a cup of tea. Robyn, you too need to get in out of this weather." He turned to the group. "Go to your homes, collect what you must bring with you and get your families to the hall as quickly as possible. Best estimate from the Met Office gives us several hours leeway to get ourselves to safety."

"But I –" Noel Cantillon began before Billy put up a hand to stop him.

"But nothing. If you want to stay with your goddamn shop, do, but don't put your family's lives at risk. Send them to safety."

"My family's already left," Noel said. "They've gone to my wife's sister in Cahir."

"Then get your ass up to the hall. And hurry. There's not much time to spare."

As he spoke, the ambulance left the pier, followed by George Quill's loaded car. June looked in the direction of the departing Quills with their luggage and their rescued daughter, but her face didn't register any emotion. Perhaps she didn't see them.

"C'mon. Let's get you warmed up. Will you come back to my place?" Tansy asked, standing directly in front of June and talking loudly over the noise of wind and rain – louder than necessary, as if she suspected the shocked woman had lost her hearing. "We'll drop by your house to get some dry clothes for you."

June nodded. A disinterested response. She would probably have done the same had Tansy asked her to jump off the pier.

"Don't stay too long in your cottage, Tansy," Billy warned. "The coastguard have told me that high tide this evening is going to swamp the coast. You'll be safe for three hours or so but get back to the hall by then."

June, who had appeared to be totally unaware, turned towards Billy.

"That means the search for Des will be called off soon, doesn't it?"

"Yes, it does. I'm sorry."

June shrugged. "He's gone."

She turned then and walked towards Tansy's car while Billy went back to the edge of the pier to keep vigil. A gust of wind blasted in from the sea, so strong that it appeared to have shape as well as an eerie high-pitched sound. Tansy's slight frame was blown against Zach and she had to cling onto him for support while he threw his arms around Robyn to shelter her and the baby. One of the flower tubs in front of the Public Toilets was tossed onto its side, spewing moss peat and broken primulas along the ground. The galvanised roof on the boatshed rattled and then screeched as one of the sheets was shorn off and lifted into the air before crashing back onto the roof and slithering to the ground. Noel Cantillon's hat, the navy peaked hat some said he had been born wearing, was whipped from his head and blown along the pier like tumbleweed before being dumped in a puddle. Noel dashed after it, his hands on his head, but it was too late for him to cover up the secret he had kept under wraps for so long.

"I knew it!" Tansy said as she stared at his bald head. "I always knew it."

"Liar! You'd have told me. You speculated that the top of his head must be bald from wearing the cap all the time but you thought his mop of hair was real."

Tansy looked at Robyn and grinned. "You're right. Who'd sell a wig like that? I thought it had to be real."

"Don't be cruel," Robyn said but her lips were twitching too as Noel dived on the hat with his hair still attached, shook it and placed it back on his head.

"Did you see that?" Kevin asked, approaching them from the direction of the boatshed. "I was almost decapitated by that sheet of galvanised."

"What were you doing over there?" said Zach. "More photographs?"

Kevin narrowed his eyes and squinted at him. "Yes, as a matter of fact. That's where the kids got the boat, wasn't it? Which reminds me, Tansy, can I use your internet? I want to send in this report for tomorrow's paper."

"Yes, sure. Just follow me. I'd better get a move on.

June is waiting for me. I assume, Robyn, you're going with Zach. See you later."

They began to walk away then, Tansy taking two steps to Kevin's every stride until she suddenly stopped, turned around and cupped her hands around her mouth as she shouted over the wind.

"Rob!"

"Yes?"

"You and Zach come over to mine when you're ready. I made soup this morning. We can have that. Build us up for whatever is ahead."

"Oh, shit!" Zach muttered but Robyn poked him in the ribs.

"Thanks, Tansy. That would be nice."

Robyn and Zach were just about to get into the Land Rover when the sergeant, Tim Halligan, approached them.

"Are you going to your cottage, Zach?"

"Yes. A few bits and pieces to do and then we'll go to the hall. It looks like the village is pretty much abandoned at this stage."

"Well, you'd better hurry. Don Cronin's truck got stuck in front of your house because that track you call a road is disintegrating in this rain. Jeff Wilcox is pulling him out now with his tractor but I'd say you'd be well advised to walk from where the tarmac ends."

Zach and Robyn looked at each other and shrugged. They couldn't get any wetter than they were now so they might as well walk from the road.

"We'll do that. Thanks for the tip. Will you be coming to the hall?"

"Later. I'll wait here with Billy until the lifeboat crew

gets back. Not long now. They've been given orders to come in."

"Have they . . . have they found Des?" Robyn asked.

The sergeant shook his head. "Not that I've been told. Poor kid. He wouldn't have had a chance against the swells out there. Such a shame. He was a grand lad."

His use of the past tense hit Robyn like a kick in the stomach. True, June had seemed to have accepted the inevitable immediately but Robyn had clung onto hope. She looked out to sea as if she could see him there, as if she could throw him a lifebelt, haul him ashore, wrap him up and present him to his mother. The wind had quietened now but the rain still lashed. Cold raindrops mixed with hot tears on her face. She wiped them away surreptitiously as she listened to the sergeant.

"This really high tide they've been talking about is due in a few hours but I'm afraid that will only be a dress rehearsal for the hurricane landfall predicted for around three o'clock tomorrow morning," he said.

"So what's this?" Zach asked, the sweep of his arm encompassing the group of rain-drenched people, the wild sea, the uprooted primulas skittering around the pier.

The sergeant shrugged. "I don't know, Zach. A taste of what's to come? As far as I can see the experts are only making educated guesses at this stage. This bloody Kimi is a law unto itself. By the way, where's June Varian now? She's not on her own, is she?"

"She's with Tansy Bingham. We'd better text Tansy before she gets bogged down on our road. Kevin Phillips too. We'll see you later, Sergeant."

"Not so fast. Are those Germans next door to you gone away, do you know? The Muellers."

Zach had seen little of Woodruff Cottage and less of his odd neighbours for the past few days. He looked to Robyn for an answer.

"They were there last night but I don't know about now. They don't welcome callers."

The sergeant gave her a very curious glance and she was sorry she had passed any remark about her neighbours. Being unfriendly wasn't a crime.

"Garda Harte called there a couple of hours ago," he said. "He got no answer but that bloody big 4x4 Mueller drives was there. That young man is still wet behind the ears. Would one of you drop by, just to check? They're probably gone but just in case."

"Will do."

The sergeant waved at them then and went off to join Billy as he waited, prayed and held onto a spark of hope that June Varian's lad might, just might, by some miracle, be on the lifeboat when it returned.

There was chaos on the coast road when Robyn and Zach got there. Tansy's car and Kevin Phillips' Cabriolet were parked on the tarmac which ended abruptly about 500 metres before the cottages. Down the track Don Cronin's truck was hitched onto Jeff Wilcox's tractor. Everybody was issuing instructions, waving their arms around and shouting. Kevin Phillips seemed to be in his element, as if he had suddenly discovered a talent for directing the release of pick-up trucks from mucky potholes. Tansy, her dark hair plastered onto her head, was standing in front of the tractor, signalling like a traffic policeman. Zach parked the Land Rover behind Kevin's car.

"I'd better go out and do a bit of waving my arms about too," he said. "It seems to be the thing to do."

"My car is parked in front of the cottage. Should we ask Jeff to pull it out to the tarmac before he goes?"

"I'll ask him," Zach said as he swung himself out of the Land Rover. "Don't you dream of moving, Rob. Stay here."

Robyn shivered as she sat there. She was very cold now. She wriggled her toes, then stamped her feet a bit but they still felt like blocks of ice.

Listening to the sound of the rain battering off the roof of the Land Rover she thought it had a mocking quality. A lively rhythm as if it was enjoying throwing itself earthwards at speed. It glistened and danced in the glow from the big tractor headlights. Their brightness made everything else disappear into the surrounding darkness. Robyn could barely make out the shore on her right or the cottages on her left.

What must it be like out at sea? If Des was still alive, was he struggling to stay afloat in the black, rolling water? Were his muscles aching and his lungs burning with every gasp he made? Was he struggling to the crest of each wave in the hope of seeing land, a light, another human being? Was he crying – after all he was little more than a child – was he calling for his mother?

His mother! June! Where was she? Robyn got out of the Land Rover and hurried to Tansy's car. She peered in and saw June slumped in the back seat, her head in her hands and her shoulders shaking. Opening the back door, Robyn slid into the seat beside her and put her arm around the shaking shoulders. They stayed like that, the mother and the mother-to-be. No words were spoken.

Robyn watched as the tractor finally got the pick-up out of the ruts and then there was another flurry as the tractor was unhitched and drew away, Jeff Wilcox waving to Robyn from the cab as he drove past. Tansy came back to her car and got into the driver's seat.

"God! Men! That would have been done in half the time if only they had listened to me."

"I'm sure you're right, Tansy. I was hoping Jeff Wilcox would move my car too but he seemed in a bit of a hurry going off, didn't he?"

"He got an urgent call from his wife to go home. Something to do with moving livestock to shelter. Don Cronin has to get back to his wife too. He doesn't have time to secure my windows." Tansy turned around and looked at June's bowed head. "Are you okay to walk to the house, June? It's not far."

June raised her head and looked around her as if only now realising where she was. Her eyes flickered towards the sea. "At least he's not suffering any more," she whispered in a gentle tone that did not seem to belong to June Varian at all.

Tansy and Robyn exchanged glances. What could they say? Pretend a hope that was tenuous at best? Their tacit agreement was that silence on the subject of Des's fate was more eloquent than any words they could utter.

Robyn squeezed June's shoulder. "Come on. You need a hot shower and dry clothes. We'll make a dash for the cottages."

Tansy carried the bag of clothing she had collected for June while Robyn led the distraught woman along. It was easy. June appeared to be glad to be brought to wherever people thought she should be. She had left her capacity to think for herself on the pier. The lights came on in Tansy's cottage and Robyn frowned as she realised Kevin had opened it up and turned on the lights. Tansy must have given him the keys. How cosy. Tansy interrupted Robyn's thought before she could decide whether she was being jealous or just bitchy.

"Don Cronin had a weird conversation with Zach."

"Really? What about? The supernatural? Porn?"

"Don't be silly, Rob. It was about the Muellers."

"Now that's proper weird."

"Don Cronin asked if Zach had ever spoken to Mrs Mueller. If he thought she might be in any danger from her husband."

They had reached the gate to Tansy's garden by now. Robyn stood still, a look of concentration on her face.

"Do you know, Tansy, that might make sense. He's a scary man with a filthy temper. We both know that. And from what little I've seen of her she seems like a very timid woman. What do you think?"

"I think you should get in home this minute, Mrs Claymore," Zach said, walking up beside her and catching her arm. "Ye'll have plenty opportunity for gossiping in the hall. See you in about an hour, Tansy. Looking forward to the soup."

Zach and Robyn walked arm in arm to their cottage while Kevin Phillips stood at Tansy's door and stared after them. He was smiling by the time Tansy and June reached him but Tansy had seen that look which clouded his eyes as he had gazed after Robyn and her husband.

Water Lily and Jasmine, Robyn's favourite bath oil, wafted in steamy puffs from the bath water. Gingerly she eased herself in and lay back, glorying in the scent and warmth. Zach had run the bath for her, insisting that she soak while he took a quick shower in the ensuite before he began to haul as much as he could from downstairs up to the relative safety of the upper floor. He didn't have to insist very much. She needed this time alone to sort through her feelings. Her fears. The gloom from the boarded-up windows added to her feeling of unease. Besides, she was beginning to feel like she was getting a cold. Maybe even pneumonia. Bronchitis at least.

Dipping her sponge, she held it over her belly and squeezed. Rivulets of suds dribbled over her rounded stomach. She smiled, whispering to her baby. An image of June Varian flashed before her, mouth open, tears streaming from her eyes, face so distorted by the deep pain of loss that she barely seemed human. Robyn dropped the sponge and pulled herself up into a sitting position. She knew that her face too would be distorted with unbearable grief if anything ever happened to end the life she could feel growing inside her. She would kill for this little person – strangle, shoot, burn and stab anyone who ever tried to harm it. Now she began to understand how June must be feeling. How she must be longing to hold her boy in her arms, to curse and scream, to tear Audrey Quill to pieces, to roll back time and have just one more smile from Des, one more sulky slouch, one second to touch his face and dream dreams of his future. Robyn understood too how June seemed so sure her son was dead despite all the assurances from those around her that he might yet be found safe and well. How could she not know? Their hearts had beat together for nine months so hers would surely tell her if her son, her baby, was no more.

Shivering despite the warm water, Robyn decided to get out of the bath and dress as quickly as possible. She must finish the packing she had started this morning, empty out perishables, organise her laptop to bring with her. Writing about what was happening would probably be therapeutic. She must remember her knitting too. She had recently started a matinee coat. White and with impossibly complicated lacy stitches. That should keep her occupied for a while. She laughed at her mental list as she dressed. Just how long did she expect to be in the hall? She heard thumping on the stairs and peeping out onto the landing saw Zach, red-faced, hauling the PC and infra-red lamp from the animal clinic up the stairs.

He stood at the top of the landing and leaned the load against the banisters. "Jeez! I'm not as fit as I thought. I'll have to get into shape before I start pushing a buggy around Felton."

"Me too," Robyn laughed patting her tummy. Then her expression changed. "Zach? Do you really believe our home is at risk?"

He came to her and put his arms around her. "Yes, Rob. I do. And I'm afraid your car is in danger too. I don't expect Jeff Wilcox will be back with his tractor. I was going to try towing with the Land Rover but the track is so bad now we'd probably both get stuck."

"Well, at least we have the Land Rover to get us to the Community Hall. With Tansy's car and Kevin's too we have plenty of transport."

"That pair appear to be getting quite cosy, don't they?"

Robyn examined Zach's face for signs of anger or disapproval at Kevin Phillips' continuing presence in Felton but his expression was unreadable.

"I was talking to one of the coastguards," he continued. "An experienced man. He said he has never seen swells so big out in the harbour. This massive high tide is heading for shore now pulled by the full moon and pushed by the hurricane winds."

"Kimi."

"Yes. Kimi in all his destructive glory. So come on. Shake a leg. We must finish up here and prepare ourselves mentally and physically for the hurricane by holding our noses and swallowing Tansy's soup."

"Hypocrite! You told her you were looking forward to it. At least it will be nourishing."

"And organic."

Zach picked up the load again and kicked open the door to the guest bedroom. Robyn was amazed to see how much he had packed in there while she had been in the bath. She spotted their television sitting on top of the bed. "Oh! I was going to check the telly weather report."

"I did before I unplugged it. This deluge of rain is countrywide – 102 mm fell on Cork in one hour – the highest ever recorded. Rivers are beginning to surge. Lucky they were so low before the rain started or some towns and cities would be flooded already. At least people have time to get out of vulnerable areas. I tried to convince Con Lynch to come with me but he didn't want to."

"He needs to be alone, Zach. Can you imagine how devastated he must feel?"

Robyn frowned as she saw him drop the equipment from the clinic onto the pristine white bedspread. She always kept this bedroom spick and span and now it was a mess. When Zach turned around she was instantly guilty about her pettiness. There was such sadness in his green eyes that she felt tears well in her own.

"I can't know how Con feels, Rob, but I can imagine how I would feel if I lost you."

She felt a cold sliver of fear slide down her back. Was this a premonition? It happened more often than we admitted, didn't it? Someone said something about loss and next thing it happened. The event you most dreaded. She walked to him and gently touched his face, tickling the palm of her hand against his stubbly cheeks, running her fingers through his still-wet curls.

"We'll always be together, Zach. Us and the baby. For as long as we live."

"Are you sure? Really sure? So what is Kevin Phillips doing here, touching you every chance he gets?"

She stared back at him, still seeing the sadness but something else now too. Jealousy? Yes, those sparks were jealousy. Mean and distrusting. She understood that too. She had envied Lisa Phillips intensely for a long time until she realised that being Mrs Kevin Phillips was probably what drove Lisa's self-destructive addiction. She smiled at Zach now, hugging him close to her.

"Don't be daft. For one thing, I have all I need here in my arms. I married you, Zach. I'm having your baby. What more reassurance do you want? I thought we had already sorted out this problem. Besides, you'd want to be blind not to see what's going on between Tansy and Kevin Phillips. I'm not the one keeping him in Felton."

"If you say so. I wonder what *he* would say though? Now come on. Time is slipping by. I must get that animal feed for the Hall from the clinic. Have you got what we need packed? Blankets? Or maybe those sleeping bags we used on our Highland trip."

No. She hadn't blankets or sleeping bags ready. Nor had she any sense that Zach trusted her with Kevin Phillips. Worse still, in a moment of honesty, she suddenly knew that his instinct was right. The passion she had nurtured for Kevin Phillips was long since buried. But not forgotten.

Chapter 20

After stacking their gear for the hall into the Land Rover, Zach and Robyn left the lights on in Woodruff Cottage while they were going next door to Tansy for soup.

"We'll need to have a quick check around the house before we go," said Zach. "Just to make sure everything's in order."

Robyn nodded her agreement.

The wind was slicing in off the sea again, slanting rain into their faces as they walked the short distance to Tansy's cottage. Even their heavy raincoats and Wellington boots seemed inadequate.

Robyn stood still and cocked her ear. "Do you hear that?"

Zach listened to the deep rumble for a few seconds and then nodded his head. "The tide. It's coming into the bay."

Wordlessly, Robyn caught his hand. She felt helpless, the sound of the ocean echoing in her head. It was a threatening noise, powerful, relentless. And yet she knew that the deep rumbling was just a whisper of what was to come.

Lights shone from Tansy's studio so they headed in that direction and tapped on the patio doors. Inside they could see June, the cat sprawled across her lap, dozing in the rattan chair Tansy had woven during her 'I'll make my own furniture' era.

Robyn frowned as she peered through the door. Tansy was sitting in front of her computer. Beside her on the long piano stool she favoured as a desk-chair sat Kevin Phillips. Their heads were close together as they bent towards the monitor, both engrossed in the images. The printer was spewing out pages and another stack, already printed, sat in a neat pile on the desk.

"I don't think they heard us with all the rain and wind," Robyn said, tapping more loudly on the door this time.

When Tansy came to the door to let them in, she had that surprised look about her which meant she had totally forgotten the soup.

"I won't be a sec heating up the soup. Come on into the kitchen. Kev, would you feed more paper into the printer?"

Kev? Robyn had never shortened his name. She had not seen him as a 'Kev' type. He was a serious, not-to-be-abbreviated Kevin.

"We're printing out information on the Maya and their Long Count Calendar," Tansy explained. "Something to read when we're in the hall."

"What's that all about?" Zach asked.

Robyn threw her eyes up to heaven in mock horror. "Don't start her off, Zach. Tansy believes the end of the world is nigh and that the Maya predicted it nearly two thousand years ago."

Zach nodded, a look of concentration on his face. "Right. I saw something on YouTube about December 2012. That Maya prediction will fizzle out when the time passes without the Apocalypse. Just like the Millennium bug did in 2000. How come the Maya didn't predict their own demise?"

"How do you know they didn't?" Kev alias Kevin asked, unwinding himself from the piano stool and stretching as if he had just got out of bed. It was always the first thing he did in the morning. How many times had Robyn watched lazily from bed as he flexed his muscles and stretched his long limbs?

"You can't be serious about this, Kevin," Zach said. "Do you honestly believe that December 2012 is going to be the end of Planet Earth?"

"No. I don't. But I wouldn't dismiss everything the Maya said. They were extremely sophisticated and cultured. Look at their writing skills. And their knowledge of astronomy was astounding considering they had no telescopes."

"Does their sophistication include the human sacrifice they practised?" said Robyn. "Children sometimes?"

"So, Robyn, you've been reading up too."

"I did history in first-year college."

Kevin nodded and smiled at her. His lovely, warm, white-toothed smile. "I should have remembered that."

Despite knowing that Zach and Tansy were both watching the exchange, Robyn couldn't help but return Kevin's smile. He should certainly have remembered. She had told him the first time they had made love. That balmy and sensual time while they had lain in each other's arms, sharing secrets, their bodies sated but their curiosity about each other insatiable. They had talked long into the night and made love again as the sun had risen on a new day. Then Kevin had gone home to his wife.

A vigorous gust of wind howled around the cottage, loud enough to wake June and even Ben. The rain hammered so insistently on the roof and against the plate-glass doors that they all peered out to see if there were hailstones falling.

"Looks like we won't have to wait until December 2012," Zach remarked. "Kimi is going to rip us apart now."

Robyn went over to June and leaned down to her. "How are you now? Were you able to get some rest?"

"I dreamt about him. Happy dreams. About when he was a toddler. A little demon, he was. Into every devilment."

Robyn caught June's hand and held it tight. She could imagine Des as a baby. He would probably have been plump and his red hair, which he slicked down with gel in later years, would have been curly. Somehow she found it easier to imagine what Des was like twelve or thirteen years ago than what June would have been like then. Maybe slimmer, her features sharper. A happy mother with a baby in her arms and a husband by her side. Why was it that some people, some families, seemed to have such tragic lives while others sailed through unscathed? Where was the fairness, the compassion, the goodness in that?

June's eyelids were beginning to droop. "I'll sleep now," she muttered. "Dream again."

She dropped off so suddenly that Robyn was worried enough to call Tansy over.

"Is she alright? She seemed to slip into sleep very suddenly. I wonder did Dr Early sedate her?"

"No. He always says there are no pills to cure grief."

"He's right of course but I'm worried that she's in shock."

"She has to be. What do you think, Zach?"

June's eyes flew open and she glared at Robyn. "I've just lost my son. What way do you expect me to be? I don't need a vet, thank you very much."

Robyn breathed a sigh of relief. That was more like the June she had come to know so well over the past few days. A fighter. She smiled at the feisty woman. "I'm sorry, June. I didn't mean to upset you. It's just that we're all worried about you and we don't know what to do to help."

"I just need to be on my own for a while."

"Soup?" Tansy asked.

"No, thank you, but I'll keep Ben with me, if you don't mind."

Ben curled closer into June and twitched a whisker as if he knew they were talking about him.

"He's too fat," Zach remarked. "Tansy, I warned you to cut down on his food."

"I've tried but he keeps looking for more. Anyway he's not fat. He's well built. I like my men solid."

"Really?" Kevin asked, flexing his biceps and grinning.

Tansy smiled back at him and if it wasn't a flirtatious smile it was a good imitation, thought Robyn.

"We'll be in the kitchen, June. Just shout if you need anything. Lights on or off?"

"Off, please," June answered sleepily. Her eyes were closed even before Robyn had flicked the switch, leaving June alone with a fat cat and her grieving.

The soup was tasty. Robyn ate hers with relish, hurrying

in case somebody asked Tansy to list ingredients. She didn't want to know.

"What's that?" Zach asked, pointing in the direction of the mini-forest which appeared to be growing on Tansy's draining board.

"My crop. My cotton crop. Just as well I brought it in. It would be destroyed by now if I hadn't."

"Cotton? That's interesting. Did you grow it from . . ."

Zach's question was left hanging in the air as a loud knock sounded on the back door. Tansy got up to answer it. Billy Moynihan lunged in, wind and rain rushing past him through the open door. He was as thoroughly wet as it was possible to be and his face had a green tinge. They all stared at what he was carrying in his hand.

"Is that the one Des was wearing?" Zach asked, never moving his eyes from the life jacket which had a strand of seaweed trailing from one of the Velcro fastenings.

"Not positively identified yet. George Quill is in the hospital in Galway with Audrey but I spoke to him on the phone. He described this jacket, down to the tear on the inner lining."

"And Des?"

He bowed his head. "They didn't find him. They couldn't stay out any longer. The swells are huge. Even the bay is rough now."

Robyn felt tears prickle her eyes. She couldn't stop looking at the jacket. Had Des already been dead when it was dragged off him or did he struggle to keep it around his body and then realise he was no match for the angry strength of the sea?

"What about a rescue helicopter?" Kevin asked. "Are they going to send one out?"

"No. The gusts are too strong. Where's June?"

Tansy nodded towards the studio. "In there. She's resting."

"I'd better tell her," Billy said but he made no attempt to move.

Robyn and Tansy looked at each other.

"We'll tell her," Tansy volunteered.

"There's no need for her to see this," said Zach, taking the life jacket from Billy and putting it into the broom cupboard. "Not now anyway."

Tansy caught Robyn's hand and led her towards the studio door. "Kev, would you heat up some soup for Billy? We won't be long."

The first thing they noticed when Tansy opened the connecting door between the kitchen and studio was the wind and cold. The double patio doors of the studio were wide open to the elements and the rattan chair was vacant.

"Shit! She's gone out!" Robyn said, racing across to the chair as if there was a possibility June might be hiding underneath the cushions.

"And Ben too," Tansy added.

They stood speechless for a moment, gazing into the darkness and the pelting rain.

"She can't be gone far," Zach said from the kitchen doorway.

Robyn turned around to him.

"She must have seen Billy come in carrying the life jacket."

"We'd better find her quickly. She's in shock now. Anything could happen to her."

Robyn dashed back to the kitchen to get her coat but Zach held her arm. "You're not going anywhere. I'm not letting you out to get drenched again. Billy, Kevin and I will go. You and Tansy wait here in case she comes back."

Robyn didn't argue. Her back was aching and she was afraid she might fall in the dark. The baby must be her priority.

"She'll be gone to the strand," Billy said quietly. "That's where she would feel closest to her son."

Grim-faced, the men got their coats.

"I've some heavy-duty torches in my car," Kevin offered. "I'll go get them."

"No camera! If I see one in your hand I'll smash it!" Billy threatened.

Kevin glared at him for an instant, then shrugged and went to his car.

Robyn noted that he still seemed to love that Cabriolet more passionately than anyone or anything else. Or maybe not. The Kevin she had known would not have been even vaguely interested in ancient cultures or search and rescue missions for grieving mothers – except as news fodder of course. Perhaps Tansy had tapped into the softer side of his nature.

"We'll head for the shore first," Zach said. "Shouldn't be long."

He kissed Robyn on the cheek and then he and Billy went out. As soon as the door closed, Tansy went to the broom cupboard and got out the lifejacket. Holding it up to her face she sobbed into it.

"Oh, Rob! Poor June. Poor Des. I've known him since he was a baby. Such a beautiful baby he was too.

Chubby and with gorgeous curly hair. June wasn't young when she had him. She was almost forty. He was a miracle and now . . . and now . . ."

Robyn held Tansy while she wept for the baby she had admired, the boy she had watched grow, and the mother from whom he had been taken.

Out from the shelter of the cottages, the full force of the wind and rain assaulted the three men, flapping their coats and trousers legs. As they headed towards the shore the gusts were so strong that at times they were almost swept off their feet.

"Jesus! If this is only the warm-up act for Kimi, I dread to think what's in store," Kevin gasped as a squall almost took his breath away.

"You don't have to stay in Felton if it's too much for you," Zach answered sourly.

"That's where you're wrong. I do. Flights out of Galway and Shannon were grounded an hour ago. I can't drive out of here either. There are already reports of extensive flooding between here and Dublin."

"You should have gone when you had the chance."

Billy shone his torch into both their faces. His own face was in shadow but his anger was so intense his eyes glittered in the darkness.

"Shut up, you pair of children! Remember why we're here. Forget your arguments and look for June. She's the one with real problems."

Zach and Kevin glanced at each other and then both looked away in discomfort.

"You're right, Billy. Sorry," Zach said. "What do we do now? Split up and search the shoreline?"

"Too dangerous. We stick together."

Nobody argued with that. The sound of surf breaking over the outlying rocks was thunderous. The inner bay was already swelling with huge volumes of wind-driven water. Zach glanced over his shoulder in the direction of his home. It looked solid, inviting. It had withstood many batterings but he shivered now as he listened to the deep roar of surf and storm. He tried to tell himself it was only a house. If the worst happened and it was destroyed they could rebuild or move. Even as he reasoned he knew he was not being honest with himself. Woodruff Cottage was so much more than just a house. It was a home. Their home. His and Robyn's and the baby's. He wanted his child to grow up here, to see it play in the sand, swim in the sea, wake up in the morning and breathe fresh air. His thoughts were interrupted by Billy.

"We'll go right first, towards the village. She might have thought of going home."

They began the trudge along then, the three torch beams swivelling around the shoreline and strand.

"He'll be carried in on the tide with any luck," Billy said. "If not it could be another nine days. Or never."

They didn't have to ask who. It would compound the cruelty if June did not have the comfort of funeral rites to say goodbye to her son.

"There! Look! On that rock."

Kevin's torch was focused towards an area where the road skirted the strand. Huddled underneath the shelter of the bank, June was sitting on a rock, so still that she seemed to be part of it. Facing the sea, she was oblivious to the rain that drenched her and the wind which whipped her wet hair around her face. Billy scampered towards her, taking off his jacket as he ran.

"You must come back with me now, June. There's nothing more we can do for Des tonight."

"We can find him."

"Not tonight. We've done everything in our power. We just have to hope."

"That's what I'm doing, Billy. Don't you see? I'm hoping to find his body and bury him beside his father. I'll wait here. I know he'll come in."

Billy draped his jacket over her, then put his arms firmly around her and lifted her to her feet. "You'll do no such thing. You're coming to Tansy Bingham's with me now. Get yourself dried off and ready for the hall. Time's running out, June."

"It's already run out for me. My time's done."

She looked at him, her agony so visible on her face that Billy lowered his eyes.

Zach and Kevin arrived in front of her and shoving their torches in their pockets, locked hands to make a fireman's lift for her. She looked at them and smiled.

"Find another excuse for holding hands, boys. I'm quite capable of walking."

She turned her back on them then and began the trudge back to Tansy's cottage.

Tansy had a scarf tied over her head as she ran out the studio door and put Ben's dish, overflowing with food, on the decking. She came back in and quickly pulled the doors shut, whipping off the scarf and shaking it out.

"Shit! That wind is going to wreck my garden. I'll be lucky if it doesn't lift the decking too. I don't know about June but I know for certain Ben didn't travel far. He hates the rain. I don't know why he went out at all."

"Maybe he has a girlfriend," Robyn suggested.

"He's neutered. Probably why he's so interested in food. If he's within a ten-mile radius, he'll sniff out his supper and come back for it."

"Of course he will."

Tansy gave a little sideways glance. "You think I'm silly about Ben but there were times when he was the only friend I had. He understands a lot of what I say to him, you know."

"I don't doubt that. Like 'chicken' and 'salmon'."

"Mock if you like but Ben's the only man who's been faithful to me."

Robyn walked over to the doors and cupping her hands around her face peered into the savagery of the storm. Rain was overflowing from the gutters on the roof and spilling onto the decking. Even Ben's dish, in a sheltered corner, was beginning to get water-logged. Down the road to her right she could see the outline of Zach's Land Rover and Tansy's and Kevin's cars. To her left the outside lights of Woodruff Cottage shone bravely. Ahead there was only darkness except for the three weak beams of torchlight from shore. Robyn took a step forward, moving so close to the glass that her nose was tipping against it.

"Tansy, look. I think they're coming back."

They watched the bobbing circles of torchlight get brighter as they neared the track.

Robyn wondered if this would be a good moment to warn Tansy again. To make sure she understood exactly what type of person Kevin Phillips was. Not kind and sympathetic like Billy Moynihan. And Zach. Or would that be interfering? Or silly. After all, Tansy and Kevin barely knew each other and maybe she had misinterpreted the smiles and gazes between them. The moment passed as the torch-light bearers clambered up to the track and headed towards the cottage.

"Thank God!" Tansy said with relief. "There are four of them. They found June."

Robyn hung her head in shame. For the past few minutes she had been so preoccupied with thoughts of Kevin Phillips that she had forgotten about June. Tansy didn't need warnings about fickleness but Robyn, Mrs Robyn Claymore, obviously did.

Chapter 21

Satisfied that June was warm and dry, Billy left for the Hall. Kevin went back to surfing the net while Tansy paid umpteen visits to the decking to look for Ben.

"He's still not back. His supper isn't touched. There's something wrong. He wouldn't stay out in that rain."

"Have you searched in here for him?" Zach asked. "I mean really searched."

"He would have come for his food if he was anywhere around."

"Not if he's afraid."

"Do you think not? Afraid of what? The wind?"

"Maybe," Zach agreed.

Robyn looked around the studio. It was huge and filled with all sorts of things for a frightened cat to hide behind. "If he didn't go out he can only be here. Call him, Tansy."

Tansy began to call and crawl at the same time. On hands and knees she looked under chairs, her bench, the cutting table and behind the book shelves. Robyn and

Zach walked around as well, lifting cushions, swatches of fabric and, in increasing desperation, magazines and books.

"Move your feet," Tansy ordered Kevin as she crawled in underneath her desk. "Ben likes to sit here sometimes."

Kevin seemed unaware, never moving his gaze from the screen.

"They're closing the floodgates on the Thames," he announced. "They reckon the rain will reach them before dawn."

Tansy, red-faced, backed out from underneath her desk and sat back on her heels. "I don't give a damn about the Thames. Ben isn't here."

Kevin looked down at her, his expression cold. "Really? I do. My wife is in London."

"Well then, so should you be. Don't go blaming me for the fact that you're here and she's there. You could have gone away early today."

"Don't you get stroppy with me just because your cat ran away. Can't say I blame him."

Zach grinned and raised an eyebrow at Robyn. "I think we have a domestic on our hands."

The row was quickly forgotten as Kevin told them more about the information he was gathering on Hurricane Kimi. "Just hours from us now and still gathering force. Winds of up to 130 mph, pressure still dropping. Imagine how that's pushing the sea surge towards us. What's happening now is only –"

"For heaven's sake, Kevin," Tansy said in annoyance, "we can do without the facts and stats. We're worried enough as it is. Get off your butt and help me find Ben."

Attention turned to June as she came into the studio,

now showered and dried off and wearing one of Tansy's hand-embroidered saris.

"Wow! That's beautiful," Robyn said, admiring the intricate work on the silk fabric and the way its soft folds flattered June's fuller figure.

June glanced down briefly at it. "It was the only thing in Tansy's wardrobe to fit me. I'll have to call home and get something proper to wear before we go to the hall."

Zach put his hands to his head. "Oh, shit! The hall! I forgot. The sergeant asked me to call in and check on the Muellers before we go. I'd better pop over to them now."

Tansy leapt to her feet. "I'm coming too. Ben could have gone over there. I've seen him climb the fence between your house and theirs. Are you sure they're home?"

Zach shook his head. "I'm not but we'll soon find out. You'd better get your boots. The track outside is like a stream at this stage."

They left in a flurry of Wellingtons and rain macs, leaving June to sit in the rattan chair staring into space, Kevin sitting in front of the computer, staring at the monitor, and Robyn standing between them both, wondering just what had happened to her peaceful, calm, existence, her certainty of just a few days ago.

Tansy called out for Ben as they waded through the muck of the track. Her words were whipped away on the wind. When they reached the Muellers' gate they couldn't make out in the dark whether the car was there or not. They stood and looked at the lights in the downstairs windows.

"Someone's home anyway," said Tansy.

"Maybe," Zach agreed. "Although all the lights are on in our house and guess what? We're not there."

"Smart ass. Will you have a bet?"

"Okay. What's the wager?"

Tansy started when a cutting blast of wind whined through the cypress trees. Timber groaned as the branches and even the trunks were bent under the force of the wind. She shivered.

"That's a horrible sound. Weird."

"The bet?"

"I bet that Horst Mueller will answer the door but that we won't see a sign of his wife."

"And if you're right?"

"Then you'll eat everything I cook for the next year without making a face."

Zach laughed. "You're on. And if I win you must put Ben on a diet."

As they walked between the lines of cypress trees towards the door they could see now that the black Hummer was parked in front of the house. Tansy continued to call Ben but was answered only by the wind.

When Zach raised his hand to knock on the door, the hall light inside came on.

"He's always watching," Tansy whispered. "He must live at the window. Probably has binoculars too."

The door opened and Horst stood there glaring at Tansy. "Not you again! Will you ever get off my doorstep? What will it take to be rid of you?"

"I think you're going about that the right way, Mr Mueller. Believe me, your doorstep is the last place I want to be."

"Why are you here and who's he?"

Tansy heard Zach's sharp intake of breath at Horst's blatant rudeness. "I'm your neighbour, Mr Mueller. Zach Claymore. The police asked me to call to you."

Horst, normally so quick with blistering replies, stood there, mouth open, eyes wide. His arms folded across his chest in an automatic gesture of self-defence. "The police?" he muttered.

"Yes. They called here earlier but got no reply. They wanted to inform you that evacuation to the hall is mandatory until this hurricane threat is over."

The slackness in Horst's features disappeared. His eyes narrowed and his mouth returned to its customary tight-lipped position. A mean mouth, Tansy thought. Cruel. She frowned as she looked at this transformation, wondering why the mention of the police had affected him so markedly. Was he hiding from them? A terrorist maybe, or a mass murderer? He certainly looked capable of taking a life and there was that conversation between Don Cronin and Zach she had overheard.

"My wife and I are staying in our home," Horst, again in control of himself, said coldly. "We're not intimidated by weather. The biggest threat to us is from interfering neighbours."

"I'm only –" Zach began but Tansy caught his arm and interrupted him.

"Mr Mueller, I wonder if I could speak to your wife, please."

Horst glared hatred at Tansy. His struggle to control his temper was visible in twitching facial muscles and the tiny flecks of spittle which sprayed from his mouth when he spoke. "Get away from my house and don't ever put a foot near it again."

"What will you do? Call the police?"

Horst slammed the door in their faces. They looked at each other and laughed, not because they were amused but because they were nervous.

"Come on. Let's get out of here," Zach said, already turning to leave.

Tansy quickly followed him.

"I overheard you and Don Cronin talking, Zach. What if he's physically abusing Mrs Mueller? Maybe he's holding her prisoner. In the cellar."

"What cellar?"

"The one underneath their cottage. Didn't you know? There are lots of stories about that cellar. Some say a tunnel leads from there to the bay. I heard one time that there's an underground passage linking it to our two cottages as well but I never found any secret doors or anything like that."

"That's ridiculous, Tansy. Our cottage was surveyed before we bought it. If there were any subterranean passages they'd have been discovered then. I'd imagine they would have undermined the foundations a long time since."

"Well, there's definitely a cellar in Muellers'. I was in it years ago. The Carmody sisters kept their store of home-made wines down there plus the ball gowns they used to wear when they were young."

They were almost to the gateway now. Zach stopped walking.

"What's wrong?" Tansy asked. "Don't you believe me? Don't you believe Don Cronin? Horst Mueller could be –"

"Sssh!"

They stood still for a moment. Then Tansy heard it

too. The sound was coming from high above their heads, it was weak, difficult to discern from the whine of the wind and the constant patter of rain, but it was unmistakable.

"Ben!" she cried, running to the base of the tree from which the meow seemed to originate. "Come on down, Ben! Good boy!"

As the gale pushed and shoved branches, she caught glimpses of Ben's white coat, high up near the tapered tip of the tree.

"Oh my God! Zach! Those skinny top branches will never hold him. He'll fall. Ben! Come down!"

Reaching up, Zach tested the strength of the lower branches, then he leaned back, looked up to Ben and shook his head. "You stay here. I'll get a ladder and a torch. Keep talking to him. He's terrified."

Tansy heard the squelchy slap of Zach's boots as he hurried away through the muddy streams of groundwater. She called to Ben again, trying to keep her voice calm. "Just hang on there, Ben. You're a good boy. Don't be afraid." He answered with a pathetic little squeak that sounded nothing at all like her spoiled and assertive cat. She stood close to the tree, her eyes fixed on the white blur at the top and continued to coax and cajole him and herself into calmness.

Horst Mueller watched from the window of his darkened dining room as the vet and the Bingham bitch walked down his garden path.

Almost to the gate, the pair stopped walking. Horst leaned closer to the window and squinted into the gloom. It seemed that both the vet and Bingham had stepped off the path and gone in under a tree. Was she having an affair with the pregnant woman's husband? Just as he decided that they must be locked in an embrace, the vet walked out from the black shadow of the tree and into the greyer dimness of the footpath. In a few long strides he had reached the gate and turned right, back towards his own cottage.

Horst waited for Bingham to appear. She was probably giving her lover a few minutes to get home before she left. He waited for her to leave. Two minutes. Two more minutes. Still no sign of Bingham emerging from under the tree. Just what was the bitch up to now? Or had she managed to sneak off without him seeing? There was only one way to find out.

Horst dashed into the hall, grabbed his parka and went out into the storm, closing the door firmly shut behind him.

Something, a step, a twig breaking, a sixth sense, made Tansy spin around.

Horst Mueller was standing behind her, his face almost hidden inside the fur-trimmed hood of a parka. Startled, she jumped back, almost falling against the tree.

"Jesus! You gave me a fright! Do you always sneak around like that?"

"Do you always trespass like this?"

He took a step closer to her and Tansy realised that she had nowhere to run. She was trapped between the tree and the man standing in front of her. The cynical smile on his face was much more terrifying than his usual glare. Words began to pour unbridled out of her mouth.

"My cat is stuck up that tree. June let him out but we got her back and I didn't know where Ben had gone. He's terrified of the wind and he can't come down."

All the time she was talking, Horst was moving closer to her. She could smell him now. A mixture of garlic and aftershave. He wasn't saying anything. Just smiling that intimidating smile. Twigs were digging into her back and waving branches of cypress slapped against her. Maybe she could make a dash past him and run out the gate. She noticed a shaft of light on her left-hand side. His front door was ajar. It was in danger of being blown off the hinges in this gale. She considered dashing in there, slamming the door and phoning the police. And say what? That he had smiled at her?

His face was almost touching hers now.

"Stay the fuck out of my life or I'll make sure you regret it."

He put his hands up, gripping onto two branches either side of her. Trapping her. Sneering. Mocking her terror. Enjoying it. She knew that shouting for Zach would be pointless. He would not hear her over the wind and rain. Straightening out her arms she tried to push Horst away from her. He was too strong. Her heart was pounding so fast she thought it would burst.

"How brave are you now?" he asked. "Where is all your curiosity gone? Your need to interfere in other people's lives? Not so smart, are you?"

She would never be able to physically ward him off. She would have to play for time.

"Zach is gone to get a ladder. He's on his way back. I can hear him."

"No, you can't. It's only you and me."

Just as she thought she would faint from fear, he dropped his arms from the tree. She was paralysed, afraid to even take a breath. He stepped back from her, far enough so that she could turn her face away from him and towards his house. His hall door was no longer open. She caught a glimpse of movement. A dark shadow moving towards the even darker shadows at the side of the house. At the same time she heard voices. Thank God! Zach. And Kevin too. She began to shake violently, overcome by the realisation that this man was capable of killing.

Horst leaned forward suddenly and grabbed a fistful of her collar, tightening it around her throat. "One word of this, just a whisper, and I'll make sure you don't talk any more. Do you understand?"

She nodded and kept nodding, terrified that he would tighten her collar more. Her hands reached up to loosen his hold but he had too firm a grip on her. She couldn't breathe and her eyes felt like they would bulge out of their sockets. The turtle-neck sweater she was wearing under her coat felt like a cord around her windpipe.

"I hear one word, just one, and I'll pay you a visit when you least expect it. You'd better sleep with one eye open in future."

He let go her collar and stepped back just as Zach and Kevin, carrying a ladder between them, came in the gate. She slumped back against the tree and breathed a huge sigh of relief.

"You alright, Tansy?" Zach asked, shining the torch into her face.

"She's very upset," Horst explained in a reasonable and pleasant tone. "I've been trying to reassure her that her cat will be alright."

"Tansy?"

She narrowed her eyes and glared at Horst. What a clever game he was playing. She nodded to Zach and tried to put a smile on her face. "Yes, I'm fine, thank you. Just worried about Ben."

"You goose," Kevin said, stepping forward and putting his arm around her shoulder. "We'll have him back to you in two minutes. As fat and lazy as ever."

Zach was frowning, looking from Tansy to Horst. "You're sure you're okay, Tansy?"

She hesitated. Why should Horst Mueller get away with threatening her like that? How would she ever have a peaceful night's sleep again, knowing that he was watching her? It was probably all bluff. Just bully tactics. But then maybe not. A bolt of lightning rent the darkness. Ben screeched. She made up her mind.

"I'm fine, Zach, thank you. Let's just get Ben down before he dies of fright."

Zach stared at her for a short moment and then turned to Horst.

"Do you mind if we put a ladder up against your tree, Mr Mueller?"

"Of course. Go ahead."

Sometime between the ladder being raised and Ben being rescued, Horst Mueller disappeared back into his house. But not before casting a glance at Tansy, so threatening that she automatically put her hands to her throat to protect herself. She knew then that she and Horst Mueller had some unfinished business.

Chapter 22

"How am I going to examine him properly if you keep hanging onto him like that?" Zach asked in exasperation.

Tansy reluctantly let go of Ben and put him on the couch so that Zach could check him out for injury. She went to the hot press and came back with an armful of fluffy towels to dry Ben off.

"Jeez! He's an animal not a child," Kevin laughed. "Next you'll be pushing him around in a buggy!"

Tansy burst into tears.

Robyn frowned at Kevin. He had no idea, and he would never understand, just how much Ben meant to Tansy and how terrified she had been of losing him. "You oaf," she said softly to him as she passed him by to go comfort her friend. She put her arm around Tansy's shaking shoulders.

"Ben's safe now. And he's all in one piece, isn't he, Zach?"

"Right as rain. Oops! Bad analogy!"

A slight smile appeared on Tansy's tearstained face.

Ben was safe. She was safe. But for how long? She couldn't get the image of Horst Mueller's threatening leer out of her mind. Nor could she bring herself to tell her friends about what had happened. In the first place they would probably think it was her overactive imagination again. Maybe not. Robyn and Zach both knew how rude Horst Mueller could be. But not how dangerous. Her throat still ached where he had tightened her collar.

"I'll be fine, Rob. Thanks. I'll just go wash my face."

Tansy rushed to the bathroom and closed the door after her. Rolling down the collar of her turtleneck sweater she leaned in to the mirror and examined her neck. There was a slight red mark, no more than might be caused by tightening her hood against the wind and rain. The turtle neck had protected her skin but it had also ruined any evidence of what Horst Mueller had done to her.

Staring at herself in the mirror she wondered for one brief second if it had happened at all. Or if she had misunderstood. She frowned at her image. No, she had not. That piece of shit had threatened her and when this hurricane was over she would have a word with the sergeant. Tim Halligan would sort the bully out. She turned on the tap and splashed cold water on her face, patted it dry and then forced herself to smile at her pale image. Her smile faded as she thought of Mrs Mueller. Ute. That shy little woman who always lurked in her husband's shadow. Tansy put her hand to her throat again and wondered how many times Horst had terrified Ute like that. Maybe even worse. Why did she stay there? Probably for the same reason Tansy had not mentioned Horst's assault tonight. Fear.

A meow outside the bathroom door brought a genuine smile back to her face. Ben might be wet and traumatised but he was hungry. Opening the door she scooped him into her arms and hugged him until he let her know, in plain cat language, that he'd had too many hugs and not enough food.

Robyn insisted on going back to Woodruff Cottage with Zach to lock up. She touched things – the kitchen table, the curtains they had bought in London, the granite counter top. When she found herself trailing her fingers over the cooker, she decided it was time to call a halt to her ritual. It was as if she were blessing the fixtures and fittings. Or saying goodbye to them.

"At least all our papers and the computers are safe upstairs," Zach said, sensing her wistful mood.

"More importantly, the cot and cradle are up there. How safe, though? The wind is so much stronger than when we went over to Tansy's."

Zach, busy putting as many things as possible up into the high presses, stopped what he was doing and turned around.

"Do you think there's something wrong with Tansy? Since she came back from Muellers', I mean."

Robyn frowned. She had expected Zach to understand Tansy's upset. "Of course there is. She got a terrible shock. You must know what Ben means to her."

"No. I don't mean that. I just thought something had happened between her and Horst Mueller when I went to get the ladder. She was very upset when we got back and I felt Mueller had a very smug look on his face."

"He was probably being his usual obnoxious self.

Tansy is well able to cope with him. On the other hand, Ben is like her child. She must have been horrified to see him stuck in the tree. Of course she was upset."

"Maybe you're right. Though Horst Mueller is a very peculiar man. We could do nothing to convince him to leave. He seems happy to put himself and his wife at risk in order to protect his privacy. I think I'll have a word with the sergeant." He glanced at his watch. "Time to leave. I'm going to throw the master switch now. You wait outside for me."

"Just one sec. June is frozen in her sari. I want to grab one of my cardigans for her. It should fit." She looked down at her bulging stomach and wrinkled her nose. "In fact any of my clothes would fit Billy Moynihan let alone June."

Getting the cardigan was just an excuse to have one last look upstairs – at their bed, the sheepskin rugs, the reading lamps. The cot. The cradle, all frills and sweet-smelling. Tears welled. Until now, she had not realised how much Woodruff Cottage meant to her. How secure it made her feel. She poked out a rose-pink long-line cardi. It would keep June warm until she got what she'd termed "proper" clothes.

Cardigan tucked under her raincoat, Robyn went downstairs, out the back door and watched as Woodruff Cottage was plunged into darkness. It seemed to disappear into the night, a black bulk standing against the wind and rain. Zach locked the door behind him and dragged the sandbags flush against the bottom of the door. He put his arm around Robyn. They stood there for a moment, neither speaking, each saying a silent and reluctant goodbye to their home.

"We'll be back tomorrow," Zach said, squeezing her shoulder.

"Will our home be here?"

"We will. And our baby. What more could we want?"

Standing on tiptoe, Robyn kissed him on cold and wet lips. What more indeed could she want?

They had just come out their gate when, over the noise of wind and rain, they heard an engine revving. They looked up the road but their Land Rover and Tansy's and Kevin's cars were in darkness. Headlights pierced the blackness behind them as Horst Mueller's four-wheel-drive sped out of his gateway and made a sharp right turn. The engine screamed as the big Hummer raced through the floods on the track. Zach grabbed Robyn and pulled her in to the hedge. Arcs of muddy water lashed them as Horst, bent over the wheel, drove like a rally racer through potholes and mud and water, almost losing control as he skidded sideways around the corner at the top of the road.

"What the fuck!" Zach swore. "Are you alright, Rob?"

Her heart was pounding. She had thought that Mueller was going to plough into them. "I'm fine," she muttered but she held very tightly to Zach's arm until they reached the safety of Tansy's cottage.

A vigorous debate was taking place in Tansy's kitchen when Robyn and Zach got back there.

"But I must," Tansy was insisting. "I need them all."

"How long do you expect to be gone, for heaven's sake?" Kevin asked with such exasperation that it was obvious this argument had been going on for some time.

Robyn burst out laughing when she saw the cause of the row. Tansy's packing looked like the lost-luggage department at Heathrow Airport. Her 'crop' was by the door, ready to travel, all six big pots plus watering can and plant feed. Ben, already in his carrying cage, was peeping out through the grille, his big fluffy tail lashing from side to side in displeasure. His blanket, basket, food and water dishes, toys and grooming kit were there too.

"How selfish can you get?" Kevin asked. "There won't be room for anyone else in the hall with you and all your trappings!"

"Twelve months. Twelve solid months I've been nurturing my cotton. I'm not going to abandon it now."

"Water them, feed them and leave them. Grow up, Tansy!"

"And be an adult like you? No, thanks."

Robyn laughed again. "Tansy, one. Kevin, nil."

Kevin scowled at her. "I should have known you'd take her side. This is mad. She can't bring all this – this clutter."

"Toss for it," Zach suggested. He drew a coin out of his pocket. "Call. Heads or tails. Tansy?"

"I'm feeling lucky since I won my bet with you. Heads."

Robyn was curious. "What bet?"

Tansy's face seemed to cloud. "It has to do with Horst Mueller," she said dismissively.

Zach smiled at her and tossed the coin. It clattered onto the tiled floor of the kitchen then rolled in under a press. Kevin was delighted.

"All bets off. The plants are not –"

He didn't finish the sentence. He stood open-mouthed as an unearthly groan, followed by an earsplitting crash rent the air. June came running in from the studio blessing herself with the sign of the cross with one hand and holding up the folds of her sari with the other.

"What in the name of God Almighty was that?"

Robyn and Zach exchanged glances, remembering Horst Mueller's recklessness as he had sped past them. Had he come back, crashed his 4x4 into the ditch or down onto the rocks?

"The noise came from the Woodruff side of the fence," Tansy said. "We'd better check."

Grabbing coats and boots, Tansy, Zach and Kevin scrambled into them. June stood pale and shaking, still crossing herself and mumbling prayers, and Robyn sat still, her eyes wide, her colour ghastly.

"Don't move until we come back," Zach warned June and Robyn.

Outside, the wind had a new energy about it. It seemed to be active on two levels, whistling high above their heads and swirling down low.

"The bang definitely came from here," Tansy said, peering into the darkness of Woodruff Cottage.

Kevin swung the beam of his torchlight all around. Everything was as Zach and Robyn had left it. "Must have been from the Muellers'."

They trooped on again, heads down against the swirling wind and feet dragging in the streams of muck and water.

"Holy shit! Look at that!" Kevin said, aiming his torch beam on the roof of Muellers' cottage. The roots of a cypress tree, with clods of earth clinging to them, glistened in the light while the rest of the tree had toppled forward, embedding itself in the roof.

"That's what caused the big bang," Tansy said,

pointing to the chimneypot which lay in smithereens on the concrete path that ran around the side of the house. "At least no one's home. Their Hummer is gone and the lights are off. He must have decided to make for shelter after all. I hope to God they haven't gone to the hall."

"I saw him leaving," said Zach. "In fact he flew past myself and Robyn. Nearly mowed us down. He was driving like a lunatic." He frowned. "At the speed he was passing it was hard to see anything – but, come to think of it, I didn't see Mrs Mueller . . . She certainly wasn't in the passenger seat . . ."

"Surely you don't think he just drove off and left her here?" asked Kevin.

"You don't know him!" Tansy answered with such bitterness in her tone that Kevin looked askance at her until he was distracted by a gust of wind so strong it took their breath away. It whipped around the garden and whistled through the tree-tops. A shrill screech rang out, like an amplified scraping of chalk on a blackboard. It was followed by a bang as a loosened slate from the roof hit the ground near Kevin's feet. He jumped back and caught Tansy by the arm.

"We're getting out of here. Now!" he said. "There's no one in that house."

"What if Ute is still inside, locked in the cellar? We should look."

"Don't be silly, Tansy. What nonsense! People locked in cellars!"

Annoyed she freed her arm. "You save your own skin if you want. I'm going to see if that poor woman's alright."

Before they could stop her, Tansy had run as far as the

front door and started hammering on it, calling out to Mrs Mueller.

"I'll look after Tansy," Kevin said to Zach. "You get back to Robyn."

As Zach walked to the gate and listened to trees creaking, wind whistling, rain hammering, and the panicked voice of Tansy calling for Mrs Mueller, he remembered his suspicion that something had happened between Tansy and Horst Mueller. She seemed terrified of Horst and considered him capable of anything – even locking his wife in a cellar. Either Tansy was mad or Horst Mueller was bad. Since he knew Tansy to be eccentric but very sane, that left just one option. Yet, talk of wives locked up in cellars was extreme, even for Tansy.

He became aware of a new sound. Rhythmic. He sloshed his way across the track, following the noise to its source. At the edge of the track he looked down onto the strand, the area which was usually golden and for the past six weeks so hot that it had been uncomfortable to walk on barefoot. It was cloaked in darkness now but the noise, the whoosh and hiss, told Zach all he needed to know. The tide was already spilling over the sand. Not in playful little white-edged waves, but in big rolling swells of water.

Quickly he recrossed the track and called out to Tansy and Kevin: "We'll have to go! The tide is almost to the edge of the strand!"

Tansy hesitated. She still wasn't sure, not certain sure, that there was nobody in the Muellers' house. Yet what more could she do short of breaking in there? If she did that and Horst found out, he would not let go of her collar the next time until he had choked her to death.

Kevin stooped down beside her as she was shouting through the letterbox. "There's nobody in that house, Tansy. I promise."

She wanted to believe him. He held out his hand to her and she took it. His fingers entwined with hers. She felt a thrill run through her body. It was a nice feeling and one she had not experienced for a very long time. She smiled at him.

"I think you're right, Kevin. And if you help me to carry my cotton crop to the safety of upstairs, I'll leave them in my cottage. Deal?"

"You're a manipulator, Tansy Bingham, but yes, I'll go upstairs with you."

"In your dreams," Tansy said but the smile she gave him was saying something different.

Chapter 23

Except that the circumstances were so terrifying Robyn would have been laughing at the sight of Kevin Phillips sitting in the passenger seat of Tansy's car, Ben's cage on his knees, the scowl on his face daring anyone to mock his misfortune. Or rather the misfortune of his precious car. The Audi Cabriolet had given up the ghost – refused to start in the rain and wind.

"Water in the engine," Tansy had announced as if she knew about these things. "Get into my car, Kevin."

He had done as he was told, turning to catch a last glimpse of his abandoned car, a scarlet slash in the greyness of the day.

They travelled slowly along the coast road: Zach, Robyn and June leading in the Land Rover; Tansy, Kevin and Ben following in Tansy's car. The wipers on both vehicles struggled to clear the rain from the windscreens. As Zach approached the area where the gorse bushes had burned, a river of water ran off the smooth slope and across the road.

"Shit! Tansy will never get through this in her car. It's running straight off the hills."

"They can come with us if they have to, can't they?"

"It'll be a squash. We'd never fit Ben and all his gear as well as the two of them. I have a tow rope. Maybe I could pull her through it."

Zach stopped, put on his hazard warnings and waited for Tansy to catch up with him. His phone rang just as headlights appeared in his mirror. He handed the phone to Robyn, pulled up the hood of his coat and got out to talk to Tansy. Robyn pressed the answer button. It was Billy Moynihan.

"Where in the hell are ye? Ye should be in the hall now."

"We're on our way."

"Is June with you? How is she?"

"As well as can be expected."

June, who had appeared to be asleep in the back seat, snorted. "Tell Billy Moynihan he'd be well advised to look after himself."

"I heard that," said Billy. "It's good to know she's still as cross as ever. Where about are ye?"

"On the coast road."

"I'm ringing to warn ye about the bridge. The sergeant says the Aban is almost ready to overtop it. He'll be putting barricades up there shortly. The sooner ye cross it the better. Don't go near Lower Street or Middle Street either. Come up the other way by the library."

"Why? What's wrong in the village?"

"The bloody drains can't take this rain at all. The water is spouting out of them. And it's pouring down off the hills. My shop's a mess. Noel Cantillon's ground floor too. Good job he off-loaded so much stock onto us!"

June sat forward and tapped Robyn on the shoulder. "I must go to my house. I need to get some things."

"Tell her she can't. There's about a foot of water on the street."

Robyn conveyed Billy's message but June got even more agitated. "I really must go home. I'll walk through the water if I have to. There are things I must have. Pictures . . ."

She stopped talking then, tears choking her words. Robyn felt her own eyes well up. Of course June would want what photographs she had of her family. Her husband and her son. Photographs were all she had left.

Billy cleared his throat, reminding Robyn she was neglecting him.

"June will probably kill me but she left her door open today when she ran out. I went back to her house tonight and secured it for her."

"That's very kind of you, Billy. I'm sure she'll be grateful."

"She'll probably blow my ears off. I went around her house and took everything I could carry upstairs. There were a lot of photos of Des. I brought them up to the hall with me. Tell her they're safe. I won't be, though, when she finds out I was in her house without permission."

June leaned forward and tapped Robyn's shoulder again. "What's that? Why am I supposed to be grateful to him?"

"He brought your photos of Des to the hall. They're safe."

"Thank God," June muttered. She sat back and closed her eyes again.

Robyn decided to embellish the truth a little.

"She said thank you very much, Billy. We'll see you in about ten minutes. How are things in the hall? Are there many there?"

"Manageable. I think. See you soon."

When she turned off the phone, Robyn rolled down her window and shouted at Zach to hurry. He and Kevin were making heavy work of fixing the tow rope from the Land Rover to Tansy's car. When Zach sat back in, he asked who had rung.

"It was Billy Moynihan. The bridge will be closed soon and the village is already flooded. I'm getting pretty scared now, Zach."

"Don't worry – we'll soon be safe in the hall. We'll have to go up by the library though. If it's that bad I'll just leave the tow rope on Tansy's car in case we hit more floods."

Plough ahead was what they had to do, through streams of water, gusts that rocked the Land Rover and nearly capsized Tansy's car, past boulders which had been washed downhill and around branches which had snapped from trees. On the bridge they were buffeted by wind and almost deafened by the roar of the River Aban surging beneath them.

Sergeant Tim Halligan stood by his squad car at the village end of the bridge, blue light twirling and barricades at the ready to block off access. He held up his hand to stop them. Zach rolled down his window a crack, squinting against the rain and wind which forced its way into the Land Rover.

"Going to the hall?" Tim Halligan asked.

"Yes, Sergeant. Looks like our cottages could be flooded before the night is out."

"Don't go by the village."

"Billy Moynihan has already warned us."

"I'll see you in the hall later. By the way, have you seen any sign of your neighbour?"

"Who? Tansy? She's behind in –"

"No. Mrs Mueller. Her husband has been through here looking for her. Keep an eye out. He says she's not too well. Suffers from delusions or some such thing."

Zach hesitated. Should he talk to Tim Halligan about his suspicions of domestic abuse in the Mueller household? But then, if Ute did have mental problems, it was possible Horst was just helping her by guarding her privacy. Besides, now was not the time with the Aban ready to sweep the bridge away. He nodded to the sergeant.

"We saw Horst alright but no sign of her. We'll keep an eye out."

The sergeant waved them on.

"So that's why Horst Mueller nearly ploughed us down," Robyn said.

"Must be," Zach agreed. "Though if his wife has run away from him, she picked a hell of a night to do it. I hope she found shelter somewhere."

It was good to see the lights of the Community Hall as they approached. Zach sighed with relief as he pulled up outside the big double front doors. "You go inside, Robyn. Take June and Tansy with you. Kevin and I will bring in the luggage."

Robyn looked around the parking lot. It was fairly full but not as packed as she had expected it to be. As far as she could see, there was no sign of Horst Mueller's Hummer.

"Most people must have left Felton," she remarked.

"I should have too," June said from the back seat. "I should have taken my son and gone. Roscommon, Sligo, Leitrim. Timbuktu. Anywhere he would have been safe. I let him down so badly."

Robyn turned around and looked June in the eyes. "Don't ever say that again, June. You were the best mother to Des. You looked after his every need. There was nothing more you could have done for him."

"I could have kept him away from that little brat, Audrey. I could have been at home with him today instead of out looking after other people."

Zach took a breath and Robyn knew instinctively he was about to reassure June that her son might yet be alive and well, sheltering in an inlet, on an outcrop, making his way towards shore. She put her hand on his arm to stop him. June was heartbroken, yes, but naïve, no.

"We'd better get inside, June. Let Zach unload."

Robyn opened the passenger door. It was torn from her hand and almost from its hinges. Wind slapped against her, so strong that it almost stopped her breath. "Jesus! We were safer in the cottage. It's vicious here."

Zach jumped out and linked arms with both women. Heads down, June trying to tame her billowing sari, they made their way to the hall. They arrived at the same time as Tansy who was clutching Ben's cage in one hand and clinging onto Kevin with the other.

"Did you hear the river?" Tansy shouted over the wind. "Wasn't it fabulous? Such power!"

Tansy didn't see the bemused looks from the others in the dark but they wouldn't have bothered her anyway. She had been getting them all her life.

Billy Moynihan must have been on the lookout for them because he opened up the door, just enough for the women to slip through. Robyn barely had time to call a quick "Take care!" to Zach before the door was slammed by a gust.

She faced into the hall and stood staring in amazement. The open space they had left today was completely filled up now with chairs, bags, blankets, a parrot in a cage, dogs on leads, and groups of people, some with the blank glaze of shock in their eyes, others laughing and talking as if they were on a parish picnic. A card game was being played in one corner, an upturned milk crate acting as the card table. The centre space was taken up by the conference table, laden with ware, bottles of water, tea and coffee pots, plates of sandwiches and packets of biscuits. Noel Cantillon hovered over it, his eyes swivelling over his stock like the revolving beam of a lighthouse. He had obviously decided to stay here with his stock rather than go back to his now boarded-up shop.

"My God, Billy! How did you get that big table out of the conference room?" Tansy asked. "In fact I never figured out how you got it in there in the first place."

"We took it apart of course. Dr Early wanted the conference room as a makeshift medical centre."

All eyes, except those of Noel Cantillon and the card players, turned towards the new arrivals. Robyn noticed some people's gaze flit briefly to June and then slide away, as if they felt guilty about her son or else they could not bear the suffering so naked in her dark eyes and pale face. Others were not as sensitive. They stared at June, drawn as some are to tragedy.

A middle-aged woman got up from her chair and

headed towards them, her hand held out to June. "I'm so sorry about Des. He was always headstrong, wasn't he?"

Robot-like, June took the outstretched hand but said nothing.

"He'll be brought in on the tide," the woman added. "Soon now. The bay's no match for what's rolling in. And the sea wall? God help us all!"

Billy nodded his head in the direction of the conference room. "Take June in there," he whispered to Robyn. "She'll have more privacy. I'll look after things out here."

He caught the other woman's arm and turned her in the direction of the table. "Have you had a cup of tea, Hanna? Come on over to Noel. He'll look after you."

As Robyn led June towards the conference room, now medical centre, she heard Hanna protest that her bladder was about to burst from all the tea Noel Cantillon had forced on her already. Her voice was lost then in the murmur of conversation from the hall and the shriek of wind from outside. The rain too, hammered on the roof and windows. Robyn felt claustrophobic, as if the air was thickened by the sounds and was weighing down on her. Her breath almost stopped completely when she heard a woman scream above the din. She twirled around to see Tansy behind her, Ben held aloft in the cage and a big Golden Labrador lolloping towards her, lead trailing and the owner in pursuit.

"Take him away! Take him away!" Tansy was shouting while various different people made a grab for the dog's lead. No one managed to catch it though. The Labrador had sniffed a cat and was determined to investigate. Only Ben, regal in his cage, seemed unperturbed.

The door of the conference room opened and Dr

Early peered out to see what all the fuss was about. The Labrador had reached Tansy by now and was standing in front of her, sniffing the bottom of Ben's cage, its tail wagging. Tansy held the cage as high as she could with one hand while, like a traffic cop, she held her other hand with palm facing the dog. She looked petrified.

"Here, Swank! Good boy. Down." The owner, a man in his thirties Robyn had not seen around before, picked up his dog's lead and smiled at Tansy. "Sorry about that. She's very inquisitive."

Without saying anything and still holding Ben's carry-cage aloft, Tansy backed into the conference room. The man shrugged and then walked back down the hall with his dog.

"It's like Noah's Ark here," Dr Early remarked as June and Robyn followed Tansy in. He closed the door, shutting out the noise from the hall.

The room seemed huge without the monstrous table taking up most of the space. Dr Early had obviously been busy because one corner of the room was transformed into a mini-surgery with first-aid equipment and medication on a wall shelf and a couch covered by a white disposable sheet underneath. Tansy took another corner for herself and Ben. She was stooping down, cooing to Ben and telling him not to be afraid.

"The only frightened one is you," Robyn pointed out, glancing at Ben's smug face as he lapped up his mistress's attention.

June made her way over to stand in front of the doctor.

"Did you hear from the hospital, Dr Early?" she asked. "How is Audrey Quill?"

"She'll be fine. How about you? I can give you something to help you sleep."

"Don't you always say there are no pills for grief?"

"Agreed. But there are pills for sleep and that's what you need now. Why don't you lie down here?" he asked, patting the couch. "Robyn, would you get a glass of water from the hall, please?"

"Don't let that bloody dog in here," Tansy said as Robyn opened the door.

Standing half-in and half-out of the conference room, the din of the hall around her, watching June being helped up onto the couch by Dr Early, Tansy moping over Ben, Kevin and Zach crossing the hall floor laden down with bags, Robyn had a bird's eye view of what the next few hours would be like. Or however long it would take for Hurricane Kimi to wreak its havoc and move on. She shivered.

There was much fussing and organising in the conference room when Kevin and Zach brought the bags in.

"Ben and me are claiming this space," Tansy said as she put the cat's carrier up on a chair and piled the space underneath with his bowls and combs.

"Don't you think there's something wrong with this picture?" Kevin asked as he watched Tansy sitting on the floor while Ben had the chair.

"Nothing at all wrong except that I can't find the printouts we did. You know, the ones about the Maya. Did you bring them?"

Kevin walked over to her and tugged at the corners of pages peeping out from underneath her. "Sitting on a document is not usually the best way to read it."

Tansy gave him a playful slap on the arm as he sat down beside her and began leafing through the pages. Robyn looked at them and frowned. On top of all the noise here, she would have to suffer through watching Tansy and Kevin flirt like two teenagers. She turned away from them and began to search her own bag for her iPod. At least she wouldn't have to listen to them. She was wondering where Zach had disappeared to when the door opened and he backed in, dragging an armchair.

"Where did you get that?"

He grinned at her. "I spotted it in the kitchen. As far as I can see you are the only pregnant lady here so it's yours. Sit down, Rob."

Robyn was about to protest but then she changed her mind. Her back was aching and her ankles felt puffy too. She eased herself onto the chair and sank into the not very well-padded cushions. It was better than a hard chair anyway.

"No sign of the Muellers' 4x4 outside," Zach said. "I had a good look around the hall. Mrs Mueller's not here. Wherever she is I hope she's safe and warm."

Tansy's head lifted from the page she was reading.

"What do you mean, Zach? Either she's with Horst or he's left her back at the cottage. Why would she be here?"

Zach and Robyn exchanged looks. Sensing that Zach was hesitating, Tansy got up from her place on the floor and stood in front of him.

"Well? What is it? Tell me."

"The sergeant told us Horst is looking for his wife. Apparently he's reported her missing."

Tansy's eyes grew huge. "I knew it! That man is capable of anything. He did something awful to her."

"Come on now, Tans," Kevin said, joining her and putting his arm around her. "He's a bully but that doesn't mean he's a wife-murderer. That's what you're implying, isn't it?"

"Maybe she's gone to friends or relations," Robyn suggested. "Although I must admit I've never seen anyone calling to their house. That could be because of her condition. Horst told the sergeant she suffers from mental problems. Delusions."

"She must have been deluded to marry him!" Tansy said.

"Sssh! Could we be quiet for a little while?" Dr Early asked. "June is just going off to sleep now."

Robyn glanced over at the couch where June was stretched out. The poor woman looked more like she was falling into unconsciousness than sleep, as if her mind had taken more shock than it could handle. She had woken up this morning, a busy, contented mother of a teenager and she was now going to sleep, childless, guilty and alone. Poor June.

On tiptoe, Zach brought over a blanket and tucked it around his wife.

"Put your feet up, Robyn," Dr Early instructed. "Those ankles look swollen."

He poked about on the shelves and then came over carrying a blood-pressure monitor. "Roll up your sleeve. I just want to check."

Robyn instantly felt blood surge to her head and around her body. My God! Her blood pressure was high. He inflated the armband and Robyn held her breath, waiting for the hiss of deflation to start. A ringing phone disturbed her concentration and made June whimper in her sleep. Kevin turned quickly and grabbed his phone out of his coat pocket which he had draped across the back of Ben's chair.

"Yes, Gemma. What is it?"

The blood-pressure monitor had started beeping. Robyn examined Dr Early's face. It was noncommittal.

"Oh, damn!" Kevin said. "I knew that might happen. Have you rung the Fire Brigade?"

Dr Early opened the Velcro fastenings on the monitor armband and smiled at Robyn. "That's fine. Perfectly normal. Just sit back there and relax."

Kevin was now pacing around the room.

Tansy raised an eyebrow in Robyn's direction.

"Gemma Creedon, his PA in the *Daily News*." Robyn said softly. "Doesn't sound good."

"Did you explain to them how bad it is?" Kevin was asking, his voice rising. He listened for another minute then cut Gemma off. "Okay, okay, I get the picture. We've already had the thunderstorm and the cloudburst here. In fact, it's still raining as hard as ever so don't expect it to stop anytime soon. Get maintenance to shut everything down, then make sure all the staff have transport home. I'll get onto the Emergency Services myself. See if I can't hurry them up."

He held the phone out from his ear as Gemma replied. Robyn and Tansy exchanged amused glances. They couldn't decipher the exact words but Gemma's sharp tone carried into the room and it sounded angry.

"That's enough, Gemma," he said eventually. "You're right. I probably should have gone back to Dublin but no point talking about it now. What are our reporters sending in? Gemma? Gemma? Hello, Gemma?"

"I think she cut you off," Zach grinned.

Kevin threw him a dirty look and then keyed in his speed-dial number for his office. He listened for a second, examined his phone and redialled. "It's gone. I can't get through."

Tansy checked her phone and held it up to Kevin. "No reception bars. My network's down. The system has either been overloaded or hit by lightning."

"Or blown away," Robyn added.

Kevin flopped down beside Tansy and sighed. He was not a happy man. "The ground floor of the *Daily News* is floating in sewage. Gemma can't even get the Fire Brigade to come out. And now the bloody phones are down too."

Billy Moynihan put his head around the door and Kevin's face immediately lit up. "Billy, do you mind if I use the hall phone? There are problems in my office."

"What phone?" said Billy, coming in.

"Your landline. Is it still working? The mobile network is down."

Billy laughed in Kevin's face. "In the first place using a phone line in an electrical storm is inviting lightning to strike you. Secondly, as you were so quick to point out, this hall is just a little village community centre in the backwoods. You should have gone back to Dublin to look after your business and left us to ours."

"Probably makes no difference anyway," Zach said. "Landlines must be down too."

"There won't be anything left standing by the time this is over," Billy agreed. "Tim Halligan's outside. The bridge is officially closed off now. It's under water. There're stories too of mudslides on The 360."

Zach who had been sitting quietly on the arm of Robyn's chair, jumped up. "The 360? Up on Lynches' farm?"

"Yes. Isn't that the only 360 we have? Some of the hill farmers are making their way into the hall because the winds are so high up there. By the way, Zach, the sergeant wants to have a word with you outside in the hall. He's just having a cup of tea to warm him up before he takes off again."

Zach stroked Robyn's hair. "Why don't you close your eyes and have a rest, Rob? I'll be back in a sec."

She caught his hand and squeezed it, so happy that at least they were together here, uncomfortable as the hall was. And about to get a lot more uncomfortable by the look of things.

"What in the hell are you up to now?" Kevin asked in exasperation as he watched Tansy pick up Ben's litter tray.

"A man's got to do what a man's got to do," Tansy answered airily as she scooped Ben up under her arm from where he regarded them all with blue-eyed innocence. "I'm taking him to the bathroom. How can he do what's necessary with all of you watching him?"

Dr Early stood in front of Tansy and tut-tutted. "I'm sorry, Tansy, but this room is my surgery for now. I know it's not exactly a sterile area but I really can't have a cat here."

"This is not just any cat, Dr Early. It's Ben."

"I'm afraid he carries the same parasites as any other cat."

Tansy looked offended. "We'll make a deal so. I'll remove the litter tray. Keep it in the bathroom. But Ben stays. Over in this corner. Nowhere near your couch and medicines. How's that?"

"As long as you put him back into his cage if I have a patient and keep him strictly on your side of the room."

"Deal!"

Zach laughed as he and Billy went out to the hall to talk to the sergeant. Tansy always won her battles without ever appearing to fight.

Sergeant Tim Halligan looked as if he had been immersed in an ice-bath. His face was white, his nose purple-tinged, his eyes watery. He was standing by the table, his hands cradled around a cup of tea. It can't have been easy, just him and his new recruit evacuating the village and checking on outlying areas. Batman and Robin, as locals liked to call them – behind their backs of course. The sergeant wasn't known for his sense of humour. Noel Cantillon was bent towards him, whispering into his ear. As Zach and Billy approached, the sergeant looked up.

"Zach, I have a favour to ask. Did Billy tell you?"

"No, he didn't. What is it?"

The sergeant reluctantly unlaced his cold fingers from around the warm cup and put it on the table. Then he caught Zach by the elbow and walked him a few paces away, probably to be out of Noel Cantillon's earshot. "I'm worried about Seán Harte – you know, the new young garda who works with me. I sent him out to check on the more remote farms. Just to be sure there weren't any elderly on their own or people who wanted to come to the hall but had no transport. The last I heard from him, he had almost finished his rounds and was heading for Con Lynch's. I can't raise him on the radio. The radios are worse than useless. The emergency frequency is so overloaded at this stage that it's collapsing under the strain. The phones are gone too so I can't contact Con Lynch."

"How long ago since you heard from Seán?"

Tim pulled up his cuff to look at his watch. "Over an hour and a half. He was within minutes of Lynches' farm then. He would be back by now unless something has gone wrong."

Zach frowned. The journey from Lynches' shouldn't take more than twenty minutes, even in this weather. "Do you think he's just trying to get Con to move? He's pretty upset about Noreen as you can imagine. I tried to get him to come with me but he wouldn't budge. He can be very stubborn when he wants."

The sergeant shook his head and smiled. "Not Seán Harte. He's not one for sitting around chatting. He's just out of training. Still does everything by the book. Besides, he knew I was run off my feet here with the floods in the village and not a snowball's chance in hell of getting a Fire Brigade to pump it out. And the bridge had to be closed off too. He'd never stay arguing while all that work was waiting. He's a good lad. Did Billy tell you about The 360?"

"He mentioned a mudslide. Is that fact?"

As softly as they were speaking it was loud enough for Noel Cantillon to hear The 360 mentioned. He came scuttling over, so interested that he momentarily forgot to monitor his stock on the table.

"Like something you'd see on television in a foreign country," he said, crossing his arms and settling in for long conversation. "The Murtaghs were driving from their place when they saw it. They said it's like the entire hillside is just snaking down. Not fast, mind you. It's crawling but the rains are swelling it all the time."

Zach felt a cold chill run along his spine. Even allowing for almost certain exaggeration, there was a strong possibility that a river of mud was sliding down The 360 with nowhere to go except the valley near Lynches' farmhouse.

"You want me to go and check?" he asked the sergeant.

"Would you, Zach? Seán has the jeep otherwise I'd go up there myself. I know the squad car wouldn't make it in these conditions."

"No problem," Zach agreed and then instantly wondered just what he had volunteered himself for. He would have to leave Robyn and, even though Dr Early said she was fine, he wasn't sure. Apart from sharing the universal fear about the weather conditions, Robyn had late-stage pregnancy and her dislike of crowds to cope with. She loved her space, her time alone. Being crowded into the conference room with other people wouldn't suit her. And then there was the Kevin Phillips factor too. Zach looked at the sergeant and felt ashamed of his thoughts. The man was exhausted from working to help the population of Felton.

"Your own family, Tim? Are they safe?"

The sergeant crooked his thumb towards the back of the hall where the card game was being played. "They're having a whale of a time," he smiled. "I'll book them on my way out. This hall has no gambling licence."

"I'll just let Robyn know and then I'll head up to Lynches'. Where will you be?"

"I must check the Emergency Exit here and make sure there's an evacuation drill in place. Then I'm going to do a last tour of the village to make sure no one's marooned there. The coastguard lads are bringing a dinghy along because the flood is already too deep in the village to walk there. I thought Horst Mueller and his wife might be here but there's no sign of them. I'll keep an eye out for them too. I hope he found her. This is a dangerous night to be out."

"What about calling in outside help?"

The sergeant laughed and shrugged his shoulders. As soon as he had asked the question, Zach knew it was stupid. The last report he had seen on Tansy's TV before they left her cottage had shown a country in chaos. Lashed by unprecedented falls of rain, shaken by thunderstorms, blown by increasingly strong winds, Ireland and its unprepared emergency services were in turmoil. And as Tim had pointed out, the worst was yet to come.

Tim held his hand out and shook Zach's.

"Thanks, Zach. And take care. Now, Noel, where's my cup of tea gone?"

Zach watched them walk back to the table and wondered what he was going to tell Robyn. A peal of thunder shook the hall. That's all they needed – another thunderstorm. He made up his mind then. This was a night when nothing but the truth would do. He would tell Robyn he was going back to Con Lynch's farm. No excuses. No lies. And then maybe, just maybe, Robyn might be honest with him too.

Chapter 24

As Zach bumped and skidded his way over ruts and through torrents of water, he couldn't get the image of Robyn's wan face out of his mind. He saw it reflected on the windscreen between the sweeping wipers and wavering in the twin beams of the headlights. She had not asked him to stay. She was too unselfish to do that. But he had felt her fear.

"Don't put yourself in danger, Zach. I know you want to help but turn back if it looks dangerous. Promise?"

He had promised her. Then he had asked Dr Early to keep a discreet eye on her. She would be furious if she knew she was being monitored.

He reached the entrance to Lynches' farmland. High up in one of the old oaks a piece of the yellow tape which had cordoned off the farm had wound around a branch and was flapping wildly in the wind. Zach shook his head at the surrealism of it all. The Bluetongue Virus drama seemed like a lifetime ago. The gate lay on the ground, torn off its hinges. At least he wouldn't have to get out to open it and be soaked again. The new thunderstorm was even more dynamic than the first. Fork lightning danced and the thunder was so loud it rang in his ears even after the rumble had stopped.

As he crested the hill and began the descent into the valley, he kept his eyes peeled for any sign of the Garda jeep. Beneath him he saw light shining from Lynches' kitchen. Overflowing ditches on the decline spilled their muddy contents down towards Con's backyard. When Zach parked near the back door and stepped out, the fast-flowing water washed halfway up his Wellingtons. Standing for one second to get his bearings in the wet and dark, he was mesmerised by the movement of the water as it coursed over the yard where Noreen Lynch's hearse had so recently stood. Debris borne along on the sweeping current was being deposited at the sides of the yard. A collection of twigs, stones, a battered plastic bottle and mud were heaped up at the base of the door. The curtain on the kitchen window twitched and Con's face appeared. Zach signalled to him that he would go around to the front of the house but almost immediately he heard the inside lock on the back door being released. He wondered if it was just a Felton quirk that none of the farmers ever seemed to use their front doors. In fact, as he thought about it now, he realised he had never actually seen the front of Lynches' house. Con opened up the door. The heap of muddy debris oozed into the kitchen. Zach dived in and, kicking with his Wellingtons, removed enough of the rubbish to quickly close the door.

"Jesus, mercy!" Con said, staring at the slimy mess on the floor and the pool of water he had not seen until now. "I've never, ever, seen that backyard flood before.

Come in, lad, and get yourself warm. What are you doing out in this weather? Why aren't you with your wife?"

"Robyn's in the hall. She's fine," Zach said as he followed the old man into the kitchen. They both sat down in front of the range and held their hands out to the heat. The glow from the embers made the puffy bags beneath Con's eyes seem darker and the lids look more red and swollen.

"Did Seán Harte call on you, Con? You know, the young guard."

"No. I didn't see anyone since you left. Sure you wouldn't put a cat out in this let alone go visiting. Anyway, what would the Gardaí be calling on me for?"

Zach hesitated. Con was a shadow of the wiry, vigorous man he had been a week ago. The old man now appeared so vulnerable that it seemed cruel to add to his worries but he would have to realise how serious the weather conditions were.

"Seán Harte came here to warn you, Con. This hurricane is like nothing we ever experienced before. You'd be safer in the Community Hall. At least that was Seán's intention. He radioed almost two hours ago that he was going to call on you but he hasn't arrived back in the village. The sergeant is concerned."

"Tim Halligan? He's always concerned with other people's business."

"That's his job. So you didn't see Seán at all?"

"No. I told you. Is that what brought you all the way up here in the wind and rain or is there something else?"

Zach took a deep breath. He would have to tell Con the truth just as he had to tell Robyn that he was going out in the storm again even though he knew she didn't want him to.

"There are reports of a mudslide off The 360."

Zach had expected shock, disbelief or even scepticism. Instead Con nodded his head as if he already knew.

"Who told you, Con? I thought you said nobody called. You weren't up there, were you?"

"Don't be daft! Of course I wasn't up there. I'm not surprised about the mudslide though because that hill was once a copper mine. Way back when my great-great-grandfather was a lad. Under the topsoil it's full of shafts and tunnels."

Zach was stunned at the idea that The 360 was just a big Swiss cheese. If Con was right, and there was no reason to doubt him, when the topsoil washed off, the shafts would fill up with water and then maybe the whole hill would collapse.

"You'll have to come back to the hall with me, Con. Your house is right under The 360."

"And where do you think the hall is? You've stood on top of that hill with me often enough. What can you see from there?"

Zach felt cold. Deathly cold. He remembered standing on top of the hill only yesterday, feeling relieved to have escaped the farmhouse and the enforced company of the Department officials, desperate that he might have contracted a human form of Bluetongue Virus. He had looked down on Felton and thought how fragile it seemed, skirting as it did the shallow bay. He knew now from watching weather alerts that the bay was more vulnerable to tidal surges because of its shallowness. He remembered too looking down at the back of the hall, thinking that

Robyn was in there. As she was at this minute. Desperate, he squeezed his eyes shut and pictured the scene again. He smiled and opened his eyes.

"The hall is raised, Con. It's up on Lookout Hill. Even if the sludge or mud or whatever it is flows down from The 360, it can hardly climb Lookout can it?"

Con gave a noncommittal grunt.

"It would flow behind Lookout, down the back road by the library. I know it would."

"Maybe it wouldn't flow in that direction at all. It might just come from this side, right down the valley and in my back door."

Zach nodded, satisfied that Con understood. "You must come back to the hall with me."

The old man glanced around his kitchen, from the pool of muddy water at the back door to Noreen's ware gleaming on the dresser. There was panic in his eyes. As if he was being torn away from Noreen all over again.

"How sure are you about the mudslide? You realise what the gossips are like. They see a trickle and they cry torrent."

Zach stood. Con was right. "I'm going out to check. I must look around too and see if there's any sign of Seán Harte and the Garda jeep. Maybe he got stuck in a flood."

Con levered himself up out of his chair. "Wait until I get my coat and boots."

"No! Stay here. I'll call back for you."

Thunder rolled down the valley so loud that Zach thought he saw the ware on the dresser shake.

"You think I'd let you go out in that on your own, lad?"

Zach knew the look in Con's eyes. It was determination.

He sat and waited for him to get ready as thunder crashed, water seeped in the back door and the wind shrieked loud and angry around the house. He thought about Robyn and how she must be feeling now. Probably afraid of the thunder, worried about him, confused about Kevin Phillips. Zach put his head in his hands and wished for blue skies, warm breezes and the undivided love of his wife. It was, indeed, a night for truth.

Despite the sergeant's warning, Horst had gone into the village. He had parked his Hummer on the high ground near the library and waded through the mean and pathetic length and breadth of Felton. Houses were boarded up. In darkness. He scaled gates and searched back gardens, peered in windows and checked porches. There was no sign of Ute.

He sat back into his car and tried to calm himself. Being outsmarted by Ute was such a shock he wasn't thinking straight. He banged the steering wheel and felt better.

He had made a mistake crossing the bridge. He had noticed that she was missing very quickly. She couldn't have gone far from the house. Not in these violent gusts and the torrential rain. If he hadn't been in such a temper he would have figured that out. Too late. There was no going back because the bridge was impassable. He had no access to the Coast Road or the cottage now.

Then, as he sat there fuming, it all became clear to him. Ute had run to one of the neighbours. Not the vet. He had seen him and his wife on the road. To the Bingham bitch. He smiled. Now he knew where to find his wife. And when he'd finished with her, he would deal with Tansy Bingham. He started the Hummer and turned it in the direction of the hall.

Robyn was trying to sleep because she had promised Zach she would. But her thoughts would not rest. Tansy and Kevin were distracting her. She couldn't drag her eyes away from them. They were both sitting on the floor, a blanket over their knees, Ben snuggled up on Kevin's lap, pages of printouts in their hands. They were engrossed in their reading, Kevin absent-mindedly stroking Ben's silky white coat. There was no doubt about it. This floor-dwelling, cat-stroking Kevin was a different man to the one he had been. When had he changed? When he had said goodbye to Robyn or when he had said hello to Tansy?

Annoyed and perplexed by her thoughts, Robyn stood up and arched her back. It was aching. She needed to walk. On tiptoe she went over to the couch and looked down at June sleeping. Curled up on her side, she had her arms folded protectively around herself. She seemed undisturbed by the rumble of thunder and the constant visits of Billy Moynihan to check on her. He popped in again now and stood beside Robyn, looking down on June.

"How is she?" he whispered.

"Sleeping. That's the best thing for her," Dr Early answered. "Sleep heals."

Robyn nodded but kept her own counsel. She knew there was not a sleep deep enough or long enough to heal the wound left by the loss of a child. Dr Early most likely did too. Satisfied, Billy scooted back to the hall again muttering about batteries and torches.

"You're right about the winter solstice in 2012," Kevin said, looking up from his page, smiling in a very intimate way at Tansy, as if the Maya and winter solstices were secrets only they shared.

"Told you! It's all confirmed by modern technology." She leafed through her pages and then pulled one out and handed it to Kevin. "Look, it says here the Maya even allowed in their calculations for the Earth wobbling on its axis long before there were instruments to observe or measure it."

Dr Early raised an eyebrow.

"Tansy thinks the world is going to end on December 21st 2012," Robyn explained, hoping the inexplicable jealousy she felt was not echoed in her voice.

"The Maya predicted it, not me," Tansy corrected her. "And you still have it wrong. They didn't say it would end, just change."

Kevin pushed even closer to Tansy and looked into her face. Feigning interest in superstitious hearsay. He must be. He was the most logical, if not sceptical, man in the world.

"So what do you think, Tansy? How will Earth change? Will it be a new energy source?"

Tansy frowned and did that annoying thing of twisting a lock of her shiny black hair around her finger. "Teleporting," she announced. "That's what it'll be. You want to go to New York. Think Times Square, blink, and you're there!"

Dr Early chuckled. "I like it, Tansy. Think, blink, and you're there. I'd teleport to New Zealand. My brother lives on the South Island. No sitting for endless hours in airports or trying to cram your feet into elasticised travel socks."

"I wonder how the powers-that-be would handle teleporting security?" Kevin asked.

Tansy gave him an elbow into the ribs. "Think change here, Kevin. There'll be no need for security because the post 2012 world will hold no threats."

"Really? So no terrorists, no ideological differences? No scarce resources?"

Forehead puckered, Tansy thought for a moment. Kevin was watching her and Robyn was convinced she saw genuine interest on his face. Maybe the world had already begun to change.

"The biggest change I believe will be in communication." Tansy nodded and then, apparently happy with her idea, she elaborated. "All arguments, and by extension all wars, are caused by lack of communication. If people communicated with each other, they wouldn't be so quick to fight. No matter how wide the differences or divergent the beliefs, sharing ideas, learning to understand the other point of view is possible."

"You mean if they *listened* to each other," Robyn pointed out. "Talking is easy. The listening isn't always."

Kevin turned towards her and narrowed his eyes. He must be remembering, as she was, the number of times she had accused him of not listening.

"Exactly!" Tansy agreed enthusiastically. "So that's why there'll be no more talk. We'll read each other's minds. No lies, no deception. No surprises. We'll just tune into each other's wavelengths and know. Yes, I think that must be the really big change the Maya prophesied."

Enjoying the flights of fancy, Dr Early laughed. "The first mind I'd like to read is yours, Tansy. It should be interesting. Then I'll take a peek inside my wife's head. It would be a relief to understand her at last."

"How about you, Tans?" Kevin asked. "Whose mind would you like to read?"

Robyn almost laughed out loud. Tans? Kev and Tans. They were like kindergarten playmates.

Tansy scooped Ben up in her arms. "Ben's of course. I'd love to know what he thinks of us all. Me especially."

"That's obvious. He thinks you're his slave. In fact he knows you are."

Tansy shrugged. "That's fine by me." She nodded her head in June's direction and then lowered her voice. "If we had that capability, I mean if we could really tune into each other's minds, and if we truly believed the mind or spirit doesn't end when physical life does, then we'd never need to say goodbye."

They were each silent, watching June relax into the escape of her drugged sleep. For an unguarded instant Robyn wanted to believe in Tansy's mad theory. How much would it mean to June to be able to communicate with Des? To know that he was happy and safe, maybe with his father in – in – where? Heaven? Another Galaxy? Or suppose she could communicate with Zach now? Confess that she'd been distracted by Kevin and the memories of what they had shared but that she loved only Zach. And you too, baby, she thought as the ache in her lower back reminded her it was there and getting bigger every day.

"Anyone like a cup of tea?" she asked. "I need to stretch my legs so I'm going out to the hall."

"Me too," Tansy said just as the door opened and two men came in, one with a big gash on his forehead and the other holding up an injured arm.

Dr Early brought his two patients over to the corner and sat them down.

"Been in the wars?" he asked. "That's a nasty gash you have there."

"We're lucky to be alive. 'Tis the most savage weather we've ever seen. We came down from our homeplace because the wind was so bad there."

"Where's that?" Robyn asked.

"Beyond the Wilcox farm. We're on the hillside, facing the sea. No protection at all. Mountains of water are rolling into the bay now. The rain is horizontal, the wind is so strong. And the lightning! It's non-stop. A tree fell on top of our Land Rover on the way here. We were lucky the roof didn't cave in on top of us."

Robyn got a sick feeling in her stomach. Horizontal rain. Non-stop lightning. Zach gone up to Con Lynch's farm. And their home! What about Woodruff Cottage?

"You're going to need a few stitches in that cut," Dr Early said to the man with the head wound.

Robyn walked quickly to the door. Tansy had put Ben into his cage, as she had promised Dr Early she would, and now she followed Robyn in hot pursuit. Kevin, looking slightly green about the gills, unwound himself from his position on the floor and then bolted for the door.

"Coward," Robyn said to him as he joined them in the hall.

He grinned at her. "Can't deny it. You saw me pass out the time I tried to do my civic duty and donate blood."

"Wuss."

"I 'spose I am but I'm a thirsty wuss. Let's get coffee. I want to ask around too. Maybe someone in the hall has a cell-phone network still working. I really need to contact the office. And Lisa."

Robyn noted the order of his priorities. First he must try to contact his office, then his wife. His mistress, when he had one, had always come third on that list.

As they walked towards the table Robyn looked around her. Conversation was all but stopped now. The floor was littered with sleeping bags and blankets but only children slept. The adults were awake and wary, many crossing themselves at each peal of thunder. Tansy put her hands up to her ears.

"I knew there was thunder but I had no idea it was so bad. The conference room must be very well insulated."

The thunder was coming from directly overhead as if it had aimed at the hall and hit the target. Rain was pelting onto the tile roof and the wind drove against the front of the building in blasts straight off the sea. Robyn looked up towards the row of small windows high up on the walls. Rain washed down the glass, lit by repeated flashes of lightning. Her hands tightened over her baby, wishing that Zach was back in the comparative safety of the hall. "Daddy will be fine, Daddy is safe," she whispered, in the belief that saying it would make it true. She started when she realised Kevin was staring at her.

"Ah! The final sign that you've lost it, Robyn. You're talking to yourself."

"I was talking to my baby, actually. Not that I'd expect you to understand that."

The background noise seemed to fade, even the thunder lull, as Robyn and Kevin stood face to face, undisguised emotion on each face. He was angry. Very angry. She was sad. And so confused. Why in the hell had she said that to him? To hurt him? To rake up the countless arguments they'd had about his refusal to father a baby? It was as if time had rolled back and they were again in Paris, Berlin, London – all the places they had gone to steal some time together away from prying eyes.

"Come on, guys," Tansy said. "I'm doing some mind-reading here and it's not – oh!"

Her sentence ended in a yelp as the lights began to flicker.

"Shit!" Noel Cantillon muttered as he dived underneath the table and came back up holding a torch.

Thunder pealed again and the hall was plunged into darkness, lit only by the intermittent flashes of lightning which appeared at this stage to be both sheet and fork and the eerie glow from the Emergency Exit sign. A gasp of panic went around the hall and a child whimpered.

"See now why this hall needs a generator," Kevin said. "We're scuppered without one."

Still trying to accustom her eyes to the dark, Robyn reached out and grabbed Tansy's arm. Noel Cantillon switched on his torch and beamed it over the table.

"I think there's a chocolate digestive missing, Noel. In fact I'm sure," Kevin said as he bit into a biscuit.

Tansy giggled. Robyn smiled and felt the tension of a moment ago fade to be replaced by fear. She felt trapped here in the darkness of the hall, afraid to move in case she tripped over someone on the floor, terrified that Zach would not be able to get back from Con Lynch's, cringing from the violence of the wind blasts and thunder claps.

"Do you think the hall can stand up to this battering?" she asked Tansy.

"Better than our cottages anyway. We're safe from the sea here. Don't worry."

Kevin slipped his arm around Robyn and pulled her close to him. "Relax. We'll be fine. And Zach will be back soon."

"You know that?"

Torch lights began to flicker into life around the hall.

"Don't anyone move until I give them a light!" Billy Moynihan shouted at the top of his lungs, as he went around the groups handing out torches from a big cardboard box. He could have spared his breath. Everyone was immobilised by fear.

The wind seemed louder, the rain more persistent, the night more terrifying. Plunged into darkness, the people in the hall now realised that the dangers they could not see were the most threatening of all.

Ten minutes before, Horst had found a parking space at the back of the hall and pulled in. He sat there in his wet clothes, shivering, more with temper than with cold. God damn Ute! She'd pay for this when he found her.

He took deep breaths to calm himself. He had big decisions to make. Vital ones. The first question was who was Ute with. She could not be alone. She was incapable of acting independently. More importantly, he needed to know what she had said. Before tonight he would have sworn she would never talk about their business but he would also have been certain that she would not have run away. She never would have either, except that he had been so preoccupied by Tansy Bingham and her ugly cat. In fact this whole mess was Bingham's fault.

His breathing was ragged and sweat broke out on his

forehead. "Enough, Horst," he said aloud. "Concentrate!"

The sound of his own voice brought his focus back to the job in hand. He had to go into the hall, where he was now certain Ute was hiding from him, and get her back. But he would have to be very careful. He had done some of the groundwork already by telling the Keystone Cop that Ute suffered from delusions. There was his dilemma. Should he go up to the door of the hall, knock on it and ask for his wife? Play the concerned husband? Would the sergeant have spread the word that Mrs Mueller was insane? Or would Ute at this very minute be whispering into her new friends' ears, telling them things that were none of their business?

His shivering returned now, more violent than before. For an instant he imagined himself standing in front of his boss, trying to explain this disaster away. Despite the cold, sweat peppered his forehead. He had to find Ute and shut her up. Whatever it took.

Pulling up his hood, he got out of his car and walked around the side of the building, passing the Emergency Exit on the way. He stopped and examined the door. It was locked from the inside. No way in there. When he reached the front of the hall he stood looking at the ugly building. The windows were small and high up. No way in there either. The front door seemed the only possibility of entry. Just as he was about to approach the door, the sky crackled in a frenzy of lightning. Thunder boomed almost immediately. The lights in the small, ugly windows flickered and died.

Horst smiled. The elements were on his side. He could search for Ute now under cover of darkness. No need for him to play any part.

His smile broadened as a lorry pulled into the parking lot. A family, mother, father and two children scrambled from the cab, raced towards the front door and hammered on it, shouting to be let in. Horst stood behind them, ready to slip into the darkness of the hall as soon as the door opened. All he had to do then was find Ute, grab her and run. And he would succeed. Of that he was sure.

When the frantic hammering started on the front door nobody moved. The banging got more frenetic. *"Let us in! Let us in!"* The words were barely audible above the noise of the wind and rain. Billy Moynihan dropped his box and with his torch lighting the way, headed for the door.

Robyn tugged on Tansy's sleeve. "Did you recognise that voice?"

"I barely heard it. Why? Did you?"

"No, but it could have been the young garda. Or maybe even Zach. I'm going to see."

"You'll do no such thing!" Tansy said. "Do you want to fall over in the dark? Stand here. I'll go."

Picking up her torch, Tansy moved off in the direction of the front door. More acclimatised to the darkness now, she made her way easily enough through the people and luggage, helped by the torches and the lightning flashes. By the time she got to the door, a whole family was milling inside the entrance, the children terrified.

Robyn had been wrong. It had not been the young garda or Zach shouting to be let in. Tansy recognised PJ Kelly, the coalman, and his family as they peeled off their sopping coats and hats.

Just as she was about to turn back into the hall a movement caught her eye. Someone slipped out from behind the drenched Kelly family and quickly eased themselves into the shadows on the right-hand side of the hall. Tansy aimed her torch in that direction and saw a door swing shut. It was the Gents'. She could hardly go in there. But she must. Or she must get someone else to go in for her because whoever had slipped in there had been wearing a parka. Of that she was sure.

Billy Moynihan would know. Tansy went over to him.

"Did someone else come in with the Kellys?" she asked.

Billy, busy bolting the door again, didn't turn around to answer. "Yes, a man came in. Don't know who it was though. Why?"

"Was he wearing a parka?"

"Isn't everyone? Stop gabbing and give me a hand to put these blankets against the bottom of the door. The gale's coming in. Rain too."

Tansy persisted. "Are you sure there wasn't a woman with him?"

Annoyed now, Billy turned around to Tansy. "I said he was alone. If you want to know anything more about him, go ask him. He's around here somewhere. Someone should get him dry clothes and a warm drink."

Tansy turned away from Billy and headed back to the centre of the hall where she had left Robyn and Kevin standing by the table. She caught them both by the arms and dragged them out of Noel Cantillon's earshot.

"I'm sorry, Rob. That wasn't Zach at the door. It was PJ Kelly the coalman and his family. And I'm certain that Horst Mueller came in behind them. He was sort of using them as a shield, as if he wanted to sneak in here without being noticed."

"Are you sure it was him?"

Tansy frowned. "He was wearing a parka like Horst does and he was roughly his height . . . it was dark of course but I'm fairly sure . . ."

"What is it with you and Horst Mueller, Tansy?" Kevin asked. "Do you not think you're a bit obsessive about him?"

"I've good reason to be wary of him. I'm not neurotic, if that's what you're hinting."

Robyn noticed Tansy begin to shake. "Are you alright, Tansy? What's wrong?"

Looking around to make sure they would not be overheard, Tansy spoke so softly to Kevin and Robyn that they had to lean close to her in order to hear.

"Horst Mueller threatened me. Told me to stay away from his house and mind my own business. He pulled the collar of my coat so tightly around my neck that he almost strangled me. And he said if I told anyone he'd make sure I wouldn't talk any more."

Robyn reached for both Tansy's hands and held them tightly.

"When did this happen, Tansy? Where?"

"Today when Ben got stuck up the tree. I was waiting for Zach to bring the ladder. That's why I was so upset when I came back. It wasn't just Ben I was crying over."

Kevin gave an angry snort. "Why didn't you say earlier what Mueller had done to you? He deserves a good thumping."

"I was afraid to say anything, wasn't I? I'm still not sure if I should have. Suppose he finds out and comes after me? And now maybe he's in this hall."

"What about Ute?" Robyn asked. "Was there a woman with the man you saw come in?"

"Not that I saw. I just caught a glimpse of someone in a parka slipping out from behind the Kellys and going into the Gents' – so I guess no, he couldn't have had a woman with him . . ."

Robyn frowned. If the parka-wearing shadowy figure was Horst, then where was his wife? Hopefully not out in this weather.

"Well, we can sort that out fairly quickly," Kevin said. "I'll go to check now. If he's there I'll find him. Then we'll see how brave the shit is!"

Tansy grabbed him by the arm. "I could be wrong. Maybe that wasn't Horst at all. Loads of people wear parkas."

Kevin caught both women firmly by the elbows. "Come on. You're going back to the conference room. Then I'm coming back out to find Horst Mueller."

"No, Kevin! I don't want him to know I told anyone. No, please!"

People were beginning to look in their direction. Tansy hung her head. Kevin wrapped his arms around her. He stroked her hair as she wept on his shoulder and Robyn tried not to watch. His voice was soft as he crooned to Tansy like you would to an upset child.

"Don't worry, Tans. I won't let anything happen to you. We'll go to the conference room. You'll be safe there. When the sergeant comes back, we'll tell him. Let the Gardaí handle it. In the meantime, I'll ask Billy to keep an eye out. Tell us if he finds him. Just neighbourly concern. Okay?"

Tansy sniffled and then nodded her agreement. The

three of them threaded their way back to the conference room.

Horst Mueller sat further back into his dark corner and glared out into the hall. People and their torches were crowded together towards the centre. Like a herd of animals they congregated, leaving the perimeter of the hall just the way Horst liked it – dark and uncrowded. The Bingham bitch shouldn't have shone her torch in his direction when he came in. She probably hadn't seen him but he had to assume she had and so leave the shelter of the Gents' quickly in case she came nosing around there. It had been easy to slip along the hall, staying in the black shadow. He had watched Bingham talk to the pregnant woman and the newspaper man who might be her boyfriend. He had warned her to keep her mouth shut. Bingham was trouble. Of that he was sure. Only for her Ute would be where she was supposed to be. Doing the job she was well paid to do.

He lowered the hood of his parka and reached into the pocket for his glasses. How inquisitive these little people with their little lives were. The world would be better if Hurricane Kimi wiped Felton off the map.

Horst's breathing got faster as his anger grew. Ute might now be just feet from him, looking all delicate and pathetic wrapped up in a cosy blanket – spilling her guts. Talking about their business. Telling some idiot about their lives. Things that had nothing to do with anyone but Horst and the people he worked for.

His shivering got more intense but it was fear that rattled his teeth now. He gritted them to stop the chattering. He must find Ute. She could not have stayed out in the maelstrom of wind and rain. Had she approached someone and asked for shelter? Had that person brought her to the hall or had she, like him, slipped in without speaking to anyone? She had an animal cunning when it came to survival.

Slowly, quietly, Horst began to edge his way out of his corner. If Ute was here, he would find her. Then, with exquisite pleasure he would punish her disobedience. When he was finished with Ute, he would show the Bingham bitch how Horst Mueller dealt with interfering busybodies.

Chapter 25

Zach's boot squelched as he pulled upward and released it from the soggy ground. With each step he was sinking deeper and finding it more difficult to move forward. He glanced at Con beside him and wondered at the strength and determination of the wiry little man. Standing still, he looked back towards where he had parked. Aiming the torch in that direction he was stunned to pick out the Land Rover, rocking in the wind and only a hundred yards away. It seemed impossible that they had spent so much energy and progressed so little.

They were crossing the meadow near Lynch's house. The one with a circle flattened by the whirling rotors of the helicopter which had taken Noreen away and then delivered her back again – dead. Their first plan had been to drive across it to the base of the hill but seeing the soft condition of the ground they had decided to go on foot.

"Maybe I should go back and get the tractor," Con suggested.

In front of them, the hill rose gently, dipped and then climbed towards The 360. To their left the ground fell away to the floor of the valley from where the River Aban wound its way into Felton. From the safety of the kitchen it had seemed like a manageable task to climb the slope and investigate the rumour of a mudslide. As Zach looked around him now, struggling to stay upright with the force of the wind, rain so driven that it was needling his face and lightning chasing his every step, he knew that going on would be foolish. Worse. Suicidal. He remembered too his promise to Robyn that he would not put himself in danger. Even though Con was beside him now, Zach had to cup his hands around his mouth and shout.

"It's too dangerous whether we have the tractor or not. We'd better turn back."

"You're right, lad. We'd be blown off that hillside. Anyway I can't see any sign of mud walls creeping down the hill, can you?"

Zach squinted into the darkness ahead, his eyes flicking along the slope when lightning illuminated it. He could discern nothing more than sheets of rain. Here and there rowan trees and gorse bushes were highlighted, bent low to the ground as if they were paying homage to the wind.

"We should go," Con said, nodding his head in the direction of the river. "That sounds bad."

Zach listened carefully, his ears less attuned to the sounds of nature than the old man's. He heard it then. A noise deeper than the wind, more constant than the thunder. The hiss and boom of the river. The Aban, so recently reduced to a trickle, was coursing through the valley – the place where he had first seen the sheep infected with Bluetongue Virus.

"At least that's the end of the little feckers," Con said and Zach knew he was talking about the midges.

"The sergeant closed off the bridge on the coast road. Judging by the sound of that river, the bridge could be swept away by now."

They turned to trudge their way back to the Land Rover.

"The lights! They're gone!"

Con raised his head to look where Zach was pointing. The farmhouse was in darkness. Con turned all round, knowing exactly where he should be seeing lights from other homesteads. They were engulfed in blackness.

"Holy shit!"

"Exactly," Zach agreed. "I hope they've plenty of torches in the hall. Robyn will be in a panic."

When they got into the Land Rover, Zach poked around looking for a towel he knew was somewhere in the back. When he found it, it felt cold and damp but at least it mopped some of the rain from their faces.

"Drive," Con ordered. "And don't stop until you get to the hall. If we can reach it now."

Zach hesitated. "What about Seán Harte? There was no sign of him on the road when I was coming up here. What other way could he have approached your house? Tim Halligan said he was only a few minutes from here when he radioed. There's a byroad that runs up to the front of the house, isn't there?"

"Agh, that lane hasn't been used in years! If you know the terrain, there are loads of different ways to get here. You can go cross-country in a four-wheel-drive. He has one, hasn't he?"

"Yes. The Garda jeep. But he's new here. How would he know those ways? I don't."

"Someone told him, of course. If he was out in the outlying farms they probably showed him some shortcuts."

Zach peered out through the windscreen and shivered. If Seán Harte had decided to drive up hill and down dale in an area he didn't know, then he could certainly be in big trouble now. A new note, a high-pitched scream in the wind, told Zach they were all in trouble. Not just Seán Harte. Kimi was here and Felton could do nothing but lie down under its might.

He turned the ignition key. Nothing happened. Taking a deep breath, he turned it again. Nothing happened. He tried to think calmly. What could be wrong? Battery. It had to be. The Land Rover would probably start with a push but how in the hell could they manage that with bog underfoot and a hurricane blowing around them?

"Forget it. No time for fidgeting," Con said, already opening his door. "We'll get the tractor. If the rain running into the yard is anything to go by we'll need it."

Zach agreed. The ditches had been full when he was driving up here. It beggared belief but the rain had got even stronger since. They plodded along side by side in silence, heads down, boots sloshing through the fast-flowing groundwater. Con tripped and almost lost his footing.

"What the fuck!"

Zach shone his torch at Con's feet. A sheep stared up at them through open, dead, eyes.

"At least it's not one of mine," Con said bitterly. "The Bluetongue saved my stock from drowning."

When they reached the yard, Con headed towards the

barn to get the tractor.

"I'll just run around to the front of the house. Check to see if there's any sign of Seán Harte on that road!" Zach called.

The lightning had stopped its incessant flashing. It was pitch black as Zach walked past the side of the house and opened the low gate into the front garden. He shone his torch around and saw Noreen's creative hand in the flower-beds and shrubs on the lawn. His torchlight picked out the front door. It was a timber door, painted green, and had a brass knocker. A very shiny knocker, most likely because no one had ever dulled it by use.

Another gate led out to the byroad which ended in a cul-de-sac a little beyond the left side of the house. Zach walked out there and knew Con was telling the truth when he said it was rarely travelled. Grass grew high through the broken tarmacadam in the centre of the road and the ditches on either side were completely overgrown. Turning right he walked a few minutes before coming to a sharp bend. He heard a throbbing in the wind and knew it was the engine of the tractor revving. Con would be another while getting the tractor out and then locking up the barn. Enough time to check around the corner just to be sure Seán Harte wasn't on the road, maybe trying to fix a puncture or, like Zach, with his car broken down. After that, there was nothing more he could do to find the young garda. He had to get back to Robyn. She must be really fretting by now.

As he walked through the inky blackness he tried to figure out what this road would look like in daylight. He knew there was a small wood somewhere in the vicinity.

Sure enough, when he rounded the corner, he heard the whine of wind through tree-tops and the creaks and groans as branches bent under the weight of wind and rain. He flashed his torch down along the road. Nothing except more overgrowth and broken tarmacadam. It had been stupid to look for Seán Harte here. The Garda jeep would barely fit on this laneway.

When Zach turned towards the house the wind was to his back. He smiled ruefully. He could take advantage of that. What was the wind speed now? 120 miles per hour? Maybe he could fly if he . . .

Zach was still smiling as the tree crashed on top of him.

Chapter 26

The gashed forehead was neatly stitched, the sprained wrist bandaged. Robyn breathed a sigh of relief as Dr Early's two patients left the conference room for the hall. Ben too was pleased to be released from his cage again. The doctor switched off his high-powered portable light and the room plunged into darkness.

"Better save the batteries in this. I've a feeling I'll need it again before the night is out."

Tansy flicked on her torch and nervously flashed it around the room.

"Horst Mueller's not in here, Tansy," said Robyn. "And Billy Moynihan assures us he's not in the hall. You're safe."

Tansy smiled at Robyn. A wan smile. "No one is safe. Too many threats. The sea, the hurricane. Horst Mueller. It's an unsafe night."

"It's an unsafe world, Tans," Kevin said with such a note of depression in his voice that Robyn stared at him.

This was indeed a different Kevin. A vulnerable man. Someone who had doubts and fears. It would be foolhardy not to be afraid on a night like this. Nature was showing the power of her anger, the force of her revenge and mankind had no defence except to curl up and rely on the primitive instinct for survival to get them through. Yes, Kevin like everyone one else was in fear. But doubts? He never speculated or debated. He pronounced. Made snap decisions and stuck to them. Was that how he had decided to marry Lisa? A wife and fifty per cent share in a newspaper – yes, I'll have that. A baby? No, thank you – I'll never have that. Cold. Self-serving. And yet he could be warm and kind. Just like he was being to Tansy now as she looked up at him with tears in her eyes.

"We'll have to find him, Kev. I won't feel safe until I know exactly where he is. I'm still convinced he came into this hall. He'd never have gone back out. You heard the wind. It wouldn't even be possible to stand up in it."

"Zach's out in it," Robyn said, panic audible in her voice. "The sergeant and the coastguard too."

Tansy got up from her place on the floor and stooped down beside Robyn's chair.

"Zach will be fine. I know he will. It's just taking longer to get back from Lynches' because of the weather conditions."

"You think so? He was going to check out The 360 too."

"Oh!"

Tansy stopped talking. For once, she seemed to be stuck for encouraging words. Her silence made Robyn even more concerned. She had so far managed to reason her way through the wait for Zach's return. The twenty-minute journey would of course take longer tonight. He probably walked around the farm to check out the mudslide. He might be driving around, looking for Seán Harte. Now Tansy's flat 'Oh!' released all the fears Robyn had been holding in check.

"Something's happened to him. I know it has. He'd definitely be back before now unless he-he couldn't . . . he might be hurt or . . ."

Robyn was on her feet even before the door to the conference room had fully opened. Don Cronin walked through, leading his wife by the hand. She was huddled into her coat, eyes downcast. Garda Seán Harte walked in after them. Robyn waited for Zach to appear. The young garda closed the door behind him.

Robyn ran towards him.

"Where's Zach? Is he outside in the hall? Is he alright?"

Dr Early flicked on his torch. Seán Harte blinked in the powerful light.

"Have you seen Zach?" Robyn asked again.

Over in the makeshift surgery, Dr Early was talking softly to Evie, Don Cronin's wife. Seán Harte was still standing there with a confused look on his face. Robyn felt like shaking him.

"He went out to look for you," she said. "Up to Con Lynch's farm."

Seán smiled then and nodded. "That explains it. I was supposed to go to Con Lynch's but I'm afraid I got a bit lost. I still don't know all the byroads and lanes around here and when the lights went, I hadn't a clue where –"

"Zach?"

"I'm trying to explain. I didn't go to Lynches' at all. I ended up at Don Cronin's house thinking it was Con's. Just as well I was there to help out. Don's house was hit by lightning. I've never seen anything like the flash. It cracked from the electricity pole outside into the house in the blink of an eye. You should see the wall sockets! Burnt to a cinder. Did you know lightning can be as hot as 30,000 degrees centigrade, five times hotter than the surface of the sun?"

Dr Early walked across to where Seán was enthusing about lightning and spoke quietly to him.

"Seán, would you mind keeping any mention of the strike down? Evie's a bit fragile at the moment."

The young man blushed and cast a sideways glance in Evie's direction. "Sorry. I didn't mean to upset her."

Dr Early patted him on the arm and went back to his patient.

"So you saw no sign of my husband?" Robyn asked.

Seán shook his head. "No. I'll go back up to Con Lynch's now if I can."

"How do you mean, if you can?"

"We were lucky to get back. There are trees down all over the place, the roads are flooded and The 360 . . ." He stopped, looked at Robyn and blushed again. "I think I should shut up. Don't worry, Mrs Claymore. I'll find Con Lynch and your husband. Just you sit down and relax."

Anxious to escape before he made more gaffes, he dashed to the door and opened it. Kevin stood up and followed him. "I'll go with you, Seán. Give you moral support."

"No. It's better if I'm on my own. I'd have to be looking out for you too if you were there. I'd best get going. The sergeant will have a fit when he knows what happened."

Robyn didn't see that Kevin would be much help in

finding Zach on the Felton hills. Seán Harte was right. He would probably be a hindrance.

"Just let Seán do his job, Kevin."

"Actually I wanted to have a chat with him. About Horst Mueller."

Kevin turned to find that Seán Harte had scooted out the door while he had been answering Robyn. He shrugged and sat down again. Tansy leaned in close to him. Kevin's arm went around her and Tansy laid her head on his shoulder.

Robyn didn't notice. She was rooted to the spot where she stood. A searing pain ripped vice-like around her lower back and her stomach. She felt a scream rise to her throat and swallowed hard to silence it. The baby! My God! The baby! She took a deep breath. She was thirty-eight weeks pregnant. The baby would survive delivery at this stage. In a hospital.

Her eyes were drawn to Dr Early's corner. His emergency surgery. June Varian was sleeping soundly on the couch and Evie Cronin had her sleeve rolled up and was getting an injection. Jesus! Would their baby be delivered in the corner of a Community Hall in the middle of a hurricane? And where was Zach? Why had he gone and left her here? Kevin hadn't left Tansy and she wasn't even pregnant.

Sweat began to form on Robyn's forehead and along her spine. She felt dizzy. Weak. Hands supporting her stomach she walked slowly towards the chair Zach had brought in from the store for her. Leaning on the arms of it she took deep breaths. She felt a hand on her back. It was Dr Early, calm and smiling.

"Keep taking deep breaths. Find a comfortable position for yourself."

Robyn looked up into the wise old face. She saw understanding and sympathy there.

"Zach," she whispered.

He didn't answer. There were no reassurances from him that Zach was fine, that he would be here any minute, that he would hold her hand and wipe her brow. That he would ever hold their child. Robyn knew then that she might never see Zach again.

Horst Mueller had seen the young garda and another man come into the hall leading a woman small enough and terrified enough to be Ute. Staying in the shadows he had followed them and seen them go into a room near the store. The door closed and Horst stood back against the wall and waited. When the door to that room opened again, he peered in from his vantage point. A bright light shone in there. The woman was sitting on a chair, the elderly doctor examining her and a younger man by her side. She was not Ute. Horst cursed. The young man was that carpenter who had called to the cottage today. The one who had seen Ute trying to wriggle her way out. Another interfering nuisance. That newspaper man was there and the vet's wife who looked as if she was just about to give birth. Also a middle-aged woman sleeping on a couch. And, yes! The Bingham bitch was in there too.

The young garda stood for a moment in the doorway, talking to the newspaper man. Horst strained his ears, but he was too far away to know if his name was being mentioned. He relaxed when the garda brushed Kevin Phillips off, came out the door and closed it behind him. Flattening himself against the wall, he watched the garda disappear into the darkness of the hall. A moment later the front door was opened, a gale blew around the hall and the door was quickly shut again.

When Horst was sure the garda was gone out he continued his search, ignoring the nagging voice in his head which kept telling him Ute wasn't in this hall. He knew where the Bingham bitch was now. But that was for later. First he must find Ute.

The sergeant shone his torch through the window of Noel Cantillon's supermarket. Water sloshed through the aisles, packets and boxes bobbing on the surface. He turned around to Ritchie Swann, the coastguard who was ferrying him.

"Right. Start her up again. No one there."

The engine on the outboard motor roared into life and the boat passed by June Varian's house and the Quills'. They knew both those houses were vacated. They also knew Des Varian would never be back there again. They approached the end of the street, where the pier was to the left and Middle Street to the right.

"I don't like the look of this," Ritchie said as a wave billowed through the intersection, rocking the little craft. "Jesus! Can you see the size of the breakers out there?"

The sergeant didn't have to look to know. The sea was coming in on Felton in gigantic swells. He was as sure as he could be now that there was no one left in the village. This was a last check. People were either gone inland, as most of them had done, or they were in the hall. From the few countrywide reports he had been able to patch together before his radio completely failed, it seemed the people who fled wouldn't fare much better than those who stayed. Everywhere rivers were bursting their banks, trees toppling, roofs being torn off. "God help us all," he muttered.

"What, Sergeant?"

"Nothing. Just talking to myself. I think we'll call a halt, Ritchie. There's no one left here now. Best get ourselves to safety. Thanks for the help."

"No problem. I'll bring you back as far as I can in this. Then I'll have to try to find a mooring for it someplace."

"My God, man! You're not going near the pier, are you?"

"What pier? It's completely submerged. The boatshed's gone too. I'll have to find a bit of high ground to secure it. Where did you leave the squad car?"

"Up behind the library."

"I might try to get this up there as well. Would you give me a hand?"

"Sure."

Tim Halligan felt a deep sadness as the boat turned and chugged down the middle of the dark street, adding further turbulence to the water which by now was five feet deep and lapping into homes and businesses. A fetid mix of brine and sewage. He listened to the angry lash and hurl of the sea against the buildings and knew that it would claim Felton for itself. It was an unequal fight. A small village versus a vast ocean.

At the end of the street Ritchie steered towards the incline on which the library stood. He cut the engine and manoeuvred the boat with an oar as the water got shallower.

"Right, Sergeant, jump now," he shouted as he heard the keel scrape on solid ground.

When they got out, the water came to mid-calf on both men. Child's play after the depths they had waded through in the lower village. The gentle rise to the library seemed steep as they lifted the craft between them. The boat was too heavy or they were too exhausted. As soon as they reached the entrance to the library they dropped it and took a rest.

"I'm knackered," Ritchie admitted. "We'll just drag it to the front of the building. I've a coil of rope. I'll tie it to the fancy pillars they built on that porch thing."

Tim looked across garden which fronted the library and thought the building seemed a long way off. The pillars Ritchie had mentioned glowed even in the pitch dark. The whole building did because it was all painted white. Wet, cold, sad, worried and fearful as he was, Tim smiled now as he remembered all the hullabaloo about the design of this library when it had been built five years ago. The village council, led by Billy Moynihan, had erected a scaled-down version of the American Presidential White House, complete with portico and pillars. It couldn't have been more out of place amidst Felton's solid granite buildings.

"They knew what they were doing when they put those pillars there, didn't they?" said Tim. "Where else could you tie up your boat in a hurricane?"

"Bloody Billy Moynihan," Ritchie muttered as he grabbed hold of one side of the boat near the prow while Tim took the other. "He has some very odd ideas."

They bumped and scraped their way along the asphalt driveway and then took a short-cut through the soaking garden. They halted when they came to the wide steps which led up to the portico and the pillars which would now double as bollards to tie up the boat. "See what I mean?" Ritchie asked. "Shagging steps now. 'Tis far from this kind of architecture Billy Moynihan was reared!"

Tim didn't answer. Instead he put his hand up to silence Ritchie. He was staring into the darkness of the fanciest porch in Felton.

"Did you hear something?"

"Jaysus! Tim, what do you mean? I hear gales screaming, the sea pounding and this blasted rain is pouring like a tap. Of course I hear something."

"No, I mean someone."

Ritchie put his head to one side and listened carefully. He still heard nothing but the raucous voice of the hurricane. Tim felt under his coat for his baton and then, holding his torch high, shone it into the porch. The light swept from left to right, highlighting the double doors, a large urn which had toppled over, spilt moss peat and plants, litter of every sort which had been blown in there and over to the extreme right a bundle wrapped in a blanket.

"I hear it now," Ritchie said as the weak noise which had first alerted Tim sounded again.

Tim began to slowly climb the steps. The blanket bundle moved and the sound got louder.

"Sweet Jesus! There's someone in there."

Tim shushed Ritchie as he approached the blanket. He could see a pair of feet sticking out from underneath the folds. A woman's feet. He stood a metre away, shining the torch.

"I'm Garda Sergeant Tim Halligan. Who are you?"

Very slowly the edges of the blanket were drawn apart and a woman's face peered through. She was terrified, her eyes glassy with shock and fear. She whispered her name so softly it was inaudible. But Tim knew who she was. He had just glimpsed her in passing but he had a good memory for faces. He remembered what her husband had said about her mental condition. He would have to be very gentle with her.

"What are you doing here, Mrs Mueller?"

The edges of the blanket were instantly drawn together again.

"You can't stay out in this weather."

There was no answer. He tried again, speaking very slowly this time, not sure whether she spoke English or not.

"The worst of the hurricane is yet to hit. Let me take you up to the hall. You'll be safe there."

The blanket began to tremble. Mrs Mueller was sobbing.

"I can't. He'll look there. He'll kill me."

So her husband had been telling the truth. The poor woman was definitely delusional.

"Who will?"

She didn't answer. Tim took another step and gently caught an edge of the blanket and noticed that it was soaking wet. He pulled it back from her face. She shrivelled into the corner as if he had been about to hit her.

"You've nothing to be afraid of, Mrs Mueller. I'll protect you."

She shook her head. "You can't. You don't understand. There are too many of them."

Ritchie and Tim exchanged glances. They understood now why the Muellers always kept themselves apart from the rest of the community.

"Ritchie here will keep a lookout too, won't you, Ritchie?"

"Of course. But not here. I'm with the coastguard and I can tell you, Mrs Mueller, the sea will shortly wash you off this step."

Tim put out his hand to her. She stared at it for an instant, then suddenly made up her mind and allowed him to help her to her feet. Her blanket fell to the ground. Both men gaped. She was holding a baby in her arms, wrapped in thick layers of clothing. Tim shone the torch onto the little face. It was waxen.

"Stay here!" he ordered Ute. "I'll bring the squad car around. Dr Early's in the hall. I pray to God we'll get there on time. Watch her, Ritchie."

He ran then, slipping and sliding over the wet ground, buffeted by the wind, blinded by the rain. He shrugged off the hurricane. All that mattered to him was getting Ute Mueller and her baby to the safety of the hall. He prayed that it was not already too late for the baby.

Chapter 27

There were tears in Con Lynch's eyes as he stood in his front garden. Tears of frustration. He was furious with himself. Why had he allowed the lad out of his sight? When Zach had suggested going to the byroad he should have just said no. He had searched the sheds, the front garden, the cul-de-sac and down as far as the corner on the byroad but there was still no sign of Zach.

Where in the hell could he have gone? Had he fallen into a ditch? Drowned in the rain and muck? This thought sent Con down the byroad again, flashing the torchlight into the drains. Rounding the corner this time, he pushed forward against the wind, pulling his peaked cap down on his head as far as it would go. Progress was difficult. Rain, cold and wind-whipped, stung his face and ears. He should have worn a woolly hat to protect his ears instead of his cap. Noreen had always thought of those kind of things. Made sure he was comfortable. Looked after his every need . . .

He stood still. Staring, yet not understanding what

he was seeing. It couldn't be! He moved forward a step and focused the beam of the torch. It was still there. The black alder tree. Lying across the road. Con could hear Noreen as clearly as if she was standing beside him. "Don't ever pass an alder tree when you're going on a journey. It's bad luck." He used to smile at her superstition. Dismiss it.

He walked forward slowly, keeping the light on the fallen tree, noting that it spanned the road from ditch to ditch, that the branches still danced in the wind and the leaves fluttered as if the tree was still alive. He knelt at the crown of the fallen giant and pushed aside branches and foliage. Zach was lying on his stomach, his arms stretched out in front of him, one cheek pressed onto the wet ground. A trickle of blood dribbled from his forehead down the other cheek.

"Ah, no, lad! No!" Con murmured as he balanced the torch in the fork of a branch and then, gently pushing back Zach's hood from his face, touched his skin. It was deathly cold. He put his ear to Zach's mouth and listened. He heard it, weak and shallow, but rhythmic. The lad was breathing. He probed around the scalp line and the skull. No cuts. The hood had protected him. The forehead gash seemed to be the only wound on his head. But what should he do now? Turn him over? Suppose he had broken bones, a fractured spine? Moving him would make the injury worse.

A groaning noise startled Con. An overhead tree had broken away halfway down the trunk, but strips of bark still held it dangling at a crazy angle. It was going to topple any minute now. Zach would have to be moved or they would both die on this godforsaken byroad. Con caught a fistful of Zach's coat and shook him more roughly than he had intended.

"Zach! Zach! Can you hear me, lad? Can you move? Zach?"

The eyelid Con could see fluttered. Zach lifted his head a little and then opening his eyes, stared at Con. He looked at the branches surrounding him, the rain pouring on top of him and back to Con again.

"You've had an accident, lad. Can you move your legs? Where are you hurt?"

Zach just kept peering at Con as if he did not know him. The overhanging tree groaned again.

"Can you move? You have to get out of here."

Still no reply from Zach. A sharp crack made Con's decision for him. Shoving his torch in his pocket, he grabbed Zach's outstretched hands. With a superhuman strength he heaved the big man from underneath the entangling branches. He kept dragging and backing away, afraid to stop, yet terrified that he was worsening any injuries that Zach might have. They were five feet back when a violent gust snapped the last of the bark from the dangling tree. It crashed onto the ground just where Con had been kneeling, sharp splinters protruding from the broken trunk.

He kept going as long as he could, pulling and dragging Zach until he had no more strength left. They were still only just around the bend and the road to the house seemed to stretch endlessly into the darkness. He rested Zach against the ditch and flopped onto the ground himself, breathless. His muscles ached and he had a pain across his chest. A few hours ago he would have been glad to suffer a heart attack. Quick and clean. He would be with Noreen again. It was different now. He must, must, get this young man to safety. Clutching his chest, Con took deep breaths. Gradually his breathing normalised and the pain eased.

"'Twas only indigestion, you old fool," he said crossly to himself.

Like an outsized rag-doll Zach sagged against briars and nettles. Con poked again at his arms and legs, searching for any sign that could tell him what injuries he might have suffered. He thought Zach's right leg was at a peculiar angle, although it was difficult to ascertain through the raingear and Wellington boots. Yet judging by the colour of the face, there were serious injuries. He tried shaking him again.

"Zach! Where are you hurt?"

The eyelids flickered. This time there was more awareness in his eyes. He focused on Con. "Robyn. I must get back to Robyn."

"You must, lad. Can you move? Can you stand up?"

Zach held a hand up to Con. Together they tried to get Zach into a standing position. He shook his head and flopped back onto the ground again.

"My leg. I think it's broken."

Con breathed a sigh of relief. A broken bone would heal. He smiled.

"You sit tight here. I've just the thing for you. I won't be a minute."

With a last check to make sure Zach was sheltered where he was sitting, Con hurried up the road, through the garden gate, over Noreen's shrubs and flower-beds and out to the barn. He grabbed a likely-looking plank from the timber pile and a length of baler twine, threw them into the big wheelbarrow and turned back again in double-quick time. He knew by the shrieking keen of the wind that shortly there would be no moving about in it. He must get Zach back to the hall before this bloody hurricane did its worst. The plank bounced in the barrow as he pushed it along, making tracks in Noreen's water-logged garden and then racing down the road.

"What do you think of this?" he asked as he steered the barrow in front of Zach.

There was no answer. "Don't turn your nose up at it. It'll do the job. Come on."

There was no sound except for the fury of the hurricane. Con stooped down and shook Zach. That had worked before. Zach fell forward, his head dropping onto his chest.

"No! You're not doing this to me or your lovely young wife, Zach Claymore! God damn you! I won't let you go."

Catching Zach underneath the arms, Con hauled him over as far as the barrow and then, with one huge effort, lobbed him into it, barely preventing it from capsizing. Zach's long legs were dangling over the edge. It was obvious in that position that his right leg was broken. Con got the plank he had brought with him and placed it underneath the leg, securing it with a piece of baler twine. He tipped the barrow and began to push. It bounced over ruts and stones jolting Zach. But Con knew there was no alternative. He simply couldn't have dragged Zach all the way out to the tractor. And that of course would be the next problem. Getting him loaded into the cab.

"By God, I'll do it!" Con muttered as he came around

the side of the house and headed across the yard to where the tractor was parked.

When they reached the tractor Con gently lowered the handles of the barrow and, leaning against the tractor wheel, rested his aching back for one brief moment. He was exhausted. He knew he did not have a second to spare but he needed to gather his strength for the almost impossible task of lifting Zach up into the cab. It helped that the big old tractor had a two-door cab and generous space. If only he could get Zach from the barrow onto the tractor. He glanced down at the young man.

Zach was staring back at him. He was conscious.

"Zach, you'll have to help me now. I must load you onto the tractor."

Expecting Zach to lapse back into unconsciousness again, Con quickly opened the cab door nearest to him and turned the barrow to face the tractor.

Zach's eyelids were drooping.

"Stay awake, man. Stay awake!" Con went to Zach's right-hand side and put his arm around his back. "Put your arm over my shoulder, Zach. Pull yourself up on your good leg and lean on me. C'mon! C'mon! Robyn is waiting!"

It must have been the mention of Robyn, or it could have been the heartfelt prayer Con said to Noreen but, whatever the reason, Zach found the strength to lift himself out of the wheelbarrow. Pushed and pulled by Con, he managed to drag himself up into the tractor. He slumped down on to the floor space between the driver's seat and the side panel, his splinted leg stuck out in front of him, his head resting against the back of the cab. Exhausted by the effort, his head fell forward. Zach was unconscious again.

Con ran around to the driver's side and jumped in. He switched on the engine. The headlights illuminated the torrents of water gushing down the incline. The yard was like a pond by now. He thought briefly of the road ahead that might be flooded and the ancient oak trees out near the entrance that might have fallen. He eased the tractor forward and felt the big tyres find traction. Glancing at his house, he wondered if he would ever see it again. He drove forward as quickly as was possible through wind and rain, his lips moving in silent prayer for the young man beside him. And for his pregnant wife who might be a widow before this terrible night was over.

The pain eased and then disappeared. Kevin was stooping down beside her and Robyn realised she had a grip on his hand. She drew her hand away.

"How are you feeling now?" he asked.

"Better. Much better, thank you. I just wish Zach was here."

He lifted his hand and stroked her hair, her cheek. "Robyn, I – I must tell you . . ."

"No, Kevin. You mustn't tell me anything. That time is past. Look, Tansy's calling you. What's she up to now?"

They both looked over to where Tansy and Dr Early were pacing and measuring and waving their arms about, the doctor in a controlled way, Tansy wildly. She was obviously in the grip of another mad idea, her earlier fear of Horst Mueller on hold.

Kevin didn't move.

"Go on. You're only crossing the room. I'll be alright."

"You're sure? I don't want to leave you. I never wanted to."

"Go."

Robyn watched as he strode across the room. Tansy looked up at him and smiled as he approached. There was warmth in her smile. Even love. Robyn smiled too, but not at seeing her best friend and her ex-lover together. The bitter little twist of her lips was a reaction to Kevin's words. So he had never wanted to leave her? Why then had he turned so cold, so unloving? Why had he always refused to bring their relationship to another level, to leave Lisa? To have a child?

He was coming back now. Standing in front of her, a concerned expression on his face as if he cared. Truly cared. Hypocrite!

"Dr Early wants to screen off the couch area. Just for privacy. In case – well, in case there's a delivery before the night is out."

Robyn's heart began to beat rapidly. This wasn't supposed to be the way it happened. She had dreamed of going to the hospital with Zach when the time came, she all serene, he carrying the maternity bag she had packed months ago and on which she now had her legs propped. She would have an easy labour, gas and air, no complications. Zach would hold her hand and smile at her. His gorgeous, fun-filled loving smile. Then his green eyes would glisten with tears when he held his baby for the first time. They would all cry for joy – Robyn and Zach and their newborn child. It couldn't be otherwise.

"No! I can't have our baby here. And not without Zach. No!"

"He'll be back, Robyn. You mustn't be upsetting yourself."

Robyn glared at him. He didn't understand. How could he when she herself hadn't understood until now? Truly understood. She loved Zach Claymore. Loved everything about him: his kindness, humour, honesty, selflessness. The way he made her feel warm and safe. She closed her eyes so that she didn't have to see Kevin Phillips. Tears welled behind her eyelids. What had she done? My God! What had she done to Zach? He knew what she had been thinking these past few days. Things she had not fully admitted to herself – how exciting Kevin Phillips was, how unpredictable, how every day with him was a challenge. That she had given herself to him body and soul and a part of her had died when he had not returned the same commitment.

"I must see Zach. I need to explain," she said, not realising she had spoken out loud.

"He knows, Rob. He knows everything about you and what he means to you."

"I didn't know. I got sidetracked. I've hurt him, Kevin. You and me both. We hurt people."

Tansy came across the room, her dark eyes glowing with enthusiasm for her new project. Robyn and Kevin looked at her and then at each other.

"Not Tansy," Robyn whispered. "She's been too hurt. Don't you dare."

Kevin nodded but said nothing. Not a man for making promises he might not be able to keep.

"How are you now?" Tansy asked, leaning over and taking Robyn's hand in hers.

"Worried about Zach. Otherwise fine."

"Don Cronin is going to make a frame to hang sheets on as soon as Evie is settled down outside. We'll find a place in the hall for June to sleep too. Then Dr Early can examine you in privacy. He said you might not be in labour at all."

"I don't want to be. Not until Zach is here."

"Isn't that up to the baby?"

The baby! Dear God! The poor baby. Head bowed, tears streamed down Robyn's face. She saw images of herself and the baby, just the two of them. She would show the child a video of Zach, photographs, tell stories about its father. 'See this man, baby, that's your daddy. He died in Hurricane Kimi. Before you were born. Before I could tell him how much we both loved him and needed him."

Kevin put his arm around her shoulder. She shrugged him off without raising her eyes to him. She did not want to see the shadow of what they had shared reflected in his eyes. A reminder of the heartbreak he had brought her and the hurt she had brought Zach.

Horst Mueller had completed a full circuit of the hall by now. It had taken some time because he had to stay in the shadows and dark spaces. Most of all he had to avoid the fat mayor who seemed to be everywhere with his blasted torch, shouting about not drinking tap water because the pumps were down and all the time scanning every face as if looking for someone.

He had seen the carpenter and his wife leave the room which he understood to be a first-aid centre. Horst had studied them as they walked around, avoiding sleeping people and luggage on the floor. They eventually found a space near the back of the hall which suited them. The carpenter settled his wife down there, then he took off again to the room Horst now knew to be the store. In fact he was familiar with the entire layout of the building at this stage. He had searched everywhere, including the bathrooms. Ute was not here. Where in the hell had the stupid woman got to?

He slid down along the wall near the store and sat on the ground. Sweat began to form in cold droplets on his forehead. He remembered how vicious the storm had been before he came into the hall. The violence of the wind, the sharp cutting slant of the rain, the taunting of the lightning as it poked lethal fingers through the black night. Ute would not survive that. Worse still, the baby would not. How could an infant breathe when the air was blasting into its lungs?

A gust of wind so strong that it rocked the building reminded Horst that the storm had graduated into a hurricane. His heart began to beat fast and his breathing grow shallow. He recognised the symptoms as panic. And it was all Ute's fault. Silly, timid, malleable Ute. Always ready to do as she was told. Always willing to obey.

A hot flash of hatred burned through him. This was because of that interfering Bingham woman and her pregnant friend. If only they had minded their own business and not come knocking on the door with dire warnings of deluges and catastrophe. It was as if they had known that Ute was obsessed with fear of drowning.

She had begged and pleaded for him to take her away from the cottage. He smiled as he remembered her kneeling at his feet, her hands joined in prayer-like fashion. "Please, Horst, please. We must leave here. The sea will sweep the cottage away. Please take us out of here." He should have videoed the scene. Especially the bit where he had made her lie face-down and beg. It would have made a great home movie. He would have done except that the Bingham bitch and her disgusting cat had taken him away from the game.

The storeroom door opened. Horst rolled himself up as small as possible and blended into the shadow of the wall. The carpenter came out carrying laths of timber. Idiot! That ignoramus had been the cause of Ute almost escaping through the door of the cottage while he was there demanding to be towed out of the mud. Fool! Horst squinted his eyes and kept his focus on the torchlight the carpenter carried. The light bobbed its way to the first-aid room. The door was opened for him when he banged his bundle of timber against it. He and the load disappeared in there and the door was closed again.

Staying close to the wall, Horst levered himself up and stood.

He had to face the facts. Ute was dead. He could get over that. The baby was dead. That he could not even contemplate. His legs were shaking and it took a while for him to recognise the reaction as fear. His fists clenched. He longed to hit someone, to inflict pain, to exploit someone else's weakness so that he could reassert his own strength. A curse on Ute!

Robyn sat back in her chair and tried to relax. Beside her, Don Cronin and Kevin were making much fuss of constructing the frame for a screen around the couch. Anyone could be forgiven for thinking they were building a suspension bridge over the Amazon.

Billy Moynihan popped his head around the door.

"I've been all over this hall. No sign of Mueller. I can't understand it. His 4x4 is in the back car park so he must be somewhere."

After a quick glance in June's direction, Billy dashed off again. A busy man.

Robyn looked down to where Tansy was sitting cross-legged on the floor, her eyes closed and her arms outstretched. In the middle of all the chaos, she was doing her meditation!

Eventually Tansy gave a long sigh then opened her eyes.

"Feeling better now?" Robyn asked.

"I'll be happy when I know exactly where Horst Mueller is. Why did he come here anyway?"

"You don't know that he's here. You could be wrong."

"No, I'm not. You heard Billy Moynihan. Mueller's 4x4 is in the car park, isn't it? And I can feel his evil presence here."

"Drama queen."

"He tried to choke me, Rob."

Robyn frowned. She hadn't meant to sound so dismissive of Tansy's fears. It was worrying to think that Horst Mueller was somewhere in the hall. Would he attack someone else as he had Tansy? Where was his wife? A cold shiver ran down Robyn's back. The world was indeed, as Kevin had said, an unsafe place.

Tansy picked up her printouts and began to read. After a while she looked up at Robyn, a dreamy expression on her face. "I must see Palenque. I will if we ever get out of here."

"Really? Is that a place you walk, sail or fly to?"

"All of them. It's in the Mexican state of Chiapas, near the Usumacinta River."

"I assume we're talking Maya again."

"Doh! Palenque has some of the best examples of Maya architecture and art. Most of it was done under a great ruler, K'inich Janaab' Pakal. Pakal the Great. He was only twelve years old when he took the throne in AD 615 and he ruled for 68 years. Imagine that."

"How could a twelve-year-old govern a kingdom? That's weird!"

"It could be that by the age of twelve every Maya child had all the knowledge they needed to lead a very fulfilled and adult life. They had female leaders too, you know. Yol Ik'nal ruled from 583 to 604."

"Good on her. Do you know yet what happened to them? Why they disappeared?"

"They didn't. Not entirely. But I think climate change affected them too. Drought in particular." Tansy suddenly jumped up and leaned over Robyn, staring into her face. "Here I am, waffling on about lost civilisations, and you're in labour. How are you?"

Robyn grinned and hugged her friend. "I'm fine. I think my pains might have been a false alarm. Probably because I'm so worried about Zach."

"Don't worry, Rob. Seán Harte will find him. He'd be afraid of what the sergeant would say if he didn't."

"I hope so."

Straightening up, Tansy looked across at June curled up on the couch. "Such a shame to wake her but we'll have to. Dr Early wants to keep the couch clear. I think he's expecting you to deliver plus an onslaught of casualties."

"We'll find a cosy space for her outside in the hall. Billy will look after her."

Tansy paled. "I'm not setting foot out there until Horst Mueller is found."

Kevin looked up from his work. "He'll never lay a finger on you again, Tansy. I'll make sure of that."

Tansy smiled at him and then, with a contented little sigh, went to wake June.

Slowly, careful to stay in the shadows, Horst made his way towards the front door. A plan was beginning to form. It was strange not to be including Ute and the child but he had to accept that they were dead.

His plan involved escape, a new identity, a new wife. A new life. He had done it before. There was a possibility the Bingham bitch had recognised him from the glimpse she got but who would believe her anyway? The idiots would conclude he probably died trying to save his wife and child. Swept out to sea, never to be found again. A nuisance that he didn't know where the bodies of Ute and the baby would turn up but no plan was perfect.

He would wait by the door until the next person came in and then he would make a dash through it. He'd go unnoticed in the mayhem caused by the Mayor each time someone new was swept in.

He found a nice dark space just beside the front door and sat down to wait. He was more controlled now, confidence returning with the plan.

A rapping on the door made him jump to his feet. He moved a bit away, knowing that the Mayor and his torch would be trundling towards the door. Billy Moynihan fussed as he kicked the draught-excluding blankets aside and fumbled with the lock. The door was lashed in against the wall with the force of the gale. People in the hall muttered as the wind whistled over them. A man in a coastguard's jacket launched himself in and grabbed the Mayor by the arm, whispering into his ear, pointing behind him into the rain and wind.

Other people were out there too but Horst couldn't see who they were. Head down, he sidled up to the door, taking care to stay in the shadows. He stopped when he was almost by the door frame and peered outside. The wind slapped into his face and whipped his hood from his head. Cold sharp needles of rain on his face made him draw quickly back. But not before he had seen Billy Moynihan, the Coastguard and the sergeant all grouped around the back door of the squad car. They seemed to be trying to coax a reluctant passenger to get out and come into the hall.

Perfect! He would make a dash now. They were too preoccupied to notice him. Just as he stepped around the frame, the Mayor turned around, shouting back over his shoulder at the others.

"I'll have to shut the door. The bloody roof will blow off. Give me a knock when you're ready."

Horst stepped back into the shadows of the hall as the Mayor came in and closed the door. Fool! Pulling his hood up again, Horst took a deep, shuddering breath. All he had to do was wait. No need for panic.

He shuffled a bit where he stood. He was frozen. The Keystone Cop should just haul the troublemaker out of the car.

Finally a knock sounded on the door. The Mayor opened up. A blanket appeared, lit by the sergeant's torch. The blanket was wrapped around a small person. Guided by the sergeant and the coastguard, the blanket and its inhabitant began to slowly walk through the doorway.

They were within a few feet of him before Horst recognised his wife. Before he realised she had the baby with her and that they were both with the sergeant. He had to grit his teeth and clench his fists tightly. He wanted to scream at her, to smash her face, to feel his fist connect with her body, to see terror in her eyes. The bitch!

The door was slammed shut by the Mayor but Horst was no longer considering escape from the hall. Not without his wife and baby.

The sergeant urged Ute on. "Almost there, Mrs Mueller. Just another few steps."

"He'll kill me," she muttered, "I know he will."

Horst cursed under his breath. Yes. She was right. He would kill her. Cut her tongue out. Make her pay for her treachery. He bared his teeth in a gesture of pure animal hatred. Ute was standing inside the door now, refusing to move forward, shrivelled up inside her blanket, small and delicate but as stubborn as a mule.

"Your husband is very worried about you, Mrs Mueller. He's out looking for you. He told me you're not well."

Horst smiled in the darkness and heaved a sigh of relief. The Keystone Cop had swallowed the tale that Ute was a complete lunatic. Even if she told the full story now, no one would believe her. Still, he wouldn't feel safe until he had shut her up.

The sergeant sounded as if he was losing patience with her. That's what Ute always did to people. "Your baby urgently needs medical help, Mrs Mueller," he said. "If you're not going to bring it to the doctor, let me take it."

Ute pulled the blanket more tightly around herself

and the baby but she allowed herself to be led slowly away from the door. They would be taking her to their first-aid room. The one over near the store. The one where that bitch Bingham was hiding. Fuck her! He would walk in there, head held high and claim his wife and child, wait for the storm to ease and then take them to where they were meant to be.

Horst began to shake again. Tansy Bingham would talk to the sergeant. That prick of a journalist would too. His story of Ute's madness might not be enough then. And there was the baby. What would Ute say? Driven by fear and urgency, Horst began to make his way back to the top of the hall, slipping from one pool of darkness to the next. He had worked too hard. Nobody, but nobody, was going to ruin things for him now.

The door of the conference room burst open. Billy Moynihan and a coastguard almost got jammed in the frame in their rush to get in.

"Emergency on the way, Dr Early!" Billy called. "A woman and a baby."

"It's the German woman and her child," the coastguard added. "Mrs Mueller."

Robyn and Tansy exchanged puzzled glances.

"I had no idea they had a baby, had you?" Tansy asked.

"No. I never heard a baby cry or saw baby clothes out on their line. I never saw their clothes line, come to think of it."

Tansy frowned and then turned to the men. "Was Horst Mueller with his wife and child?"

The coastguard shook his head. "No. Only herself and the baby. Pitiful they are. The sergeant is trying to coax her in. She's terrified. It's one step forward and two back. I'll go see if he needs a hand."

Billy went with him, muttering about looking after June outside in the hall.

When they walked off there was silence in the room. Kevin was the first to speak.

"Do I understand that nobody knew the Muellers had a child? Not even you, Robyn, right next door?"

"I'm stunned. I had no idea."

"I'm not surprised," Don Cronin said. "There could be anything in that house but 'twould be a brave person would try to get in past Mueller." He put the last staple into the sheets he was fixing to the frame then and stood back to examine it. "Will this do the job, Dr Early? It's as close as I can get to a hospital screen with the materials to hand."

"It's great, Don. Thank you."

"I must get back to Evie. If there's anything else I can do give me a shout."

Don had to stand aside at the doorway, to let the sergeant and what appeared to be a walking blanket through. Ute Mueller was shivering so much that her teeth were rattling. Dr Early walked forward to meet them. He put his hand on Ute's shoulder and she jumped with fright.

"Don't be afraid, Mrs Mueller. I'd like to help you. And your baby."

The small woman looked up at him, her eyes huge and her narrow features pinched with cold and something else – perhaps terror.

"I'll take the baby now," he said, his arms outstretched.

Ute sighed. A long shuddering letting go. She handed the baby to the doctor.

Robyn levered herself up from her chair and walked over to Ute.

"Sit down there, Mrs Mueller. And take off that blanket. It's soaking."

Ute didn't move. The sergeant caught her arm firmly and led her to the chair. She made no attempt to resist. Robyn got a dry blanket to wrap around her. As she fixed it around the bony shoulders she felt the woman shiver with fright – just as Tansy had done at the mention of Horst Mueller. Robyn had no doubt now that Ute was terrified because of her husband.

"You're safe here, Ute," she said softly. "We'll take care of you."

"He'll kill me," she muttered. Her voice was husky, a slight trace of a foreign accent in her pronunciation.

Behind her back, the sergeant was pointing a finger to his head and twirling it to indicate that Ute was quite mad. Dr Early frowned at him, obviously displeased with the sergeant's less than professional diagnosis.

"When you're finished with Dr Early you should have a shower," Robyn suggested to Ute. "We'll find something dry for you to wear, won't we, Tansy?"

Tansy didn't answer Robyn. She was staring at the baby as Dr Early unwrapped the layers of clothes around him.

It was a beautiful little boy. Maybe about three months old. An Asian child. He coughed as the doctor took his temperature and put the stethoscope to his chest.

The doctor straightened up. "I don't like the sound of this. I'll have to give him an antibiotic. Has he any allergies, Mrs Mueller?"

Ute twisted her fragile hands and wriggled uncomfortably in her chair. "I-I don't know. I don't think so."

"Has he had antibiotics before now? Penicillin?"

Ute hung her head. Dr Early nodded to Tansy to hold onto the baby. He walked over to Ute and stood in front of her.

"Has he had his vaccinations? His BCG? Six-in-One? Who's your GP?"

Ute continued to wring her hands and keep her head bowed.

The doctor stooped down to her. "I'm trying to help, Mrs Mueller. I think your baby has pneumonia. I need to know his history before I treat him."

"I-I don't know. We only have him three weeks. My husband has the papers."

She began to cry then, muffled sobs as if she was used to keeping her despair quiet. Kevin, who had been listening in, came over to her.

"You adopted this baby, Mrs Mueller? A foreign adoption?"

There was no sound from Ute except her sobs, which were getting louder.

"Is he yours? Did you adopt him?"

When Ute still did not reply he leaned down to her until their heads were almost touching.

"Did you adopt him? Is he legally yours? Tell me, Mrs Mueller."

"No point in badgering her," Robyn said. "Dr Early just needs medical information about the baby."

Kevin glared at her. "But she hasn't got it, has she? She knows nothing about this child. He's not hers. Whose baby is it? What do you think of this, Sergeant?"

Tim Halligan looked down at the pathetic little woman sitting in front of him. "This woman isn't well.

Her husband said so. That's why he's out in the storm looking for her."

"He's not," Tansy said quickly. "He's here in the hall."

"And he should be in police custody," Kevin added. "Do you know what he –"

"He'll kill me, he'll kill me," Ute began to mutter again.

Kevin's face was flushed with anger by now. "The baby shouldn't be in this woman's care. There's something very wrong here. I'm going to find that husband of hers."

"Just leave it to us, Mr Phillips," the sergeant said stiffly.

Robyn leaned down in front of Ute and caught her shaking hands. "Horst is a bully, Ute. You've no need to fear him any more. The police will deal with him. But you must tell Dr Early what you know about the baby. What's his name?"

"I don't know. I call him Hans. I call all the boys Hans and the girls Zelda."

Even the wind seemed to still as everyone in the room gaped at Ute. All the boys! All the girls! What was going on in that cottage? Or was Ute, as Horst had claimed, quite insane?

"How many babies do you have now, Ute?" Dr Early asked softly.

She lifted her head and looked up at him, responding to his gentleness. "Just Hans. Always only one. Except the time we had the twins. They came from Vietnam."

"How long do you keep them?" Kevin asked.

Ute quickly bowed her head again and began to twist the blanket in her hands.

"How long?" Kevin asked, less gently this time.

"He gives them away. He gives them all away."

Robyn could feel the colour drain from her face. She was following Kevin's line of questioning and her mind had leaped ahead to where it led. No! Her eyes met Kevin's and she saw revulsion and anger blaze there.

"I knew it!" he said." How many, Ute? What do you do? Smuggle the babies in here and then sell them on like disposable commodities! That's evil!"

"And that's enough, Kevin," Dr Early said firmly. "We have a sick baby here we need to treat. Mrs Mueller needs attention too. I don't think she's responsible for anything she's saying now so don't go jumping to conclusions. And you must stay calm, Robyn. The recriminations can wait."

Kevin nodded. "For now. I'm going to find Horst Mueller. Are you coming, Sergeant? I've things to tell you about Tansy and Robyn's neighbour. We'll search the hall first."

"How do you mean first? Have you any idea what it's like outside? It's nearly impossible to even stand up with the force of the wind and every place is flooded. If Horst Mueller is out there, he won't last long . . ."

Tim Halligan stopped talking when he saw the terror in Robyn's face.

"Zach is still out," she said. "And Seán Harte too."

"Holy God!"

The pain began again. Stronger, more urgent this time. Robyn felt warm fluid gush down her legs. The little baby named Hans cried and Robyn did too.

Chapter 28

Con leaned forward, his knuckles white as he gripped the steering wheel. They were making progress, slow but sure. He took his eyes off the road ahead to glance down at Zach. The young man looked ghastly. Con cursed. He couldn't go any faster than what he was doing now. The road, or what he could see of it, was like a river and the wind rocked the tractor cab as if it was teasing, seeing how frightened it could make them before finally tipping them over.

Cursing done, Con prayed. His hands relaxed a little on the wheel. They had made it this far. His biggest dread had been the old oaks at the entrance. He had fully expected one of them to tumble on top of them as they passed. The trees had threatened, branches scraping against the cab, but the tractor had ploughed safely through. He knew now when he rounded the next bend, the library would be in view. It would just be a quick run uphill then to the hall.

"We're almost there, lad. Hang on," he said, glancing again at Zach.

As he turned the wheel to steer them around the bend, Con became acutely aware of the pulled muscles in his back. He knew he had done himself damage as he had hauled Zach from the wheelbarrow into the tractor. He took a deep breath. Time enough for giving in to his own pains and aches when he had got help for the lad.

Something felt different. Con felt the tractor slide to the left. He jerked the steering wheel but the slide continued. Then he remembered that you should steer into a slide. But that was for ice, wasn't it? The only curse this hurricane had not thrown at them was ice. He tipped the brake. The slide continued. Peering through the cascades of water on the windscreen he stared at the surface on which the huge tractor tyres were trying to find purchase. Jesus! They were skating on mud! He jabbed the brakes hard. They were almost in the ditch when the tractor gripped and began to respond to his frantic turning of the steering wheel. Just in time, it skimmed past the ditch and rounded the bend.

Con jammed on the brakes. This time they came to a halt. He gaped, not believing what he was seeing. Zach groaned. Con dragged his eyes away from the nightmare ahead.

"Where am I? What happened? Where's Robyn?"

Leaning over, Con looked into the young man's face. Zach's eyes were flicking around, confused, unfocused.

"We'll see your wife soon. Just you rest there while I try to get us out of this mess."

Zach's eyelids drooped and his head nodded. He was asleep again. Or unconscious.

Pulling his cap as far down on his head as he could, Con opened the door of his cab. The wind grabbed the door and tore it off the hinges. It flew into the darkness. Holding onto the frame, he climbed up on the hood of the tractor. The headlights illuminated a hellish scene. A tree which must be at least one hundred years old lay across the road, its thick trunk forming a blockade between the ditches. Sections of the stone ditch were no more. They had been dismantled by the weight of the mud oozing down from the valley. Boulders, branches, whole trees, pieces of timber, dross of every description floated past, piling up against the fallen tree and in the places where the ditch still stood. As he watched in disbelief, a dead dog floated past him. The 360! The mud was sliding off the hill, down the valley and heading for the back of the library. Con stared at it, confused by its slow, deliberate progress. Everything else, the wind, rain, water, was racing, lashing, whirling, rushing. The mud slid ponderously by, hypnotising him. He stood trance-like, and stared.

He should have attached the shovel to the tractor. He might have been able to shift the tree with it. He should have gone to Dublin with Noreen. He might have been able to save her.

As he watched, the level of the mud was visibly rising. They would have to get out of here soon or else they would end up floating away like the dead dog. Gripping the frame tightly to hold himself steady in the vicious wind, he looked around him, searching for an escape route. The tree was too tightly jammed and too thick to be shifted. Maybe if he managed to slide the tractor through a gap in the broken ditch, he could access the road again further down. The mud was about eighteen inches deep now. The tractor could cope with that. Satisfied that he had a viable plan, Con carefully began to climb back into the cab. Something caught his eye. A flash of light. No! Two lights! Headlights. Swinging himself up again he squinted his eyes and peered over the fallen tree. There was a blue light now. Twirling. The Gardaí! The lights stopped moving, coming to a halt a few yards on the other side of the blockade. He shoved his hand into his pocket and grabbed his torch, switched it on and began to wave it over his head, to reassure himself as much as the person on the other side of the tree that he was still alive and well. Almost well. He shouted as loud as he could even though he knew he could not be heard above the keening of the wind.

The door of the Garda jeep opened. Con got down from the hood of the tractor, put his foot on the step and slowly lowered his other foot into the mud. It sucked up to the top of his Wellingtons, so unexpectedly powerful that it would have knocked him had he not been holding onto the tractor. He shone his torch on Zach. He was ashen, his lips blue-tinged. Con took a deep breath, lowered his head and began the strenuous trudge towards the fallen tree.

On the other side, Seán Harte too was struggling against the wind and rain. The mud was not as deep on his side. The fallen tree was forming an effective dam, with only slicks of mire seeping underneath the tightly jammed trunk. He held his torch up and flashed it on and off a few times just to let the tractor driver know he had been seen. He knew it was Con Lynch. It must be. Seán's heart skipped a beat. Where was Zach Claymore? There was only one person on that tractor. He could see nothing now but the image of the vet's pregnant wife, he could feel nothing but guilt. If only he had not been so stupid and had found Con Lynch's farm, then Zach Claymore would not be missing.

As far as the fallen tree now, Seán stood, holding onto a branch so that he would not be blown off his feet. His guess had been right. Con Lynch was trudging through the mud on the other side, struggling to drag his feet through the thickness of the sludge. When Con reached the tree, he too grabbed hold of a branch and took a moment to get his breath back. Seán shone his torch on him.

"Are you alright, Con? Are you hurt?"

Still leaning against the solid trunk, Con looked up at the young guard. "I'm fine. Zach Claymore is not. He's injured. Badly injured."

"Jesus! No!"

"He's in the cab. Can you help me get him out? What's it like on your side there?"

"A lot of water running down, some loose stones and branches, but passable."

"Good. Come on over so. We'll have to lift Zach to your jeep. And hurry."

Without waiting to hear more, Seán climbed over the fallen tree, pushing aside branches. Con had already begun the walk back to the tractor. When Seán reached there he was shocked at the condition of the vet. A loud rumble added to his shock. The mudslide from The 360 was gathering pace and strength. No longer sluggish, it was whipping around their legs.

"You take him under the arms," Con ordered. "I'll take his legs."

Zach's head lolled as they lifted him up. Seán wondered if it was already too late for him. The mud rolled up to his knees and he wondered if it was too late for all of them.

Kevin had managed to borrow a baby carrier from someone outside in the hall. Despite her panic and pain, Robyn had to smile when she saw him come into the conference room with the carrier in one hand, nappies and baby clothes in the other.

Tansy, holding Ute's baby wrapped in a soft towel, flashed him a grateful smile. She was a lot more relaxed now since both Kevin and the sergeant had combed the hall and assured them that Horst Mueller was not there. It wasn't that she didn't trust Billy, just that she trusted Kevin and the sergeant more.

Robyn was glad to see the terrified look leave Tansy's face, though she herself was even more gripped by fear. She believed she knew now why Horst was so protective of his privacy. He had a lot to hide. Despite the fact that Ute appeared to be mentally unbalanced, Robyn believed her. There was something sinister going on in that house and it involved many babies named Hans or Zelda who stayed for a short while and were then moved on. Probably for huge sums of money. Robyn shook her head. Zach would say she was as fanciful as Tansy for believing Ute's ranting. He would laugh at the idea of baby-smuggling in Felton. Right next door to them and they had never heard a baby cry. And yet Ute was here with a baby she knew nothing about, and Horst appeared to be willing to go to any length to protect his secrets. Even as far as killing his wife if Ute was to be believed. Robyn shivered. The sense of evil Tansy seemed to have shrugged off now hung over her.

"Do you think you could rustle up a few baby blankets too?" Tansy asked Kevin sweetly.

"Hold the blankets until his temperature drops," Dr Early called from behind the screen where he was treating Ute. "It's still very high."

Robyn began to walk around the confined space. She felt more comfortable when moving. She heard the murmur of Dr Early's voice as he spoke softly to Ute, asking her how she got this and this. It was obvious to Robyn that the doctor was asking her about bruises, welts, scars, marks of brutality inflicted by Horst. Animal! Ute was not replying.

Tansy was crooning to the baby as she dressed it in the borrowed clothes. She handled the child as if she was born to the role. More surprising still was Kevin's active participation, the gentleness with which he touched the baby's face. Robyn stood still and watched. Tears came to her eyes. Where had this Kevin been hiding? The gentle caring person? The man who was now cradling the little baby in his arms while Tansy closed the fasteners in the lemon babygro.

"You're good at that," Robyn heard herself say.

Kevin raised his head. There was a terrible sadness in his face. "I had plenty of practice. On my son."

Son! Had he said '*my* son'? His son? It couldn't be. He and Lisa had never had a child. She must have misheard.

"What did you say, Kevin? I didn't hear you properly."

Tansy was still fiddling with the fasteners on the babygro. Kevin looked over her black, curly head and met Robyn's gaze.

"I said I had plenty of practice on my son. You heard me right. My son."

Robyn stared open-mouthed. A pain stabbed her but this time it was in her heart. A searing physical pain as intense as her contractions but more hurtful. It was the agony of being cheated, the despair of knowing in one split second that she had thrown away a chunk of her life on a lie. It was the ease with which he said it now in a roomful of people as if she did not even deserve the courtesy of privacy to mourn the loss of her self-respect. Unable to breathe, Robyn stared at him. His expression changed from one of sadness to shock. Perhaps he had not meant to tell her at all. This night, this wild and vicious night, was bringing them all face to face with their realities, whether they wanted to or not.

Finished with the fasteners, Tansy took the baby from him. "Out there," she said, pointing in the direction of the door. "You and Robyn have things to talk about."

Kevin raised an eyebrow and Robyn nodded. They both walked towards the door.

"Ten minutes, Robyn," Dr Early said, popping his head out from behind the screen. "I'll be finished with Ute then and I want to check you out."

"Ten minutes," Robyn agreed but she felt like shouting. Ten minutes to sort out a ten-year deception? A minute per year. Ten minutes to come to terms with the fact that she had been lied to in the most despicable way? A lifetime wouldn't be long enough.

As soon as the door of the conference room closed behind them, Robyn turned to Kevin, her eyes blazing.

"When? When was your son born? While you were

with me or before that? How old is he? Where do you hide him?"

Kevin glanced around him. People were scattered all around the hall, some visible only as a darker shadow in the blackness.

"We can't talk here," he said, holding her arm and leading her towards the storeroom. The smell of a meaty soup heating in the kitchen almost made Robyn sick. Despite the hurricane, the floods, the tragedy of Des Varian and perhaps more tragedies to come before the night was out, a happy group had gathered in the kitchen, laughing and chatting as if this was the social occasion of the year. She heard someone say that Billy Moynihan was cuddling June Varian, comforting her. The voice sounded like Noel Cantillon's. That would have brought a smile to her face a few minutes ago. Now it left her unmoved as she followed Kevin into the quiet of the storeroom.

He closed the door and flashed his torch around the shelves and boxes. They were alone.

"Well? You have some explaining to do, Kevin."

He dropped his head so that she couldn't see his eyes. "I tried to tell you earlier. I want to explain."

"Earlier tonight? That's ten years too late. How could you have let me go on, longing to have your baby, asking you, begging sometimes, while you were insisting it was wrong, even criminal to bring a child into the world. And all the time you were a father to this mysterious son. Where is he? Who's his mother? Not Lisa. Everyone in the office would know. Besides, she's too busy drinking herself to death to look after a child."

"Lisa was my son's mother. Don't talk about her like that. You know nothing about her."

That was the deepest hurt of all. He had respect for his wife. He defended her and he could not even tell Robyn the truth.

"For Christ's sake, Kevin! You let me make a fool of myself. You deceived me. How could you? Why did you do it?"

He raised his head. The torchlight cast shadows on his face, making him seem older. Vulnerable. But no less contemptible in Robyn's eyes.

"Answer me. Try to give me a reason. Any reason to make sense of this."

"I had a vasectomy after my son's birth. Long before I met you."

"Oh, Jesus! It gets worse. You let me spend ten years hoping to have a baby with a man who'd had a vasectomy. You're a – a – low-life. Scum!"

She felt like hitting him. Pummelling him with her fists until he begged for mercy. A strong spasm in her lower belly took her breath away before she could demean herself even more by resorting to physical violence. She waited until the pain eased before looking at him again.

"So that's what all the preaching was about? A cover-up. The 'I couldn't bring a child into this terrible world' farce. While I didn't agree with you, I respected your principles. I can see now you have none."

"I had my reasons, Robyn. I-I just couldn't tell you. I couldn't tell anyone. My brother –"

Robyn held up her hand. "Hold it there. This is between you and me. You're not going to lay the blame on someone else. You lied to me and you'll take the blame. Anyway, what brother? You never mentioned him before. Another lie?"

"He died when I was eleven years old. He was four."

She sensed the pain in his voice.

"I'm sorry," she muttered.

"So am I. Now. But I wasn't then. I hated him. I hated the way he took my parents away from me. The way they abandoned me, sent me off to boarding school when I was only seven so that they could devote all their time and affection to him."

His feelings were so intense that his voice shook when he spoke. There was no doubt in Robyn's mind he was telling the truth now. At last.

"Why did you hate him and what has it got to do with the lies you told me, the way you cheated and stole ten years of my life?"

"He was sick."

"You hated him because he was sick? How noble of you. Tell me about your son. Do you hate him too?"

"I loved him. I really loved him. I-I . . ."

He began to cry. Robyn watched as his shoulders shook. She felt an instinctive urge to take him in her arms, to comfort him, but her anger boiled too hotly.

Kevin sniffed and wiped his eyes with the backs of his hands. "He was also four when he died."

She stared at him, trying to take in what he had said. He had fathered a child and buried that same child and never told her. God! She had bared her soul to him, told him everything about herself and had thought he had been doing the same. And yet he had kept a son, a brother and a vasectomy secret from her.

"I'm sorry about your son but I still don't understand

why you lied to me. Is it coincidence that both children died when they were four?"

He peered at her and touched her on the arm. She immediately stepped back from his touch.

"Are you alright?" he asked. "Do you need to sit down?" He flashed his torchlight around. "There must be something here to sit on."

"I'm fine, thank you. I just need the truth."

"The truth is, I'm a carrier of Tay-Sachs disease and so is Lisa. My brother died from it and Lisa and I passed it on to our son. The odds were stacked against that happening but it did. A small gene defect in chromosome 15 with huge consequences. So now you know. I live with the guilt of hating my little brother and the agony of having brought a child into the world just to suffer for the duration of his short lifespan."

He was telling the truth. She had no doubt about that. Why had he hidden it from her for so long? She pitied him. Of course she did. But she still resented him for deceiving her. She still felt a need to hurt him too.

"Is that why your wife drinks herself into a stupor? And you stay with her to ease your guilty conscience?"

"Maybe."

She had achieved her goal. The man standing in front of her now, tears clinging to his eyelashes was vulnerable and devastated by grief. She had hurt him and she felt a momentary satisfaction.

He gripped her wrist and pulled her towards him. "I loved my son, Robyn. Kaleb. His name was Kaleb. I will always love him."

She nodded. The love he felt for Kaleb was easy to read in his eyes. She pulled her wrist away from him.

The pressure of the baby was too uncomfortable for her to remain standing in one position. She walked carefully back and forth in the cluttered room as she let Kevin's revelations sink in. One thing was sure, tragic as the history of the two dead children was, it didn't excuse the way he had deceived her. He hadn't even thought her worth the truth.

"What was I to you, Kevin? A tart? The clichéd bit on the side?"

"I love you, Rob. I always have since the first day we . . ."

She didn't hear him finish the sentence. Dazed, in both physical and emotional pain, she stumbled out of the storeroom and back to the conference room. She met Dr Early just outside the door. He was on his way to collect her.

"Come on, Robyn. I want you to hop up on the couch. Let's see how things are progressing."

As Robyn went into the conference room with him, she sought and met Tansy's eyes. Tansy knew. It was evident in the soft sympathetic glow of her dark eyes. Kevin had told Tansy, whom he barely knew, and yet for ten, long, passionate and sometimes despairing years, he had kept the truth from her. Damn him! Damn all men! And with that thought came tears and a longing for Zach so strong that she could almost feel his arms around her, soothing her, telling her he loved her.

"I want Zach," she sobbed.

Dr Early patted her hand and smiled at her. "I know, Robyn. I know. But now we must look after his baby."

His words hung in the air with the resonance of an unfinished sentence. Unbidden, the conclusion formed in Robyn's mind. They must look after Zach's baby because it might be all that remained of him. She climbed onto the couch and for the first time in many years, began to pray.

Chapter 29

Horst had pins and needles in his feet. Dust tickled his nose and he was afraid that any second now he would sneeze. That idiot journalist was standing here in the storeroom, in the dark, sniffling. Through a slit between the boxes he could see him. How much longer would he stay? He should have followed his girlfriend out – the snooty vet's wife – his 'bit on the side' as she had called herself. There was a limit to the time Horst could stay squeezed into the narrow space between the stacks of cartons and the wall. He had found refuge here while the sergeant and the blasted journalist had searched for him but now he felt trapped. He smiled, thinking it had been worth the discomfort to hear that smug journalist confess he'd had a snip. And to know that Mrs Claymore had a very interesting past.

Another minute dragged slowly by and still Kevin Phillips did not move. Horst wondered what Ute was saying in the room next door. He had come here thinking he could put his ear to the dividing wall and listen to what was being said. Not a sound seeped through. One thing they could do well was insulation. She was probably ranting away in that husky voice of hers, her eyes huge, her bony little body curled up into a shaking mass. He knew both she and the baby were still there. In the emergency medical centre. A pretend hospital. A farce. Just like everything else in Felton.

Very slowly and carefully, Horst raised his hands and scratched his nose. He felt less itchy but more helpless. He could feel his anger boiling. Yet again one of these morons was thwarting his plans, giving Ute more time to ruin what they had worked so hard to achieve.

Kevin Phillips flicked on his torch. Horst scrunched himself up smaller. Phillips gave one last sniff and then threw his shoulders back. He was obviously preparing to face back out to his moronic friends. Someone tapped on the door. The journalist strode over and opened it up. It was the Bingham bitch. His fingers itched. He longed to wind them around her skinny neck.

"Are you alright, Kevin?" she asked in the whiney voice Horst was growing to detest.

"I'm not sure, Tans. But you were right. I should have told Robyn a long time ago. I'll never forgive myself for being so unfair to her. She'll certainly never forgive me."

'Tans' stood on tiptoe and kissed him on the cheek. Horst had to smother a laugh. Was this guy sleeping with both women and a wife as well?

"She will, Kev. Have you told her the full story?"

"Yes. Everything. No more secrets."

"That's good. Truth heals. Dr Early says her labour is advanced. He wants us to bring Ute and her baby into the hall. The sergeant says Horst is definitely not here but he wants us to keep an eye on her just in case."

Horst had to restrain himself from jumping up. Was there no end to this bitch's interfering? He should have finished the job when he'd had the opportunity.

As the door closed behind Tansy and Kevin, Horst came out from behind the cartons and flexed his cramped muscles. He took a breath and calmed himself. He would get his chance. Horst Mueller always did.

Gravel slapping onto the sides of the jeep added to the clamour of the storm. Seán Harte took the corner approaching the hall car park recklessly. Every time he glanced in the rear-view mirror he thought Zach Claymore had breathed his last. He drove the jeep straight at the front door and jammed on the brakes at the last possible second.

"Stay with him," he ordered Con Lynch. "I'll get help."

Not waiting for Con's answer, he leaped out and was instantly blown up against the jeep. It took minutes of struggle against the wind to cover the few steps to the door.

"*Help!*" he called out as he banged his fist on the heavy wood panel. He hopped impatiently as he heard someone fumbling with the bolt inside the door. Billy Moynihan's face appeared and the sergeant loomed over his shoulder.

"Seán!" the sergeant said. "Thank God you're alright!"

Seán took a breath to calm himself but he couldn't keep the panic out of his voice.

"Zach Claymore's in the jeep. He's badly injured."

"Sweet Jesus!" Billy muttered.

Tim Halligan dashed past him, a blanket in his hand. "We'll carry him in. Go tell Dr Early."

When Billy turned around, June Varian was behind him, an expectant look on her face.

"It's Zach Claymore, June. They say he's badly injured."

"I'm sorry to hear that."

Billy gave her hand a quick squeeze. He knew she had been hoping the knock on the door would have brought her news of her son. "I must let Dr Early know. He's got Robyn in there. I must warn him."

June nodded and then went in search of a bed. A folding bed, a camp bed. Any kind of bed she could bring into the conference room for Zach since Robyn would need the couch. The room was becoming a hospital ward. She would not allow the thought that it could soon become a morgue.

Kevin carried the Muellers' baby while Tansy led Ute from the conference room into the hall. Ute walked reluctantly along, chanting "He'll kill me, he'll kill me!" Tansy, still reeling from Dr Early's whispered news that Zach was badly injured, ignored her.

"We'll bring Mrs Mueller over to the kitchen," Kevin said. "She'll be safer there because people are in and out all the time."

Tansy nodded agreement and followed Kevin. She couldn't concentrate on Ute or even on her own fear of Horst Mueller. All she could think of was Robyn. Poor Robyn, in labour with no epidural, no gas and air. No husband to hold her hand. She heard Billy Moynihan's excited shouts as he approached from the front doorway, clearing a pathway ahead of him. He was followed by a dark clump of people, indistinguishable in the shadows. It wasn't until they were right next to her that Tansy saw Zach, lying on a makeshift blanket stretcher that was being carried by the two gardaí and two other men. He looked lifeless, his right leg strapped onto a board and sticking out at a peculiar angle. She looked at the inert figure and put her hands to her mouth to stifle the scream she felt well up. The little troop and their burden moved on. A cortege. The surrealism was compounded when the rear was brought up by June Varian, struggling with the weight of a fold-up bed.

"You take her," Tansy said, guiding Ute towards Kevin. "I'm going back to be with Robyn."

Without waiting for his answer, she grabbed one side of the camp-bed from June and together they followed Zach towards the room where his child's life was about to begin and his, quite possibly, was about to end.

When Billy Moynihan had come bustling through the door of the conference room for the umpteenth time, Robyn did not take much notice. She was leaning forward gripping the arms of the chair Zach had found for her. She got ease from the pain in that position. Maybe the comfort came from the fact that she felt a physical connection with Zach by touching the piece of furniture he had so recently handled. She was glad of the demands the contractions were making on her attention. They kept her from speculating about Zach's situation and from murdering the deceitful, cowardly Kevin Phillips.

Billy whispered to Dr Early before scuttling out again. Robyn smiled. The hurricane seemed to be a coming-of-age for Billy. He had at last found his niche in Felton. Master-in-chief of hurricane management.

Dr Early came to stand by her side, a pocket watch which looked like a family heirloom in his hand. "You're doing very well, Robyn. You're dilating nicely – seven centimetres last check. The baby's heartbeat is normal and it's presenting head first." He snapped the case on the watch shut. "Contractions five minutes apart. No problems so far."

The deep, regular breaths Robyn had been concentrating on taking became ragged and shallow. She straightened up and looked into the old man's face.

"What do you mean 'so far'? Do you anticipate a problem? My God! There can't be. I have no way of getting to a hospital. Damn it! I should have gone when Zach said!"

"Sit back, Robyn. Continue your breathing exercises. You're fine. So is the baby. I must tell you something now though that may upset you. Zach is being brought in here."

She felt the baby press downward, blinding her with white pain, robbing her of breath. She stared wide-eyed at Dr Early, the question in her eyes. He caught her sweaty hand in his warm, dry one.

"Your husband has been injured. I don't know any more details."

Her lungs sucked in a huge breath, taking the edge off her physical agony but bringing the emotional pain into sharp focus. Her thoughts began to race along illogical paths.

Had she thanked Zach for getting her the upholstered chair? An act of kindness so Zach-like. Had she thanked him for painting the nursery, remembering her birthday, tolerating her mother's biting sarcasm, massaging her back when it ached? For not hating her when she allowed Kevin Phillips back into their lives?

"Try to stay as relaxed as possible, Robyn. The labour will be easier on you then. I can, if I have to, give you some painkillers but I'd prefer not. Think of your baby."

"Is Zach dead?"

As soon as she blurted out the question, Robyn covered her ears. She didn't want to hear the answer. The door opened and Billy Moynihan walked through. A sombre, downcast Billy who averted his eyes when she looked at him. Con Lynch came next, hunched over, drenched, a soggy cap pulled down low over his face, muddy Wellingtons squelching as he walked. She caught the arms of the chair and heaved herself up when a group of men carried a blanket stretcher in. She gasped, or maybe it was a scream escaped her. Zach, blue-lipped and waxen, was in the blanket. Somebody put their arms around her. Soft, gentle arms. She smelled oil of roses and knew it was Tansy. Lovely Tansy, all scents and ideas and fun and love of life.

"Calm down, Rob. Dr Early will look after him. Think of your baby."

Robyn did. She thought of her baby like they were all telling her do. For an instant she hated it as passionately as she had yearned for it for the past almost nine months. What child would choose to be born in the middle of a hurricane on the night its father died? As if to punish her for her shameful rejection the muscles of her lower body contracted with such force that she almost fainted with the pain. She heard a groan and thought it was her own. When she heard it again, she knew it was Zach. In pain but alive! She took a step forward to walk to where he had been carried behind the screen. Her legs were weak and her abdomen felt as if it was being squeezed by red-hot bands of steel. What little breath she had dispersed in one puff when she saw June Varian setting up a camp-bed with an orange frame and a mattress covered in a Superman motif.

"Oh, fuck! This is too much. I'm going mad!"

With surprising strength, Tansy held onto Robyn and turned her around so that her back was to the screen behind which Zach lay.

"We're going to do our breathing, Robyn. I'll take Zach's place and help you until he's able to. That means I'll take no nonsense from you. Understand?"

No. Robyn didn't understand anything. She didn't know why Zach was all white and blue, why the baby was coming early, why June was making up a Superman bed or why gentle Tansy was suddenly like a major domo. And she hadn't the strength to work it out. She was tired and weak, yet her body was making demands for huge amounts of energy she no longer had. Her mind was asking questions she couldn't answer. She needed to lean on the strength Tansy suddenly seemed to have found. She smiled at her. At least she tried. Her facial muscles were in spasm too.

"Help me, please, Tansy."

"Of course I will. Now, down on your hands and knees. Bum in the air. We're going to do this as nature intended. It's the best way."

Tansy helped Robyn down then joined her on the floor. Together they inhaled, held and exhaled to the rhythmic chant of Tansy's one, two, three count. June continued her busy assembling of the Superman bed and

Con Lynch seemed to shrivel in misery until he was nothing more than a cap and Wellington boots.

When the noise and the heat of Robyn's pain abated, she crawled on hands and knees to the screen and pulled it back. Tim Halligan and Seán Harte stood at the end of the couch. They saw Robyn and stepped quietly away. Dr Early was leaning over Zach, lifting his eyelids and shining a light into his eyes. Robyn saw a piece of timber on the couch under Zach's right leg. Someone, probably the doctor had cut Zach's jeans, exposing a badly swollen and misshapen leg. Clotted blood from a wound on his temple streaked his cheek. Zach blinked. His eyelids fluttered and then they opened. Leaning on Tansy for support, Robyn pulled herself into a standing position. She stooped over Zach and touched his face. He was so cold!

"I love you, Zach Claymore," she whispered.

His eyes turned in her direction. His beautiful green eyes, confused now. They cleared for a moment and gazed at her with such love she felt it touch her soul. She lowered her face to his and kissed him gently on the forehead. He sighed. A gentle, tired sigh. His eyelids drooped and closed.

Horst had no idea what time it was now. He hadn't remembered to put on his watch when he left the house, in his rush to pursue Ute. It was still dark. Blacker here in the storeroom. The only noises he could hear were the howl of wind, the clatter of torrential rain and occasionally a piercing sound from overhead. He thumped the wall in frustration, not caring now if somebody heard. He was getting desperate, his earlier confidence fading with each passing minute.

He stood and walked over to the door, double-checking that he had bolted it from the inside. He had been lucky so far. Nobody had come to the door and wondered why it was locked. That's why he had chosen the store.

He began to pace between the cartons and paint tins. Every time he thought of Ute spilling her guts to the police, he trembled with temper. But maybe she had said nothing about their business arrangements with the Americans. That was the biggest curse. He didn't know and he couldn't take the chance. If Ute had indeed blabbed their business Interpol would be on the lookout for them, hurricane or no hurricane. Why had she run away? Did she intend delivering the child to the contact in the UK and collecting the money herself? He shook his head. Ute wouldn't have the brains to work out that plan. Then why had she gone? And more importantly how was he going to get her back and shut her up? The Bingham bitch had said she was bringing Ute out to the hall but just going out there and claiming his wife and child was too risky.

Keeping the beam aimed low, he shone his torch around the store, desperately searching for some inspiration. He saw packing of every sort, bits of timber, reams of paper, cans of alcohol-based polish, varnish.

Plenty of material to start a fire. A funeral pyre!

The idea made him smile. What justice it would be to burn the whole building to the ground and all the little people in it. The Bingham bitch, the fornicating journalist, the vet's wife with her butter-wouldn't-melt appearance and her interfering ways. Ute and the baby too. All gone. Ashes to ashes.

He paced faster. The idea excited him. Going to the centre of the store he shone his torch up to the ceiling. A fire alarm. Behind the door was a fire extinguisher. The whole building would be alarmed and fitted out with extinguishers. Of course it was. It would have to be. Fuck! They would have the fire out before it could take hold. There was the emergency exit door too and the evacuation drill that loud-mouth Mayor had been shouting about. The idea was dead even before he had time to think it through properly. A pity. He allowed himself to think of the panic the sound of the fire alarms would cause. The Mayor would probably have a heart attack. Preferably not immediately fatal but very painful and prolonged. The whole place would be in uproar, people running around terrified for their lives, forgetting their evacuation drill, afraid to stay in the hall and afraid to go out into the hurricane. What a shame it couldn't work.

His ears began to buzz. He hated that. So did Ute. She knew what buzzing ears made him do. He kicked a can. The buzzing was getting louder and his head was beginning to ache. It was harder to think. He flashed his torch high up on the back wall where the small windows were. Not even bony little Ute could escape through them. Despite his anger and pain Horst laughed. The Mayor must have designed this shit-hole. The laugh turned to rage. He put his hands to his forehead and squeezed hard. It didn't help. He knew his hands would shortly begin to shake. That's what made him most angry. That loss of control.

Needing to rest now, Horst sat on the floor, bent his knees, rested his head on them and sobbed as he hadn't done since he was a child.

Kevin held the baby carrier while Ute ate the stew someone had given her. It was warm in the kitchen, heat coming from the gas cooker and the people who seemed to be perpetually milling around there. Head down, she shovelled the food ravenously into her mouth. He tried to pity her but then he looked at the baby, the little tummy rising and falling quickly as he battled to get air into his diseased lungs. Where had Hans come from? Cambodia? Vietnam? Thailand? And what about his mother? A child, a young girl forced into prostitution? A mother mourning the loss of her baby or a hard-hearted woman who had sold her child for profit?

"Who organises this scam, Ute? Where do the babies come from and go to?"

She stopped eating and looked up at him. He saw nothing in her eyes. Just blankness.

"How long do you keep them for?"

"Until we're told to deliver."

"Who tells you?"

She bowed her head and began to eat again. Her plate empty, she held it towards Kevin and asked for more. He put the baby carrier on the floor beside her and went to the big pot bubbling on the cooker to ladle some stew onto her plate. When he turned back she was staring intently at him. Daring him to outstare her.

He put the plate of stew in front of her and stooped down close to her ear.

"They all feel sorry for you, Ute. I do too for the beatings your husband gave you. He's an animal. But he couldn't have carried on his despicable baby trading without you. I'm watching you. I don't trust you."

She picked up her spoon and stirred her piping hot stew to cool it. Then she smiled at him. Her mouth smiled. Her eyes still held the same blankness.

"Horst Mueller is not my husband," she said.

He nodded. That figured. They might even be brother and sister. Business partners. Soul mates in sickness. Kevin shrugged.

"Eat up. I'm taking you back to the hall."

He picked up the baby from the carrier and turned his back on Ute as she dived into her second plate of stew. The child was feather-light in his arms. He drew a finger gently across the silky skin of the baby's face. His eyes filled with tears of regret and guilt and mourning for opportunities lost and mistakes made. He rocked the nameless baby in his arms and remembered his own son. How beautiful he had been when he had been born. How much he had suffered by the time he died.

"I'm finished," Ute said.

Kevin put the baby back in the carrier and caught Ute by the arm. She shook off his hand and walked beside him to the hall. Kevin narrowed his eyes as he watched her. Now that she was fed there was something different about her. Less vulnerable. There was definitely more to Ute Mueller than met the eye.

Chapter 30

Robyn felt the baby move with energy, grasping hold of the life on which its father had such a tenuous grip. She inhaled, exhaled, counted and cried. She thought she heard Dr Early ask June for a packet of frozen peas. She inhaled, exhaled, counted and cried again. She heard Zach moan and then call her name. The doctor appeared from behind the screen and immediately she called him over to her.

"How is he? Do you know yet?"

Dr Early looked at her, frowning, his lips sealed. Then he suddenly made up his mind. "You realise, Robyn, I don't have the benefit of hospital technology here. My diagnosis is purely on the physical exam I've done and my experience."

Robyn nodded, not sure where this was leading. Tansy caught her hand and she clung on.

"Zach is hypothermic and has suffered a concussion. The wound to his temple is superficial but he has a displaced fracture of his right leg. It's a closed fracture which is good but there's a lot of swelling."

Tansy nodded. "Aah! The frozen peas."

"Basic but effective. I'll try to get some of that swelling down before I set the bone and put on a cast. Luckily I have a suitable plastic one in my emergency supplies. Though I must say Con did a great job with the piece of board."

"And the concussion?"

The doctor hesitated. "I don't want to make a definitive diagnosis at this early stage but the signs are good. Under the circumstances, I'd like to reassure you that I see no immediate threat to your husband's life, Robyn."

Robyn exhaled the breath she hadn't realised she had been holding. Tansy should be proud – the whoosh of air lasted to a count of five.

"Can I see him now?"

He held his hand out to her and helped her up from the floor. "Tansy, you go with Robyn. I'll just chat to Con Lynch for a minute."

The walk as far as the screen seemed like a marathon. As soon as Robyn laid eyes on Zach, her heart couldn't help but jump. His colour was less deathly and a neat dressing covered the wound on his temple. She reached out shaking fingers and touched his cheek. It still felt cold.

"Zach? Zach, can you hear me?"

His eyelids flickered. His eyes opened, awareness dawning slowly.

"Rob! Are you alright? I'm sorry, Rob. I shouldn't have left you. The baby. How is the baby?"

"Our baby is fine, Zach. Just anxious to be born. You rest now and we'll talk again soon. I love you."

"How's Con? Is he safe?"

"He's fine. He's here. Do you want to talk to him?"

His eyes began to close, then flew open again, panic in them this time. "I must paint the shelf before the morning!"

Tansy and Robyn exchanged terrified glances.

"Reassure him," Dr Early said from behind them. "He could be like this for a while."

"A while? How long is that?"

"Maybe twenty-four hours."

Robyn caught Zach's hand in hers. "The baby is well, Zach. Tansy and I are taking good care of it. Now you rest and we'll talk soon."

June came in with the bag of peas and handed it to the doctor. He wrapped it in a towel and placed it on Zach's swollen leg. Zach didn't react. He was already in a deep sleep.

"June, the sergeant and Seán Harte have gone out into the hall. Would you find them for me, please? I'll need them here. When Zach's leg is set we'll move him over to your very colourful camp-bed. Then I'll need to see you behind the screens, Robyn. We'll soon be turning this area into the maternity ward."

With a last look at Zach, Robyn took Tansy's arm and returned to the other side of the room. She had seen the misshapen leg and knew Dr Early needed Tim and Seán to help with setting the bone. Maybe to hold Zach down. She shivered. Then all thoughts of everything except her own pain left her head as a heart-stopping, nerve-shattering, contraction whipped her breath away.

Con Lynch was sitting on a chair beside the camp-bed, wrapped up in a warm rug. The shivering had stopped now. He watched June Varian straighten out the sheets on the bed and wondered where she got the strength. She smiled at him.

"You look a bit better now, Con. You and Zach were so lucky to get here. You saved his life. Noreen would be proud of you. But then, she always was."

Con bowed his head. That was true. It's what made his failure to be there when she needed him most so very hard to bear. June put her hand on his shoulder and rested it there. She didn't say anything. She didn't need to. By osmosis they shared their guilty thoughts, one for failing a wife, the other for failing a son.

Eventually Con stood up. He nodded his head towards where Robyn was sitting in her chair, her feet up on a bag, Tansy Bingham behind her, massaging her shoulders.

"It's time I wasn't here. I'll go out into the hall. I just wanted to be sure that Zach was alright."

"Did you get anything to eat, Con? There's plenty of food in the kitchen. I'll go with you."

Tansy stopped rubbing Robyn's shoulders. "June, would you mind if I went with Con? Could you stay with Rob? I'll only be a little while."

June walked over and waved Tansy away. "Go on. We'll be grand here."

She began immediately to massage Robyn's shoulders, her touch stronger and firmer than Tansy's. Con Lynch was standing hesitantly near the door, embarrassed to look directly at Robyn.

She called him over and smiled at him. "Con, Seán Harte told me how you found Zach and loaded him onto the tractor and brought him to safety. I'm very, very, grateful to you. Zach will be too when he wakes up. Thank you."

The old man shuffled uncomfortably but he returned her smile.

"He's a grand lad, your husband. He was good to me too. We won't know until this blasted hurricane is gone but there's a fair chance my house has been buried in the mudslide. If he hadn't come for me I might have been buried there too."

"By the sound of the wind and rain, it seems this hurricane will never –"

Robyn had to grit her teeth as another contraction took her breath. She longed to howl. Bay like a wolf. She grimaced silently instead. Con mumbled something and scurried away, Tansy trotting after him.

June laughed. "It's his age," she said. "He probably thinks there's something sinful about the birthing process."

"There bloody is!" Robyn gasped and this time she did howl.

Tansy left Con Lynch in the kitchen being fussed over by Noel Cantillon and his army of helpers. She looked out into the darkness of the hall and wondered where Kevin had settled with Ute and the baby. She had forgotten to bring her torch with her and had to depend on the sporadic light from other people's torches. She stood for a moment, listening to the wind, quaking before the deep roar of power in every gust.

Standing in front of the storeroom door she thought she heard a noise from inside. Had Kevin gone back in there? Pressing down the door handle, she pushed. The door didn't budge. It was locked. She listened again, certain that she had heard something from inside.

A high-pitched screeching sound echoed through the

hall, followed by ripping and tearing. Stunned, everyone looked upwards from where the sound had come. "The roof!" someone said and another sobbed in fear. Tansy tried to remember the details from when the hall had been built. It was a tiled roof. Sheets of plastic tiling. She remembered now. That meant if a sheet had come loose, it would uncover a good area of the roof. With wind this strong the whole roof could lift. Where would they go then with all the evacuees – Zach injured, Evie Cronin having a nervous breakdown, not to mention Robyn about to give birth?

She dropped her hand from the storeroom door. Obviously the noise she had heard had not come from there but from the roof which was about to blow away. She began to feel panicky, seeing nothing in front of her but dark blotches. She must find Kevin, let him know how Zach was and then get back to Robyn.

Even as she began to step her way through the encampments people had set up around the hall, she knew she was not being entirely honest with herself. Kevin would want to know about Zach, of course he would. And how Robyn's labour was progressing. Especially how Robyn's labour was progressing. But it was Tansy herself who had the greatest need. She must, just must, see Kevin, talk to him, know that he was alright. "Silly fool," she muttered to herself. "Once bitten and then back for more." She wasn't listening to her own warnings. This was different, somehow ordained. By Maya gods? She hadn't figured it all out yet, but Tansy knew that in some grand blueprint, she and Kevin Phillips had been meant to meet and connect in the way they were doing now. Poor Kevin. Poor guilty Kevin.

It was the baby carrier she saw first. Kevin was sitting beside it, gently rocking the child to sleep while Ute lay on the floor curled up underneath a blanket. Tansy flopped onto the floor beside Kevin.

"How's little Hans?" she asked, leaning over and looking at the sleeping child.

"He's cooler. Seems to be breathing easier too."

About to pass a remark on his experience with babies coming in handy, Tansy, out of character, stopped herself in time. The pain of watching his child suffer and eventually die in his arms was not something he needed to be reminded of. She smiled at him.

"I came out to tell you the great news. Dr Early says Zach's injuries aren't life-threatening. Concussion, hypothermia and a broken limb."

"Ouch! God! Poor Zach. It's very good news though. How's Robyn?"

"Coming up to the end stages. Dr Early is setting up the couch for her to deliver. I think it will be quick."

Kevin laughed. "You're a midwife too?"

"It's a natural process."

"Just like your cooking!"

"You're laughing at me. Brat!"

"No. I'm not. Tansy Bingham, you're the wisest woman I've ever met. One of the most beautiful too."

"I'll ask you to repeat that under better weather conditions. When you're not hurricane-shocked. Did you hear the noise on the roof ? Do you think it's going to blow off?"

As if to help Kevin make up his mind the screeching noise came from the roof again. A frightened murmur went around the hall. Ute stirred and then curled up smaller.

"I don't know, Tans. Kimi has blown all my certainties away."

They both laughed as they listened to Billy Moynihan, his voice like a foghorn, scuttling around the hall announcing that nobody was to panic about the roof. The more he shouted the more panic he spread.

"If Billy says the roof won't blow off, then I 'spose it wouldn't dare," said Tansy.

Tansy glanced to where Ute was sleeping. Her gaze softened as she saw the child-woman curled in the foetal position, the blanket held protectively under her chin. She shook her head.

"Poor little Ute. What must she have suffered at the hands of that barbarian!"

"Hmm."

Tansy looked sharply at Kevin. "What does that mean? Surely you must have sympathy for her."

Kevin shrugged. "Call it a hunch but I'd like to know a lot more about her before I'd feel sorry for her. From what I can gather she's never tried to stop Horst. She's not his wife either, or so she says."

"Really? But none of us are what we appear to be on first acquaintance, are we? I'd better get back to Rob. Do you want me to take a message to her?"

Kevin's head dropped. He sighed, then looked up. "Just tell her I'm truly sorry and I hope everything goes well with her delivery."

Tansy stood up. "I'll give her your message, of course. But you will talk to her yourself, won't you? Neither of you will be able to move on until you do."

Kevin stood too and put his arms around her. His lips brushed against hers. The merest gossamer touch but it set her heart pounding. Someone wolf-whistled and Tansy was glad of the dark to cover her blushes.

"I'll hop back again later to let you know how Robyn is doing," she said.

She was excited as she turned to head back to the conference room. Robyn's baby would soon be born. A new life. In her heart she could also feel the stirrings of a new start in her own life.

Tansy smiled in the darkness as she carefully picked her way towards the top of the hall.

Chapter 31

As gently as if they were handling Belleek china, Tim Halligan and Seán Harte lowered Zach onto the camp-bed. He looked a lot more comfortable now with padding and a plastic splint supporting his broken leg. Seán Harte was still pale after witnessing the setting procedure.

"I'll hear that bone crunching for the rest of my life," he whispered to the sergeant. Jesus! And the roar he gave! God! I could nearly feel the pain myself."

Tim winked at him. "We'll get out of here now. His wife will be doing her own bit of roaring soon if I'm any judge. And I should be, with four kids."

June, busy with her self-appointed task as sheet-changer, heard them and gave a 'What could a man know about labour pains?' type of snort. Then her face changed and suddenly crumpled. She was remembering when Des had been born. The long labour, the worry that he would be healthy, the joy when the red-haired boy was placed in her arms. And why had she suffered all that pain? Just to sacrifice her baby to the sea? To have the body she had nurtured and cared for nibbled by fish and broken against rocks? She felt like screaming now, as loud as Zach had while his broken bones were being pushed back into place. She turned to Dr Early. The old man looked tired. And no wonder.

"You delivered my Des. Do you remember?"

"I do. I remember well. He was a big baby. Over nine pounds, wasn't he?"

"Yes. Nine two. He hurt like hell then. He still does."

Dr Early caught June's hand and patted it. "You're doing well, June. You're a terrific help here and a godsend to Robyn. But don't try to be too brave. Cry if you need to. And don't lose hope."

"I'll have a lifetime to cry. And there's a distinction between hope and fooling yourself. He's gone, Dr Early. No amount of hoping will bring him back."

June returned to putting the sheet on the couch.

Robyn saw and heard all this through a haze. She was totally possessed by pain and she welcomed every searing bolt. Her mind had no space for treachery or wasted years or secret sons and brothers. Kevin Phillips was blanked out by the demands of her body. By the urgency of her baby's need to enter this world of broken promises and shattered illusions.

Dr Early caught her arm and led her towards the couch.

"I want to see Zach first," she said.

Slowly, they detoured by the camp bed. Zach was sleeping peacefully. She reached out her hand and touched his hair. It was damp with sweat, as was hers.

"We're a pair," she whispered to him. "You and me, Zach. Always."

His eyes opened and he smiled up at her. An aware but very tired smile. "You should be resting, Rob. I'm sorry to have put everyone to such trouble. Would you thank Con and Seán for me? And thank you too, Dr Early."

"I will," she said. "Go back to sleep now."

"You too. I love you."

He was asleep almost before the words had left his mouth. Robyn kissed him on the forehead and then allowed Dr Early to help her up on the couch. June stood behind her, gently stroking her face and hair.

Dr Early said "Hmm" a few times before finally raising his head from the examination.

"Well, Robyn, that was quick. You're fully dilated. The head is engaged. Very unusual for a first baby."

"Is that wrong? Is there something not right with the baby?"

"No. Everything's perfect, no foetal distress. Unless of course you were looking forward to a really long labour. Then you'll be disappointed."

"Where's Tansy? I need her to breathe with me."

"I'll go get her," June volunteered.

Robyn grabbed her hand. "No! Please stay, June. I feel safe with you here. Tansy will come back when she's ready."

Robyn forgot about Tansy then, about June and Kevin and even about Zach. Her world was populated by excruciating pain and her urgent need to deliver her baby.

She heard it again as she passed by the storeroom. She stood and listened. This time Tansy knew it wasn't the sound of the roof being torn off. It was more like the thump of solid objects being thrown around. Looking around she checked to see if there was somebody nearby who would either confirm or deny what she was hearing. She was alone in the dark shadows. She could walk back to the kitchen and ask someone to come out. Annoyed with herself for needing someone else's opinion before making up her own mind, she put her hand on the door handle. It was still locked. Hairs stood on the back of her neck. Who was in there? Why was it locked? She should find Billy and ask him. He had all the keys. When she heard him shouting from somewhere in the hall, assuring people in his panicky way that the roof was designed to withstand all weather conditions, she decided not to disturb him. She rattled the handle and called out hello. The banging stopped. She heard a bolt slide back. Glancing over her shoulder, she checked to see how far away Kevin was. She couldn't pick him out in the darkness. The door opened a crack. Suddenly Tansy felt very alone in the crowded hall. She was isolated in blackness. And that was when she allowed herself to examine the thought she had pushed away the first time she heard the noise. Even though the sergeant and Billy assured her Horst Mueller was not in the hall, she knew he could very well be. In the storeroom banging things.

She took a step back just as a hand reached out and grabbed her by the wrist. A strong hand. It caught her unawares and jerked her inside the darkness of the storeroom. She heard the inside bolt being snapped into place again. Somebody swung her around, grabbed her from behind and locked his arms around her. A hot breath wafted over her. It was a mixture of aftershave and garlic. She tried to scream but he clamped a hand over her mouth while still keeping a tight grip around her waist with his other arm. She felt her knees go weak and her heart pound. She was dizzy, longing to sink into the weakness which was enclosing her in a deeper darkness, but her survival instinct came to the fore. She must stay conscious and aware. It was her only chance. She bit a finger of the hand across her mouth. He yelped but didn't let go, tightening his hold over her so powerfully that she thought her jaw would break and her ribs crack. She gasped as hot needles of pain stabbed her. She stamped down on his foot. He laughed as her shoe glanced off him.

"You'll have to do better than that, you interfering busybody. Didn't you ever hear that curiosity killed the cat? And not just your big, fat, ugly cat."

Sweat was beginning to trickle down her back. She thought of Ben, safely in his cage in the conference room. This bastard couldn't touch him. She thought of Robyn in labour and wondered if she would ever see the baby. And Kevin. How cruel to die now just when she had sensed the start of something very meaningful between herself and Kevin.

"This is your own fault," her attacker said. "Why couldn't you just have left us alone, you and that other nosey bitch?"

His hand was up under her nose so that she was finding it difficult to breathe. Somewhere in the back of her mind she remembered reading that you should try to engage your captor in conversation. She had only skimmed through the article, never believing she would need the information. She spoke against the pressure of his hand, not knowing whether he could decipher her words.

"Your wife is out in the hall. And the baby. The police know about you. All the roads are blocked off. You have nowhere to run."

He pushed her so hard and so unexpectedly that she was lying on the floor before she knew what had happened, Horst straddling her back, pinning her to the ground. Mouth free, she opened it wide to yell for help. The scream was torn from her throat just as another, louder and more violent tearing sound came from the roof. Before she could get her breath back to scream again, Horst had slapped a length of insulating tape around her mouth. The strong adhesive stuck painfully to the tender skin of her lips and prickled the soft hairs on her face. She kicked and bucked but he maintained his control over her while he jerked her hands behind her back and taped them together. Quickly shifting position he turned his attention to her legs. He hummed while he taped her at ankle and knee. He stood then and surveyed his work.

Horst Mueller smiled. A job well done.

"I can't. I just can't. No more strength," Robyn gasped.

"Pant," June advised. "It will help."

Robyn tried to think of her baby and of Zach. She tried to be maternal and selfless. Her generous thoughts were gone. All she wanted to do now was to rid her body of this unbearable pain. How could her child do this to her? And Zach, sleeping so peacefully while she was dying. She hated both of them. Tears welled in her eyes. This wasn't how it was meant to be. It wasn't as she had planned. And where was Tansy? Such a fair-weather friend. All wisdom and support and then when the going got tough, Tansy ran.

"Keep up with your breathing, Robyn," Dr Early said.

Robyn found the strength somewhere to do as she was told.

"Good," he muttered.

Robyn felt like hitting him. Weak, she leaned back against her pillows, her body sweat-drenched.

"Where's Tansy?" she asked as June wiped her forehead with a cool wet cloth.

June frowned. "I don't know. She's gone a long time. Didn't she say she was just taking Con Lynch to the kitchen?"

"Kevin Phillips," Robyn said. "She'll have gone to see him. Find him and you'll find her."

June gently pushed Robyn's now wet, blonde hair back from her face. "I'll go get Tansy. I won't be long."

Dr Early mouthed to her to be quick. June understood. Robyn Claymore was about to deliver her baby.

There was no time to waste. Grabbing a torch, June ran out into the hall. She panicked then. It was a sea of shadows and swathes of deepest black. Torches shone here and there but mostly people just sat on chairs or lay on their makeshift beds on the floor and all the while the wind howled eerily and pushed against the building with such force that the solid structure shook. She didn't know where to start looking. She heard Billy Moynihan's voice booming from the end of the hall. She began to make her way towards him. Billy would know where Tansy was.

When she finally got within calling distance of him, he rushed towards her.

"Are you alright, June? Don't worry about the roof. As I've been telling everyone –"

"I don't give a fiddler's about the roof. Robyn's about to deliver and I'm looking for Tansy Bingham. Have you seen her?"

"Last I saw of her she was bringing Con Lynch into the kitchen. Did you look there?"

"Not yet."

Billy caught her by the elbow. "Come on. I'll help you find her."

He guided them expertly around all the obstacles. The kitchen was quieter now than it had been, with only a handful of those who could not rest in the dark of the hall sipping cups of tea. Noel Cantillon was as alert as ever, still doing an inventory of his stock. He looked up from his task as June and Billy came in.

"I've set aside some milk for the children. We're going through it at an awful rate. I'll have to ration it soon."

"Whatever," Billy said dismissively. "We're looking for Tansy Bingham. Have you seen her?"

Noel frowned and then nodded. "Yes, she was here with Con Lynch. But that was a while ago. I don't know where she is now. Why?"

Billy turned to June and raised an eyebrow. She hesitated but then decided she should answer.

"Robyn Claymore is about to deliver her baby any time now. She wants Tansy there."

Noel leaned forward, the glint of new gossip in his eyes. "The poor girl. And I heard it's touch and go with Zach."

Annoyed, June snapped at him. "I hope you're not

spreading that story. Zach's going to be fine. Do you know where Kevin Phillips is? The journalist from the *Daily News*?"

"He was in here with Mrs Mueller and her baby. She was starving. She had two plates of stew."

Billy caught June's elbow again. "I know where they are. Come on. I'll bring you there."

June allowed herself to be led along, silently praying Robyn had been right and that Tansy was indeed with Kevin. She felt a bit confused by the relationship between the three of them. It had seemed to her that there was a history between Robyn and Kevin Phillips. A more intense relationship than employer and employee. Now it appeared that Tansy too had something going on with the man from Dublin. June dismissed these thoughts. How could she understand these young people when she hadn't understood her own son? Poor Des. A sob escaped from her into the darkness. Billy tightened his hold on her elbow.

"Almost there now," he said, shining his torch straight ahead.

June was surprised to see Kevin Phillips holding the Muellers' baby in his arms while Ute slept on the floor beside him. He looked up at June and Billy, a confused expression on his face as if he was coming back from a long way off.

"I'm looking for Tansy," June said. "Have you seen her?"

"She's in the conference room. She went there to be with Robyn. How is Robyn? Do you know?"

Billy and June exchanged a worried glance.

"What's wrong ?" Kevin asked.

"Tansy hasn't come back to the conference room. And Robyn needs her now. Her time to deliver the baby is almost here."

"But she left me to go to Robyn and that was over . . ." Kevin stopped talking and a look of terror crossed his face. "Are you certain Horst Mueller is not in this hall?" he asked Billy.

Billy puffed out his chest, offended that his word was being doubted. "I told you the sergeant and myself searched every nook and cranny. So did Seán Harte. We looked outside too at the front of the building as much as we could with the blasted wind. It nearly lifted us off our feet and we're solid men. Horst Mueller is not here."

Ute stirred and began to mutter again. "He'll kill me. He'll kill me."

Kevin stood, put the baby into the carrier and handed it to June. He turned to Billy. "Where's the sergeant? Get him. And the young guard too. We must find Tansy."

"Calm down, Kevin. She certainly wouldn't have left the hall. A little scrap like her would be whipped away by the wind. She'll just be chatting to someone about one of her mad ideas. You know Tansy."

Kevin took a deep breath and tried to do as Billy advised, but his heart would not stop beating too fast and his mouth was dry. He knew for certain that Tansy would not stay in the hall chatting when Robyn needed her. The other shattering truth was that Kevin realised now, without any doubts, that Tansy Bingham was the only person who made him see the joy in life, the happiness which had evaded him since he had been a child. He had just found her and was not going to lose her. Just as terrified but sounding calmer, he spoke to Billy.

"Let the sergeant and Seán Harte know. I'll start the search at the top of the hall. You three start from the back."

"Why don't you shout, Billy?" June asked. "Call Tansy. She'll surely hear your big voice."

Billy looked askance at her but nevertheless, he opened his mouth and roared.

"*Tansy! Tansy Bingham! Where are you?*"

People looked curiously at him but there was no answering call from Tansy. Just the scream of the wind which was even louder than Billy Moynihan.

"*Tansy! Tansy Bingham*!" Billy yelled her name again. "*Has anyone seen Tansy Bingham?*"

No response other than murmured denials.

"That's it," Kevin said. "There's something wrong here. I agree with you, Billy. She most certainly won't have left the hall. But where is she? Come on, June, I'll help you take Ute and the baby to the conference room. Then we'll find Tansy."

June turned behind her to get Ute. Her blanket was still on the floor but Ute was gone. Billy scratched his head. "Jesus, another woman on the missing list! What in the hell is going on here?"

"Maybe she's gone to the bathroom," June suggested. "Or the kitchen. Noel Cantillon said the poor woman was starving."

"Forget about her," Kevin said "She can look after herself. Just bring the baby. Hurry!"

June looked at Billy and shook her head. She had just

decided that Kevin was a kind man and now he was being heartless about the unfortunate Mrs Mueller. She followed Kevin as he hurried off to the conference room and she tried to rid herself of the fear that this awful night would never end.

Chapter 32

Tansy was gone beyond fear and into the realms of terror. The man holding her captive in the storeroom was irrational. Totally mad. She knew he could decide to kill her at any moment and she was helpless to defend herself. For one thing he had manic strength – for another, he had her trussed up like a turkey, sitting propped against shelving, while he paced and ranted.

There were times when he went quiet. Those were the saner moments when he discussed his dilemma with her as if they were having a civilised conversation. He needed to find Ute. If she had not spoken to the police about the baby-selling operation, he would let her live. He would punish her, of course, but he would not kill her. On the other hand, if she had blabbed, she was a dead woman. Tansy realised that she too was on his execution list. He would not be so openly discussing his criminal baby-selling operation with her unless he intended killing her. He stooped down in front of her, his eyes gleaming fanatically.

"I can tell you all this because you won't ever get the chance to repeat any of it. Whatever happens, you deserve to die. Slowly."

Tansy nodded her head. She had found that appearing to agree with him kept him calm for longer.

"But I must get the baby. He's worth fifty thousand euro to me. Don't you see? Can you understand why I must find him and deliver him?"

She nodded furiously again.

"You have no idea how the people I work for treat those who don't do their job properly. They're ruthless bastards. There's no escaping them. They'd hunt me down."

His voice was rising and she knew he was about to slip into another manic phase. Tears seeped from her eyes and slid down her cheeks and nose. They itched but she could not wipe them away. Her tears cooled, depositing salt tracks on her already irritated skin. Behind her back she constantly strained against the binding on her hands to no avail.

He was banging his forehead now with the heels of his hands. He jumped up and began to stride around the room, knocking things off shelves, opening boxes and emptying them. He passed her by and kicked her outstretched legs. She whimpered as the heavy sole of his shoe made contact with her shin. That seemed to please him. He calmed down a little and continued a more methodical search.

"There must be something here," he said and Tansy knew he was looking for a weapon. She cried again.

"Two more jobs. That's all we had left. We're going to Mexico, Ute and me. Retiring there. We've worked hard. We deserve it. At least I do. I don't know about her now, do I?"

She grunted an answer. Mexico? She knew that had a significance but she was too focused on her survival to work it out. Then she heard something. A muffled shout from the hall. She tilted her head to the side and listened intently. She could hear Horst clattering and banging things around the store, the wind shrieking, rain hammering on the tiled roof, and yes! There it was again! Through all the din she deciphered her name. Someone was calling for her! A male voice, though she could not hear clearly enough to identify the caller. She peered in Horst's direction. He was continuing as if he had not heard. Terrified, angry and clutching onto any sliver of hope, Tansy tried to do something to attract the attention of the caller in the hall. She banged her bound-together feet on the ground with as much strength as she could. The drumming sound they made was drowned by the strident voice of Hurricane Kimi.

"Aah! Found it!" said Horst.

He came to stand in front of her, a Stanley knife in his hand. He flicked the blade open and ran a finger tenderly along it.

"Good and sharp too. I'll make a nice neat cut with that."

Tansy shook.

Horst stooped down in front of her and grinned. "You've got a scrawny neck. It won't take much cutting."

She felt nauseous and wondered whether, if she got sick, she would choke because of the tape around her mouth. At least there would be some satisfaction in cheating Horst out of the pleasure of ending her life. She had always believed she would live to be a very old woman and would just drift off to sleep one day and never wake up again. She had thought to die with dignity after a full life. What a foolish notion that was. He leaned forward and touched the blade to her cheek. She felt the sharp point break her skin and blood begin to trickle.

"You see, nosey bitch, I can do what I like with you. Use you any way I want."

Tansy nodded and the point of the blade dug deeper into her face.

"I'd like to be rid of you here and now but I can't. You must help me first. Understand?"

He suddenly took the knife away from her face and waited for her to nod. She did, unable to dim the gleam of hope which lit her eyes. If he wanted to keep her alive for a while longer then there was always the chance that someone would search for her or even that somebody would notice the storeroom was locked. She got angry when she thought of them all out there, sipping tea and having babies while she was fighting for her life. Even the caller seemed to have lost interest in shouting her name. Where did they think she was, having a stroll in the hurricane? The possibility crossed her mind that, like a parched desert wanderer conjuring a mirage, her mind had conjured up the caller. She rejected the thought. It was more than fifteen minutes since Horst had dragged her in here. She had to cling onto the only hope she had.

Without warning, Horst plunged the knife towards her legs. With a deft flick of his wrist, he cut the tape around her knees. She sat still, afraid to react in case that tipped him further into his manic phase. He smiled at her.

"I have plans for you. You'll love them when you hear them."

The handle of the door rattled. Someone shouted. Tansy heard her name being called again. No illusion. She began to sob. In one swift slash Horst cut the tape around her ankles, dragged her to her feet, spun her around and held the knife to her throat. She felt the coldness of it against her skin and almost fainted. His breath was coming in short, garlicky puffs, adding to her nausea.

The rattling of the door handle stopped. Tears ran down Tansy's face. She felt abandoned. Betrayed. How could whoever it was have walked away and left her here? Didn't they know this door shouldn't be locked?

She closed her eyes then and prayed that death, if it had to come, would be as quick and painless as possible.

Ute tracked Kevin Phillip's every move. She had seen him bring Hans and the plump woman to the door of the medical room. She crept after him as he searched the top of the hall, shining his torch into faces, tripping over sleeping people, getting more anxious by the minute. And he had every reason to. Ute also believed that Horst was somewhere in the hall. He would never let the child escape. He would go to hell and back in order to protect the fifty thousand euro he would get when he handed Hans over. Any obstacles in his way would be eliminated and he would take particular pleasure if that obstacle happened to be Tansy Bingham. He hated her and her interfering ways.

The babies had never been anything more than a business to Horst. It might have been different if they'd had children of their own. Ute smiled, a bitter little smile. Horst, the powerful man, the bully, was impotent. All-powerful outside the bedroom, powerless in bed. A powerlessness which drove his hatred and anger.

Standing in the shadows she watched Kevin try to open the storeroom. He shook the handle impatiently and called his girlfriend. Tansy. What a silly name. She was a silly woman anyway, all smiles and energy and laughs. Only a fool could laugh in a world where people like Horst and his bosses lived their evil lives and prospered.

Kevin strode away from the door. Ute could feel his fear and anger. She was good at that. She knew fear and anger intimately. He would be back, of that she was certain. He knew, as she did, that Horst was behind that locked door. She leaned into the shadows to wait.

June glanced at Robyn's sweat-drenched face and then looked at Dr Early, an eyebrow raised.

"We're doing fine," he said. "Everything going according to plan."

"Asshole! What do you mean 'we're doing fine'? *I'm* the one in agony here!"

June tut-tutted. "Robyn! I'm surprised at you talking to Dr Early like that."

The doctor laughed and shook his head. "If I had a euro for every time a woman in labour cursed me, I'd be a very wealthy man. I'm just hopping around the screen to check on Zach and little Hans. Won't be a sec."

Despite the doctor's reassurance, June was worried about Robyn. She looked very pale and weak. She had such a slight build, it would be a miracle if she had the strength to deliver the child herself. June took up her position behind the couch again and began to massage Robyn's shoulders.

"Come on now, Robyn. It's time we got back to our breathing. Are you ready?"

Robyn turned her head around to look June in the eyes.

"You're not telling me the truth about Tansy. There's no way she's in the bathroom having a shower and washing her hair. Not when she knows I need her here."

June tried to return Robyn's look as steadily as possible. "She'll be here in a few minutes. Now stop worrying. We have work to do."

Robyn started her breathing count but she did not stop worrying. There was something June wasn't telling her. Something horrendous. She thought about what it might be until the next wave of pain rid her mind of all coherent thought.

Kevin charged to the end of the hall, aiming towards the sound of Billy Moynihan's voice. He ploughed through and over things, leaving a trail of irate people in his wake. The sergeant and Billy Moynihan looked at him in surprise when he asked for the keys of the storeroom.

"Is it locked?" Billy asked. "It was open when we were looking for Horst Mueller earlier. Anyway I've got the keys and I didn't lock it."

"Can it be locked from the inside?"

Billy took a large bunch of keys from his pocket and singled one out on the ring. "There's a bolt fitted to the inside but I don't know why. Who'd want to lock themselves into the store?"

"Someone who wanted to hide," the sergeant said quietly. "Maybe Horst Mueller."

Kevin swore. He grabbed the keys from Billy and

began the return journey. The sergeant took a moment to post Seán Harte at the front door before he and Billy Moynihan followed. Kevin was breathless by the time he reached the storeroom. He stood still, his ear against the door, listening for any sounds inside. He heard the infernal wind, the rain, the mutters of people he had trodden on in his rush and the pounding of his own heart. He could not distinguish any sound from behind the door.

The sergeant came up behind him and took the keys from his hand.

"Stand back, Kevin. I'll do this. We don't know what to expect here."

"We do! That creep Horst Mueller and Tansy. He has her in there, I know it. Maybe we're too late."

"Step to the side, Kevin. You go to the other side of the door, Billy. Don't move 'til I tell you."

The sergeant unclipped a baton from his belt, then quietly, with great deliberation, he put the key in the lock.

Tansy and Horst were standing just inside the door of the storeroom, one of his arms tightly around her waist and the other holding the blade of the Stanley knife to her throat. Her legs were unbound but the insulating tape still burned into her mouth and wrists.

"It won't be long now," he whispered, releasing another stream of garlic-laden breath over her. "The nosey fuckers will soon be here. You know what you have to do?"

Tansy nodded. She knew. All she had to do was die. A sacrifice on the altar of Horst Mueller's madness. A pawn in his determination to get his wife back, kill her and sell baby Hans on. Her legs were so weak that she would have fallen except fear of the knife to her throat kept her upright. Her hands were taped so tightly together behind her back that they were numb, the blood flow cut off. She tried to move them and loosen the binding. It bit tighter into her skin. She cried with helplessness and terror.

Horst's breathing was very ragged now and she knew he was out of control. But not enough so that she could try to escape from him. He was more focused than ever on slitting her throat. In his own time. When she was no more use to him. There was a sound from the other side of the door. The metallic scrape of a key being fitted into the lock. Tansy stopped crying and held her breath.

"I knew it! I knew it!" Horst said triumphantly.

He pushed her a step forward and, jamming her against the door, took his hand from around her waist and slid the bolt back. He pushed the knife a little deeper as if he had read her fleeting thought of escape. He slid his strong arm around her waist again and dragged her back into the depths of the room. He stopped moving when he reversed into a pile of some of the clutter he had scattered on the floor.

"This is far enough. You try anything smart and you're dead."

Only the reality of the pain in her bound wrists and the sting of salty tears in the cut on her cheek convinced Tansy that she had not already died and been banished to hell.

Both Tansy and Horst stood still, breathless, staring at the door. An eternity of stillness passed before very slowly, carefully, the door opened a crack.

It took all Kevin's strength not to push the sergeant aside and rush through the door. Tim Halligan was now flattened against the door, pushing it open slowly, his baton at the ready. Staying close to the wall, Kevin edged right up to the door frame. The sergeant continued the slow pushing open. Kevin peered around the door frame but could see nothing except blackness inside. He reached for his torch but his hand froze on the switch when he heard a voice, high-pitched and excited, coming from the storeroom.

"Aah! The rescue team has arrived. Come in."

A cold sweat broke out on Kevin's forehead. For an instant he was paralysed with that shock peculiar to your worst fears becoming reality. That was unmistakeably Horst Mueller's voice. In that instant too, Kevin knew Tansy was in there with him. What he didn't know was whether she was dead or alive.

The sergeant flung the door back. Brandishing his baton, he stepped into the store. Kevin dived in after him and aimed his torchlight into the darkness. The light wavered as Kevin's hand shook. He stared at Tansy, her eyes glittering with tears and terror, a trickle of blood running down her cheek, black tape around her mouth and a knife held to her throat. Worse than all that was the evil face of Horst Mueller, leering over her shoulder as he held Tansy close to him. He grinned at Kevin.

"She'll have no interest in you now that she's had a real man. You'll have to make do with your own wife or the vet's."

Kevin lunged towards him, blood pounding in his head. For the first time in his life he felt capable of murder. The sergeant grabbed him and hauled him back just as Tansy gave a cry of pain.

"Look what you made me do!" Horst said angrily. "This is your fault."

Billy Moynihan had just come in. He stared at the fresh wound on Tansy's neck. "Jesus Christ! What in the fuck do you think you're doing, Mueller?"

The sergeant spun around and spoke quietly to him. "Get Seán Harte. He's down by the front door. Clear everyone back from the top of the hall. Make sure there's no one around the store. Quick!"

He turned back to face Horst.

"Right. Let's talk, Horst. What do you want?"

Horst laughed into his face. "So you watch TV, do you? You know all about hostage negotiation. You're going to broker a deal and become a Felton legend."

Kevin took a step towards Horst. Tim Halligan caught him roughly by the arm. "You'll either stand and do nothing until I tell you or else get out of here."

"Don't be too hard on him, sergeant," Horst said. "He has a lot to cope with. Bad genes, you know. He passed them on to his son."

Kevin went cold. So Horst had been in the storeroom all the time. He had been listening to his conversation with Robyn. What scum! Kevin's fists clenched and he imagined them smashing into Mueller's face. He looked at Tansy and saw the plea in her eyes, begging him not antagonise her captor. He bunched his fists into his pockets. Tim nodded to him and then turned his attention back to Horst.

"Shut up, Mueller, and listen to me. I know about your scam. Ute told me everything. I contacted Interpol. You have no bargaining chips left. Let Tansy go now and save yourself another charge."

"You're lying. Fool! You didn't believe a word Ute said. I heard you talking to her. You believed me when I told you she was mad. Well, you're right. She is. But I'm not, so don't bullshit me. Interpol know nothing about me. You can't contact them anyway. Communications are down."

The sergeant nodded his head. Mueller was sharp. He would have to try a different tack.

"How about you tell me what you want? Then we start to talk."

"I want you to bring my wife to me and the child."

"And what then? Surely you don't think you can get out of Felton?"

"Yes, I can. I'm not afraid of a storm. I've been through worse. I'll be taking this bitch with me until I'm clear of this stinking country."

"It's not a storm. It's a mighty hurricane. You're trapped here, Horst. We all are."

Tansy made a weak little sound like a baby whinging. Desperate to do something, Kevin flashed his torch around the room, looking to see if there was any way to get into this room from the back and maybe surprise Mueller from behind. The place was in chaos, shelves mostly bare, things scattered on the floor, boxes upended.

"Turn off that fucking light!" Horst screamed. "I'll rip your girlfriend apart if you don't."

Kevin instantly switched off his torch. He stood there, feeling as helpless as he ever had in his life.

"Suppose Ute doesn't want to go with you," the sergeant said. "What then?"

"She will. She knows who's boss. She's nothing without me. She'd just end up back where I found her."

"And where was that?"

"Wouldn't you love to know? Bet you'd like to know

who we really are too. Way above your head, Sergeant Plod. Just stick to putting down traffic cones and get me my wife. Now!"

Standing out of the beam of the sergeant's light, Kevin was very slowly inching his way into the room. He tried to remember what he had seen on the floor. His path was obstructed by boxes and everything thrown around. The last thing he needed to do now was reveal his position by tripping over something. He peered into the darkness and tried to picture the exact layout. Shelves lined the walls all around. Cartons were stacked against the back wall. He remembered some free-standing shelves too but couldn't recall their exact position. The sergeant must have sensed what was happening because he kept Horst busy with conversation.

"I can bring Ute to you, Horst, or bring you to her. That might be better."

"Really? You think if you got me out of here, you could more easily overpower me. Maybe you could but the instant I feel any threat, I'll slit this bitch's throat. Is that what you want?"

"Of course not! There's no need for threats. We can work this out."

Kevin was so near them now he could smell Tansy's flowery perfume. It was infused with a garlic odour which he assumed must be from Horst. If only he could work his way behind them, then maybe he could grab Horst around the neck and give Tansy a chance to run. Something brushed against his shoulder. Suddenly a tin of paint which had been protruding from a shelf crashed to the ground.

"What the fuck was that!" Horst shouted, tightening

his grip on Tansy. "Is that you, Phillips? Get the fuck out of here!"

Kevin made a dive back to the doorway, flicked on his torch and shone it up into his own face. "I'm here, Horst. Look."

"Do you think I'm an idiot? You were creeping around. Trying to be the hero, are you? Too late for you now. You're a failure. Always will be."

Kevin felt the words as sharply as if he had been stabbed with a knife. Mueller might be totally insane but he had a talent for cruelty. And in an odd way, truth. He was right. A failed marriage, a dead son, a failed ten-year affair. And now he was failing to help Tansy. That made Kevin Phillips a failure.

A gust so violent that the building seemed to bend under it made an eerie keening sound. It hovered over them and ended in a piercing shriek. They all looked up towards the roof, even Horst. A blast of wind swirled from the back of the room, followed by the tap-tap of rain as it dripped onto the exposed insulation.

"A tile sheet gone there," the sergeant said, pointing to the back of the room. "We'll have to get out of here."

"Is this another trick?" Horst asked. "Trying to get me into an open space, are you?"

"Look! That insulation is all that's keeping the hurricane out of here. See the way it's bulging with the weight of the rain. The next gust will probably rip off another sheet. This room will be open to the elements. Do you honestly think Ute will come in here if it's flooded?"

Horst stared up at the roof where the sergeant was focusing his torch. He wondered how this moron knew about Ute's dread of drowning. Had she told him every blasted detail of their lives? Even about . . . He stopped that line of thought. He didn't want to consider it at all. Just to make himself feel better, he pushed the blade a little harder into Tansy's neck. Enough to hurt but not kill. She gasped in pain. Horst smiled.

"Alright," he said. "You, Sergeant Plod, and you, Romeo, go first. Then I'll follow. Just outside the door. And remember, I have the knife to her neck. I can draw it across any time I like."

The sergeant nodded to Kevin and together they began to back out of the room. After two steps they waited for Horst to move. He did, pushing Tansy, her eyes terrified above her gag. Two more steps brought Tim and Kevin to the door frame.

"I'm holding this door open until you come out," said Tim.

Horst looked at the sergeant, opened his mouth to say something and then seemed to change his mind. He nodded and pushed Tansy through the door. Tim slammed it shut behind them.

Seán and Billy had done a good job of clearing the top of the hall. The only light came from underneath the door of the conference room and the greenish glow from the exit sign on the emergency door. All else, even the kitchen, was in darkness.

"Where is she? Get her now. If I don't have Ute and the child in two minutes, I'm going to slice this bitch."

"I'll get her," Kevin said. "I'll look for her now. It might take longer than two minutes to find her. Give me more time." He shone his torch on Tansy's face and winced at the terror he saw there. "Just hang in there, Tans. We'll get you out of this."

Horst laughed. A mocking laugh. "You let them all down, didn't you? Your brother, your son, your wife, your mistress. What makes you think you'll be able to help 'Tans'?"

Kevin had to use all the will power he had to turn his back on Horst Mueller. He started to search for Ute. He knew the baby was in the conference room. He was safe there. But where the fuck was Ute? And what if he found her? What would he do? Hand her over to her lunatic husband, if he was indeed her husband? Would they be able to free Tansy and at the same time save Ute from this monster?

Frantically, Kevin shone his torch on abandoned beds and chairs, blankets and sleeping bags and all the while Horst's words echoed in his head. The madman had spoken the truth. Kevin had let everyone down. But he was determined, whatever it took, that he would not be found wanting in his efforts to save Tansy from a horrible death that looked more inevitable by the minute.

Ute smiled as she heard the door to the storeroom bang. This was better. She sidled along the wall, deep in the shadows. She was almost as far as Horst now. She could smell his peculiar scent. Reaching into her sleeve she wrapped her fingers around the handle of the bread-knife she had taken from the kitchen while the snooty journalist had been filling her plate with disgusting stew. Horst was right. They were all idiots here. She took another few steps. She could hear the frightened sobs of the girl Horst was holding hostage. Ute didn't feel sorry for Tansy Bingham. She should have minded her own business and then she wouldn't have ended up in this position. None of them would. She and Horst would have delivered Hans and collected their money, as they always did. Horst would have continued beating her, as he always did. Torturing her and making her and the babies stay in the cellar of that horrible cottage.

Ute's breathing quickened as she thought of the hours she spent locked up, released just so that Horst could take the only pleasure he knew or when he needed her by his side to play the part of the devoted wife and allay suspicion. How she would love to make him suffer too. To feel humiliated and powerless. She smiled. She would have to forego that satisfaction but she would get to keep the money. His precious hoard. Enough to live in luxury for the rest of her life.

She was standing directly behind Horst now. The garda was holding a light which shone onto Horst and the girl. Ute knew the policeman would see her when she made her move so it would have to be quick. She tightened her grip on the knife, angling the blade so that it faced downward. She took a deep breath and ran.

The sergeant saw something move in the shadows behind Horst and Tansy. He raised his light. "Stop!" he shouted as he saw Ute Mueller lunge at her husband, a knife in her hand. He was too late. With a strength driven by revenge, Ute raised her arm and plunged the knife into her husband's back. He screamed. His eyes bulged and the Stanley knife clattered from his hand to the floor. Tansy stood immobile, shocked.

The sergeant dashed towards them and reached them just as Ute plunged the knife into Horst's back for the second time.

"Run!" he shouted to Tansy. She looked at him,

confused. He grabbed her, pulled her away from Horst and behind himself, shielding her with his body.

Horst made a gurgling sound. Pinkish bubbles frothed out of his mouth, his knees bent and he collapsed onto the floor.

Chapter 33

Kevin heard the sergeant shout for Dr Early. His heart almost stopped with fear. He raced back in the direction of the store. He saw Horst lying on the ground, the sergeant leaning over him. Beside them, Tansy was frozen in place, her eyes focused on the handle of a kitchen knife which protruded from Horst's back.

"Ute," the Sergeant said as he looked up and saw Kevin. "Nothing I could do to stop her."

Kevin recalled Ute's change of character after they had left the kitchen. So his hunch had been right. The Muellers were a devil couple.

"Get Dr Early! Quick! Take Tansy with you. Take her away from here."

Kevin reacted instantly to the sergeant's orders. He took Tansy's hand and gently tugged her along with him. She was stiff, holding herself away from him. He released his grip, trying to imagine how repulsed she must be now by the touch of a man.

As soon as she saw the light seeping out from under

the door of the conference room, she stood and pointed to her mouth gag. Kevin understood but could do nothing about it. The adhesive tape was solidly glued to Tansy's skin. If he tried to rip it off now he might damage her skin permanently.

"Dr Early will have to do that, Tans. He'll probably need to use a solvent."

She stamped her foot and mumbled into her gag. Kevin nodded.

"I know you're worried about upsetting Robyn. She's behind the screen Don Cronin made, isn't she? I'll bring you over to your own corner until you're ready for Robyn to see you. Okay?"

She nodded, content to go along with that. When he opened the door he was met by the sight of Zach sleeping on the camp bed, his splinted leg propped up on pillows, Hans snuggled into the baby carrier on the floor beside him. From behind the screens came the voices of Robyn and June, puffing and panting and counting. A weak mew reminded him that Ben was still here in his carrier. Just what Tansy needed now. As he led her over to Ben, Dr Early appeared from behind the screen. The doctor's always impassive face showed horror as he looked at Tansy, bound with black tape, blood streaming down her cheek and a wound to her neck. He came towards them.

"You're needed urgently in the hall," Kevin whispered to him. "Horst Mueller has been stabbed. He's in front of the storeroom."

Without a word, Dr Early went to get his medical bag from behind the screen. Kevin heard June ask him who had come in. He muttered about having to check on a patient in the hall and that he wouldn't be long. She must have been satisfied with his answer because she immediately got back to her sing-song counting with Robyn.

On his way out, the doctor stopped in front of Tansy and examined her face and throat wounds.

"Nothing too serious," he said quietly. "I'll attend to them as soon as I can." He handed Kevin a small sharp scissors. "Cut the binding between her wrists. Just enough to free her hands. Don't pull any tape off her skin and don't go near her face. I'll do that when I get back."

Kevin stood Tansy where she could see Ben's carrier. Kneeling behind her, he began to snip, millimetre by millimetre, at the insulating tape. It took some minutes but eventually her hands parted. She flexed her wrists and stretched her arms, then stooped down and pushed a finger through the mesh on the carrier. That soft, furry contact with her beloved cat seemed to unleash all her pent-up fear and horror. She stood and threw herself into Kevin's arms. Silent sobs wracked her body. She clung to Kevin as tears washed away the initial horror of her ordeal. Kevin gently held her, afraid to stroke her face or hair in case he frightened her. When the sobbing stopped, he sat her on the chair. She was trying to brush away her tears with shaking, swollen hands, her wrists still covered with the black tape Horst Mueller had so gleefully applied.

"I'll get tissues," he whispered to her.

He heard someone swear. He turned around to see June Varian, white-faced, staring at Tansy. He put his fingers to his lips in a shushing gesture and nodded in Robyn's direction.

The door opened and Dr Early came in. He shook his head.

"Gone?" Kevin asked.

"Yes. Lung puncture," he replied. He saw June then. "Back to your job, June. I'll be with you shortly. I'll just see to Tansy. Won't be long." He turned to Kevin. "Tim Halligan wants you outside. Don't worry about Tansy. We'll take care of her."

Robyn heard the door open and close again as Kevin left. She smiled. She could have her baby now. Zach was safe and Tansy was back.

The sergeant and Dr Early had draped the body of Horst Mueller in plastic sheeting which was splattered with Magnolia paint.

The sergeant hurried towards Kevin when he saw him approach.

"We must find Ute. She may have more than one weapon."

Kevin looked into the blackness of the hall and cursed. "She could be anywhere now."

"She's not in the store. Or the kitchen. We've searched them and locked them. She's not in the conference room, is she?"

"No. Definitely not."

"I asked Dr Early to lock it from the inside in case she goes after the child. Seán Harte is guarding the front door and I have a man keeping an eye on the emergency door. She can't escape."

Kevin did not think this was true. The Muellers seemed to have an affinity with dark shadows. They could shrink into them and disappear.

"Where do you want me search?"

"You take the centre of the hall. I'm going left and Billy Moynihan right. And be careful. She's a very dangerous woman. Flash your torch for help if you find her. Don't try to tackle her yourself."

Kevin thought of the way she had deceived him. She must have got the knife from the kitchen when she had sent him to get food for her. He would love to tackle her. Then he remembered the sight of the knife embedded in Horst's back. Tackling Ute didn't seem like a clever thing to do. He nodded to the sergeant.

"Right. I'll switch my torch on and off three times if I see her."

"Get going," the sergeant said, then he too disappeared into the shadows.

Ute was near the front door. A policeman was standing in front of it. Her hands were sticky with Horst's blood. She wiped them on the cardigan someone had given her to keep her warm. The garda was a young man. Strong, alert. She knew she could neither overcome him nor dupe him. She shrugged. There was no hurry anyway. The hurricane was still raging. Perhaps the sea was lapping right outside the door. She shivered. She was tired now. The tremendous burst of energy she had used as she buried the knife into Horst had drained her.

She looked back up the hall. Several torchlights were bobbing around. They were looking for her. For one unguarded instant she turned to Horst to ask him what she should do. She smiled at her own stupidity. He was dead. No more beatings. He had got what he deserved.

She began to work her way back up the hall, trying to

remember exactly where her blanket was. She moved slowly, exhausted from all the planning and plotting. With each step she realised anew that Horst was dead. She was alone. By the time she found the blanket she had abandoned, she was weak and lonely. She flopped onto the floor and wrapped the blanket around herself. She needed to think, to plan her escape, organise the rest of her life, but she needed sleep more.

Ute tucked the blanket under her chin, held it there with her bloody hands, and fell into a deep sleep.

Like a criminal returning to the scene of the crime, some instinct brought Kevin towards where he and Ute and the baby had been sitting. He shone the torch on her blanket. She was lying on her side, curled up as peacefully as a child. Blood glistened on her fingers which held the blanket to her chin. The contrast of the innocent face and bloodstained hands confounded Kevin. This tiny little woman was at once a victim and a perpetrator. He examined her features, so neat and even. Ute must once have been very pretty. There was too much tragedy in her face now, too many secrets pinching her face into viciousness.

How had she become involved with Horst? Why had she never left him, looked for help? How could she have allowed him to buy and sell those babies? Kevin shone his torch on her and thought of shaking her awake, forcing her to answer his questions. He remembered the sergeant's warning. She was dangerous. Perhaps she had another knife clutched to her bony chest.

He took a step back from her, not out of fear of what she might do, but out of fear for what he himself could do. He wanted to shake the truth out of her, to know in detail about the Muellers' illegal trade in babies, to see her charged and imprisoned for the rest of her life. She had spared Horst that punishment. He would never now have to answer for his crimes.

Kevin felt his foot move towards the sleeping figure. He imagined what it would be like to see fear in her eyes, to make her feel the terror Tansy had. Bile rose in his throat. He felt dirty, lessened by his vicious thoughts. Ute had, after all, done what he could not do. She had saved Tansy's life by removing Horst.

He raised his torch, pointed it towards the back of the hall and flicked it on and off three times. While he was waiting for the sergeant to reach him, he watched Ute sleep and knew there had been a moment when he too could have crossed that line between what is right and what is unspeakably evil.

Chapter 34

Robyn thought she was going to die. The pain of her baby pushing down the birth canal was ripping through her like rods of white heat. She wanted to scream but knew Zach was sleeping and that Dr Early was attending to Tansy. She had to push again and this time a scream was torn from her mouth involuntarily.

"Dr Early!" June shouted, such panic in her voice that Robyn knew there must be something wrong. She began to bargain with the god she had not visited for many years. "Please let the baby live. Take me. Let my baby live. Please, God."

Dr Early appeared at the foot of the couch, snapped on surgical gloves and bent to examine Robyn.

"Aah!" he said with satisfaction. "You've crowned. I see the baby's head. You're doing very well, Robyn. It won't be long now."

Robyn felt a new strength surge through her. Their baby was almost here, hers and Zach's. Kind, loving Zach. She squeezed her eyes shut and pictured him, his clear green eyes, his curly hair, the breadth of his shoulders, the warmth of his smile. He had fought for his life in the hurricane and she knew he had not been thinking of his own survival but of getting back to her and the baby who was now about to be born.

June ran a cool cloth over her face. Someone caught her hand and gripped it tightly. Tansy smiled down at her, a dressing on her cheek and at her throat, a band of inflamed skin circling her lower face.

"Tansy! What in the hell happened to you? Are you alright?"

Tansy smiled. "I'm fine, Robyn. Just fine. Now stop slacking. Push!"

Robyn did. Again and again.

As soon as the sergeant and Seán Harte reached Ute, Kevin left her to them and went to the bathroom. He washed his hands, face and neck as thoroughly as he could in the dark room. He felt cleaner, though still tainted with the scent of Horst, Ute and evil.

He made his way to the conference room, dashing the last few steps as he heard a piercing scream. Someone must have told them that Ute had been captured because the door was no longer locked. He threw it open. Zach was struggling on the camp bed, trying to sit up. Hans had woken and was looking around him in fear. Kevin's lips tightened as he saw the little mite, terrified of his strange surroundings yet more afraid to cry. For a second he regretted restraining his urge to hurt Ute.

He couldn't see Tansy. He panicked, dashing over to the chair where he had left her as if she was still there but invisible. Then he heard her voice from behind the screen.

"One more push, Rob, and that's it. We're almost there."

Kevin walked back to the camp bed and put his arms underneath Zach's.

"Lean on me," he ordered as he hauled Zach off the low bed.

Awkwardly holding his splinted leg off the floor, Zach draped his arm over Kevin's shoulder and hopped towards the screen.

"June!" Kevin called. "Can you come here, please?"

June popped her head around the screen and then her face broke into a smile. "Great timing, Zach. Come on. I'll help you."

Kevin waited until Zach was supported by June, then he stood outside the screen and listened. He heard Robyn's cry of joy when she saw her husband, followed by a cry of pain as her baby took her attention.

He turned his back on them and went over to Hans. Picking him up from his carrier he took the frightened child in his arms and sat on the camp bed. The baby stared at him for a while, motionless, waiting.

"We're a pair, Hans. You and me," Kevin said softly. "We don't know where we belong, do we? Misfits, the two of us."

The terror dimmed in the baby's eyes and the sadness eased in Kevin's heart. Even when Robyn gave an ear-splitting roar, even when the cry of a newborn baby filled the room, Hans and Kevin did not flinch. They had found strength in each other.

Robyn heard her baby cry through a haze of pain and weakness. It was a lusty cry. She lay back against her pillows.

"A girl," Dr Early said. "A fine healthy little girl. I'd estimate around seven and a half pounds. Congratulations!"

He stood beside her and laid the baby on her breast. She felt the warm weight of her baby against her and the comforting feel of Zach's arm around her shoulder. Tansy and June were both sniffling.

Robyn lowered her head and looked into her daughter's face for the very first time. She was beautiful: button nose, round cheeks and a mop of dark, still sleek hair. Tenderly, her heart bursting with a protective love for this miraculous scrap of humanity, Robyn touched the minute fingers. They reacted to her touch, grasping hold of her index finger. A bond was formed, binding mother and daughter so strongly that Robyn knew nothing, not time or distance, living or dying, would ever break that bond.

Zach kissed his wife on the cheek. She turned to him. There were tears in his eyes. Just as she had imagined there would be. Robyn kissed him, laughing and crying at the same time.

"This was how it was meant to be, Zach. How it was always meant to be."

Tansy smiled at the Claymore family, mother, father, daughter, and thought her heart would burst with the beauty of new life and love. A pain darted through the cut on her cheek reminding her instantly of death and evil. She shivered.

"What are you going to call her?"she asked.

Zach and Robyn looked at each other and shrugged.

"We had decided on Alison for a girl," said Zach, "but I don't know now, do you, Rob?"

Robyn gazed at her daughter again and then looked up at Zach. "She's not an Alison, is she?"

"Whatever you want to call her, she needs to be washed and dressed now," Dr Early said. "And we still have a bit more work to do to tidy things up, Robyn."

Tansy slipped outside the screen. Her job here was done. She saw Kevin sitting on the camp bed with Hans in his arms. She sat down beside them.

"Robyn had a daughter."

"So I gathered."

"How do you feel about it?"

He rocked Hans gently and stared into the child's face. Tansy put her hand on his arm and gave it a squeeze. He looked at her, a deep sadness in his eyes.

"I'm very happy for her and Zach. They'll be great parents. She's a lucky little girl."

"But?"

"I feel sad too, Tans. You know that. And not because the baby is not mine. I can't come to terms with how I deceived Robyn for so long. It was wrong."

"We all do wrong. Make bad decisions. Hurt people. It's part of the human condition."

"Maybe, but my bad decisions have affected so many lives."

Hans whinged. Just a tiny little noise but a sound nonetheless.

Tansy smiled. "See! No matter what has happened in the past, there's always a way back, Kev." She stood up. "Now come on out to the kitchen. Hans is telling us he's hungry. We must make a bottle for him."

Kevin took her hand, still tender from being bound,

and kissed it gently. "You're an amazing woman, Tansy Bingham."

He put Hans in the carrier and together, arm in arm, they left the conference room. Tansy's step was light, her head held high. She did indeed, at that moment, feel like a much traumatised but yet amazing woman.

Chapter 35

A weak grey light was beginning to seep through the small windows. The blackness in the hall was not as impenetrable as it had been. Unnerved by Horst's death, everybody with a torch had switched it on. Kevin and Tansy saw that the area around the store room was roughly cordoned off with an array of chairs and boxes. In the centre lay Horst's covered body.

"Not even a hurricane prevented the sergeant from preserving the crime scene," Kevin remarked.

Tansy looked sharply at him, not sure if his tone was admiring or sarcastic.

"Or the criminal," she said, pointing to where Seán Harte sat on the floor, handcuffed to the sleeping Ute Mueller. "Poor Ute."

Kevin shrugged. His new insight into his own failings didn't include sympathy for Ute Mueller.

When they got to the kitchen, it was crowded. The one topic on everyone's lips was the murder.

"I always knew there was something wrong with the

Muellers," Noel Cantillon was saying. "Why didn't they buy their groceries from me like everyone else? Why did they have to go to Galway?"

"That's only because you're too expensive," someone said. "You rob us with your high prices."

In the laughter that followed, Tansy recognised the loud guffaw of Billy Moynihan. She made her way towards him.

"Robyn's had a little girl," she said.

"Are they alright?"

"Mother and baby are both doing well."

Billy threw his head back and roared the news to the whole room.

When the oohs and aahs had died down, Tansy whispered to him. "June could do with a bit of support. She's been with Robyn all the time. It's tough on her seeing a new life being born when . . . well, you know."

Billy was gone before she had finished the sentence. Tansy went to the cooker to heat Hans' bottle, leaving Kevin to find a space for them to sit in the crowded room. Noel Cantillon stared intently at her.

"Jesus, Tansy, what are you doing here? You shouldn't be walking around with all those stab wounds and stitches. Twelve, isn't it?"

"I have two little puncture wounds and no stitches, Noel. Now I need a saucepan of hot water to heat a bottle for the baby. Is that okay?"

"Of course, of course," he muttered but yet he examined her closely, still looking for evidence of the rumoured twelve stab-wounds.

They had just settled down, Hans snuggled into Tansy's arms sucking his bottle hungrily, Kevin sitting contentedly beside them, when Con Lynch began to behave oddly. He was standing in the middle of the room, his head tilted to one side, shushing everyone.

"Listen, do ye hear it?" he asked when the room was quiet.

There were little sounds. The gas hissing in the cooker, feet shuffling, someone coughing, Hans sucking.

"I don't hear anything," Noel Cantillon said, his tolerance for silence having reached its limit.

"Exactly!" Con answered. "Nothing. No wind. No rain. It's over. The hurricane has spent itself!"

Kevin and Tansy were almost knocked over as the crowd swept past. Tansy raised an eyebrow in query.

"Yes, why not?" Kevin answered.

Hans still feeding happily in Tansy's arms, they made their way down the hall in the wake of the crowd. The front door was opened up. Tansy wrapped Hans' blanket closely around him before they stepped outside. She raised her face skyward and closed her eyes. A gentle breeze touched her skin, soothing the wound on her cheek. Kevin put his arm around her shoulder.

"We made it, Tansy. We survived."

She opened her eyes and looked up at him. "This time."

"What do you mean?"

"Kimi was just a warning. What about the next hurricane and the one after that? The next drought? We're on the cusp of destruction, Kevin."

He looked sharply at her, worrying that she was still being affected by her ordeal with Horst Mueller. Of course she was. She probably would always be. Even so, it wasn't like her to be so despondent. So hopeless.

"What is it, Tans? What about the great changes you were talking about? Teleporting and reading each other's minds? The new world the Maya predicted after 2012?"

She smiled at him. "We've made a mess of this one, haven't we? But you're right. We must look forward."

He looked down at Hans, so cosy and safe in Tansy's arms. "There is a future for Hans and for Robyn's baby. There must be."

The sky was beginning to lighten towards the east. People started to venture into the car park to check if their vehicles had survived intact. Tansy handed Hans to Kevin.

"Here, I must get Ben. Won't be a minute."

On her way back to the conference room, she met June and Billy on their way out. He had his arm around her shoulder, comforting her as she sobbed. Tansy felt her own eyes well with tears. The search for Des would soon be resumed. This was the end of the hurricane and most probably the end of any hope that Des had survived the savagery of Kimi.

"It's really over?" Billy asked.

Tansy nodded and not knowing the words to say, squeezed June's hand and moved on. Ben mewed in protest when he saw her. "I know," she crooned. "Believe me, Ben, I know what it's like to be caged up but I'll let you out soon."

He mewed more angrily this time, not in the least impressed by her excuses. Before she picked up the cage, she popped behind the screen again, unable to resist another peep at the baby.

She stood still at the sight which greeted her. Robyn was sitting on the side of the couch. Fully dressed. Zach was leaning on a make-shift crutch – an inverted sweeping brush, the head under his arm. The baby, on the couch beside Robyn, was all rosy and clean now and snugly wrapped in the baby nest Robyn had included in her maternity bag.

"Where are the Claymore family off to?" Tansy asked.

"Just like everyone else," Robyn answered. "Out to see if this hurricane is really gone. I won't believe it if I can't see it for myself."

"Are you mad? You've just had a baby and you, Zach, have just nearly died."

"Exactly!" Dr Early agreed. He looked exhausted. Worn out from birth and death.

"You're the one, Tansy, who told me that women in the Korku tribe return to work in the fields immediately after giving birth." Robyn said. "I'm talking about walking a few metres, not digging a furrow."

Robyn had a glow in her skin and a sparkle in her eyes. She had never looked more beautiful. Or more determined. Tansy held out her arm.

"C'mon, then. Let's dig some furrows."

She offered her other arm to Zach.

"I suppose I'm left holding the baby," Dr Early laughed, taking her into his sure and steady hands.

Ben turned his back to Tansy as she passed his carrier. He didn't want to hear any more excuses.

They headed out through the hall, a motley crew of two women, an old man carrying a baby and a young man hobbling along with the aid of a sweeping brush. By the time they stepped outside the door, the sun had begun to infuse the eastern horizon with tints of yellow and orange.

"The dawn of a day we never thought we'd see," Dr Early said.

Robyn and Zach looked at each other and then at their baby.

"Dawn," Robyn said. "Dawn Claymore. What do you think, Zach?"

He nodded his agreement and their daughter was named.

Tansy slipped out from between Robyn and Zach. They didn't need her any more but, judging by the lost look on Kevin Phillips' face, he did. He stood to the side of the door, Hans in his arms and a lost air about him.

"Are you coming to see Robyn's baby?" she asked when she reached him.

"Soon. Tans, we need to talk. About you and me, our future."

She raised her hand and pressed her fingers to his lips.

"You've a lot of thinking to do. Fences to mend and ghosts to banish. That will take time."

"But I wanted to tell you . . ."

"We'll talk later. Much later. After the events of this awesome night have settled into a comfortable place in our memories."

He narrowed his eyes and peered at her. "You're not giving me the brush-off, are you? I don't think I could handle it."

She stood on tiptoe and kissed his cheek, fighting her urge to throw her arms around him and hold onto him forever.

"You know where to find me if and when you feel ready."

"You're going to stay in Felton?"

"I belong here."

Tim Halligan came rushing up from the car park, anxiety written in every long stride he took. He stood in front of the crowd around the door, his face grave. "My radio is functional again. Patchy but enough for me to learn the news from around the country. I have to tell you all that it's very bad. Ireland has been devastated by Hurricane Kimi. Towns and cities flooded, buildings collapsed, power down, emergency services totally overwhelmed."

"Dublin?" Kevin asked. "What's the news from there?"

"Pretty grim. You can add looting to the problems they're having. I was able to let them know about the Mueller affair. They'll get help here as soon as possible. I've arranged for the child to be taken into care."

Tansy took Hans from Kevin. The baby cuddled in close to her and looked up at her with solemn eyes. She couldn't help the sob which escaped her.

"What's going to happen to him, Kev? Will he spend the rest of his life being passed from one care home to another?"

"He might be sent back to his rightful home. We don't know whether he was willingly sold or kidnapped. Maybe some girl or woman is praying this minute that her son will be returned to her."

Tansy touched the baby's silken cheek. He smiled at her. A glorious, toothless smile as radiant as the rising sun. Through her tears, she smiled back at him, bent her head and kissed him on his forehead. He snuffled, then closed his eyes and went peacefully to sleep.

"Did you notice your car, Tansy?" Billy Moynihan asked her. "It's blown over on its side. Lucky it didn't blow away altogether!"

Tansy shrugged. What was a car in comparison to the losses other people had suffered? She glanced at June and saw in her drawn face the suffering she would endure for the rest of her life. She thought of Ute Mueller and, despite what Kevin thought, she pitied her. An abused and demented woman who had lost both her torturer and the last vestiges of her sanity to the hurricane so aptly named Kimi after the God of Death.

The sun was pushing up over the horizon, spilling light gradually over the land. Silence fell on the gathered crowd as the sea beneath them danced out of the darkness in orange tinted swells. The rain had dried up, the wind blown itself out, but the mighty ocean still heaved with awesome power.

"The village!" someone gasped and all eyes were drawn to where the village should be. Still was – but under water now.

"My shop!" Noel Cantillon cried with the wail of mourning in his voice.

"My son," June said so quietly that only those nearby heard the depth of her pain.

Robyn and Tansy exchanged looks. They both knew the cottages were submerged. They had to be, situated as they were on what used to be the edge of the ocean.

The sun rose higher and the devastation became clearer. Chimneypots of the houses on Upper Street appeared and disappeared as swells rose and fell, trees lay low, torn by their roots from the earth. Rivers of water cascaded down the hillsides and splashed into the sea, adding to the already swollen volume.

"She'll not go back now," Ritchie Swann, the coastguard, said with the certainty of someone who knew the sea intimately. "She's carved a new shoreline for herself. She has buried Felton in a watery grave."

Heads bowed and people thought of their homes. The budgeting, planning, hopes and dreams they had invested in them – all gone; cushions, chairs, pictures, fridges, tables, gardens – all gone; the safe, almost smug feeling of opening your front door and closing the world out – all gone; the familiarity of the creaking step on the stairs or the cracked tile on the kitchen floor – all gone; certainty and the illusion of permanence – all gone.

Con Lynch, hands behind his back and cap pulled low on his forehead, rounded the corner of the hall to the sight of the silent gathering. He went to stand near Zach.

"You've been around the back of the hall, Con?"

"I have and there's good news and bad."

"Get the bad over with," Robyn said. "We're all so shocked it won't hurt."

Con lifted his cap and scratched his head, then slapped the cap back on again as if to trap his thoughts.

"Horst Mueller's Hummer is parked around the back. The tile sheet that came off the roof was blown clean through his windscreen."

"Is that the good or the bad?" Noel Cantillon asked.

Con ignored him and continued.

"The mudslide. 'Twas a devil of a thing. It came down the valley and took all before it. I could see its destruction as far as the library. There's walls of rock and mud piled up against the building. 'Tis ruined."

"The good news?" Zach prompted.

"My house is still standing. The 360 held out. If the mine shafts had collapsed, well, God knows what would have happened. The hill is almost bare of topsoil. It's an ugly sight now." He shuffled from one foot to the other and squinted at Zach. "I was thinking, lad, that your house must be under water. Why don't you and your missus and baby stay with me until you get on your feet again?"

Zach looked at Robyn. She appeared frail. Whether she realised it or not, she needed her mother now.

"Do you want to go to your own home, Robyn? Your mother could help you with the baby. Look after you until you're strong again."

Robyn peered into the baby nest. Dawn was sleeping soundly, her tiny lips puckered into a rosebud shape. She looked at Dr Early, daring him to defy her and then at Zach.

"I *am* home, Zach. Everything I need is here. You and Dawn and our friends."

Con smiled and raised his eyes towards the morning sky. He didn't see the streaks of red, the yellows or the clear white light. He saw his beloved wife there and he sent her a message of thanks.

"That's settled then," he said. "And I was thinking that maybe Tansy might like to come too. There's plenty of room for you all."

"What do you think, Tansy?" Robyn asked.

Carrying Hans in her arms and dragging Kevin along behind her, Tansy went to Con, and much to his embarrassment, kissed him on the cheek.

"Thank you, Con. I wonder if I could bring Hans too until they collect him? And Ben, my cat."

"Of course. I'll have to get a few milk cows. We'll need them with all these babies."

He sounded as if he was complaining but he looked as if he had just been presented with the most precious gift in the world.

"No worries," Tansy said blithely. "I'll do all the cooking. And you, Zach, can't turn your nose up because you promised."

While this conversation had been going on, Kevin had been inching nearer to Robyn and Zach. He held out his hand.

"Congratulations, Zach. And you too Robyn. I was told your daughter is very beautiful."

Robyn looked into his eyes and saw regret there. She felt an answering tug in her heart. But it was not regret that their affair had not worked out. It was an admission by both of them that they had travelled the wrong path for too long. Zach took the offered hand and shook it.

"Thank you, Kevin. Yes, Dawn is as beautiful as her mother. A bit more wrinkled at the moment but time will iron out those creases."

Robyn smiled. How wise Zach was. Time would indeed, iron the creases and heal the hurts.

A throbbing sound overhead attracted everyone's attention. Looking up they saw a helicopter appear, circle a few times and then slant off to the east.

"Television," Kevin said.

Tansy shivered. With that one word she sensed Kevin being pulled back into the world he had so briefly left behind. He turned to her.

"I'm going now, Tans. I'll try to find a way to get to Dublin. See what's happened with the *Daily News*. I must contact Lisa too."

She nodded and held more tightly to Hans. Kevin

stooped down and whispered in her ear. "I love you, Tansy Bingham. I'll be back soon."

He turned then and walked through the car park, his stride determined. He sat into the squad car with Sergeant Halligan and together both of them left the safety of the hall to venture into a world torn and tattered by avenging nature.

"The end of an era," Robyn said as she watched the car disappear over the brow of Lookout Hill.

"The beginning of a new one," Tansy answered.

They looked at each other and smiled, at once fearful and excited by what lay ahead.

"A new day, a new way," Tansy said. "We can do it, Rob."

Robyn looked at Zach and then at her daughter, at Con Lynch and June Varian, Dr Early, Billy Moynihan, Tansy and Hans. At where Felton used to be. It would be a different life to the one she had planned. Just as Dawn's birth had been different but no less wonderful. She nodded. "Of course we can do it. We must."

They went into the hall then to collect the few possessions they had left. Help would come soon. They knew that. Rebuilding would start. But they did not know when the next storm would lash, the next drought scorch.

The only thing they knew for certain was that, together, they would survive.

Epilogue

Nine months later

Tansy closed her eyes and turned her face up to the spring sunshine. It warmed her right through to her heart. She sensed the promise of flowers yet to bloom and buds to unfurl.

She was standing on Lookout Hill in front of the Community Hall. Opening her eyes she faced towards the sea. The tide was out, or as far out as it went these days. The wreckage of Felton village wallowed in silt beneath her, rooftops with barnacles, paneless windows curtained with fronds of seaweed. It was better when the tide was full in. At least then the village had the dignity of burial at sea.

That thought reminded her of Des Varian. It had recently been learned that Des had been picked out of the water by a Spanish fishing vessel on the day Hurricane Kimi churned up the sea. How his heart must have leaped with joy when he saw them throw him a lifeline. How grateful he must have been to the strangers who saved his life. And how cruel the fate which then sank the trawler with all hands, including Des, on board. June found the news oddly comforting. "At least he didn't die alone," she said. The trawler, like the village, remained buried at sea. Des had been laid to rest beside his father, while the bodies of the Spanish men he had not known at all, yet with whom he had shared the most intimate and profound experience of dying, had been taken back to their homes.

Tansy glanced at her watch. She was running late, as usual. Going into the hall, she made straight for the section where Noel Cantillon had set up shop – a temporary arrangement until the shape, size and location of the new Felton village was finally decided. Noel was reading a paper when she approached. The *Daily News*. Because she was strong, determined and in control, she banished the thought of Kevin Phillips, slaving over his newspaper, editing copy, chasing stories, forgetting about Felton and Tansy and the promises he had made while wind howled and rain lashed.

"How many eggs did Con send me today?" Noel asked.

"Three dozen. The hens are beginning to lay well."

Tansy frowned as Noel began to count out money. "When are you going to stop this silly carry-on? You go to all the trouble of paying for the produce and I just hand the money back to you for something else. Why don't we barter? A clean swop. I need washing powder and flour. You need eggs. Fair exchange. Deal?"

"You think I can go to the wholesaler with a bag of spuds under my arm, a chicken in my hand and a few eggs in my pocket? Would they give me my supplies?"

Tansy laughed at the mental image. She put out her hand for her money, then duly paid it back to him for the things she needed.

"How are your wife and family doing?" she asked and was immediately sorry when she saw his mouth tighten and a flush spread over his cheeks. It appeared that Mrs Cantillon and the children were getting far too cosy in her sister's house in Cahir.

"They'll be back when I get the new shop built. I know they will. If only the insurance and the bloody planners would stop dragging their heels, I could have it done already."

She nodded to him and packed her shopping. Pointless telling him yet again that the country was still reeling from the effects of Hurricane Kimi and that, as usual, the centres of population would have the benefit of priority services. Little townlands, like Felton, and there were many of them, especially around the coast, would have to literally sink or swim on their own. She hoisted her backpack on and waved him goodbye.

Robyn, her daughter at her breast, relaxed back into the old armchair in Con Lynch's kitchen and absorbed the peace. The only sounds were the ticking of the clock, Dawn's suckling and the odd crackle from the logs burning in the range. She sighed with deep contentment.

Zach and Con had gone back the road to where Don Cronin and his crew had begun work on the new houses. Two cottages, side by side, one for the Claymore family and one for Tansy. There was a rightness about it all. The cottages were being built near the spot where Zach had almost lost his life. One of the felled trees crackled in the range now. Burning away the memory of what could have been.

Robyn put the warm weight of Dawn against her

shoulder and began to pat her back. The baby snuggled her soft face into her mother's neck. Dawn burped and spat some milk on Robyn's shoulder just as a knock sounded on the door. Startled out of her peaceful moment, she grabbed baby and towel, dabbing at the milky stain on her sweater as she went to answer the knock.

Kevin Phillips stood in the doorway, as handsome as ever but leaner, older. Robert Redford matured. They stared at each other, Robyn very conscious of her baby-sick sweater. He smiled at her.

"You look more beautiful than ever, Robyn. Motherhood suits you."

"You're the same as ever. Still trotting out the clichéd lines."

He laughed. "Agreed. Next I'll be asking do you come here often."

"That's my line."

"Is Tansy around?"

Robyn realised then that they were still standing on the doorstep. "Come in. She's just gone down to the hall. Noel Cantillon has his shop there for the time being."

She sat back into the armchair and waved Kevin to the seat opposite. Dawn burped and they both laughed.

Kevin looked closely at the baby. "Last time I saw her, she was just a scrap and had a mop of black hair."

Robyn ran her hand tenderly over the blonde fuzz on Dawn's head.

"I think she's going to have blonde curls. Just like Zach when he was a baby."

"You and Zach . . ."

"We're very happy, Kevin. It frightens me sometimes when I think how near Zach came to dying. We would never have known – well, we would never have known what we have now. And you? How's Lisa?"

"Lisa's well. I think she's going to make it this time. She's dry for almost a year now. Getting her life back together."

They were silent then. Not a comfortable silence. They no longer felt at ease in each other's company. Perhaps they never had. Robyn stood.

"Can I get you something? Tea? Coffee?"

He shook his head.

"If you'll excuse me so, I'll just change Dawn and then I must go to see the foundations. We're building a new house just down the road from here. Tansy too."

"If you don't mind, I'll wait here for Tansy."

Robyn looked at him. At his startlingly clear blue eyes, his still thick blond hair and his chiselled features. She asked herself the same question. Did she mind that the man she had given ten years of her life to was waiting for her best friend, the sister she never had? The answer came to her loud and clear. She stooped and kissed him on the cheek, not caring that he almost gagged from the smell of baby-sick.

"No, Kevin. I don't mind at all."

She changed Dawn's nappy and her own sweater and headed down the road to Zach.

The copse was alive with the growl of the cement-mixer and the excited voices of the men as they shouted above it. Don Cronin, Con Lynch and Zach had their heads together, pouring over the plans. Robyn looked at Zach's animated face and thought she had never seen him so content.

Theirs was a difficult life now, there was no doubt about that. The insurance company had agreed to pay some compensation for the cottage but not the full amount. Most of the people who had left Felton before Kimi struck had not come back. They had nothing to come back to. With them had gone the bulk of Zach's small animal clinic. Luckily the farmers, for the most part safe on the slopes of the hills, had stayed. He still had some work and the government were grant-aiding those who rehoused themselves.

And yet, for all the financial worries and concerns about the future, they had found peace here in Con Lynch's house. They were a happy group, Con and Zach, Tansy and Robyn, Dawn the glue that held them all together. Billy and June would be building in the copse too. "More convenient to share a house under these circumstances," Billy liked to say. "But separate bedrooms of course." He always looked to June hopefully when he said this but she hadn't yet contradicted him. Robyn was sure she would in time or else the bedrooms would have connecting doors.

Zach saw her and walked across to her. "How are my girls?" he asked, stooping to kiss Robyn. He gazed at Dawn, now sound asleep in the baby sling, her face snuggled against Robyn's breast.

"We're very well, thank you. How's the work coming along?"

Zach threw his eyes up to the heavens and laughed.

"Too many chiefs. Everyone has a different idea how things should be done. It's starting to take shape, as you can see. And the best news is that plans for blasting the old mine shafts in The 360 were finally approved by the Department of the Environment today. That's one less threat to cope with in the future. It's full tilt ahead now, Rob."

When she didn't answer, he asked her what was wrong. Robyn hesitated, reluctant to introduce a note of discord. She cleared her throat.

"Kevin Phillips is up at the house. He's waiting for Tansy."

Zach's eyes narrowed and he shifted the weight on his feet, as he sometimes did now since he broke his leg.

"I hope he's not going to upset her. Or you."

"He has no influence on my life any more, Zach. He's not part of it. I'm sorry that he ever was."

Zach looked into her eyes and then nodded.

"I know, Rob. But don't be too judgemental. He's a good man, you know. He just hasn't fully grown up yet. What about Tansy? Do you think she'll want to see him?"

Robyn shrugged, disturbing Dawn who opened her blue eyes, stared and then went back to sleep again.

"Don't know. Kevin Phillips is the one topic we don't discuss."

"That says it all."

Robyn smiled and kissed him on the mouth. Wise Zach. Beautiful, kind, generous, wise Zach.

When Tansy crested the hill to begin her descent into the valley, she saw a car parked in Con Lynch's yard. She stumbled over a stone and almost fell. The car in the yard was not a red Cabriolet but there was something about it – its sleekness and the way it was parked at an angle – that made her sure she knew who owned it. Kevin Phillips.

Her breath caught as thoughts scampered through her head.

Why was he here? Had he come to see her or Robyn? Would he remember that he had promised her love? Would he offer her the little of himself he had given Robyn for ten years – a few stolen weekends, a handful of passionate nights and loneliness in between?

She raced downhill, gravity adding to her already quickened pace. Then she slowed her descent.

Why did she think it was him? Wish fulfilment. And, even if it was him, he might have come to tell them about Ute and Horst. Maybe he had news of little Hans. Or wasn't it possible, probable, that he was just chasing a story? A feature on how the ruined village of Felton was struggling to survive.

Fixing the straps of her backpack firmly on her shoulders, Tansy began a more sedate and thoughtful descent into the valley.

When she reached the yard, she checked out the strange car. Yes, it had a Dublin registration and it was stylish enough to be Kevin's, but it probably belonged to one of the engineers or architects who were doing work on the building of the new houses. She was deluding herself to think that Kevin would at this stage be coming back to Felton.

The house was empty when she went in. She put away her shopping and, before going outside to look for Ben, brushed her hair and dabbed on some oil of roses to cheer herself up. Ben spent his time now out in the front garden. He was sleeker, always busily involved in hunts and cat adventures.

She opened the front door and almost fell over Kevin. He was sitting on the step, stroking Ben's silky fur.

He looked up at her and grinned.

"He's lost weight at last. He's a beautiful cat now."

"He always was."

He pushed over on the step and Tansy sat beside him. He smelled nice. A clean, fresh scent. She felt the heat from his body and scrunched herself up so as not to touch him. Glancing at him she saw new lines on his face. He looked older. Very handsome, but older.

"How have you been, Tansy?"

"Busy. And you?"

"Very busy. The *Daily News* sustained a lot of water damage in the storm."

"The hurricane."

"In the hurricane. We're just getting back to normal now. It takes so long to get anything done."

"Yes, it must be very inconvenient having to wait in line while people have their homes rebuilt."

He caught her hand and her fingers stiffened at the touch. She felt vulnerable, thoughts of Ari and how he had cheated on her worming their way to the surface from where she kept them hidden. She couldn't, she mustn't, ever allow herself to be hurt like that again. She drew her hand away.

"Tansy, I'm sorry I didn't . . ."

She stood and looked down at him. "There's no need for you to explain anything to me. It doesn't matter."

Jumping up he caught her by the arms. "It matters to me, Tansy Bingham. Stop being so stubborn and listen. I didn't want to contact you until I had everything cleared up. We agreed that, didn't we? You told me to sort out my life and I have."

"Really?"

"Yes, really. I've divorced Lisa. Set her free like I should have done so many years ago. Guilt it was that kept us together and guilt destroyed us. She's doing very well now. She doesn't need to drink anymore. Not so far anyway."

Tansy sat down again and took Ben onto her knee. He curled up and began to purr. Kevin sat beside her, his face open, vulnerable like she had never seen before. There was only one way to get an answer to the question that would not let Tansy be.

"Do you still love Robyn?" she asked.

"Yes. I always will. But for her goodness and her intelligence and charm, her little pixie face. I love her just like you do, as a very good friend."

Tansy thought about this. It was true that Robyn was the type of person who attracted devotion. Her petite frame and shy manner belied her strength. You drew Robyn in out of sympathy and you held onto her out of admiration.

"So what now for Kevin Phillips? Expanding your empire?"

"I don't have one. According to our agreement, my shares in the *Daily News* reverted to Lisa on our divorce."

Tansy's eyes widened. "So you have nothing! That's some serious life-changing!"

"I got a very generous settlement. I'm not pauperised. I wouldn't ask you to marry me if I was."

Tansy started. Ben mewed and jumped off her knee. She focused on the daffodils which were beginning to push up through the lawn. Drank in the reality of them. She heard the cement-mixer in the distance, churning the sticky mess that would become the foundations of her new home. A house for her and Ben. Beside Robyn and Zach and baby Dawn. Safe. Secure. She turned to Kevin and looked into his eyes.

"No, Kevin. Don't ask me. I've been married. You have too. We both carry the scars and will do for the rest of our lives. I will never marry again."

His face paled. "I thought you felt like I do."

She leaned towards him and put her hand on his shoulder. "I do, Kev. I want to spend the rest of my life with you, to wake beside you in the morning, to kiss you goodnight. But I don't want to marry."

He smiled at her then. "I have something else to tell you, Tansy. Will you hear me out and then reconsider my marriage proposal?"

Her head on his shoulder, the sun on her face, a warm feeling in her heart, Tansy listened carefully to what Kevin had to say.

The house came to life a short time later as Robyn, Zach, Con and Dawn, now sleeping in her father's arms, trailed in. All except the sleeping baby were talking about the new houses. The troupe stopped still at the kitchen door when they saw Tansy and Kevin, arm in arm standing in front of the range.

"I've got something to tell you all," Tansy said, her eyes glowing. "Kevin is coming to live with me and he's going to write a book. Probably about Hurricane Kimi."

She stopped to draw breath. Robyn looked at the happy faces of Tansy and Kevin. Zach was smiling too. Only Con Lynch looked serious.

"More babies," he muttered.

Robyn flinched. That must have hurt Kevin. But he was smiling.

"Yes, Con. I hope so. There's a lot of bureaucracy to sort through but after Tansy and I get married, we hope to adopt the baby the Muellers had. Hans' mother doesn't want him back and is willing to have him legally adopted here."

Robyn threw her arms around Tansy. "I'm so happy for you, Tansy." She turned to Kevin and took his hand. "Mind her," she said. "She's precious."

He smiled and Robyn saw in his eyes that Kevin had found with Tansy the true happiness she had with Zach.

"I'm glad," she whispered.

Con Lynch picked up his wedding photo and smiled at his wife's black-and-white image. She would be so pleased if she was here now, her house full of young people. And she was. He could feel her gentle presence. Just as the presence of Hurricane Kimi would always be with them too. That one night of savagery which tore the village apart and brought the people together.

"Anyone hungry?" Tansy asked. "I'm cooking."

They all laughed, except Kevin. He had yet to learn the awesome depth and breadth of Tansy's culinary skills.

to adopt the [illegible] and [illegible] the
[illegible] between [illegible]
[illegible]

[illegible]
[illegible]
[illegible]

[illegible] and [illegible]
[illegible]
[illegible] murmured.

Cody [illegible] and [illegible]
in the [illegible] she would [illegible] so
[illegible] as [illegible]
[illegible] and [illegible]
[illegible] the presence of Lynch [illegible] would [illegible]
with [illegible] the [illegible] of [illegible]
"[illegible] and brought [illegible] the [illegible]
[illegible] the

They all laughed except [illegible] the [illegible]
[illegible] Lynch's [illegible]

If you enjoyed

Time and Tide by Mary O'Sullivan

why not try

Under the Rainbow also published by Poolbeg?

Here's a sneak preview of Chapter One

Under the Rainbow

MARY O'SULLIVAN

POOLBEG

Chapter 1

He accidentally spilled my drink in a Dublin club one wet February night. Not a very auspicious beginning but that's how I, Adele Burke, met Pascal Ronayne. He ticked all the boxes. He was tall, dark-haired, at twenty-six the same age as me and, I guessed instantly from his cultured accent, wealthy too. I was almost right. Pascal, like his father, was an architect. A very successful one. He worked in his father's company designing prestigious new buildings in Dublin city. Some day, Pascal would inherit the company and then he too would be rich. This was a man with dark brown eyes, broad shoulders and prospects.

I believed, on that wet February night, that Pascal was the man I had spent my life waiting to meet. I still believed it two years and three weeks later when I came home early from my teaching job. I had picked up a tummy bug from my seven-year-old pupils. Feeling nauseous, I turned the key in the door to the apartment Pascal and I had shared for the past year and wondered if I'd make it to the bathroom before being sick.

I stood in the open doorway, unable to move. From where I was, I had a perfect view into the kitchen. A girl was lying across our kitchen table and Pascal was leaning over her. Neither of them was wearing clothes. My first thought was how inappropriate it was for them to have sex where I ate my cornflakes in the morning and my pizza in the evening.

Pascal turned towards me and I tried to see shock and embarrassment on his face, even some sign of apology. His expression was blank. Calmly he stooped and handed the girl her clothes from the floor. She was young. Maybe about twenty and very beautiful. Blonde and blue-eyed. A slut who looked like a virgin. It must have taken her minutes to dress but it felt like hours to me as I stood in the doorway, unable to leave or to speak any word of condemnation or disgust or anger. When I looked away from her, I noticed that Pascal too had put on his clothes. His jeans which fitted so snugly and his expensive cashmere sweater.

He kissed the slut-virgin on the cheek and murmured something into her ear. The girl walked towards me, sneering. "Loser!" she muttered. The only word I ever heard the girl speak. An ending to my relationship with Pascal Ronayne which was even more inauspicious than the beginning had been.

I rang Carla and Jodi. We had always been best friends, Carla, Jodi and me. Born within three months and three miles of each other in the seaside town of Cairnsure, we had been destined by fate to share whatever life had in store for us.

Carla, pregnant with her second child, and Jodi, wearing a designer suit and a laptop as accessory, came to Dublin to help me curse Pascal Ronayne and the blue-eyed blonde. I had by now discovered that the girl had been his regular bit on the side, or on the table, for the last six months of our relationship. The three of us sat around that same table while Jodi and I got very drunk and Carla sipped orange juice and patted her bump.

"You must get out of this apartment straight away," Carla advised. "Don't be under any compliment to him."

"No! Stay as long as you need to," Jodi insisted. "Let him wait. In fact, just squat here for ever."

It was a messy situation and thinking about it now still makes me shiver. It was Pascal's apartment and I'll have to acknowledge that he was gentleman enough to allow me to stay there until I found somewhere else to live. Until I crawled away in disgrace, humiliated. Which is exactly what I did two weeks later.

This time I bought a property. A one-bedroom apartment which the estate agent described as bijou. Probably because he was too embarrassed to call it a shoebox with plumbing, but it was what I could afford. It was mine. Just me and the hurt I carried from Pascal Ronayne.

I then entered my celibate period. I had been deeply hurt by Pascal. I was twenty-eight, single, the proud owner of a mortgage and teacher by now to a group of eight and nine-year-olds who thought they already knew it all. There were many bleak evenings. Just me and my books and television in my little apartment. Some hectic evenings too, rushing to night class for Russian or chess, tai chi or art. Whatever the interest of the moment happened to be.

In London, Jodi was promoted by her accountancy firm again and this time became head of her own department.

She never mentioned any romantic interest in her life. Neither Carla nor I asked. It was obvious that Jodi's first and only love was work. It was equally obvious that Carla's first and only work was love. Four months after her second baby was born, Carla fell pregnant for the third time. She and Harry decided to move to Cairnsure, our home town, to live. They bought a site and built a house so big that I thought they were definitely aiming for a score of Selby babies. The birth of their twins, Lisa and Dave, confirmed that notion in my mind.

Somehow, Carla, Jodi and I had managed to pass through school, college and most of our twenties in the blink of an eye. Here we were, Carla no longer nursing, married to Harry Selby and mother to a nursery full of babies, Jodi married to her work . . . and me – I was drifting. My apartment seemed to be getting smaller, the children I taught more demanding, the city streets meaner. There were men. A few. Adele Burke was not made for permanent celibacy. Nothing serious though.

I went to London to visit Jodi and spent a week luxuriating in the clean, white space of her waterside apartment. She took me to the theatre and parties and shopping. I came back to Dublin with the same unsettled, uneasy, dissatisfied feelings as when I had gone away. My world consisted of my small apartment, evening classes, precocious children and solitary nights. It was time to face the truth.

I, Adele Burke, was almost thirty. My life was halfway through and I had to admit Part One had not lived up to expectations. I was not over-enthusiastic about facing into Part Two. I was at a crossroads.